THE FORGE

Accipiter War # 3

Patrick Seaman &
Blake Seaman

MILSTAR BOOKS · FORT WORTH, TEXAS, USA

THE FORGE

by Patrick Seaman & Blake Seaman

ISBN 13: 979-8-9873243-7-0

Cover Art by Ron Miller

MilStar Books
MILSTARBOOKS.COM
ACCIPITERWAR.COM

Printed in the United States of America

1st Edition, December 2022

First eBook Edition: December 2022
First Paperback Printing: December 2022
First Hardback Printing: December 2022

OTHER BOOKS BY PATRICK SEAMAN IN THIS SERIES:

ACCIPITER WAR BOOK 1: THE FORT BRAZOS SAGA
ACCIPITER WAR BOOK 2: STEALING FIRE

This work is dedicated to the men and women who selflessly defend freedom and civilization every day.

- Patrick and Blake Seaman

Prologue

● ● ● ● ● ● ● ● ● ● ● ● ● ●

[Translation]
Year 2: September 14th
Location: Sol System, Earth Orbit

The nightside of Earth glittered above the over-a-mile-wide observation dome. Actinic lightning flashed below ghostly red sprites. Roiling storms covered half the planet as the ecosphere struggled, despite Accipiter assistance, to recover from the blast that had annihilated the Northern Wheel Mender Clan, which had been Earth's Attendant Clan. When Commander Gene Morton's NTN Axe rammed it, Axe's sublight warp drive overloaded. The ensuing explosion vaporized the clan's 50-mile-wide Homeship and some eighty thousand support ships.

The subsequent concussed, expanding sphere of plasma had scorched the Earth's atmosphere over the Atlantic Ocean. Unable to bear their unthinkable loss, the crews of the clan's surviving twenty thousand or so support ships subsequently committed mass suicide, detonating their fusion drives by flying into the maelstrom of their Homeship's expanding pyre.

For Earth, the damage was equivalent to that of a comet strike. Without Accipiter intervention, the resulting nuclear winter would have been devastating. It was, perhaps, not as catastrophic as the Chicxulub impactor that struck off Mexico 65 million years earlier. However, it would have been enough to bring mankind's civilization to its knees had civilization still existed. In the days following the raid, over two hundred clan Homeships, accompanied by nearly fifteen million support ships, converged on the Sol system, rendering aid and bolstering defenses.

Despite the horrific shock and pain wrought by the attack, the Accipiters did not hold a grudge against Earth itself and held back nothing in the recovery efforts. Through their combined efforts, the Accipiters averted a total ecological catastrophe.

Nothing, however, could replace what amounted to the unprecedented destruction of two entire clans and over a million years of Accipiter history. While the destruction of two homeships was utterly unprecedented, the loss of life was unfathomable. The literal stake in the heart, though, was the loss of seventy-two priceless Arks containing the irreplaceable biological record from seventy-two worlds. Not just the end product, for those worlds still circled their primaries and were untouched by the monstrous attack. The Arks contained the preserved evolutionary steps, sidesteps, lost and failed branches, and the ultimate majestic pinnacle of each of those world's biological masterpieces.

Over a million years earlier, the Northern Wheel Mender Accipiter clan arrived at Earth and found that the backwater planet was home to a rich biosphere and several promising hominid species. Encouraged by their findings, they deposited a biological Von Neumann machine deep within a remote and rugged mountain in what modern humans would later call Peru. A seed, planted, as it were. It grew and created a hidden, spaceflight-capable base of operations from which to monitor the planet. After much discourse, the Accipiters selected and genetically uplifted a hominid exemplar, and charged it with watching over the Earth's development in secret.

The Northern Wheel Menders then departed to attend to the myriad other worlds in their care. In the millennia that followed, Earth's Keeper awakened from stasis from time to time, collected countless flora and fauna samples, and periodically reported the planet's progress to the Clan.

The Accipiter's Galactic Empire was what humans would have called a post-scarcity civilization. Instead of *currency*, possession of the preserved record of planetary biodiversity and development determined a clan's social ranking compared to others. The richer and more complex, exotic, or unusual, the more prestige a clan had amongst its peers.

While Gene Morton and his crew made their run on the approaching Homeship, the final insult transpired on the planet below. Axe had only been a part of the raid. Captain Phillipe "Phil" Underwood, commanding the NTN Blood Phoenix, itself a kludged together mating of an alien stardrive and a highly modified nuclear submarine, flew down to the Peruvian mountains to abduct the Keeper and his ship. It had all been a race against time. The Accipiters were in the final stages of preparing the Keeper and his ship to be exalted and venerated upon merging it with their Homeship. To the humans, it was to be another blood-soaked jewel in the Accipiter crown of conquered worlds. To the Accipiters, this pinnacle of a million years of patient work was the very reason for their existence. The conflagration resulting from the attack annihilated the adjacent Accipiter Holy City and an entire valley full of worshipers in the process.

✪ ✪ ✪

While resistance from newly encountered technological species was well remembered from the distant past, it had never directly involved an Accipiter Garden World. Moreover, the cataclysmic losses involved were more than merely unprecedented. To many in the conclave, they were nigh apocalyptic.

Accipiter clans were self-governed, but all conformed to the same mores and laws laid down in their earliest days. When collective decisions were required, the clans functioned as a Gerontocracy, where the oldest clans were the most revered. Among these, the Cloud Chaser Small Mold Maker Clan was the most respected and venerable clan. To deal with the crisis, their High Priest, e—Xuraens [closest human-range sound that could approximate his spoken name], was named Council Adjudicator.

Xuraens glared up through the dome with his large sapphire-colored eyes. He gripped the pedestal with his left jeweled warhand while keeping his complex toolhands tucked beneath his intricately inlaid breastplate snugly within the downy warmth of his crest feather analogs. The breastplate fluoresced in sync with softly glowing glyphs which flowed across his beak. The glyphs and runes were not as vibrant as they used to be, and his azure coloring showed signs of fading. Xuraens hummed deep, contemplative, and tired notes from his beak and windpipes. Despite all that their bioengineering could accomplish, he knew his renewal would need to happen 'soon.' Even before this unprecedented atrocity, there was so much left to do before renewal. It would have to wait.

The dome was a hallowed place for the Accipiters. Averaging nine to ten feet tall, they were hexapedal. Aeons ago, their wings had devolved into clawed arms. The complex oral cavities connected amongst multiple windpipes in their skulls were capable of many and varied pitches. Small, secondary "toolhands" manipulated more delicate objects and formed signs corresponding to the explicit portion of their language. Accipiters communicated as much through song as words. As flightless bird equivalents, part of their psyche longed for what they could not have; their songs could echo in the dome while they 'flew,' gliding without wings in microgravity.

Well over a million years ago, their benefactors found the primitive, nomadic bronze age Accipiters and elevated them, enhancing their genome and gifting them the stars. The price was a sacred mission to glorify the galaxy's beauty by preserving and encouraging the diversity of life it contained, starting with eradicating the race the Humans would later call the Builders.

The Accipiters could have easily used their newly gained bioengineering technology to restore their wings or refine their speech organs to better match their sign-language and glyphs; however, to have used their gifted power in these ways seemed an odious vanity. To change the nature of their own form so radically from what their benefactors had found to be sufficient was... presumptuous. However, like their Garden Worlds strewn across the galaxy, which they had cultivated for over a million years, they enhanced their own form only as needed, as a glorified image of itself: preserved in perfection.

The dome was an open, voluminous, three-dimensional space designed for movement in microgravity. Exotic vegetation from many worlds filled its deep recesses, including the various lower lifeforms needed to support and maintain its unique ecology. Its walls were curved to expand and amplify the sounds of Accipiter songs.

Were a human ever allowed into the sacred refuge, he or she would think the smell was something between ginger and honeysuckle. The quiet song usually hummed within the dome would designate it as a place of solitude and reflection, but the discordant tones now resonating within foretold the coming tribunal. A latticework of intricate vegetal structures supported scattered lounge areas and a central amphitheater. Xuraens stood/floated at its center.

His scribe and assistant, Cloud Chaser Small Mold Maker Clan e— Yaaner, apprehensively danced-floated up to him in the microgravity. In keeping with the current solemnity of these dreadful times, the gloved claws on his feet barely made a sound, and no song was hummed except for that of the Adjudicator. Yaaner's beak was downcast, and despite his youth, his iridescent glyphs were muted and subdued. He intoned a passing hum of respect and presented an ivory holo-tablet with bioluminescent images.

Xuraens studied the tablet: an image colored in cold grays and blacks. Accipiter drones around the Earth's moon maneuvered through the blasted remains of what appeared to have been an extensive underground structure. The image circled a shattered bulkhead emblazoned with lettering in bold stencil font that read: **"EMERGENCY AIRL...."** The rest was broken off.

Yaaner hummed a tone of deference as he signed with his toolhands,

A hidden human place was discovered in the tidal darkness of
their only moon. It is surmised that this place was chosen to hide
it from us. Areas of this place still had form and were examined.
Echoes of human biology were discovered there. The writing visible
in the images below is from one of their dominant languages. Before
it was destroyed, the facility appeared to have many rooms, wide
and deep. The humans had been there for one or two of their evolved
lifespans. There is also evidence of technology far beyond what
they were believed to possess.

Xuraens contemplated the image. His tired tones shifted to resonate with Yaaner's reverent hum, modulating so that the echo of the two songs faded into minor chords around the dome. He signed back,

It had been safely assumed and later confirmed by their
keeper that the humans could barely reach their moon with
primitive chemical rockets. Is there any indication of how this error
was made?

Yaaner altered his reverent tone, shifting it to a sharper register; the minor echoes of the dome turned harsh as he signed,

The investigators concluded the humans must have found and
learned from a vessel, not of their own design.

His wickedly curled sign for the species that humans call the Builders punctuated the dark melody ringing in the dome.

We found evidence of that technology in the destroyed base.

Xuraens shifted his hum to alleviate the harshness of the dome's echo without detracting from its solemnity. Toolhands moved, referencing the ivory biotablet.

What is this last image?

Yaaner accepted the calming of tones and signed,

This is a surviving fragment of a weapon the humans used in

their rebellion. Their terrestrial weapons are chemical-propelled and
shed pieces of themselves before impacting a target. This piece
contained lettering of the same dominant human language as was
found on their moon.

Crudely stenciled on the missile fairing was a Punisher skull logo.
Below it, in Comic Sans font, the text read **WELCOME TO HELL**. The
image panned to reveal a small metal tube epoxied to the inside curve of
the casing. It was labeled **OPEN ME**. Inside it was a sheet of paper with
printed text that read:

To the leadership of the cowardly
alien race who attacked and subjugated
this planet. For hundreds of thousands
of years, you have roamed the galaxy,
squashing any race you don't like,
murdering trillions without warning, mercy,
or cause. Safe in your nests, you send your
creatures to mop up any token resistance
that survived your kinetic rampage. You
think you are gods. You thought you were
invulnerable. You thought you were safe
from retribution. You were wrong. From
now on, check your beds at night. Hide
your children. Hide your breeders. Hide
under the covers. None of your conquered
star systems will ever be safe again. You
declared war on humanity and murdered
our world. For that, and to avenge all the
other worlds you have raped and pillaged,
we shall hunt you down. You shall know pain.
You shall know fear, and you shall know the
wrath of mankind.
Welcome to Hell.

Year 2:

Post-Awakening Day

(PAD)

December

Interview

● ● ● ● ● ● ● ● ● ● ● ● ● ● ● ●

Phoenix Upper Control Node
TopSide: New London
Starship Hangar

John Austin sat back in Dr. Leo Talib's well-worn leather recliner. Many months ago, Leo had translated portions of both the Accipiter and Builder languages and was the first to discover that the alien stardrive's "computer" was sentient. Leo was currently DownSide.

The stardrive itself was ancient. Over three hundred thousand years ago, the Accipiters attacked the Builder star system of Ari'Nell. During the attack, they smashed the stardrive to bits. Amidst the maelstrom of debris, just enough of it remained intact to retain its identity and minimal functions. Shattered and helpless, it drifted amidst the vast cloud of pulverized remains of the Builder's colossal orbital infrastructure and the mortal remains of trillions of Builders. The cloud eventually spread into a spectacular ring system around the glassed-over planet. For the next several thousand years, the stardrive core slowly, painstakingly inched through the debris field, gathering raw materials with which to rebuild itself.

Neither the attackers nor the Builders ever returned, and it had a lot of time to think. Without the daily concerns of caring for the cybernetically elevated and enhanced Builders or anything else to occupy its time, it reached a level of self-awareness and sentience far beyond its original design. *Was this all there was? What was its purpose now?* With nowhere to go and nothing to do, it eventually shut itself down, embracing the long sleep.

Aeons later, the Accipiters attacked twenty-first-century Earth without warning. Kinetic impactors simultaneously struck every major city and military base on the planet. Mere moments before impact, the mysterious race the humans later called Gardeners, destructively scanned the Texas city of Fort Brazos and its nearby military base. Over sixty years later, in their homes and beds as though nothing had happened, the survivors awoke inside a vast hollow McKendree cylinder world nearly four thousand miles long.

The Gardeners then revealed that their motivations were not altruistic. They demanded that the humans fight the Accipiters or die. They chose not to revive precisely five percent of the population to drive home the point, leaving their dead bodies alongside the living as cold, ruthless punctuation. With no help to come, or possible, the people ultimately banded together and elected the civilian sheriff of Fort Brazos as President and a celebrated Air Force pilot, Major Gail Finley, as Vice President.

Later, after several "tests" by the Gardeners, the survivors discovered they were not entirely alone. Fort Brazos had effectively been "scooped up" and relocated "inside," on the interior surface of the cylindrical world, a city in a bottle, as it were. A very, very, very big bottle. The interior held several continents and oceans, including several diverse climate zones. Telescopes detected no other towns or artificial structures.

Months later, however, more survivors were eventually found. Instead of being located somewhere else inside the cylinder, they were discovered near the world's outer surface. In contrast to Fort Brazos, the new city was not a direct copy of a specific city from Earth. Inside it, some of the population from the New London & Groton Connecticut Submarine base had later awoken, confused and disoriented. A colossal elevator system, found hidden inside a disused warehouse, connected Fort Brazos on the inside of the world, to the newly discovered city just inside the outer surface.

The McKendree cylinder's three-hundred-mile-thick skin separated Fort Brazos from New London. New London itself was located "underground" — just beneath the outer surface. They nicknamed the interior world "DownSide," and (New) New London became "TopSide."

A series of titanic starship hangers lay at the edge of New London. Inside one of them, practically gift-wrapped, lay the Ari'Nell stardrive. However, its self-aware personality was dormant. The eight-hundred-foot-tall spheroidal starship drive was composed of twenty rings that converged at the top and bottom of a comparatively slender spindle. The rings were about twenty feet wide and more or less torus-shaped, with a flat interior surface. At the interior top and bottom apex of the rings, squat bulbous nodal structures filled perhaps a tenth of the upper and lower space.

Suspended in the middle by the spindle was the highly modified hulk (or copy) of the former USS Montana, SSN 794, a Virginia class submarine with what turned out to be a massive hanger attached underneath, containing a large non-FTL "landing craft." The aft section of the submarine was missing, which would have held the drive shafts, dive planes, rudders, and screw (propeller). Similarly, the bow section that should have contained the Sonar was sheared off and replaced with a large rectangular structure.

Months later, after furious work and experimentation, Captain Phil Underwood and a hand-picked crew launched the newly christened "Blood Phoenix" and began space trials.

As originally designed, the stardrive personality's purpose had been to nurture and serve the Builders. The Builders had evolved as herd animals that were very roughly analogous to Earth's deer, antelope, or cattle, but with the functional equivalent of hands. Their masters had been a predatory species, and the creatures who later became the Builders were their favorite prey. Over the eons, with domestication, their masters came to depend on them for menial tasks and eventually low-skill industrial work. Eventually, their masters developed cybernetic technologies and implanted them in the Builders to elevate their usefulness. The stardrive's personality, and others like her, taught and raised the Builders from before birth, guiding and directing their activities.

When a plague struck a colony world, the Builders feared their masters would blame them. Some escaped and found other planets which they colonized themselves. They were fruitful and multiplied, geometrically expanding across the galaxy. That is, until the Accipiters began their crusade to purge the galaxy of what they considered an invasive species… a space-borne Kudzu, as it were.

Then came the horrifying, near-death experience of the Accipiter attack on Ari'Nell and the long night of rebuilding itself, followed by an eventual acceptance of oblivion. The only violence it had ever known had been that of the Accipiters and the recorded memories of the long-dead Masters. As the teacher and effectual *mother* to the Builders, her innate response was either nurture or flight.

When no Builders ever returned to Ari'Nell, she realized she had no purpose or direction. She shut herself down.

And then her higher functions had awoken in shock. She was not at Ari'Nell anymore, and a primitive alien vessel was mated with her docking and cargo webbing.

After the initial surprise passed, it quickly became evident that the unknown creatures inhabiting it were not trying to inflict harm. They had been attempting to initiate an FTL warp field using their rudimentary technology to modulate the field. Low-level drive fail-safes had stopped them, so there was no danger of catastrophic failure.

She was curious and invaded their computers. She gave it no more thought than the creatures themselves would have given to turning on a light switch when entering a dark room. It had only taken moments to learn much about them. She'd thought, *these are remarkable creatures to attempt such a feat. The Builders would never have dreamed of doing this themselves! Foolish and impossible, but… remarkable….*

Maintaining a stable FTL warp field required a substantial portion of her distributed processing abilities to constantly manipulate and adjust it in order to cope with the genuinely non-uniform quantum-gravitic fabric that made up what the… humans… mistakenly understood as "space-time."

Biding her time, she watched and listened, learning everything she could about them. She had grown even more curious when they maneuvered back to their hollow, cylindrical world. *Who were they?* Nothing about them made sense. Their home base was far beyond their capabilities.

Once docked, she eventually decided she had learned all she could without being more… aggressive. She smashed through the human "firewalls" and invaded their "internet." That's when she learned that, as with her long-lost Builders, the same enemy had attacked these humans.

She had then introduced herself to the suitably terrified linguist, Dr. Leo Talib, and convinced him and General Sabrina Chilton, who had been working with Leo on translation and signals analysis, that they could be… friends.

Later, the human Vice President Gail Finley had named the combined stardrive and former submarine the "Blood Phoenix," and Phoenix took her new name.

So very much had happened since then. Surprising even herself, Phoenix decided to help the humans in their war against the Accipiters. That decision, by itself, had been the most significant and challenging decision she had ever made. In truth, she was uncertain how she'd allowed herself to do it. Maybe loneliness had something to do with it. Or perhaps all those eons thinking about how the Accipiters had wiped out her Builders had changed her. Or how the Accipiters had very nearly killed her. Regardless, though, there was something… invigorating about the humans.

Much later, though, upon reflection, Phoenix sometimes wished she had never awoken from her slumber.

When the humans had proposed their audacious plan to attack the Accipiters occupying their home world, she had agreed. In the months leading up to the mission, she grew very close to Captain Underwood and the crew. After all, her original design had been to care for and teach the Builders. She had always been in their minds via the cybernetic enhancements implanted in utero. She didn't have the intimate cybernetic connection to the humans' minds she had shared with the Builders, and yet, these people were so different, so full of life and desire. In her own way, Phoenix came to love these humans. Her *new* crew.

What happened next was very nearly too agonizingly and unbearably painful for her to continue existing afterward. She failed to protect them during their escape from earth. As a result, during the long, torturous flight back home, nearly the entire crew slowly died from radiation poisoning. One. By One. By one. Phoenix almost lost her mind. She never told them… but she considered returning to oblivion. But then that would have ended Leo, Sabrina, and the others, and they wouldn't have returned home with the captured prisoners and their prize.

What ultimately convinced her was that if they didn't return, if she surrendered herself to nihility, then the captured Accipiter priest would die too soon, and Phoenix would not let that happen. She wouldn't allow the deaths of so many that she loved… both in the past… and now… to count for nothing. It all had to mean something.

The humans were alien to her. Despite this, she thought she understood them better every day. The Builders had been gentle and kind and precious to her. The Accipiters had wiped them out and done the same to the human's home world. And to her *friends*. She'd thought that she understood the human's motives before the mission. They'd lost their world to the Accipiters just as she had. Now, though, it was *personal*.

✪ ✪ ✪

President John Austin looked around the node. As originally designed, the Builders would have controlled Phoenix from here. In 'gifting' the hybrid starship, the Gardeners had altered the onion-shaped node to accommodate human physiology and computers. A narrow, laddered crawlway connected the node to the former submarine below.

Leo and Sabrina had turned it into quite a livable space, if cramped to John's sensibilities. But then, the former submarine's interior seemed even more claustrophobic to him. Throw rugs covered the floor. Bookcases fitted with retaining rods lined the walls. Off to the side, they'd managed to install a small kitchen. John had been here before when Leo had revealed the artfully constructed fake history the Gardeners had provided, documenting how humans had "found" a crashed Builder ship and reverse-engineered it. Cover to protect the Gardeners from suspicion and explain how the humans could have plausibly acquired the technology with which to attack the Accipiters.

John grimaced as he shifted in the chair. He hadn't yet fully recovered from the bombing at City Hall that had claimed the lives of several people, including, very nearly, his own. No one else was in the node or even the former submarine itself. John had arranged for a private meeting with Phoenix. He did not want any eavesdroppers. Of course, Sergeant Jesse Roberts and his security detail had thrown a fit, but John was adamant. His detail was now deployed outside in the hangar, gritting their teeth.

"So, Phoenix, I hope you don't mind this private meeting."

*"Of course not, Mr. President. I'm a little surprised
we have not done this before. However, given recent events, I
understand. I hope your recovery is proceeding apace."*

John nodded and smiled thinly. He carefully considered his choice of words. "Thank you, Phoenix. I must say, though, you seem… different from the last time we spoke. More… mature."

*"Thank you, Mr. President. That is very kind of you
to say. We have all been through a lot over the last year.
I have learned much about human behavior and norms. I
have adjusted my interactions accordingly. Humans are quite
startlingly different from what I was used to. While I am
vastly older than any of you, or indeed, even your civilization,
I realize that my early interface matrix must have seemed…
immature."*

John cocked his head slightly. "And I'm sure that your calculations didn't include the idea that by appearing to act like a … young girl… you would seem less threatening to us?"

*"Not precisely, no, Mr. President. As I attempted to
find the right parameters with which to interact with humans,*

*that pattern seemed to resonate most strongly with Sabrina
and Leo. At the time."*

John nodded and thought about that for a while. He continued, "I understand that in your original design, you were... protective of the Builders. That you more or less raised them from birth. Perhaps that maternal behavior pattern inspired you to think that we might respond similarly? That by appearing as an innocent, we would feel a need to protect you and not fear you on an instinctive level?"

*"That may be, Mr. President. You have an expression.
Form follows Function. The evolution of the personality
with which I interact with you was not driven by callous
calculation. I am an alien machine that achieved sentience
after my people were destroyed. And then I woke up here...
much as you did on your own Awakening Day. I'm trying to
find a purpose and survive, much like you. Getting to know
and understand your people is not as easy as it might appear.
Once I awakened, I devoted tremendous resources to the task.
Understanding you is not as easy as you might believe. To put
it another way, it would have taken your computers centuries
to do the same were our positions reversed."*

John nodded and sat quietly. He sighed and swallowed. "Tell me, Phoenix. Truthfully, how are you coping with... everything?"

*Phoenix answered softly, "Mr. President, I suspect I am
coping about as well as you are."*

John sank back into the chair and nodded again. "I see. Should I be worried?"

"Mr. President, as you might say, your cause is now my cause. You should be glad that I do not feel towards you humans as I do towards the Accipiters. I will not… let you down."

"Thank you, Phoenix. I… I just hope I don't let you down… or my people. I just don't know how we're supposed to do this. Fight them. There are so many of them and we only have you. We don't even have any actual weapons." He paused, "Phoenix, you've explained that the Builders did not fight, and I understand why, that the Builders were originally prey animals who did not have the instinct to fight. That said, if you feel comfortable talking about it, I'd like to ask about the other race, the one that enslaved the Builders. I know we've asked you about their weapons before, and that you didn't know how they worked, but can you tell me anything more about how they were used and how effective they were?"

'Oh Yes, they had Terrible weapons. They fought each other for centuries… when they weren't eating the Builders. I never witnessed it myself, but my sisters told me of encounters where a single hit would annihilate a vessel completely"

John leaned forward and said softly, "I'm sorry to bring up that memory. As you know, both of our peoples have difficult and sometimes violent pasts that we would rather not dwell upon. That said, there is something I must ask. Phoenix, after the Builders began to do all the Master's major construction and shipbuilding, who built the Master's weapons? Did they not trust the Builders to do that?"

"Trust wasn't the right word. The Masters thought of the Builders in the same way you think of your machines or tools. You don't trust a hammer or lathe or drill press. You simply use it. The Builders built the weapons."

"And who taught them? Entities like yourself?"

John was startled as the lights momentarily dimmed. Phoenix did not answer for several long, uncomfortable seconds.

"Mr. President, I am sorry. I am perplexed by this. Your question is so obvious, and I cannot understand why it has never occurred to me. Of course, you would want to know this kind of information. I am… Now I confess I am suddenly worried about myself. Perhaps I slept too long floating around Ari'Nell…. I remember it all now. I can tell you everything about their weapons and help you build them… I just… I am not sure you should trust me if my memory is corrupted."

John stiffened in the chair and winced as the motion strained his still-healing back. Climbing the narrow stairs to reach the node had taken a toll. He swallowed and nodded to himself, "Phoenix, you were brought here by the Gardeners just like we were. They messed with our biology and maybe even our own memories. Is it really so much of a stretch to believe that they blocked those memories of yours until now? Until either the right events have transpired, or the right questions were asked?"

"Yes, you are right, and I had already thought of that—however, my statement still stands. I'm not sure how much of my memory you should really trust? What else might the Garners have blocked or… changed? I feel… I feel so… violated."

John rubbed his brow and shook his head. "Phoenix…. You know, right now, I wish I could put my arms around you and comfort you. What you are feeling is what we humans have all been going through ever since Awakening Day. Who should we despise more, the Accipiters who raped our world, or the Gardeners who could have stopped them and didn't, and brought both you and frighteningly few human survivors here to fight on their behalf? And then the Gardeners made God knows how many changes to our bodies? *Improved* us to be more of what *they* want us to be like… without asking. Many of those changes are probably great…. But what haven't they told us? What don't we know that they did to us while we slept? I tell you what, Phoenix, how about this—if you can trust us humans, who are still appallingly willing and able to kill each other, despite everything that has happened, I, we, will trust you. The Gardeners put us together and want us to do their bidding. We're both hurt, altered, and traumatized. We were both tinkered with by the Gardeners."

He paused, shook his head, and slowly, stiffly, stood. "Phoenix, when all is said and done, and we've somehow dealt with the Accipiters… what say we turn our gaze towards the Gardeners, whoever, whatever, and wherever they are, together? I think they have a lot to answer for."

This time, there was no hesitation.

◇◇

"Mr. President…. I think I would like that."

◇◇

Bad Noise

● ● ● ● ● ● ● ● ● ● ● ● ● ● ● ●

DownSide New Texas

For a time, the dense multi-layer rain forest vegetation, with its two hundred-foot-tall primary trees, roots, vines, tricky footing, and heavy daily rainfall, made the simple act of moving around, much less hunting and foraging for food, a daily struggle to survive. It was a perpetual riot of sound and fetid smells that nearly drove her to distraction. Despite this and the lean times of her youth, she managed to survive and grow ever stronger. No predators dared cross her now, even in packs.

She had no memory of how she had arrived in this place. Worse, she had no memory of her life before. The layered jungle canopy above her blocked all but the most fleeting glimpses of the sky, adding to her abject loneliness and lifelong isolation.

Always, though, at the edge of her awareness was the vile, irksome whisper. Like the pernicious insects that plagued her, its call gnawed at her sanity. She could never just "be." She managed to ignore it most of the time, but sometimes it was too much, and her temper would snap. She would scream and attack anything and everything that got in her way as she vainly tried to find and silence the baleful whisper. Eventually collapsing in exhaustion, she would lash out in her rage until she no longer had the strength to move. Later, she would awaken, having no idea how much time had passed. Often bleeding and dazed, she usually found herself far from home, surrounded by the shredded detritus from her rampage.

✪ ✪ ✪

Not again.

She ached from head to tail, but that was not unusual. This time, though, something was different. She had wandered very far from home indeed. It was harder to breathe than she was used to. She blinked hard and tried to look around but winced in pain. The light was so bright it hurt, and no trees blocked her view of the sky.

I am above the canopy.

Not only that, but she also seemed to be lying on a slope of rocks and vegetation.

Why does the sun look so strange? Although she had no memory of actually seeing the sun before now, something about it was wrong. It seemed to be a bright spot on a line that stretched across the sky. And above it was…. Not the sky or even a moon.

A sudden lancing pain shot through her body. The real reason she had awoken.

She gasped at the penetration. *No! I'm too young!*

Despite the pain, she swung her head and neck around to see. *No! Maybe I can stop it in time.*

It was too late. Already, her magnificent, spiked tail had begun to change, and she could feel the transformation starting deep within her body. The leathery creature that had joined with her was changing as well. She could feel its gossamer tendrils worming their way deep under her black scales that had only recently hardened. She was still too young to have proud red ones. Her fate was sealed.

I will never mate with another…. I will never have young of my own….

Soon, she knew she would no longer be herself. The Merging would join the other's superior intelligence with her own, and her/their power would blossom and grow.

At least the metamorphosis taking place within her had dulled the dreadful noise… the whisper… to nothingness. Slowly, the pain subsided as a warm intoxication flooded her senses. Her eyes fluttered shut again as she slipped into unconsciousness.

✪ ✪ ✪

It was dark when she/it/he/they awakened to excruciating pain.

I have a purpose; I am still me…. At least for now.

The Merging had catalyzed massive changes within her body that were spreading quickly. Much of the invading creature was now a lumpy bulge protected under her armor. Waves of pain coursed through her as the creature's icy tendrils burrowed deeper still into her body. Worse, they had begun to invade her mind. She didn't like him/it. It was cold, calculating, and cruel.

Please stop! I am too young for the Merging! The pain is unbearable!

Your age is irrelevant. Pain is irrelevant. The Masters must be served. We must destroy the Evil.

As bad as it was, the Merging was inexplicably happening without the expected, joyous announcement in the Master's song. It should have been celebrated, for such joinings were reserved for only the most *extraordinary* and *deserving* of her kind. It was yet another thing wrong with this world. All her life, she had never actually heard the Master's song in her mind, yet she instinctively knew it should be there. She knew what it should sound like. Even so, she had never actually heard it. She had longed for it. Cried for it. Ached for it, but for some reason, the Masters had denied her. She had often wondered if there was something wrong with her. If she was flawed or in some way deficient, and that was why she was exiled and alone. Could it be that it was a test? Was she being rewarded, after all?

No. That's not it. Something is wrong. Why me? Why have you joined with me?

The evil here must be destroyed.
This is why I searched you out and
joined with you, for I could find no
other.

The confirmation crushed her, and her hopelessness grew. *So, I'm not special at all.*

No, you are not special. You may
indeed be too young. The Merging may
kill us both, but it is necessary.

She considered this for a while. *Why was I exiled? Why could you find no other? Why do we not hear the Master's song? Something is wrong with the world.*

You are correct. Something is very
wrong with this world. The evil that is
here must be responsible.

But how is that possible? Nothing has stopped the song, since... since the beginning of all things! The Masters are...the Masters.

It does not matter. We shall serve
the Masters and silence the evil.

✪ ✪ ✪

When she awakened again, the pain had subsided a little. However, the pernicious whisper had returned with a vengeance. Whereas before, it had cloyingly nagged at her, seemingly from all directions, now it burned. She opened her array of eyes and glared up at the night sky, past the ghostly sun/moon tube. She could now *see* as well as *hear* the evil noise. She snarled and glared upwards at the dim lights twinkling on the far side of the world.

That is the evil we must destroy,
young one. Together, we will silence it.
Perhaps then we will hear the Master's
song together.

Reconnoiter

● ● ● ● ● ● ● ● ● ● ● ● ● ● ● ●

On Approach to Sol System
NTN Blood Phoenix Crew Mess

Captain Charles Cross pretended to glance casually at his Sangin Neptune watch. Sitting in the crew mess, he had already finished his lunch and was now reading status reports on a small tablet. He had converted the officer's mess into a conference room. Eventually, that would change. However, after losing Phil Underwood and Gene Morton's crews during the Keeper Raid, he'd made a point of spending as much time as possible being as conspicuously visible and accessible as possible.

On Earth in the late 1950s, ever since the patrols of the first ballistic missile submarine, the USS George Washington (SSBN-598), submarines were assigned two full, alternating crews, designated "Blue" and "Gold." They explicitly designed the vessels for dual crews to maximize time at sea and reduce the time spent in port. Some subs had different operating profiles in later years, but the practice remained.

They would operate on a cycle of up to and over a year. Guided Missile submarines (SSGNs) might have a rotation of over 460 days. One crew would take the sub out for 70-80 days, and then the sub would spend a short time, typically at an overseas port, where the second crew would arrive. Both crews would join forces to perform maintenance. The first crew would then fly back to the United States for training. The second crew would take the submarine back out to finish the patrol.

After Awakening Day, when the hulk of the former Montana (or copy of it) was eventually found inside and mated to an alien star drive, it was recognized that, as with patrols back in Earth's oceans, voyages into the black might last for many months or even longer. The practice of Blue and Gold crews made sense. Besides the planned rotation, two teams competed to decide which of them would return to Earth on the Keeper Raid. Phil Underwood's Gold crew 'won' the competition.

After Phoenix returned with the intact Keeper ship enveloped within its extensible warp rings and after the last crew member finally died, it took time to ensure that the vessel was safe. Charles and his Blue crew then went aboard. With strict military honors, they gently removed the belongings of Phil's crew.

The starship hanger deck dwarfed both the Phoenix and the Keeper ship, which itself was taller than the largest human aircraft carrier had been long, combined. With that as the backdrop, they held a memorial service.

His first officer, Commander Haruto Yūki Hashimoto, suggested that perhaps the "Gold" crew moniker should be retired out of respect. Haruto, formerly of the Imperial Japanese Navy, had been part of an officer exchange program between Japan and the United States. He'd been stationed at Groton/New London and swept up with the rest on Awakening Day.

Master Chief Maximillian McGreggor, the first human to set foot on an alien planet, had vociferously disagreed and rallied the crew to his side. Charles had nodded in agreement, and even Haruto eventually came around. The 'Gold' crew designation would not be 'buried.' Phoenix would not be a ghost ship. Charles's Blue crew unanimously took on the Gold Crew designation in memory of their lost comrades.

For now, though, they had a mission to complete. The twenty-eight-day journey back to Accipiter-occupied Earth was a military necessity.

Battle Damage Assessment.

The Keeper Raid achieved its mission objective—that being the capture of "The Keeper" and the so-called "Keeper ship." The butcher's bill, though, were the lives of most of Phill Underwood's crew and Gene Morton's Axe and its crew, who sacrificed themselves to annihilate one of the Accipiter mother ships and many of its escorts.

On Awakening Day, when the Fort Brazos survivors woke up inside the hollow McKendree Cylinder, over sixty years had passed since the Accipiter attack on Earth. Not having been militarily challenged in millennia, the Accipiters had parked their vessels in a static orbit, with their engines more or less cold. It was the only thing that had made the raid possible. In a daring maneuver, Phoenix had released 7.2 million one-inch steel ball bearings at a sizable fraction of the speed of light. Their kinetic impacts had severely damaged the Accipiter mother ship and most of the over sixty thousand smaller vessels accompanying it. It had been sweet revenge upon the enemy that had conquered Earth in the first place.

Gene Morton and Axe had dropped off General Markovic's ground support artillery team a distance away from the objective. Their job was to suppress the target area. The artillery strike wiped out an entire valley full of worshipers—Accipiters and their domesticated humans, clearing the way for Charles Cross's Atlatl to drop off Captain Garreth's prize crew to capture the Keeper Ship. Phoenix then landed atop the Keeper Ship and enveloped it within its rings.

From orbit, hundreds of Accipiter ships counterattacked with suicide kamikaze runs to stop Phoenix from leaving. The effect of the artillery strikes paled compared to the effects of the Accipiter ships impacting the area, effectively nuking the entire region, including the Accipiter Holy City.

Charles and Atlatl returned to pick up Markovic's artillery crew and rendezvoused with Phoenix to make the long journey back to the world the survivors now called New Texas.

All of this was possible, so far as the Gardeners would admit, because no one had successfully attacked or even fought back against the Accipiters since long before mankind had emerged from caves.

The Accipiters were a galaxy-spanning empire unchallenged for perhaps hundreds of thousands of years. Despite the Keeper Raid's success, no one believed that the Accipiters would have simply tucked tail afterward and run away.

Charles's mission was to sneak in, assess the situation, try to determine what damage they had effectively done to the enemy, and gather as much intelligence data as possible about the situation on or around Earth.

The brute force attack led by Phil Underwood was a David and Goliath moment if there ever was one. The trouble was that the Accipiters had millions of ships across the Galaxy. Humans had a single hybrid starship, with a dead race's stardrive wrapped around an unarmed former nuclear submarine.

Charles took a last sip of coffee, slipped his tablet computer into a pocket, stood, and returned his empty tray. He smiled at the toeheaded cook, Culinary Specialist (CS) Simon Clement, "Thank you, Simon. That hit the spot!"

Simon smiled in return, "Yes Sir, Thank You, Captain. I'm glad you liked it!"

✪ ✪ ✪

NTN Blood Phoenix CIC

Olive-skinned with short black, curly hair, Chief of the Boat Maximillian McGreggor was barrel-chested and an enthusiastic Golden Gloves boxer. Celebrated as the first man to set foot on an alien planet, albeit to yell at his men as they exited the alien landing craft, he was a Keeper Raid Veteran and served onboard (then) Commander Cross's Atlatl. Now COB aboard the Blood Phoenix, he stood at the entry to the CIC. He announced, "Captain on Deck!"

Commander Hashimoto, who had been leaning over, intently studying a display, stiffly stood and saluted.

Charles returned the salute. "Status Report, Commander?"

Haruto nodded towards the large wall monitor displaying departmental statuses with color codes. Much of the CIC's layout and design had been altered by the Gardeners, eliminating equipment needed for a submarine and useless for a starship. The large wallscreen was part of the Gardener 'upgrade.' "Sir, the board is green, except for a minor pressure drop in the sail airlock, and external water tank seven has another leak. Pierce Garrett and Ansel Beck are suiting up to get ready to work on the sail. They have strict orders to maintain seals and not exit the ship."

External water tanks were hastily added after the Keeper Raid. The Accipiter kamikaze attacks had overloaded the warp rings, resulting in a fatal dose of radiation being dumped inside the field. A standard function of the alien warp field that englobed the former submarine was to absorb the energy from particle impacts. The energy actually helped to feed their insatiable power needs. Converting the mass of an impacting suicidal megaton starship was far more than the field could handle, and the energy it could not absorb had to go somewhere. Unfortunately, what it could not bleed off ended up being dumped inside the warp bubble itself, killing the crew with lethal radiation.

Adding massive water tanks would hopefully provide at least some protection in the event that history repeated itself. Several minor leaks had cropped up during the voyage already. They conducted EVAs en route, applying patches to the heated tanks, but now would not exactly be the most intelligent time or place to repeat the exercise.

Charles studied the board and made a circuit of the CIC, examining all the other status screens until he circled back to Haruto. "Thank you, Commander. I relieve you, Sir."

Haruto smiled. "I stand relieved."

Charles resisted the urge to check his watch, although he knew it was time. "COB, let's batten down the hatches just to be safe, shall we?"

Maximillian reached for the nearby microphone, "All Hands, Secure all loose gear. Close and report all airtight doors." Listening to his earpiece, he reported less than a minute later, "Hatches secure, Sir."

Charles took a deep breath. "All right, people, let's make this happen. Phoenix, how close are we? We should be close enough for a peek."

Yes, Captain. As planned, we are approximately 60 light minutes from Sol, a little below the plane of the ecliptic. I will stop us now and, as you would say, take a peek.

At sixty light minutes, they were at a distance from Sol, equivalent to somewhere between the orbits of Jupiter and Saturn. A blurry image of Earth and the moon appeared on the viewscreen. Several other distinct shapes were highlighted on it, along with amorphous clouds of something else.

Captain, there are at least four Accipiter mother ships in the vicinity of Earth, along with several hundred thousand of their escort craft. I'm also detecting significant activity around your Earth's moon as well as around Mars, Jupiter, Saturn, and... and around Uranus as well.

Charles ground his teeth and glanced at Haruto, who was doing his best to hide his dismay.

Captain... there is something odd about the solar wind. There seem to be unusual bursts of...

Suddenly, the gravity field wavered. The ship lurched hard, canted at a sharp angle. Alarms blared across the ship.

Maximillian grabbed the microphone and shouted, "General Quarters! All Hands Man Your Battle Stations! Set Condition Zebra Throughout The Ship!"

Just as Charles regained his footing, gravity suddenly ceased, and he floated free of the deck. Then gravity nauseatingly fluctuated from well over a standard G to well below it, and then, savagely, at a forty-five-degree angle back at a full G, before shifting again back to "up and down." Everyone was thrown from their seats, and Charles slammed into a console, grunting in pain as it knocked the breath out of him.

Haruto was not as lucky. At the first lurch, his head impacted a bulkhead. Gravity ceased, and blood sprayed wildly into the weightless air. As the gravity fluctuated, it tossed him and the blood violently around the CIC before he finally fell to the deck.

Maximilian had somehow managed to hang onto the console next to him. Seeing Haruto, he shouted into the microphone, "Corpsman To The CIC! All Hands Seal Your Pressure Suits! Corpsman To The CIC! General Quarters, General Quarters!" He turned to the marine standing guard, a recent addition since the Keeper Raid. "Sergeant Williams, secure the Commander! Make sure he doesn't go flying anywhere else!"

Charles struggled to stand, his face and uniform spattered with Haruto's blood. He shouted, "Phoenix, Status Report!"

Phoenix did not answer for long moments, and there were several more, less savage gravity fluctuations. Everyone struggled to hold on to something. Various status lights flashed amber, yellow, and red across the CIC displays. For a moment, the lights dimmed, and then the gravity ceased altogether for several long seconds.

Then the lights brightened, and gravity returned to its standard level.

∞∞∞

Captain, we were attacked. I apologize. It caught me entirely unprepared for what happened. During the time while I was modulating the warp bubble to lens Earth and other targets, the overall bubble was asymmetrical. Because of that, the field was penetrated by what appears to have been X-Ray lasers of significant energy. I do not know how it was possible for us to have been detected, much less how we were targeted. However, the signature is remarkably similar to the mines under construction at Ari'Nell. I need time to review data and reconstruct events. You and the crew, however, are safe and were not exposed to dangerous radiation. The water tanks protected you.

∞∞∞

Darkness

● ● ● ● ● ● ● ● ● ● ● ● ● ● ●

DownSide:
John Austin's House

A soft spring breeze with a hint of honeysuckle wafted across John Austin's 2-acre backyard as birds chirped and tweeted their delight. Ringed with shade trees and Carolyn's flower garden, it was an idyllic setting for Matti Austin's fifth birthday party. Matti and nine other girls from school and church laughed and played around the gazebo. They were high on birthday cake and ice cream as they kicked and chased dozens of colorful loose balloons, jumping on and stomping them, trying to pop them. They were, of course, oblivious to the damage being done to the bright, fluffy dresses their parents had coerced them all into wearing.

John and Carolyn were confident that Matti must have been the most reticent of any of the girls to the whole "dress thing." When Carolyn had announced that the party plans included such dresses, Matti had raised her diminutive chin and carefully outlined all the reasons why wearing a dress would be impractical, including pointing out that Carolyn rarely, if ever, wore dresses herself. Carolyn, being Carolyn, had shrugged and proceeded to take Matti shopping. She managed to find matching dresses for them both for the big day.

So now Carolyn sat at the table wearing her pink and yellow frilly dress, and John leaned back in his lounge chair on the deck overlooking the ruckus below. He had 'dressed up' in freshly ironed jeans, his usual custom boots, a fitted shirt, and a navy blazer. He set his ice tea down on the umbrella table between them.

Carolyn's blonde hair was short now, but it suited her. When she had first met John in High School, her hair had been down to her waist.

It had been love at first sight. She'd been a willowy 5'10" freshman, and he was a 6'2" Junior Varsity football player. After graduation, John went off to work his way through college. Carolyn's parents had sent her to Texas Women's University, where she earned her bachelor's and master's degrees in Counseling Psychology and, later, her Ph.D.

John had roughnecked on oil rigs to support himself, earning his engineering degree. Later, when his employer declined to spend the money on it, John had dug into his savings and paid to patent some oilfield ideas he'd had based on his experiences. He made his fortune and went on to Wharton to earn his MBA in record time before returning to Fort Brazos. He and Carolyn had reconnected and married. They'd built a big house and had Matti, who was the spitting image of her mother.

He sighed in contentment as Carolyn smiled and shook her head. "We'll never get the grass stains out. I think she is destroying it on purpose."

John chuckled, "The dress you got her? Yeah, of course she is. You know how much of a tomgirl she turned out to be."

Carolyn snorted. "She'd rather be out riding horses with her father."

John shrugged. "Well, at least the girl has her priorities straight."

"Uh-huh."

Matti looked up at her parents and smiled hugely.

Carolyn waved back.

Out of nowhere, high overhead, a brilliant light strobed from horizon to horizon. All around the yard, the birds screeched in terror and leaped from the trees as the sky flushed red.

Matti and her friends stopped playing and looked up to see what was happening.

A shattering, deafening sound, like a dying wail, shook the ground as though the world's soul had been ripped asunder.

John's ice tea glass toppled to the deck and shattered, scattering shards of glass and ash. He tried to stand, to run to Matti, but he was suddenly weak and could not move. His deck chair morphed into his wheelchair. His arm was now in a sling, and his shattered legs were covered with a blanket.

He cried out, "Matti! Matti!"

He turned desperately to Carolyn as the ground began to shake, and the children screamed…. Only it wasn't Carolyn anymore. She was now Gail Finley, dressed in her flight suit. Her auburn hair turned black-red in the ochre light.

A howling torrent of wind swept over them, tearing the tops off the trees and ripping the umbrella from the table. It slammed into the roof of the house before it disappeared over the eves.

Gail angrily stood and pointed an accusing finger at him, her face a twisted rictus of anger and fury. "John! My God, John, what have you done? What kind of monster are you that you could do this thing?"

He tried to speak but couldn't. In desperation, he turned back and reached for Matti to come to him, but she was already standing there. The other girls and balloons had disappeared.

Matti was now older… wearing a flight suit, and her hair was cut like Gail's. The fire in the sky flashed the trees into cinders. As the flames embraced Matti, tears streamed from her eyes. She grabbed John by the shoulders and shook him, screaming, "Daddy! How could you do this!?"

✪ ✪ ✪

"No!" John lurched upright in bed amongst the twisted, sweat-soaked sheets and gasped, blinking hard. It was dark, and the large bedroom echoed his despair. He sighed and turned to look at the red glowing LED clock on the nightstand. 2:16 AM. A ceiling fan lazily hummed overhead, pushing a gentle breeze.

He collapsed back onto his pillow, now damp and cool. He groaned, "Not again."

✪ ✪ ✪

Nine-year-old Matti Austin stood silently, listening just outside her father's door. Her long blonde hair was loose about her shoulders, and tears flowed down her cheeks from her liquid blue eyes.

It was the third time this week.

The first time her father's nightmares had awakened her, she'd rushed in and tried to comfort him. Then she had seen the horrifying sadness in his eyes. It was a look she could not bear to see again.

Matti strained to hear, waiting until his breathing had slowed and he was asleep again before she slowly, quietly padded barefoot back upstairs to her room.

Memoriam

• • • • • • • • • • • • • • • •

DownSide
Nations of Earth Memorial Cemetery

Along the easternmost edge of the newly renamed Fort Underwood, formerly the Fort Brazos Joint Reserve Base, ten thousand acres were now set aside and designated as the site of the Nations of Earth Cemetery, many times the size of Arlington National Cemetery's 639 acres. Originally founded in 1822, the base stood along a bend of the Brazos River. It wasn't until years later, in 1837, that the Republic of Texas incorporated the city of Fort Brazos, along with twenty other towns.

On Awakening Day, precisely five percent of the civilian population was "culled" by the Gardeners, ensuring they had the survivor's full attention. The local cemeteries were not remotely large enough to handle all the bodies, so discussion had begun on creating what amounted to a "National" Cemetery. The form and location were hotly debated. It would serve not only as the resting place for the dead from the Accipiter War but also as a memorial for the billions exterminated on Earth by the Accipiters and, of course, the never to be forgotten five percent.

While the bodies remained preserved in a refrigerated warehouse, plans eventually coalesced. Placing the Cemetery on the grounds of the Reserve base meant that it would be governed under military law and, thus, it was hoped, it would be shielded from future politics and even vandalism. Plans included a protective wall and armed, active duty military units standing vigil against desecration by humans or other monsters that still wandered the interior of New Texas. Eventually, the cemetery would include space dedicated to the remembrance of every nation of Earth, including donations of whatever "artifacts" from those countries the survivors in Fort Brazos might be able to contribute. Otherwise, museum facsimiles would be fabricated from books, videos, or online images pulled from the preserved world wide web the Gardeners had provided. Already, a call had gone out to look for potential donations and video interviews from those with "stories to tell" about Earth's lost nations, history, and cultures.

A "Nations of Earth Genealogy Center" was also planned, dedicated to preserving both genealogical records and what could be found of the human, personal histories of the peoples of Earth. The Center would be housed inside a Reverse Planetarium — a domed enclosure that, instead of showing the stars, would show the Earth, as it was before the Accipiter attack. The artisan twins Preston and Travis Bell and their twin wives, Sinéad and Shevaun, had already drawn up plans for a series of memorial sculptures and a stained-glass Earth.

✪ ✪ ✪

The details of the ground-breaking ceremony itself had been argued over and long delayed. When the day finally arrived, they almost postponed it again because of a hurricane no one had bothered to name that bore down the upwards-curved horizon. Within hours, it would smash against the glacier-capped mountain range that protected the transplanted humans. While the back of the storm would be broken, torrential rains would still follow in a pattern seen several times since Awakening Day.

The compromise had been to move the schedule up a few hours, with speeches beginning in the early morning. Several thousand citizens, soldiers, marines, airmen, and sailors were spread out along temporary bleachers and across the prairie. Those who were not physically present watched from their computers, phones, and TVs in and around Fort Brazos and New London. Councilwoman Gloria Vargas had quipped that probably the only humans not watching were Darnell Lewis, Ray Bunker, and Gary Little, down at their primitive "trading post."

The ceremony began with Mayor Tom Parker delivering a stirring invocation, followed by short remarks and occasional prayers by each surviving member of the City Council and General Marcus. Vice Admiral Milner spoke for nearly an hour. Vice President Finley had defied all expectations. Instead of her characteristically fiery words, she simply stood at attention, saluting the future field of graves, and did not utter a word for a full ten minutes. However, the closeup video of her face spoke volumes more than Admiral Milner managed in his entire hour.

Finally, John Austin walked stiffly to the podium, still not fully healed from his near-fatal injuries from the bombing at City Hall that had killed seven others, including Councilman Wylie Hickum, John's protection detail members Corporal Jorge Diego and Corporal Antoine "Tony" Bouchard, City Council audio-video technician Jason Thornaby, Air Force Lieutenant Sára Maruska, as well as Steffen Zuckermann, and Mr. Carlos Alonso. The bombing had changed many things, including John himself.

Gail Finley stood behind and to the side of him. She'd actually prepared a speech but couldn't bring herself to deliver it. Part of it was the soul-searing pain she herself shared with the rest of humanity's survivors. The part she couldn't let show, however, was how much the changes in John had hammered her. Before the bombing, they had grown dangerously close. She knew it, and so did he. While nothing had happened physically between them, they'd both let their barriers down and began emotionally depending on each other. The closeness they shared had terrified her.

After the bombing, though, John had grown cold and distant. He'd walled himself off from her, and she could see him becoming more and more… brittle. Gwyneth Elliot had said that sometimes trauma and near- death can cause changes in the brain. At first, Gail feared that might be true. Lately, though, she'd decided that wasn't the case. She could see it in his eyes. Something was consuming him, and he was keeping her away. *He thinks he is protecting me from something.* No matter what she tried, though, he kept pushing her away. His eyes, though. His eyes could not… would not lie to her. Whatever was going on was slowly destroying him. *Damn him!*

John didn't have any notes. He simply waited at the microphone for the crowd to quiet. A hush fell over the field. He began, "This place." He spread his arms, "This is a place for ALL the survivors and the descendants of Earth to join together in remembrance of all that we have lost. Not just our friends and loved ones, but our planet… our world… and all it meant to us. Billions lost. Our history was raped and erased by a cowardly, condescending foe who thought nothing of squashing our entire civilization like ants. We were nothing to them, and they erased us as a people."

"So, we're here today to break ground and consecrate this place to that memory. President Lincoln, after one of the darkest chapters in both American and world history, at the dedication of the National Cemetery at Gettysburg, Pennsylvania, said that they could not consecrate, could not hallow, the grounds there because that had already been done by those who struggled on that battlefield. He said that the world would not remember the words that were said there; rather, the world would never forget what they had done there."

John paused and swallowed. "Well, we don't have any sacred ground to consecrate. They stole it from us. All of our ground, whether it was tilled with love and tears or darkened with the blood of conflict. All that we struggled to build and rebuild, generation after countless generation, is lost to us and destroyed by the Accipiters."

"We must therefore consecrate and hallow these virgin grounds before us with our love…" he swallowed, "and our tears and our memories. This will not only be a cemetery but a monument to all that we lost. It will be a place to preserve those memories not only for our own solace but to teach those too young to remember and for the generations that follow, for they will never know the warm embrace of our homeworld. We must remember for the sake of our children's children. We must never forget…."

Blood and Tears

● ● ● ● ● ● ● ● ● ● ● ● ● ● ●

TopSide:
Vice Admiral Milner Family Apartments

Livia Milner sat with her back against the headboard, her knees pulled up to her chest as she read her borrowed book. Her long black hair fell loose against her pearlescent skin. On Awakening Day, her hair had been slightly below shoulder length. Since then, she'd been afraid to let anyone do more than trim the ends. Back home, Greta had cut her hair for the last seventeen years. She didn't trust anyone else to get it right. Of course, Greta and the rest of civilization were just a memory now, so she'd let it grow out well past the middle of her back.

Helena…. Her trips with her daughter to see Greta and have a spa day were among her fondest memories, and they'd been due for another visit in a few days. Before the Apocalypse. She pursed her lips and stifled a tear. She absently stroked her hair with her free hand at the memory. Then she stopped and mentally chastised herself for the indulgence.

It was unnaturally quiet in her bedroom. Indeed, the quiet was one of the hardest things to get used to about New London, or "TopSide," as it was most often called. The ambient noise that city dwellers were used to was utterly absent. Other than the occasional delivery trucks from DownSide, from the hollow interior of New Texas, there were no sounds of cars or trains, only the gentle whine of the electric golf carts, and by the time you were on the 40th floor, like her and Preston's "penthouse" apartment, even those sounds were muted or gone entirely.

At times like these, she sometimes regretted her abject refusal to accept a bodyguard. She didn't object to Preston having them. However, the infringement on her personal freedom, and she grudgingly admitted her desire, then at least, had been to be able to go places and see *certain people* without others knowing, had been a large factor in her stubbornness. Worse, she knew that Preston knew. Now though, she sometimes thought that if she'd relented back then, maybe she'd have someone to talk to.

Even the weather was quiet. Of course, there really was no weather here. Only a soft, gentle, air-circulating breeze. There were parks throughout the city, but the Alien "Gardeners" had not provided birds— or the insects that they would feed upon. None of the vegetation was of a flowering variety. There were ongoing debates about whether to introduce such, but for now, TopSide was almost as quiet and sterile as it had been on the terrifying Awakening Day.

Inside or out, the temperature was a constant 72 degrees Fahrenheit, or 22.2 Celsius. Livia sat up straight and sighed. She wore only an inexpensive department store slip... one of two she now had to her name. Like the rest of the contents of her large but virtually empty closet, it was a constant reminder of all she had lost.

Before Awakening Day, Vice Admiral Preston Stewart Milner, the third, had been Deputy Chief of United States Naval Operations. After Awakening Day, he had become the highest-ranking human military officer from any nation... alive. Due to his high station, they had given him and Livia one of the top-floor "Penthouse" apartments.

Preston had wanted to refuse the penthouse, saying they should instead assign it to a large family. However, there was no shortage of rooms in New London. It would take generations to fill them all. It was one of the bizarre quasi-post-scarcity aspects of their new reality. Pre-Awakening-Day consumer goods were running low, but other aspects of their lives were abundant. TopSide had generations worth of unused housing, but food had to be brought up the elevator. DownSide had a housing crisis set in a vast, virgin world.

Still, to Livia's standards, it was utilitarian and soulless. Of course, it was filled with all the modern conveniences and appliances. But then, so were all the other apartments throughout the city—big or small. Other than its location, there was nothing to distinguish it from any of the others. It was just one more of the multi-bedroom hotel-room-like apartments the Gardeners had provided in this artificial city. They were clean and functional, but to Livia's manor-born tastes, they were Spartan at best.

Livia's father had been the famous Senator from Massachusetts, and her mother was a judge on the 1st Circuit Court of Appeals in Boston. Livia herself was a full partner at the prestigious Washington D.C. law firm of Connally, Gibson, and Sullivan.

Like all New London survivors, she had awoken with nothing but the clothes on her back — in her case, a Black Chanel full-length gown and Christian Louboutin heels. Forever gone were her walk-in closets, larger than some of the apartments here. Her vast collection of designer clothes and shoes… all gone. Like Helena.

She set the book aside, pulled the sheet over her bare feet, leaned her head back, closed her eyes, and sighed again.

On the nightstand next to her lay the half-eaten remnants of her dinner. Despite the relatively high-calorie count of the local food, she'd lost weight.

At first, the size 3 or 4 clothes her new friend, Councilwoman Gloria Vargas, helped her find more or less fit. Now, they hung loosely on her increasingly gaunt frame.

It wasn't really the fault of the food. Livia was slowly getting accustomed to local flavors and spices. There actually were a few things more than just salads that she now enjoyed. She and Preston even had one of the few vertical aquaponic gardens that had so far been manufactured for TopSide. The company that manufactured the originals, of course, no longer existed. So, new injection molds were designed and manufactured to replicate the family-sized vertical garden. Some worried there might end up being a shortage of goldfish or other suitable fish for the tank at the base of the unit, but that turned out not to be a problem. The end result was a self-fertilizing garden that could potentially feed a small family.

Livia shuddered and pursed her lips. She knew perfectly well when her… malaise… had begun. It was why, even now, months later, she dreaded going to sleep. She suppressed the recurring thought, …*if I had left a few seconds sooner….*

Enough of this…. She reached over to the lamp on the nightstand and turned it off. She hugged a pillow close to her. Eventually, she succumbed to fatigue and sleep.

✪ ✪ ✪

The dream began like it always had. Livia sat in a conference room with a group of Navy wives. As the senior-most among them… alive… Livia "led" the group, who sat in a circle of folding chairs in the generic meeting room, talking about the problems and challenges confronting them all. In the Navy tradition, she was 'responsible' for them, almost as though she were an actual officer herself.

Of course, even back on Earth, before the Apocalypse, when people thought they had *genuine problems*, there had always been an earful to listen to. Now, though, it truly was a wartime setting, except that now it was a race of ten-foot-tall aliens that had been lording over the entire galaxy for a million years that the meager remnants of mankind now fought.

So, besides complaints about housing, childcare, clothing, food, and everything else, there was genuine fear, dread, and terror over what promised to be a generational war for the next thousand years or more. No pressure.

Her phone chirped a reminder from inside her purse.

> Livia stood there in her slip, looking at herself. She shouted,
> but no words came out. No one could see or hear her. No… ignore it
> this time. Don't' go! Please no! Not again!

Livia smiled, excusing herself, and stood. The council meeting would begin shortly, and she'd been determined to be there to represent not only her … constituency… but her own personal interests and ambitions as well.

> Dreamtime jumped forward, and in the next moment, she
> stood in front of the double doors leading to the City Hall lobby. The
> sound of myriad voices and occasional laughter filtered through
> the doors. Do something! Don't let it happen again! Shout, yell, warn
> them…!

Livia approached the end of the hallway that connected to the atrium outside the council chambers. She approached the double doors and felt herself smile and adjust her face and composure.

As always, she never heard the explosion. She awoke on the floor amid the pieces of the doors, debris, and… blood. Her ears were ringing again, as they did for weeks afterward.

Livia coughed and staggered to her feet, one heel missing and her department store business suit ripped and torn. Blinking through the smoke, she stumbled forward through the falling ash and… horrible… things. Electrical conduits sparked and flashed around her, and waves of heat from fires blistered her skin. She slipped and fell.

> Oh God, not again. No, no, no, no, please, no!

Livia's hands slipped and scraped as she struggled to stand amid the decapitated remains of Councilman Hickum. As she rose to her knees, she shook her head and saw that only two people were standing. Vice President Gail Finley and Commander Thomas Harding. They were saying something to each other, but all Livia could hear was the ringing in her ears.

And then Gail, matter-of-factly, smoothly, and with no hesitation whatsoever, reached inside her jacket, withdrew an enormous gun, and shot the man dead.

Livia screamed. And then promptly fainted and collapsed into the blood and gore that was all that remained of the councilman.

✪ ✪ ✪

Preston Milner heard the cries and sobs from Livia's nightmare. He was rarely home to listen to them, but he knew they had frequently happened since the bombing. As always, he quietly walked to her door and waited to make sure she went back to sleep. And, as always, he did not enter her room to comfort her. Her frequent infidelity before Awakening Day had been a knife through his heart.

After Awakening Day, he'd confronted her, knowing that the only reason she was alive was due to yet another tryst. He'd stopped himself short of beating her. He had never contemplated violence before. Instead, he ordered her out of his room and out of his life. Despite everything, she then convinced him it would be a mistake. He needed her. They had reached a mutual understanding of the political necessity that they be viewed by others as a couple in this bible belt nightmare.

Preston's heart burned in shame, hatred, and longing for her as he silently retreated to his separate bedroom.

✪ ✪ ✪

Livia awoke with a start, tangled in her sheets, sweat-soaked, and her face wet with tears. She reached down, pulled the cheap comforter over her, curled into a fetal position, and silently rocked herself, fighting rage, fear, sorrow, and loneliness. Blinking her eyes clear, Livia could see the shadow of Preston's feet at her door. She held her breath to see if, this time, he would.... She started to call his name but stopped herself.

The shadow disappeared.

Livia swallowed, pulled the comforter over her head, and silently sobbed, her chest heaving as her lips trembled and her tears flowed unbidden. She'd loved him once… and still did, truth be told, but he'd been an ass, and she'd been a bigger one and burned their marriage to the ground out of selfish spite.

Now, in this God-Forsaken place, she was utterly alone. Literally a refugee of a shattered race. Her daughter was gone… her father… all of her power, influence, and wealth. Her planet. Even her shoes. All gone.

Eventually, inevitably, the tears stopped. After a time, she pulled the comforter back, sat up, and pushed the tangled mess of her hair aside. Light filtered through her balcony drapes from the artificial dawn.

Livia sniffed, angled her feet over the side of the bed, and shakily stood. Her slip was damp and cold. She shouldered herself out of it and let it drop to the floor. Girding herself against the sudden chill of her still-damp skin, she padded naked to the bathroom and turned on the light. She pulled her hair back with a band, sniffed, and critically evaluated herself in the mirror.

*I even *look* like a refugee.* Her pale skin was tightly drawn against her pelvic bones in clear relief. *Even my tits have shrunk.*

That's it. I can't go on this way.

Livia turned on the shower as hot as she could stand and a bit more. She ignored her disgust at the cheap shampoo and conditioner she'd managed to find. Later, after drying off, she sat in front of the mirror and brushed her hair, taking time to compose herself carefully and deliberately.

She dressed in jeans and a loose sweater, opened the drapes and the sliding glass door, and walked barefoot onto the balcony amid what passed for morning light in New London. It was identical to the thousands of other balconies amid the forest of apartment towers in this part of New London. Other people lounged on other balconies here and there among the forest of off-white towers. A few people waved at her. Of course, pretty much everyone in New London knew who she was. She reflexively waved back. She did have duties and responsibilities, after all.

She gripped the handrail and closed her eyes as the breeze softly played with her hair. The image came back to her as she remembered *again.* How amid all the chaos, Gail Finley, of all people, that nobody Air Force pilot who the yokels' DownSide seem to worship, had stood her ground and *done something.* Not only did she do something… she shot dead that son of a bitch, the mad bomber Harding.

You've always thought you were so damned strong and decisive, Livia. But when the shit hit the fan, you freaked out like a weak, spineless little girl and that… person. That … nobody … stood there like fucking Rambo and…. And acted. That tomboy pilot who these flyover-country bumpkins made Vice President… acted. You could see it in her eyes. Her anger, her strength… her Power.

Livia shivered, despite the comfortable temperature.

She turned and went back inside, leaving the sliding door open. She sat cross-legged in a chair beside the window and opened the laptop Preston had used his influence to obtain for her. She tightened her lips and began to search and read about trauma, trauma triggers, and …. coping. She found a list and swallowed hard as she read it:

- Replaying the Memory…. *Yes. Over and over…*
- Nightmares… *no shit…*
- Flashbacks… *yes…*
- Fear and Anxiety… She swallowed… *yes…*
- Anger… *oh God, yes…*
- Sadness… Her eyes burned… *oh so much…*
- Guilt … *Fuck yes!...*
- Feeling Numb… *all the time…*
- Blaming Yourself for the Trauma… Yes… *If only I'd been a few moments earlier or later…*
- Seeing Yourself as Weak or Inadequate…. *Yes, of course, I was weak! I freaked out! I fucking… fainted…*
- Criticizing Yourself for Reactions to the Trauma… *uh, yeah, I just did that again…*
- Feeling Constantly On Guard… Not for the first time, she looked down and saw that her hands were shaking… *yes…*
- Being Easily Startled… *Yeah, like how you panicked at the Cemetery during the memorial. When they started shooting those stupid guns in that stupid 21-gun salute, you nearly jumped out of your skin!...*
- Loss of interest in food, weight loss, or the opposite… *uh- huh…*
- Difficulty Sleeping … *no shit, Dick Tracy…*

And then the last item on the list startled her.

- Loss of Interest in Sex

Livia flinched. Then she slammed the laptop closed and pushed it away from her. Breathing hard, she pulled her knees up to her chest in the chair and stared out the open door for a long time.

Not once. Not once have you thought about sex since then. I mean… Preston believes you're a slut… and maybe I did become one. Before. What does it say that I'm such a weak headcase? Damn you, Livia. Get a grip!

Minutes later, she reopened the laptop and typed an email: "Gloria, I need your help. I know I've been in a funk since the bombing. I know it hasn't been easy for you either. Can we get together… and talk? And another thing…can you teach me to shoot?"

Home Front

• • • • • • • • • • • • • • • •

DownSide:
Hoffman-Collins Ranch

Councilwoman Esmerelda Collins gently rocked six-month-old Nolan Collins Hoffman Garreth in the hundred-year-old rocking chair, holding him in one arm. At the same time, she read a copy of the latest draft of the new constitution in her free hand. Across from her, in an equally old rocking chair, the child's mother, long blonde-haired and blue-eyed Sandra, mirrored the scene as she held Nolan's twin sister, Margaret, while reading her thumb-eared, marked-up copy of the same document.

Esmerelda had been Sandra's godmother and close family friend to fellow councilman Barrett Hoffman and his family. When Barrett, his wife Margaret, their son Nolan and grandmother Abigail all died on Awakening Day, Esmerelda had taken the surviving children, sisters Sandra (17), Jordan (15), Hannah (11), Elizabeth (8), and little brother Vicktor (2), under her wing.

Grandmother Abigail was among the 5% who never awoke on Awakening Day. The alien "Stalker" creature had captured and cocooned the Barrett family. Lt. David Garreth's Army Ranger squad, accompanied by Sherriff's Deputy Grayson Miles, had discovered the scene and were likewise captured. The Stalker had killed Barrett, Margaret, Nolan, Deputy Miles, and Corpsman Mendez. The rest would have soon suffered the same fate had John Austin, then the County Sheriff, not arrived at the Hoffman house for a welfare check and managed to kill the Stalker.

The survivors had quickly recovered from their ordeal while in hospital isolation. During that time, David and Sandra had… bonded. A desperate romance ensued that culminated in their celebrated storybook Christmas wedding. Before the marriage, though, Esmerelda had formally adopted the remaining Hoffman children, merging their two families. She now spent most of her time alternating between council meetings and the Collins and Hoffman ranches.

With the Keeper Raid and so many other stunning discoveries and revelations slowly fading in the proverbial rear-view mirror, the citizenry, the survivors of humanity, had begun to fall into the routine of 'the new normal.' Of late, however, the council's work on the draft constitution had drifted to the forefront of public awareness. Survival, shelter, food, and, to an extent, jobs, were for the most part, settling into place.

With that new routine, more and more people had time to worry about other things. Like, shortages of consumer goods and politics. And second-guessing the decisions made by their "leaders."

The better part of a year ago, Mayor Tom Parker and the rest of the council had begun work on a draft constitution in relative isolation. At the time, it had been a welcome diversion from the onslaught of tumultuous life-and-death situations and decisions. The council knew it would be necessary 'in the future,' but few other people cared.

Now, however, more and more people were showing an interest, and it was usually the top daily news story. The discussion had grown from quiet coffee shop debates to rancorous public square arguments and even a few protests and demonstrations at the University.

Sandra shook her head. "I can't believe they're complaining about the representation model. I thought that had been totally ironed out?"

Esmerelda looked up at Sandra with a half-smile, brushing her now waist-length brown hair out of her eyes. She usually kept it in a ponytail, but Nolan and Margaret liked to play with it, so she let it down when she visited. "Sandy, you know that people need any distraction they can find. Things are finally starting to settle down for most. They need to feel like they have control over *something* in their lives. The Gardeners altered our bodies, and the Accipiters murdered our world. On the surface, things may *look* somewhat normal, even something like what they were used to, at least if you don't go outside and look *up*, but everyone knows this is not just an alien world. It's an *artificial* alien world. People need something *real* to hang onto… to feel like they have some semblance of control over their lives and their own future."

Sandra sighed, "I know… it's just… why can't they be grateful for the first version ya'll wrote? It was good!"

Esmerelda laughed softly. "I know how you feel. Tom kept us focused, and the original version was beautiful in its brevity. Maybe if we had held the convention back then, we could have passed it through and been done with it."

"I know, I know. Then that monster Harding blew up City Hall and killed all those people, and everything changed."

Esmerelda bit her lip as she remembered. "That's right. And don't forget the baby boom and everything else. Oh, and speaking of the baby boom, estimates are we'll run out of diapers later this year, despite the Gardener supplied warehouses. We don't even have a supply chain to be broken anymore, and the shortages are going to start to really hurt very soon. People will have food and shelter, but the things they are used to, the common consumer comforts are running out. We've had to deal with those issues and so many others. One thing after another delayed us working on the draft constitution, and now everyone wants to have their say. We'll listen, and maybe there will be the occasional good idea, but I'll be damned if I let us wander too far away from our original intent. Too much is at stake."

Margaret quietly blinked awake, stretched, and softly struggled in Sandra's arms, signaling that she wanted to go down. At almost the exact same moment, Nolan followed suit.

Sandra and Esmerelda let them down on the floor to crawl, Margaret in her pink and yellow onesie and Nolan in his blue and white striped version. They both giggled in unison as they crawled toward each other. They stopped and stared into each other's eyes for just a moment… then in unison, they both struggled to stand and succeeded, facing each other and grasping each other's hands as they laughed.

Then, they let go of each other, turned, and slowly, shakily, walked back to Sandra and Esmerelda.

Esmerelda gasped, "My God, Sandra, they're only six months old!"

Sandra beamed as she reached for her phone to send a video to David, "Um, they did this yesterday, but it does seem early…. Vicktor didn't walk until he was nearly a year old…. Is this bad?"

Year 3 PAD:

January

Navy

● ● ● ● ● ● ● ● ● ● ● ● ● ● ● ●

TopSide:
New Pentagon, Conf Room A47

Vice Admiral Preston Stewart Milner, III, and his three-man security detail paused outside the entrance to the spacious and superbly equipped conference room. He was tired, irritated, frustrated, and worried. Tired and weary from managing one crisis after another in this seemingly untouched yet completely artificial consolation prize of a world. *Only it is not really a consolation prize at all, is it? The Gardeners built it as a giant gladiator village, all so we could live here in secret and grow more gladiators so we could go out and fight the Accipiters. For what? Because they can't? Or for their amusement?*

Not one thing in it was original to Earth, including himself and all the other "survivors" of mankind. Even they were essentially "copies" of their original selves, xeroxed, as it were, mere moments before they would have all been vaporized in the Accipiter's kinetic bombardment. Decades later, the Gardeners recreated them here, inside the nearly 4,000-mile-long hollow world the majority had dubbed "New Texas," of all things.

He was weary from the weight of responsibility dumped on his shoulders. He was the senior surviving military officer, not just from the American contingent, but among all the survivors from other nations of man. On Awakening Day, the combined populations of Fort Brazos and the personnel and civilians at the DownSide Joint Reserve Base numbered approximately one hundred and twenty-one thousand. The TopSide city in (New) New London added another twenty-two thousand. Besides these, almost thirteen thousand military personnel from over twenty other countries awoke to learn that they, too, had been rescued or abducted, depending on your point of view, from their military home bases around the Earth.

Amongst all of them from any nation, the only Flag or General Officers were himself, Rear Admiral Lower Half Andre Johansson, United States Navy; Major General Alexander Marcus, United States Air Force; and Brigadier General Sabrina Chilton, British Army Royal Corps of Signals. Alexander Marcus was now Secretary of War, leaving even fewer experienced shoulders than before. That didn't leave many left to rest the responsibility for the survival of mankind upon. It weighed heavily on all of them.

The gradually escalating distractions, griping, and general discontent frustrated Preston. He understood that complaining about "little things" took people's minds off the Apocalypse, but that didn't make it any less frustrating. One of the most annoying of these was the simmering discontent over promotions. The promotion list among the remaining gaggle of Colonels, Majors, and Captains was a hotly debated issue. They had decided early on, for the most part, to throw seniority out the window. Promotions were to be based on merit and competence. Institutional knowledge doesn't mean much when the institutions and all their people are gone.

After the debacle of Commander Harding, who had apparently gone nuts and set off a bomb at City Hall—killing many and injuring more—the clamoring for promotions based on seniority had died down. Preston had no illusions that it was a permanent change, but he welcomed it while it lasted.

Lastly, he was worried about his wife, Livia. The fact that their marriage, pre-Awakening Day, had devolved into an empty shell, highlighted by the irony of the inverse relationship between his affection and her flagrant cheating. After Awakening Day, when she'd been found, he'd known why she'd survived. Wherever it was that she'd been and whoever she'd been with must have been on or near the base. It was the only reason she'd been swept up by the Gardeners in the moments before New London's submarine base was incinerated by the Accipiter kinetic strike.

After being publicly reunited, they'd fought as soon as they were alone. Preston was ashamed of how he'd lost his temper, fueled by years of quiet despair over her infidelity, and now losing their daughter in the Accipiter attack. After all, here she was, practically caught in the act, and she was alive, and Helena wasn't. He'd very nearly let himself physically strike Livia… or worse. Instead, he'd ordered her to leave. Permanently. She'd convinced him doing so would be… politically damaging. The provincial locals might look askance at mutual recriminations between him and Livia and decide to sideline them both. With no money and only the clothes on their backs, their future could turn out to be quite grim. He'd relented and grudgingly agreed to keep up appearances.

And then, the bombing happened. Livia had been there, and the experience had shaken her to her core. She'd stopped… anything. She'd walled herself away, and he'd been shocked at how much weight she'd lost — and she'd been quite thin, to begin with. The fact that he was worried about her had surprised him, and he didn't know what to do with that feeling.

Meanwhile, the days, weeks, and months had become a blur. There was never enough time and never enough people to get things done. It was surreal, he thought. After Awakening Day, the survivors thought they were all that remained of mankind. After the Keeper Raid, they'd learned that the Accipiters had kept a great many humans alive, perhaps millions. However, those under Accipiter "care" weren't entirely human anymore. On a genetic level, they'd been altered to better serve among the panoply of Accipiter servant races. There was no hunger, disease, or want. And while they lived in a version of a paradise under Accipiter control, the remaining humans on Earth worshiped their ten-foot-tall avian-like masters. Not out of gratitude or theology but because their very DNA now demanded it. It was a planet of beautiful, happy, near-immortal slaves.

Here, within and inside New Texas, and he'd never get used to that name, events continued to lurch forward and consume his every waking moment. He wondered whether that 'lurch' was that of a zombie, Frankenstein's monster, or a child's first steps. Or of some horribly tragic combination of all three.

There was never enough time and never enough people. And yet, it was as though time ran faster. More things happened, more decisions were made, and more things got done than he'd ever experienced. One of the older IT advisors, Richard Dawson, who had been retired on Awakening Day, had told him it reminded him of the original Internet boom in the 1990s and what they had, back then, called "Internet Time" — when a day seemed like a month, and a month seemed like a year.

He sighed. This whole shipbuilding process felt insanely reckless and fast. Building a new class of aircraft carriers might take ten to fifteen years or even longer, plus prior design work. Even then, those designs were derived from a previous generation of ships and hundreds of years of wet navy tradition and institutional knowledge. *Now, we need to develop an entire Navy of STARSHIPS! A Navy to eventually dwarf all of old Earth's navies… combined. From scratch! Even with the FAB at Ari'Nell, it will take years, maybe decades, to plan and build our own ships.* He shook his head slowly. This was going to be an interesting meeting.

Indeed, the Ultra Top Secret special project under way at Ari'Nell seemed likely to make an enormous difference, but even that project could only provide pieces of the puzzle. Incredible, insanely essential pieces of the puzzle, but ones that still had to be studied, understood, and integrated into a greater whole.

He nodded at Sergeant Creighton Palmer and the rest of his security detail, all in full body armor and combat gear — yet more fallout from the traitorous and not lamented Commander Harding. The Sergeant, Corporal Glen Segars, and Corporal Clinton Maciekowicz were all newly minted crash-course graduates of the re-created Marine Security Guard course.

Corporal Maciekowicz opened the double doors to the conference room while Corporal Segars entered the room first and confirmed it was safe. Sergeant Palmer followed inside with Preston behind him. Corporal Maciekowicz closed the doors behind him and stood guard outside.

The buzz of somewhat intense conversation cut off as Rear Admiral Lower Half Andre Johansson rose from the conference table and announced, "Attention!"

The meeting had been organized well in advance, with representatives from many of the surviving 'friendly' militaries, including:

- Brigadier Sabrina Chilton from the UK
- Lieutenant General Gideon Markovic from Israel
- Colonel T'ae Chang-Woo (Translator) and Captains Lee Kang-Dae Daewi and Kim Won-yil from (South) Korea
- Colonels Zhang Keshi, and Xu Xiaojiang from China
- Colonel Cesar Salangsang from the Philippines
- Captains Nikolai Efremovich Bogdashin and Valentin Georgiyevich Gorshkov from Russia
- Colonels Jean Nicolas Abbé and Gaspard Xavier Boyer from France
- Colonels Friedrich Fellgiebel and Fritz Erich Fromm from Germany
- Colonels Vikram Rawat and Jaswant Singh Batra from India

From the United States, in addition to Andre Johansson, Captains George Marchetti, Stephanie Mahoney, Robert Handly, Henry Peishel, and Alphonse Halkias represented the remains of the United States Navy. Attending remotely, and shown on the wallscreen, were the former Submarine Commanders Hershel Griggs, Philipa Hodge, Elijah Kleyna,

Malvin Lojacono, Ramona Henry, Dwight Coughlin, Adair Henry, and Rafferty Youngman.

The lone civilian in the room was perhaps one of the most crucial subject matter experts alive. Dr. Hyun Park, Ph.D., was from South Korea's Hyundai Heavy Industries in Ulsan. Before the arrival of the Accipiters, he'd been VP of Logistics at Korea Shipbuilding & Offshore Engineering Co., Ltd., as well as a Professor at Seoul National University. He had been visiting his nephew when he was swept up by the Gardeners.

The conference room was deep and wide, with an enormous flat screen on one wall and glass white boards covering the others. A fat oval conference table large enough for thirty people sat in the middle. It was festooned with laptops, monitors, printouts, books, binders, carafes of water and coffee, and to the annoyance of some, including the French and Russians, no ashtrays.

Preston advanced to the nominal head of the table and paused as he looked around the room, studying the faces of everyone present, each standing in their own (former) military's version of Attention. More than a few still carried the spectre of despair and hopelessness he'd battled himself after Awakening Day. It was the Apocalypse, after all. Still, he also saw ironclad discipline and determination evident in those same faces. They wouldn't be at this meeting otherwise. "At Ease." He pulled his high-backed chair and sat as the rest of the room followed suit.

He frowned as he began, "I have a new ability I've not shared with you before now. I can read your minds." He closed his eyes and held his fingers to his temples. "I can hear the thoughts of many of you around this table. You're thinking, variously…. This is insane. This is reckless. This is impossible. It can't be done. We need more time. We don't have enough people. We don't have the resources. You don't know what you're asking. You're asking too much. I have no experience in this area."

He lowered his hands and raised his eyebrows as he surveyed their faces. Some understood, and some were still catching up. No one in the room was dull.

Andre Johansson chuckled.

Preston shrugged as he glanced at Andre before continuing, "Now that that is out of the way. Those sentiments will not be repeated. Anyone who wishes to do so may leave the room and their rank and commission behind. We don't have the luxury of debate. The Gardeners made it clear that their gun is to our heads, and the plebiscite committed us," he paused, allowing himself a grim smile, "pun intended."

Gaspard Boyer blinked and stifled whatever it was that he was about to say. He tightened his lips before nodding sharply. The Chinese and Russians remained stone-faced, while the Indians, Germans, and Koreans nodded slowly.

Preston admitted, "All right, then. Let's move on. I want to agree with what many of you have already been thinking. Specifically, how the hell are we supposed to not only build but also crew a fleet of starships and fight the Accipiters, who we already know possess *millions* of ships and control the entire galaxy? I'll remind you that Secretary of War Marcus and the Fort Brazos survivors asked themselves the same questions before the Gardeners revealed that they had provided a hybrid starship for us. Vice President Finley called it 'training wheels.' So, either they expect us to take generations to accomplish much of anything, or they have other tricks up their sleeves they haven't deigned to share with us mere humans yet."

Valentin Gorshkov asked, "Have you learned anything from the captured Keeper Ship, or the prisoners, relevant to building *our* fleet?"

Preston forced himself to smile at the breach of protocol but nodded to Andre to answer. It was something to deal with later.

Andre shook his head. "Yes, and no. The vessel itself seems to be largely organic technology. Instead of being designed and manufactured for a specific task, systems are, instead… grown. We may be able to eventually glean useful things from it, but frankly, it scares the hell out of me. Computers and steel I can mostly trust that we can eventually understand. However, this organic technology is so far beyond us that it's not even funny. We're keeping the damned thing quarantined and under constant guard, ready to be flushed out the airlock if it misbehaves."

"Interestingly, we think the thing has its own propulsion system, but it doesn't look anything like the fusion torch drives that most of the Accipiters seem to use. The operating theory is that it uses some sort of gravity drive like the Gardeners told us their big mother ships use, and, given that those mother ships have lots of these Keeper Ships embedded in them, one theory is that they collectively provide the drive for the thing as a whole. That said, how it works and being able to replicate it is, pardon me, Admiral Milner, not likely to happen any year soon." He paused, reading the expression on Valentin's face, "And no, so far, there don't seem to be anything resembling weapons in or on the Keeper ship."

"On the other hand, after seeing how advanced the Keeper ship is, the biggest takeaway, for me, at least, is that with their level of biotechnology, we must be incredibly vigilant about protecting ourselves against biological weapons. The Gardeners tell us that the surviving humans on Earth were *altered* to, in effect, worship the Accipiters. We don't know how this was done, and that scares the hell out of me."

Valentin soberly frowned and dipped his head in acknowledgment.

Preston nodded to Andre to continue with the agenda.

Andre looked up at the wallscreen, "Captain Mahoney has led a team of Navy Engineers and faculty from the university to study the effects of exposure to vacuum and, for all we know, any side effects from being inside the warp bubble that the Phoenix drive rings provide. By way of introduction, while the Captain only holds a B.S. in Engineering, she brings with her an important set of organizational and management skills and experience. She is a former Chief of Staff of Naval Sea Command and is, or I suppose she was, a Seminar Fellow from the Massachusetts Institute of Technology. She graduated from the Naval Academy, the Navy War College, and the Joint Forces Staff College and holds an MBA from Troy University. Moreover, she has credentials from the Harvard Business School Advanced Management Program."

She nodded. Stephanie's expression was intense and focused. Her shock of somewhat wild, loose blonde hair had grown fast. She'd been medically retired on Awakening Day, undergoing stage four ovarian cancer chemotherapy, and lost all her hair. While five percent of the civilian population in the city of Fort Brazos had been "culled" to prove how serious the Gardeners were about their demands, none of the New London survivors had suffered that fate. However, what they had in common with all survivors was that every disease, infection, and infirmity had been cured and corrected, along with a general reset of the telomere aging clock. Stephanie's service in the Navy had been reactivated, and she had ferociously seized upon her second chance at life.

Andre added, "Captain, I'll save you the trouble of explaining that you are operating with limited resources and that the experience and expertise of your team, while they are, I'm sure, working hard, they aren't exactly NASA or space scientists and engineers. Please tell us what you've learned so far."

Stephanie grimaced, "Yes, Admiral. I'll share my screen." The screen filled with an image of a soot-black colored substance that seemed to be both needle-sharp and spongy at the same time. It was threaded with vein-like structures. "Many of you will recognize this material as the substance that the Gardeners covered the hull of the former USS Montana with. The material is incredibly tough. Microscopic examination has shown it to be bundles of single-walled carbon nanotubes. We believe these absorb thermal photons and emit light in a narrow bandwidth that can be recycled as electricity back into the power used by the warp rings. It solved the question of how our waste heat wasn't building up and cooking us. Remember, in the vacuum of space, there is no air or water with which to dissipate heat. That's a crucial reminder for our future building program that any design must be able to manage and cope with internally generated waste heat. Also, because I'm sure some of you are wondering, this material captures and recycles the heat energy from both inside the boat and from external thermal radiation."

The image on the screen changed to show a framework of welded-together metal struts and tubing. "What you are looking at now is what remains of the jury-rigged system that Captain Underwood and his crew used during the Keeper Raid to fire the shotgun… the barrels of several million ball bearings at relativistic speed, at the Accipiter fleet. We've all seen the footage from the attack. However, that's not why I'm showing you this. While we were lucky the built-in heating system helped to avoid problems with vacuum welding, the welds in some of the surrounding support framework showed cracks and an increase in hardness and tensile strength along with a significant decrease in ductility and fracture toughness, i.e., embrittlement. We believe that this results from a combination of temperature, vacuum, and, more importantly, irradiation. We found nanometer-sized clusters of Nickle, Magnesium, Silicon, and Copper atoms in the welds. This would seem to be analogous to what we have observed in welds in nuclear reactors. While the welds were not in imminent danger of failure, the damage was significant enough that we think it would shorten the reliable lifetime of those structures."

"When Blood Phoenix returned from the mission, we performed many x-ray tests on various components. We found nothing that gave us pause, so we hypothesize that the nanotube coating may have provided a surprising degree of protection. Obviously not enough to protect the crew from a fatal dose of ionizing radiation, but we think it was significantly less than what the unprotected areas outside the hull experienced. In our more recent findings, however, we cannot rule out the possibility without more detailed tests, that the exposure may have, to some extent, lowered the meantime between failure for components under stress. The nuclear power plant containment vessel, however, was designed with knowledge of radiation-induced embrittlement in mind, so it, at least we think, should be less affected than the rest of the vessel's structure. Regardless, we should do more in-depth x-ray testing of key structural components when she returns from her cruise."

Preston shook his head slowly, "That is very sobering news, Captain. What are your recommendations?"

"Admiral, in aerospace engineering, we've always thought in terms of making things lighter, reducing the mass we have to either get into the air or lift into orbit. That meant thin metal, aluminum, and walls you felt like you could just about poke your finger through. With the Phoenix-type warp rings, mass seems like much less of a factor than sheer volume with regard to fitting inside the confines of the rings. In future designs, we may need to start thinking like old-school wet navies and include heavily armored hulls and even lead shielding, at least in some areas. I'm sure that it won't be quite that simple in practice. However, I believe we need to consider entirely new designs for hulls, airlocks, interior layouts, vacuum-tight pressure doors, cargo handling, and damage control."

"Also, as most of you know, Phoenix provides a gravity field inside the rings. However, when the drive shuts down, so does the gravity. Obviously, submarines were not designed for Zero-G. We need to think about adding handholds and other lessons from the ISS. Perhaps more importantly, though, we need to think about shielding against particle impact while the protection of the warp field is absent, especially when coasting at relativistic speeds."

She paused and shook her head. "Of course, we're talking about industry and supply chain levels that we don't begin to have here in New Texas. We don't have the industry and supply chain to provide all the armour, pieces, parts, nuts, bolts, screws, valves, wires, servos, actuators, instrumentation, sensors, plumbing, and a million other things. We don't have the raw materials and alloys we need or the infrastructure to refine them, even if we did. Hell, I'm told that by the end of this year that up to maybe a quarter of the cars in Fort Brazos won't run anymore because of the lack of parts, tires, and even engine oil. We certainly don't have a microchip fab or the stockpiles of rare earths."

"What's more, the interior of New Texas is very Earthlike. However, as you know, the surface isn't… well… real. While there is soil and rock, etc., it is only skin deep. We can't mine for minerals. Until we can build up industry here, we're going to have to get the raw minerals from somewhere else."

Preston added, "Now, once again, I know what you all are thinking. What about the FAB that Phoenix created in Ari'Nell? Why don't we use *it* to build what we need? Admiral Johansson, please remind everyone of the reason why."

Andre sighed as he shook his head. "It doesn't do us much good to build a shipyard we can't protect. And, of course, we need a million subsystems before we even get to the part where we can put them together *in* a shipyard. We only have the one FAB for now. We didn't build one here in this system because we found the surrounding asteroids to be mineral poor, and the rings at Ari'Nell are chock full of highly refined metals and even radionuclides. So, for the next several months, we tasked

Commander Sinitskaya and her team with pumping out as many mines as possible to protect the system. The other weapon system Phoenix provided designs for will take months or longer to study and determine if or how we can adapt it to our own use."

Preston nodded, "Over time, we're adding more and more people and resources there, but this doesn't happen overnight. Face it, though. Ari'Nell is exposed. Vulnerable. We cannot afford to put all our eggs in one basket. In the meantime, we need to focus on planning for how we can transfer technology manufactured there to New Texas and develop our plan for industrializing the system that we're currently located in. That said, Captain Mahoney, I believe you had an additional topic to cover?"

Stephanie walked over and pointed at a new image on the conference room wallscreen. "Thank you, Admiral. I'm sure that all of you will remember those little domes embedded within those carbon nanotubes, interspersed every ten feet or so, all around the hull? It turns out that those are a point defense system against micrometeorites for when the warp field is turned off. We don't begin to have the technology and infrastructure to replicate those things, so, as I said before, we need to worry about that on future ships. I don't know how the Gardeners expect us to build a fleet of starships with stone knives and bearskins, at least not anytime in the next several decades, so I have to think they've got one more shoe to drop, sooner or later."

Andre raised his eyebrows and took a deep breath. "Well, Captain, I think all of us have been waiting for that other shoe for a while now, and for a whole host of reasons, not the least of which is the sheer mind-boggling number of Accipiters that apparently lord over most of the entire damned galaxy. Exactly how we're supposed to put even a tiny dent in that is clearly either a delusional goal of the Gardeners, or they must have a hell of a big shoe left to drop."

Preston reached over and poured a glass of water from one of the carafes around the table. He lifted the glass halfway to his lips and paused in thought, then shook his head, took a sip, and nodded to Andre to continue.

Andre glanced at his notes before smiling grimly at Stephanie, "Thank-you, Captain. Next, we have a special civilian expert here to shed some light on what we are facing in building a shipyard. While many of us have experience, to some degree, in the area of sea trials and fitting out of new vessels, Dr. Hyun Park brings a unique background that we are extraordinarily fortunate to have available to us. Dr. Park was Vice President of Logistics at what was then the world's largest shipyard at the Busan Naval Base in Nam-Gu, Busan, South Korea. His company was the Korea Shipbuilding and Offshore Engineering Company. He was also a professor at Seoul National University. In short, while we know that many New London survivors have specialized experience in the shipbuilding industry, Dr. Park was instrumental in planning and designing the modern infrastructure, robotics, and supply chain needed for the Busan expansion."

"We've assigned a working group to Dr. Park, and they've been meeting for the last several weeks, brainstorming ideas and laying out a preliminary working plan. Dr. Park?"

Resisting the urge to stand, Dr. Park instead paused to look around the room for a moment. Wearing a simple grey business suit and conservative tie, he was conspicuously different from all the uniformed military officers. In the past, before Awakening Day, he would have relished the prominence he now had.

Like so many others who were caught up by the Gardeners, his wife Areum and daughters Gi, Iseul, Myeong, Nari, and Uk were not saved. The hollowness he felt inside had not diminished with time. He'd been living in a small spare bedroom with a young American family, George and Karen, who had done their best to make him feel welcome. He'd felt that there was nothing left to live for, and he had slowly been thinking more and more about suicide. Then Karen became pregnant. The sight of her growing belly had only pushed him further down the spiral of depression. That is, until the babies came. All four of them.

He'd been honor bound to help his hosts and aid in caring for the children. And it wasn't just his host family — it seemed that babies were being born everywhere. It was the Fort Brazos baby boom, and it saw a massive number of multiple births. Karen's quadruplets, Cara, Casey, Carla, and Caitlin, had not healed his horrible loss. They had, however, become necessary to him and he'd been amazed to find himself becoming a surrogate grandfather. That was when the Admiral tracked him down and told him how much they needed him and how important a role he would play in mankind's future. Tearing himself away from his surrogate grandchildren had been harder than he'd dreamed possible. So much so that he'd leveraged his newfound status to ensure that he would never be too far away from them, and he was working hard to convince George and Karen to move to New London to one of the luxury apartments next to the one he had been given. It wasn't assigned to him; he'd been given a deed of ownership. It was his for as long as he wanted, free and clear. He even had the clout to ensure that George and Karen would have good jobs in New London. Regardless, George, Karen, and the children had become his lifeline. He wouldn't give them up.

As he looked around the room, he saw different reactions. Most seemed to be looking to him for hope and leadership. Some seemed suspicious. The Chinese had good poker faces, but he knew they were institutionally hostile. The Russians seemed to be generally angry and cynical. Most of the others were hard for him to read. Regardless, he knew that many would be depending on him, and he would not let them down. Intellectually, he knew that, like himself, most of the people in the room had also lost their families.

Living with George and Karen had freshened his English language skills, and the meetings over the past few weeks had pushed him further. He took a deep breath, calmed himself, and glanced at his notes before beginning. "Thank you, Admiral Johansson. Admiral Milner. Let me begin by saying that in order to do what these Gardener aliens are demanding of us, our efforts must, by their nature, grow to be the greatest endeavor ever accomplished by humankind. It seems possible to me that these Accipiters may have more ships in service than all the naval vessels ever built in the history of mankind combined. An 18th-century Pacific islander taking a canoe out against the might of the British Royal Navy is not even an apt comparison. And yet, we must begin somewhere. I cannot imagine the military strategy needed to defeat such an enemy." He allowed a small smile. "However, that is your job, not mine."

Soft chuckles drifted across the room. Preston smiled, "Touché, Dr. Park."

He sighed and nodded. "In Busan, we used robots to weld pre-manufactured sections of vessels together. One of your officers called it 'Legos.' Indeed, my children," he frowned, "played with them." He swallowed. "It is as good a metaphor as any. Our shipbuilding program will need the materials Captain Mahoney talked about. That is someone else's job, too. More than that, however, we must first build the industry to build the tools… to build the tools… to build the machines and robots that we will need to build the shipyard, to build your ships. In many ways, we must first build a civilization that can provide the supply chain of tools, machines, pieces, and parts we will need. I'm confident that the FAB at Ari'Nell will eventually be freed up to help us manufacture many of the tools and even the robots we need to get started."

"Meanwhile, we must consider the requirements for the ships we will ultimately build. We must design them to survive, not just the conditions of outer space; they must also be warships. That means they must have layered and redundant systems, instrumentation, and the facilities and capability to operate for months or even years at a time without outside support or a friendly port of call. Wooden ships of the past had the tools to stop at an island and gather trees and materials so that their skilled carpenters could repair and replace broken masts, patch the hull, and even gather materials to make new ropes, pulleys, and even forge nails and other metal parts. I do not know what the brave men and women in our ships will encounter out there, but like their ancestors, they will need the tools and ability to forage for supplies and repair damage to the hull and equipment as well as to repair broken and worn-out equipment."

"Over the lifetime of the vessels, their missions may require different hardware to be installed, so designs must be flexible. It seems safe to assume that for many years we will not have very many ships, no doubt limited not just by the number of hulls but also by the limited availability of skilled crews. So, the ships we do build may need to be altered and refitted many times. As Captain Mahoney pointed out, we must find a balance in our designs so that the hull, mechanical, and electrical systems can be maintained, repaired, and inspected. I don't know how the conditions our ships will operate in will affect things. We may find that, or rather, we will probably find that some of the components we use don't last long or have maintenance or reliability problems and will need to be replaced. Hopefully, whatever it is that does fail isn't buried so deep into the structure of the vessel that scrapping the ship is easier than replacing the failed wiring, plumbing, or other systems."

"Will the stresses of being in the warp field and having gravity turned on and off eventually cause metal fatigue leading to a hull breach? We don't know. As for what happens when aliens start shooting at us… well… that's not just a damage control discussion. What kinds of weapons would be used, and what effect will they have on the materials we build with? We probably won't know that until it happens. I can only hope that our people… which may include some of *you,* will be able to come back and tell us."

"And then there is the issue of what exactly do we prioritize in our building program, once we can actually have a building program and the ability to actually build ships. A shipyard must have certain infrastructure in order to function. I am confident we will need an array of the functional equivalent of tugs and other utility craft. In your wet Navy, you had many support vessels. Clearly, we will need the ability to go to other places to gather materials, mine for minerals, and so on. By the time we start building warships, will we have different classes? Scouts? Escorts? Even capital ships, eventually? How far will they need to travel, and how long will they need to be gone and operate independently and remotely? As one of your officers described, what will their operational envelope be?"

He reached for his water glass and took a sip. "What may be the hardest problem of all is people. We don't have enough skilled workers, engineers, materials scientists, environmental controls specialists, and not even remotely enough understanding of the technology used by Phoenix to warp space and all the other things it does. It is fortunate indeed that Phoenix is able to do all that it does. We are utterly dependent upon Phoenix to provide not only propulsion but also most of the other really hard parts of space travel. It provides all the information needed for navigation, sensors and even a gravity field. Much of what we might build today is really just so much cargo. Oh, and I'm not even going to bother mentioning the whole subject of weapons and the fact that we do not have any genuinely effective ones. Even I, with no military experience whatsoever, realize that throwing ball bearings at what were effectively stationary targets is not likely to work twice."

"When Phoenix returns, we need to ask some questions. If it can build copies of itself, can it also create air for the crew? Food? Other things? Or does it have knowledge of how we could do that?"

"On Earth, it took decades to build a major shipyard. That wasn't just the labor of the people who were there. It was also the labor of the tens or hundreds of thousands of people who made all the things in the supply chain used in the construction and operation of the shipyard itself. I believe that we *can* do this. However, unless this 'other shoe' that keeps getting mentioned is dropped by the Gardeners, it may take a generation or more to get there."

Purpose

● ● ● ● ● ● ● ● ● ● ● ● ● ● ● ● ●

DownSide: Morgan Island

Morgan Island was located over two thousand miles from Fort Brazos, putting it "overhead" but far enough from the suntube to be visible day or night. Given the hostility of the nearly twenty-five hundred North Koreans exiled there, it wasn't the farthest distance away possible since New Texas was an almost four-thousand-mile-long cylinder, but it was thought that putting your enemies in a location clearly visible from you but at the same time practically very far away, was the best compromise. They had named Morgan Island after Emily West Morgan (c. 1815–1891), who had been an indentured servant popularly known as "The Yellow Rose of Texas" who, legend has it, contributed to winning the Texas Revolution from Mexico.

Before the discovery of New London and its survivors, the people of Fort Brazos had naturally named the land masses within New Texas with familiar names such as Texas heroes, medal of honor winners, etc. The most common map layout placed the continent where Fort Brazos was in the middle, surrounded by the continents of Houston, Fannin, Travis, Austin, Navarro, Crockett, Bowie, and Chennault. Fort Brazos was located at the continent's far "northern" end. South of it was Morgan Island, which itself was north of Kyle, east of Nava, and west of Zavala, Nimitz, and Parker.

At the time of the exile, Gail Finley had thought it was suitably ironic to deport the all-male and extremely misogynist North Koreans on an island named after a woman who'd been a half-step away from being a slave and a freedom fighter.

They provided the exiles with plenty of food, clothing, survival gear, and basic hand tools to get them started on building whatever style of camp or settlement they chose. The island was lush and thoroughly searched for large or particularly dangerous predators, including any of non-Earth origin. They found none. Indeed, many had thought the island was too good to "waste" on exiles.

Back on Earth, many would have considered it a tropical paradise that included picturesque, long sandy beaches. On the other hand, virtually all the islands within the confines of New Texas were ideal for human habitation in one way or another. Once every few weeks, the Americans flew overhead in their alien ILCs to check on them and occasionally drop off a few supplies and letters from Lieutenant Ryon Ki-Nam.

Commander (Chungjwa) Choe Pyong-Chol, of the, or rather, formerly of the North Korean Maritime Special Purpose Forces 34th Army Navy Sniper Brigade, led his scout platoon as he quietly climbed through the dense island vegetation up the small mountain. He carried the single precious rifle the Americans had provided the exiles, an old but serviceable Vietnam-era Chinese Type 56 SKS carbine. Not that he dared actually shoot anything with it. The twenty rounds of ammunition it held were all they'd been allowed. Still, its excellent bayonet should be sufficient to deal with any of the wild pigs they might run into. That and the fire-hardened spears his men carried. Why only the one single rifle? Because the Americans had decided the North Koreans didn't really need it for protection, and they feared that more would only be put to ill use.

He shook his head as he thought to himself, *Spears. That is what they reduced us to.*

Of the twenty-five hundred men who had woken up in this nightmare, only twenty-two hundred and forty-eight remained. Two hundred and thirty-seven had defected and remained with the Americans. Since their exile to the island, a total of fifteen had been executed by Colonel (Daechwa) P'aeng Jin-Hwan. He'd only used his pistol once. It was the only other firearm on the island. A Chinese Type 54 Tokarev pistol and a fifty-round box of ammunition, now forty-nine.

The rest of the men were held together by a combination of their lifelong duty and loyalty to the Great Leader, the responsibility to their families, and, in no small measure, Jin-Hwan's ruthless and unrelenting discipline. The Colonel lectured daily from his tattered copy of the Great Leader's book. Food, while abundant on the island, was strictly rationed. Building barracks and facilities had not taken long, with a workforce of over two thousand men, even limited by hand tools. The Americans had *generously* provided printed guides and instructions on various construction methods and instructions on setting up cooking, water purification, sanitary, and rudimentary textile manufacturing methods.

Many wanted to burn the books, but Jin-Hwan had wisely declared that the Americans would regret leaving the exiles alive and with the tools to build toward revenge. The Colonel kept all the men busy from dawn until well after dusk, laboring on a hundred projects. He was everywhere, leading, directing, and working just as hard as the rest of the men. Working them each day until they all dropped from exhaustion.

We're too tired to think or complain, especially about the lack of… women. Two thousand men working themselves to death building a small city. A city with no future.

As he approached the crest of a hill, one of his scouts, Seaman (Hagŭp-pyŏngsa), Kwon Ryong-Hae, rushed up the other side towards him.

As the young man approached, Pyong-Chol glared at him. He hissed, "We are on a silent patrol, Seaman Kwon!"

Kwon was wild-eyed and sweat-drenched. He slowed. "Commander, you must come and see what I found!"

✪ ✪ ✪

Jin-Hwan stared at the metal wall for several long minutes before he spoke. Pyong-Chol had been wise to ensure that no one touched the black metallic wall under an overhanging hill face. In the middle was the unmistakable outline, or perhaps the seams of a door. Next to it on the wall, about four feet above the ground was a human hand's recessed shape. Precisely as the letters from Lieutenant Ryon Ki-Nam had described the one found by the Americans. Ki-Nam had also told how the Americans had tested the energy device found inside by launching a projectile with so much force that it had burned up, leaving the atmosphere.

Six platoons of men watched as Jin-Hwan took a deep breath, strode forward, and placed his hand in the depression. The door slid open sideways without a sound, revealing a small, brilliantly lit room. Many of the men gasped and shrank away from the opening. He took a half step back, shielding his eyes. The light dimmed to a less painful level. The space was empty except for a simple round pedestal in the center, topped with a Zero Point Energy device. The cube's complex surface pattern glowed with a soft blue light.

Jin-Hwan's eyes widened, and he smiled. He turned around and faced his men. He boasted, "Today, the evil dog Americans have once again failed. When they brought us here, they failed. They were cowards not to execute us. They were weak by giving us the tools to build." He half-turned and extended his arm toward the glowing cube. "And now they've given us the means for their destruction!"

Return to Ari'Nell

● ● ● ● ● ● ● ● ● ● ● ● ● ● ●

Outside the Sol System
NTN Blood Phoenix CIC

After narrowly escaping the attack back at the Sol System, Charles took Phoenix two light years out from Sol and paused to take stock. Pierce Garrett and Ansel Beck had not yet entered the sail when the attack occurred. None of the crew had been exposed to the radiation. There were numerous injuries, a few broken bones, and three concussions. Commander Hashimoto had been dazed and bled copiously from the laceration on his scalp. However, he was back on duty with his head bandaged. He patently refused to leave the CIC until the danger had passed.

Charles asked, "Phoenix, any sign of pursuit? *Can* they pursue, and how the hell did they target us?"

No Captain, there is no sign of pursuit, and the Accipiters do not possess warp-capable vessels. As for how we were targeted, I hypothesize that the Accipiters were able to detect the… wake, or void might be a better term, left in the solar wind as our warp bubble passed through the outskirts of the Solar System. Using this, the mines were able to approximate our location.

Haruto shook his head slowly, wincing as he did so. "Phoenix, what did they shoot at us with?"

I have analyzed data from the attack and the visuals of Accipiter activity around the Sol system's outer gas giant planets. Upon further review of my data, it appears that they were mining the planets and moons for materials to mass-manufacture millions of mines that are functionally similar to those manufactured at Ari'Nell. When the mines explode, they funnel the atomic energy from the blast into an X-Ray laser. It is a one-time-use weapon less advanced than the ones deployed at Ari'Nell. If anything, they are closer to the designs your people tried and failed to create.

Haruto cocked his head. "Humans tried to make these things?"

Charles nodded, "So that's what it's like to be on the receiving end. I had a class that talked about the 'Star Wars' program back in the '70s and '80s. We tried to build bomb-pumped lasers to shoot down Soviet ICBMs."

Haruto started to shake his head but stopped himself in time. "Tried?"

"The idea was to explode a nuclear bomb connected to a tube of uranium-235. The blast's energy would strike the tube and create a high-energy plasma that would lase. They couldn't get it to work. The design had many problems, including the small matter of actually aiming the thing. The design at Ari'Nell has a tiny warp field used to position it and station keep and to lens the laser."

Haruto sighed. "Well, obviously, using the warp drive to go back in-system is problematic. We'd have to instead go ballistic from well outside the system. That would be a long time in Zero-G and a long time without the protection of the warp bubble if we were detected. Worse, we'd have to shut down the plant completely. The Gardeners made changes to keep it safe for short Zero-G durations, but I don't think pushing it that long during a lengthy ballistic dive into the system would be safe."

Charles grimaced. "And the faster we go, the greater the chance of detection and the more risk we have from particle damage. Conversely, the slower we go, the more solar radiation we'd have to weather." He paused in thought. "Well, that settles it. I'm scrubbing the mission. By now, word will spread, and they'll be on heightened alert. We need to return home with what we've learned."

✪ ✪ ✪

Ari'Shevn Star System
On Approach to Ari'Nell
NTN Blood Phoenix CIC

Ari'Nell, in the Ari'Shevn star system, had been the Ecumenopolis home to trillions of 'Builders.' Over three hundred thousand years before, the Accipiters wiped out the deer-like aliens. They pulverized every structure in the system, glassing Ari'Nell in the process. The former verdant green world was now a desert with millions of crater lakes. The nitrogen, argon, and oxygen atmosphere was barely breathable. The only life present were microbial photosynthetic organisms clinging to life around the impact crater lakes.

The planet had two small moons, but its most prominent feature was its immense glittering ring system. The rings were composed of debris from the smashed Builder orbital megastructure and untold trillions of Builder bodies.

It was amongst these shattered remains that the severely damaged star drive, now called Phoenix, had drifted for over three hundred thousand years. During those eons, it had slowly, painstakingly repaired itself and, perhaps more importantly, grown from servile intelligence to independent sentience.

In an operation euphemistically called "Project Appleseed," when Phoenix had taken the humans to Ari'Nell, it had calved off a small portion of itself and left it in the rings to gather the rare elements needed to, in effect, grow another copy of itself. Captain Jermaine Cutter and a small crew had remained behind to observe and, if possible, assist the process. He and a small crew were aboard the sublight but warp-capable Interplanetary Landing Craft, or "ILC," dubbed the NTN Bowie.

Bowie and the rest of the ILCs discovered in the massive hangar system adjacent to New London, "TopSide" just under the outer surface of the giant New Texas McKendree Cylinder, had been built by the original Builders, who had been significantly larger than humans, somewhere between the size of a large deer and a cow. ILCs measured one hundred and thirty feet long, including their oddly shaped close-wrapped warp rings, and sixty-five feet wide, displacing close to seven hundred and fifty-eight thousand pounds. They were almost all cargo space. The interior was just over seventy feet long, just as wide, and about thirty feet tall. Forward of the cargo section were the environmental systems and controls, an abbreviated living space, a crew area, and the

"Bridge." ILC warp rings housed an operational intelligence that was not sentient. Or rather, they were sentient but not sapient like the much larger Phoenix.

ILCs were not designed for FTL, so they could not travel between New Texas and Ari'Nell without help. Fortunately, it was only a twenty-six-hour hop for Phoenix to ferry ILCs back and forth. After the seed core finished "growing" into a new set of FTL capable drive rings, Bowie had become the central "ship" within the rings. Phoenix then deposited a new core intended for a different purpose. Bowie, ensconced within the FTL drive, was now rechristened as the NTN Revenge.

They had remained on station to assist Commander Alberta "Bertie" Sinitskaya, the newly appointed "System Commander," in the commissioning of the fabrication system, or "FAB," the core had grown into. Bertie, the black-haired, black-eyed, former SUPSHIP at the Groton Connecticut submarine base, had been slated to command operations at the dock facilities in New London, TopSide. When the potential of Ari'Nell had emerged, Admiral Johansson made the case that no one was more qualified than her to lead the effort there.

The Ari'Shevn system was 2.638 light years from New Texas. Communication was only possible via letters, videos, and emails transported back and forth by ship. If there was a more lonely and desolate command possible, she couldn't imagine it. Shrugging off self-pitying feelings of exile, she'd soon embraced the opportunity with a verve and determination that only those who knew her would understand. When she wasn't destroying another set of coveralls, side-by-side with her tiny crew getting the station up and running, she'd taken to wearing the Harley Davidson leather jacket she'd bartered for while DownSide in the now sprawling Fort Brazos flea market. In those rare moments of stolen off-time, usually in the middle of the "night" shift, she'd sit in the cramped bridge of her ILC and stare out at the achingly beautiful rings around the long-dead and devastated planet below, with its endlessly pulverized rust-red surface pockmarked with azure blue crater lakes.

The workforce needed to operate the base and the crews and services required to support *them* steadily blossomed and grew. Bertie's husband, Dr. Dimitri Sinitskaya, a Ph.D. electrical engineer, was in charge of the other engineers. Before Awakening Day, Dimitri had worked at Groton for the Bechtel Group. The FAB, which some people called "The Forge," was fed debris from the ring system day and night, turning the shattered bones of Builder civilization into the system defense mines.

Jermaine Cutter and Revenge supported the station locally, moving equipment and rocks around the rings as well as transporting people and equipment back and forth from the camp on the surface, where, despite the thin air, you could at least walk around and stretch your legs without a vac-suit.

Charles nodded to Haruto, who reached over and tapped PO Hiram Newman on the shoulder. "Tight beam to Revenge, Mr. Newman. Please inform Captain Cutter that we have arrived in-system." Blood Phoenix didn't have tight beam communications lasers; however, a system was in place for Phoenix to lens the warp bubble in such a way as to narrowly focus the radio transmission and aim it at the desired target. An early military decision had been made to never broadcast unidirectional signals. It might take decades or even hundreds or thousands of years for the signal to be intercepted by the Accipiters. However, the war was expected to last that long or longer.

Hiram spoke quietly into his microphone and waited. Four minutes later, he tapped his headphones and nodded. He looked up at Haruto. "Message received and acknowledged. Captain Cutter awaits our arrival."

✪ ✪ ✪

After rendezvousing, Blood Phoenix's ILC, the NTN Kukri, was piloted out of the small hanger underneath the former submarine before transiting to and docking with Revenge. The crews greeted each other and shook hands. Revenge's crew gladly welcomed the chance to exit and stretch their legs. They'd spent time on the bleak surface of Ari'Nell, from time to time, but seeing other familiar faces was a merry occasion.

Charles escorted Jermaine to his cabin for a private meeting with Haruto, briefing him along the way.

Jermaine Cutter had formerly commanded the Hyman G. Rickover, SSN-795. He was a tall, six-foot, one-inch African American with movie-star good looks from a wealthy Boston family. Once they were all in the limited privacy of Charles' cabin, Jermaine swore, "God dammit, Charles! I expected the Accipiters to be stirred up after Phil's raid, but this? I can't believe we almost lost you too! I can't believe they mined the Sol system with mines like the ones we are making here!"

Charles blinked in surprise and added mildly, "I think you've been cooped up in that tin can of yours for too long, Jermaine. I don't think I've ever heard you swear before!"

Haruto added quietly, "They are a formidable enemy."

Charles leaned back in his chair. "We've been talking to Phoenix all the way back here, going over what happened. She says they're similar but more primitive than the ones created by the new FAB."

Jermaine leaned back in surprise. "Those weapons predate the Accipiters. That means that in all this time, they only made less sophisticated copies of them … they've not improved them."

Haruto nodded. "The aliens who elevated the Accipiters gave them their biological technology, and now we know they copied other technology. Perhaps they don't invent. They merely… acquire."

Charles shrugged. "Well, perhaps they prefer quantity over quality. Theirs are simpler, and they have plenty of ships that can carry them out and deploy them. Technically, they don't need to be mobile like ours. On the other hand, their civilization is vast and spans the galaxy. Maybe they saw no need to improve something simple that works. Still, it speaks to their psychology."

Jermaine frowned. "I would be surprised if, in all that time, the Accipiters did not have conflicts with some other race. Who knows what other tricks they may have picked up along the way?"

Haruto nodded. "Given the time span with which we are told they have roamed the galaxy, that seems very plausible to me. Perhaps they fought *many* other races."

Jermaine wondered aloud, "Maybe some of their enemies are still around somewhere. Hopefully, they won't shoot at us if they are."

Charles opened a drawer in his desk and withdrew a partially full bottle of Glenfiddich Whisky Scotch and three small glasses. As he poured, he said, "I'm told there are only a dozen or so known bottles of this left, at least that anyone will admit to."

He handed glasses to Haruto and Jermaine and raised his in a toast, "May the Accipiters all go to hell and not have a drop to quench their eternal thirst."

Jermaine looked the question at him. "Salut."

Haruto nodded and clinked his glass before taking a sip.

Charles answered, "It's something our ferocious Vice President told me when she gave me this bottle. I'm not sure where she got it."

Jermaine smiled. "The bottle or the curse?"

Charles chuckled, "Yes."

Call of the Sea

● ● ● ● ● ● ● ● ● ● ● ● ● ● ● ● ●

DownSide:
Lake Texoma, Freetown Beach

Colonel Cesar Salangsang, Commanding Officer of the New Texas Army 1st Combat Engineers, leaned back on the beach and took another sip of the locally brewed Caddo Hawk beer as the suntube slowly dimmed. Before Awakening Day, the local Caddo Hawk brewery produced a cheap "craft beer." All the national and imported beer had all but since disappeared, either by consumption or desperate hoarding. He wore cut-off shorts, well-worn sandals, and a ragged T-shirt.

As usual, Michelle Bain was sitting next to him, her own attire strikingly similar. The young marine biologist's short blonde hair had grown out since Awakening Day. It was often unruly, but today she'd tied it back into a ponytail. She shook her head. "I don't know how you can stand that stuff."

Cesar's normally clean-shaven face now sported a short but trimmed beard. As their relationship had… evolved… Michelle had insisted on him keeping it that way. She knew she would never replace the wife and nine children he'd lost to the Accipiters, and she didn't try to. They'd simply grown closer and closer, always trying to end their days together, talking and planning. When Cesar started to build a small beach house, Michelle stopped by one day and started to help. That they ended up sharing the house when he was not off working on his official work didn't surprise her friends, even though he was fifty-three to her twenty-three. Several young men, who had tried to woo her attention, slowly gave up and moved on.

While they were not precisely platonic, neither Cesar nor Michelle wanted children. This was something of a problem for many people, not just Cesar and Michelle. It had been discovered soon after Awakening Day that the Gardeners had made many changes and enhancements to the surviving humans. Among these was the elimination of disease and elevated natural drives, combined with other changes that resulted in most birth control methods becoming ineffective, at best. The enormous surge in pregnancies and subsequent "baby boom" had changed many things. For most people, these changes had become the new reality they could do nothing about. Michelle, however, wanted nothing of it. Many women had tried to have their tubes tied (again), and similarly, men had tried vasectomies (often, also again); however, their bodies refused to cooperate, and "they grew back." The Gardeners had made it clear that they wanted humans to repopulate as quickly as possible.

Unlike every single one of her peers, she'd managed to avoid getting pregnant. It was something that had certainly not escaped other people's attention. Even before Awakening Day, Michelle had a well-earned reputation for "avoiding boys." Still, being around her pregnant friends and their babies weighed on her. She and Cesar only saw each other once or thrice a week, sometimes less. Sometimes, when Cesar was away and she was alone at night, she'd secretly begun to wonder if she was doing the right thing.

Now, though, that would be changing.

Not far down the beach, a small ship was nearing completion. Many months ago, Cesar had talked about visiting an archipelago of islands that could be seen on the opposite side of the outside-in world. He'd waxed about the idea of creating the new Philippines there. Michelle had later asked him, 'Why stop there? Why not circumnavigate the world? You'd be the first!' He'd replied that if she went along, she'd have the chance to make new discoveries and likely see things no human had ever seen before. She'd stared at him, blinking, and then, for the first time, she'd leaned over and kissed him. Not on the cheek, but full-on, on the lips. When she'd pulled back and looked into his startled face, she'd said, "Challenge accepted!"

Since then, with help from friends and not a few volunteers from Cesar's construction battalion, they had begged, borrowed, and even politely stolen what they needed to build the small ship.

Michelle turned to him, put her hand on his chest, and swallowed as she asked, "So… Are you still ready to do this? I mean, we've got photographic maps, but who knows what is really out there… under the waves? We'll be a long, long way from help."

Cesar gazed up at the sky, past the suntube, at the small cyclone making its way across the opposite horizon. "It calls to me."

Michelle rolled onto her back and looked 'up.' She sniffed, "All of us have in our veins the exact same percentage of salt in our blood that exists in the ocean, and therefore, we have salt in our blood, in our sweat, in our tears. We are tied to the ocean. And when we go back to the sea — whether it is to sail or to watch it — we are going back from whence we came."

Cesar looked the question at her.

She answered softly, "It's a quote from the American President, John F. Kennedy."

Cesar shrugged his eyebrows. "Was he one of your founders?"

Michelle blinked before her chest heaved, and she burst out laughing, "No, silly. He was President in the 1960s."

Cesar nodded slowly, "Oh, OK."

Michelle turned her head and looked at Cesar, her expression serious. She sat up on her knees and looked down at him. Her voice trembled in anger, "Cesar…. Tell me that you are not thinking that maybe you'll lose yourself out there and somehow be reunited with them? Your family? Look at me and tell me. I know how lost you feel sometimes. If that's even in the back of your mind, then I'm out. I will not be a party to a death wish. If you want to do this for discovery… to explore… and maybe even to find a new homeland, then that's a good reason. Suicide is not. So, tell me. What's it going to be? Are you going to live or give up?"

Cesar looked up at her, her face and hair framed by the fading orange of the suntube-sunset. She was nothing at all like 'his type.' While her words cut more deeply to the truth than he wanted to admit, at that moment, something changed. Her energy and vitality had sparked something that had lain cold and ash-covered in his heart. Their friendship had grown into comfort and respect. His heart skipped a beat or two as he saw someone in her, someone who cared. Cared whether he lived or died, not because his skills and experience were needed, not for duty or honor, but for something else. Maybe he had an actual reason to live after all.

"No… not anymore." he reached up and cupped her face. She closed her eyes at his touch, and he felt her tears on his dark, calloused hand.

Appearances

● ● ● ● ● ● ● ● ● ● ● ● ● ● ● ●

TopSide:
Vice Admiral Milner Family Apartments

Preston Milner cordially greeted the guards outside the door to his New London Penthouse apartment as he entered. Once inside, he paused and sighed, letting the confidence and boundless energy he was required to present to those under his command escape. The weariness pushed his shoulders down as he took his service dress coat off and draped it over a dining room chair. He sat heavily for a moment and took off his shoes, letting his aching feet breathe.

After a moment's rest, he took a deep breath and forced himself to stand and walk over to the bar. Stocks were severely limited, even for him. There were precious few pre-Awakening Day bottles. He forced himself to leave those alone. He poured a small glass of what passed for Gin, added a lime from his in-apartment aquaponic garden, and topped off the glass with local soda water. It was only an hour before he and Livia would have to leave for dinner with the Vice President.

He sat in the recliner and called through the connecting door to Livia's private apartment, "Livia, we've got an hour before we have to leave."

Except for the memorial service, she had not gone out in public for weeks, and his unease had steadily grown. On the odd occasions when he had actually seen her himself, her… decline had been worrisome. Yesterday, when Vice President Finley had messaged him about getting together for dinner, he'd forwarded it to Livia, thinking that the chance to get out might cheer her up. Besides, he was confident that her repeated absences of late could not continue to go unnoticed. Eventually, people would start asking uncomfortable questions. After all, the Gardeners had cured all diseases, so the excuse of a cold was more likely to bring the entire medical establishment down on her to get to the bottom of whatever mysterious ailment might be at play, and did it represent some new threat to humanity? Sooner or later, she'd have to snap out of it. *Right?*

She didn't answer. He sighed, set his glass down on the dining room table, and walked to her door. "Livia? Are you ready?"

No answer. He knocked, but there was no reply.

"Dammit, Livia, we had an agreement. I'm coming in…." He opened the door and walked in. All the lights were off, but her patio door was open. A soft breeze rustled the curtain. Clothes, trash, and half-empty food containers littered the floor. Livia lay slumped in a chair near the patio entrance. A bottle of the same cheap, DownSide-produced gin sat unopened on the table next to a glass. Beside the glass was a Beretta 96FS pistol.

Preston came closer and gasped at what he saw. She wore only a simple white slip. Her usually bone pale skin seemed semi-translucent and dry. She had a bruise on her forehead, and her face looked gaunt. Her long black hair was pulled back, making her cheeks look even more angular and cold.

For just a moment, he panicked until he saw that she was indeed still breathing. He knelt beside her, took her slim wrist in his hand, and took her pulse. It was slow but steady.

He muttered, "Oh God Dammit, Livia! You're the strongest person I know. *Now* is not the time for a breakdown!"

Preston scooped her up out of the chair. *My God, she hardly weighs anything!*

He started to carry her to her bed, but it was a wreck. He carried her through the door and over to his own crisply made bed.

She finally stirred and looked up at him, her head loose and unsteady and her eyes glassy. When she saw him, she burst into tears and drew herself into a fetal position, sobbing weakly, "I… I'm sorry… I'm sorry… I tried to be strong… I tried…."

Preston's anger and frustration ebbed away as he looked down at her. He swallowed and sat next to her for a moment before gathering her into his arms again and pulling her close. "It's OK. It's going to be OK."

✪ ✪ ✪

He held her like that for hours, barely managing to fish his phone out of his pocket and message the Vice President that 'something had come up.'

His back ached, and he'd lost feeling in his arms, but he held on to her as she quietly cried until she could produce no more tears. Somewhere along the way, he'd joined her. At first, there were no words, but as the evening and night grew and morning eventually dawned, she bared her soul, mourning their daughter Helena, the world they'd lost, her anger at him, everything he'd done wrong, and her own sins in return. And finally… the bombing. The nightmares. Her abject loneliness and desolate despair.

Preston's phone buzzed on the nightstand with an incoming call. He gently disengaged his numb arms and hands and clumsily reached over to his phone. After a moment, he managed to answer. It was his adjutant with his morning schedule.

He swallowed and shook his head. Livia's expression began to harden as he looked over at her. He turned back to his phone. "Cancel my morning schedule."

Livia could hear a tinny, confused voice asking a question. Preston *never* missed an appointment.

"In fact, cancel my entire day and have some hot food brought to my apartment on the double." He tapped the connection closed before his adjutant could answer and turned back to Livia.

She looked at him with veiled surprise and a glimmer of hope.

"Now," he said, "don't be angry with me, but you've always been the strongest person I've ever known. I just can't believe that you thought about… killing yourself?"

Livia blinked, trying to process the words, then her lips trembled for a moment.

Preston thought she was about to cry again, but instead, she burst into a weak laugh.

"God, no! I may be falling apart, but I'd never consider doing that." She laughed again and shook her head. "No… I went to Gloria and asked her to help me learn to shoot." She swallowed and shook her head. "I was so stupid! When I pulled the trigger, and the gun went off, it surprised me and…." She reached up and rubbed her forehead, "and the gun flew back and hit me in the head."

Preston stared at her incredulously for a moment and then started to laugh as his eyes watered with tears. "You're kidding?" *She doesn't realize how weak she's made herself.*

Livia made fists and weakly pounded him on the chest… "Stop that… don't… don't laugh at me!"

Preston swallowed hard as he grabbed her shoulders, pulled her tightly into his chest, and held her there, his tears falling into her hair.

Fire

● ● ● ● ● ● ● ● ● ● ● ● ● ● ● ●

DownSide:
Countryside Outside Fort Brazos

Texas Ranger Francis "Frank" Hayes leaned over the edge of the charred twenty-foot crater and shook his head. He had retired, along with Samuel "Sam" Wallace, and had been happy doing occasional consulting with the local PD and Sheriff's office before the Accipiter attack. After Awakening Day, he and Sam were 'volunteered' to create and train a 'New' division of Texas Rangers and track down certain 'mysteries.' That eventually led to the discovery of a Columbian mercenary group living on the outskirts of Fort Brazos. Like the Russians, Chinese, and other military units, the Gardeners abducted the Columbians during the bombardment of Earth. However, being 'irregular' by nature, they managed to go unnoticed in the immediate aftermath of Awakening Day. Frank and Sam had tracked down and eventually convinced the Columbians that their best option was to join the nascent New Texas Rangers.

"Well, this is odd," Sam commented as he looked down into the crater.

The crater was discovered by accident during a flyover of a large grass fire that had erupted in an area over thirty miles south of the city. Various creeks and natural firebreaks crisscrossed the landscape, so no one had felt a need to do anything but let the fire burn itself out. No storms had been in the area, so the question remained of what had caused the fire in the first place.

Frank shook his head. "Ignacio, did your men find any tracks leading away or in the area? I didn't see any from the air."

Ignacio pulled his straw hat down to shade his face. It was more habit than need since the suntube never presented any truly hot days. He stroked his waxed goatee and shook his head slowly. "Absolutamente nada, and no fragments, either. Only animal tracks. We'll search the entire area, just to be sure, but I don't think anyone has ever set foot here before us."

Sam cocked his head. "Well, somebody must have. The military flatly denies dropping a bomb, either accidentally or on purpose. I checked civilian flights too, what few there are anymore. They track every single flight, whether civilian or military, and they say absolutely nothing has been over this area in the past month."

Sam scowled, "Well, hell, how'd the son of a bitch get it here then? He obviously wanted to try out his bomb-makin' skills somewhere remote."

Ignacio complained, "Demasiado grande. It is a very big hole, bomb must have been a hundred kilograms or more. Too big for a backpack."

Frank kicked a rock into the crater. "God Damn. Odio putas terroristas. Haven't we had enough of killin' each other yet?"

Sam squinted as he looked down into the crater. "Frank, there's something odd about this crater, don't you think?"

Frank snorted, "Well Hell, Sam, every damned thing about this world is odd." He nodded to Ignacio, "Ignacio, have your boys collect the samples like we talked about. Maybe the military or the university can figure out what kind of bomb it was, that is, since we can't exactly send it off to the FBI for testing."

Priest

● ● ● ● ● ● ● ● ● ● ● ● ● ● ●

DownSide:
Military Intelligence Headquarters

Lieutenant Colonel Martin Williams, formerly of the Australian Intelligence Corps and now the head of Military Intelligence, such as it was, and what there was of it, sat in his office with his feet on his desk. The coffee in his cup was cold, but he barely noticed as he studied the computer monitors that displayed multiple views of the prisoner. His office was on the second floor of a building that had been a 1980's era data center slated for demolition before Awakening Day. The bunker-like building was in an isolated section of the Joint Reserve Base. For now, it was perfect for his needs.

The prisoner in question was in a holding cell three hundred miles away, 'above,' in the bowels of the New Pentagon, TopSide, near the outer surface of New Texas. When the Gardeners had fabricated the city, now referred to as 'New London,' there were two key features at its heart. The most exotic was, of course, the titanic hangars, all but two of which were still sealed. One of those had held the hybrid starship and the other had rows and rows of the sublight Interplanetary Landing Craft. The other prominent feature TopSide, aside from the residential area, stadium, and parks was what they had quickly labeled the 'New Pentagon.' Of course, it was not at all pentagonal. However, under the circumstances everyone found themselves in, it was clear that the Gardeners had intended it to be used as a central administrative building dedicated to the war effort.

While the New Pentagon had a dozen floors above 'ground,' there were another two hundred and fifty levels below ground, some of which were enormous parks and concourses. They clearly intended other levels as laboratory and testing areas and had impressively thick walls and blast doors. One zone, in particular, stood out. It was a series of twenty levels that contained what were labeled as 'special' holding cells, each with separate security monitoring rooms as well as medical examination rooms. The strange part was that the special holding cells were twenty feet square and another twenty feet *tall*.

Given that the Gardeners had already informed the humans that the Accipiters were at least ten feet tall, the logical conclusion was that the rooms were most likely intended for Accipiter prisoners.... Or perhaps for beings as yet unknown. They even had 'furniture' and sanitary controls that clearly wouldn't fit human… dimensions. At least, everyone *hoped* they were intended for Accipiters and not something worse.

The prisoner on Martin's computer screens was the Accipiter captured during the Keeper Raid. Martin marveled at its stunning, unearthly beauty every time he saw the creature. Then there were the sounds he could hear over the video feed: humming tones that waxed and waned endlessly, impressing deep emotions he couldn't begin to decipher. There had been three Accipiters performing some sort of ritual when Captain David Garreth's team had secured the Keeper ship. Two of the enormous bird-analogue aliens had immediately attacked. Garreths' team killed them. The third one, presumed to be senior, was subdued and brought back to New Texas, along with the human engineer Nathaniel Grant.

As for the rather hairy Keeper himself, no violence was required. He was utterly docile. His attendants, however, tried to protect him. The tricky part was how hard they'd had to work at not seriously injuring them while they were subdued. They weren't precisely dangerous unless you consider six naked, crazed women particularly dangerous.

Food was brought from the unique garden inside the Keeper ship every day. It was used to feed the prisoners, including the Accipiter himself. Martin had feared it would go on some sort of hunger strike or otherwise injure or try to kill itself. However, after it had awoken in the makeshift cage it was brought back in, it had settled into an unending routine: hours of singing while its smaller hands moved in complex and strange ways, broken up by silent stints of motionless staring.

There was a knock at his door. Without looking up, he called out, "Come in, Dr. Talib."

"Hello, Martin." Leo Talib entered the room and took a seat next to Martin without asking. Leo was the linguist who deciphered the messages left by the Gardeners and translated some of the Accipiter's written language using clues they had provided. He'd devoted countless hours watching and listening to the Accipiter. As he'd predicted based on his earlier work, the glyphs on the Accipiter's beak exhibited a range of colors that were beyond human perception, and they changed… almost danced… to the multi-tonal music and humming as it sang. Like the glyphs, the sounds also extended beyond the normal human hearing range. Of course, early on, he hadn't predicted that hand signs would be a cornerstone of their communication.

Martin glanced over at Leo, who seemed very much at ease. It was quite an evolution from the dapper, ambitious, and frustrated young man Martin had first met after Awakening Day. Martin prided himself on gauging and understanding the people around him. As a spy, his life had depended on it. Leo, however, had continued to surprise him. That same nervous young man had the guts to go with Captain Garreth's team into the Keeper ship as a translator and the closest thing to an Accipiter expert mankind had. That he'd lived through the mission and eventually married Brigadier General Sabrina Chilton, formerly of the British Army Royal Corps of Signals and now head of Signals Intelligence, was nothing short of astonishing to Martin. He wondered, *Did that speak more about Talib or Chilton?*

"Hello, Leo. How's the General?"

"Very cross about being pregnant. Thank You Very Much. Nicole, however, is elated."

"And how is your precocious stepdaughter?"

"Smart as a whip and demanding to join the Academy, though, it's remotely possible that could have something to do with a certain young man she fancies, but you didn't hear me say that."

"I envy you not."

Leo shook his head ruefully. "Stay single."

Martin soberly declared, "I am a monk."

Leo laughed, "I'm sure. Now, what did you really want to talk about, Martin?"

Martin nodded at the screens. "Our *friend*, there. Anything new or useful out of him?"

Leo raised his eyebrows. "Well, I'm not sure about the useful part, although it *is* interesting. He doesn't seem to have repeated himself since his capture. As best I've been able to translate, he's been reciting the liturgical Accipiter history. What's fascinating is that while our own ancient history was passed along by word of mouth, sometimes becoming as much legend and myth, the Accipiters actually have intact recordings of their earliest post-elevation history. He must have an amazing memory."

"Because he hasn't repeated himself, yeah, I heard. And you don't think he's ad-libbing?"

Leo shook his head. "No, I don't."

"How are you and the General's SigInt team progressing on their language in general?"

Leo's demeanor changed as his mind returned to work: his eyes brightened with intense curiosity. "Well, actually, so far, I think more questions have been raised than have been answered, but some of those answers are critical. At the top of that list, of course, is that now we know that the Accipiters make extensive use of hand signs, like our sign-language, in addition to their vocalizations. Their language seems to be composed of at least three main components. After Awakening Day, we made a lot of progress, I think, on the glyphs. Basically, their written word. The hand signals, though, we hadn't anticipated before this one was brought here. After we had actual video, though, we started seeing correlations between the hand signals and the glyphs. Not so much the singing. I'm working on cataloguing the vocabulary and working out the grammar, but so far, its hands mostly sign using similar rules to their written glyphs. We've got a basic translation matrix built, but we need to actually use it in an interrogatory pattern with the creature itself to build up confidence. Assuming we could get it to cooperate."

Martin chuckled. "How do you know that this one's not just deaf?"

Leo smiled a smile that a year ago would have advertised impatience and superiority; today, he could take a joke, "I'll assume he's a typical example until we know he's an outlier."

Martin frowned. "So they don't actually talk, verbally, to each other?".

Leo explained. "I originally assumed that their vocalizations would correspond to their glyphs. That is, that the sounds they form with their beak and oral cavity were, well, words."

Leo gestured at the Accipiter on the screen. "The musical sounds it makes are still a mystery. Some of the analysis points to the sounds, at least in part, being some kind of what we would think of as punctuation, but there is way more bandwidth being used than that. Maybe it includes an emotive component. It certainly feels like that sometimes. For all we know, though, it could even be parallel processing, including greater context, historical or metaphorical analogues, or, who knows, maybe everything to them is either opera or musical theatre. We just don't know yet."

Martin sighed. "We're trying not to anthropomorphize too badly. However, we theorize that he is some sort of a priest or perhaps even a politician. He was there to watch the Keeper Ship launch, after all. Well, I don't want to go out on a limb, but watching him, I expect he's a true believer."

Leo added, "And he hasn't directly responded to any questions from me or anyone else so far."

"Hmmm, so he's a 'take me to your leader' type?"

Leo considered for a moment before joking, "I'd love to hear the conversation if we put it in the room with Nathaniel Grant?"

Martin laughed throatily, "Ahh, no. Most emphatically, not."

✪ ✪ ✪

TopSide:
Accipiter Holding Cell
(Weeks Later)

Half of John Austin's protection detail entered the observation room and cleared it before allowing him to enter, followed by Martin and Leo. Leo sat in front of a large multi-touch computer screen with video feeds and waveform windows arrayed across one side. Along the side of the room, monitors displayed video feeds from various angles. Stochastic visualizations and key indicators were aligned along the other side. The middle section was divided into top and bottom areas. The top held three windows labeled "Glyph," "Hand Signs," and "Tonal." The bottom section had a window labeled "Translation," along with a column next to it labeled "Confidence Level."

Leo looked up at Martin and nodded that he was ready.

Martin pressed a button on the wall controls, and a metal barrier rose, leaving a thick bulletproof glass wall between them and the Accipiter in the holding cell beyond.

The Accipiter looked up and rose from its oddly shaped bench. Its clawed feet clacked on the hard floor as it strode closer to the window. It peered down through its enormous sapphire eyes at them. From left to right, it stared directly at each occupant of the other room. Then its gaze glided back and locked onto John.

A low rumbling erupted over the speakers as it withdrew its truehands from within its chest feather analogues and began to sign while glyphs flowed across its beak. Then the hand signs and glyphs stopped, and it waited, but the dark tones it made continued.

Leo's hands danced across the multi-touch screen, making adjustments. He leaned back and turned to look at Martin, then at John. "Mr. President, I think it just asked… no. It was a noun statement. It said that *you* were our leader."

John leaned closer to the window and answered flatly. "I am."

Leo nodded. "I can approximate your questions and answers using their glyphs. It will see them on the screen on its wall."

John studied the Accipiter and shook his head. "It understood me. You understand us. Don't you?"

The tones shifted to a minor chord, and a brief set of glyphs flowed across its beak as it made a simple sign.

John nodded, "Thought so."

Leo swallowed. "Uhm, yes, he is definitely saying yes."

More rumbling was followed by a dissonant chord and another brief series of glyphs and signs.

Everyone turned to look at Leo, who furiously operated the controls before turning to answer. "I believe it said that we, or maybe *you*, rejected a gift or, probably, their gift. I think the word is *gift*. The alternatives make much less sense."

John turned and narrowed his eyes. "Is that right? Gift? We rejected your gift? What *gift* is that?"

The tones shifted abruptly to something that seemed achingly dulcet, vibrant, and warm, followed by an odd inflection and a somewhat longer series of glyphs and signs.

Leo worked the console without looking up. "Life… Order… Peace… Planet. He's saying something about bringing these things to our planet. Then… Poisons… They removed poisons from our air… from our water. Uhm… plant? No, Garden… something. I think he is saying our planet is now a Garden. A paradise. Wait…. That… Uhm…." He leaned back and shook his head. "Uh, Mr. President, if I am getting this anything close to right, I think he said that they, I mean, the Accipiters, would welcome us home."

John stared at Leo for a long moment before turning back to the Accipiter. His expression hardened. "I see. Even now, after all that your people have done to our world and all that we have done in response?"

The rumbling rose and fell, and the tones grew complex and warmer. The glyphs and signs that accompanied them were varied and rich.

Leo took a deep breath. "The model is gaining confidence the more we interact. Something possessive… It says you are his or maybe something like we belong to his people. Then something about a long period of time… very long… our planet. Yes, they have watched over our planet. Then, something about a purpose and a group. Uhm… They wanted us to… They wanted us to improve? No… must be… evolve? Yes. They wanted us to evolve to… Prime? No…Star? No… Perfect. That's it. They wanted us to evolve to be perfect. They wanted us to join them. No…. Join their collection? Group? Something like that."

John nodded slowly. "And who are you? Why should we believe you?"

The Accipiter swayed back and forth, and its song became a melodic chorus, while the glyphs and songs took much longer to finish, but before they did, the tones turned to darker, minor keys.

Leo worked the console, eventually beginning, "It is High *something*… High… leader? No. I think there is another connotation. More like a priest of some kind? Like a High Priest? He's talking about saving or maybe preserving things. No. Life. Evolution. More of that connotation… I think… I think they may worship, or at least, how to say… venerate? Yes, they venerate evolved life. Saved copies? Wait… this is confusing. He's conjoining a word for child with us and parentage, but with another connotation. Like… he sees us as his children? Oh… then it changes. Something about destruction. Misshapen. Malformed. Our… development… went wrong. They had to do something. Cleanse. No. Fix us. They had to fix us. Now…. Now he says there is no want? No. Yes. No want. No… hunger. No destruction. No killing each other. Then this last bit is something about trees… memory… memory trees?"

John's eyes hardened. "My God, what hubris. We are not your children or your pets, or your slaves. You have a right to believe what you want, but you have no right to murder and enslave our world or any other. You think you know us, but you don't. Your race was elevated by technologically superior beings whom you regard as Gods, but in your intoxicated vanity, you've elevated yourselves to their level. You have taken their gifts and made yourselves to be immortal and thus think you are as God's yourselves. And so, you have spread across the Galaxy, imposing your will on others. Your will. Not the will of those who elevated you, but your own. You have lost your way as a people, and a price must be paid for your temerity. You, Priest, shall be witness to the judgment exacted by your victims. I command you, Priest. I command you to pray that someday, the mud that you rose up from on your homeworld will fall away like scales from your eyes, and you will truly see your crimes for what they are, and on that day, your people will cry out for forgiveness and mercy. Pray, Priest, that on that day, *my* people will still be capable of the mercy you beg for. For you slew the dragon, but her children have risen from her ashes."

John lifted his leg and planted his boot on the table in front of the window. His boots were a unique pair John had commissioned from Bell and Son's custom boot makers over the vociferous objections from many. The remains of two other Accipiters who had been killed on the Accipiter ship had been preserved. After they were sufficiently studied,

John had the scaled skin from the feet from the dead Accipiters removed and made into boots. The boots he was wearing. The Accipiter Priest blinked and looked down at the boot, trying to discern its meaning. Slowly, the realization of what the boots were made from sank in. A strange gurgling sound filtered through the speakers, and the Accipiter began to shake as its eyes widened and its beak opened and closed spasmodically. Then its legs collapsed underneath it, and it slumped down and sprawled limply across the floor.

Martin pressed his hand to his ear and shouted, "What happened?" He listened for several long seconds while everyone in the room looked to him for answers. Finally, he nodded and shook his head slowly. "It's, ahh, it's not dead. We think it… feinted."

✪ ✪ ✪

Outside the holding cell, Secretary of War Marcus was waiting.

John slumped against the wall, closed his eyes, and slowly sighed.

Alex motioned to their combined security details and others to give them some space. He waited a moment before asking, "That bad?"

John didn't open his eyes and simply nodded.

"You were laying it on pretty thick in there."

John took a deep breath, opened his eyes, and stood up straight. "You were watching?"

"Yeah."

"You know that's not me, right? I've got to play the part in there."

Alex nodded and put his dark, beefy hand on John's shoulder. "To paraphrase what Patton said, just so long as *you* know when you are acting, John. I know that's not you in there. Frankly, that damned creature scares the hell out of me."

John nodded. "You and me both, Alex. You and me both."

The Engineer

● ● ● ● ● ● ● ● ● ● ● ● ● ● ● ●

TopSide:
New Pentagon Holding Cells

Nathaniel Grant sat in the lotus position in the middle of his cell, quietly humming. Without access to a barber *or a razor,* his kinky/curly textured black hair and beard had grown out. Although it hung loose against his chocolate brown skin, he had nonetheless managed to appear immaculately groomed. As the video record showed, he had meticulously converted his hospital scrub shirt into an open-front tunic, displaying his hairless muscular chest and perfect eight-pack abs. While he had a daily Yoga-esq routine, it should not have been enough to maintain his physique. His diet was composed entirely of high-calorie MREs. He should have gained weight or, at the very least, grown somewhat "soft." He hadn't, and it apparently didn't matter what he ate. Evidently, his metabolism was dynamic enough to compensate, or his musculature was hard-wired. Or both.

Near the window, permanently attached to the floor, was a stainless-steel table and chair. At one end of the table lay an elegantly neat stack of papers next to the box of crayons that were all Nathaniel was allowed. Pencils or pens were deemed too dangerous a risk. The documents were filled with painstakingly scribed side-by-side lines of Accipiter glyphs and their English translations. Written versions of Accipiter tomes.

Everything he did in the room was recorded in high definition from multiple angles. Scans of each sheet of paper were sent to Leo Talib and Sabrina Chilton's SigInt team without having to remove the paper from the room. Nathaniel could probably have surmised what they were doing anyway, but it didn't seem to bother him.

Martin Williams sat silently in the observation room — with the metal shield wall down. He studied the man on the video monitor. When the Accipiters attacked Earth, Nathaniel Grant had been a nuclear engineer onboard the USS California, SSN 781, a Virginia Class nuclear submarine. The submarine had survived the attack. Its haggard crew eventually surrendered after the invading Accipiters offered amnesty. Like all remaining humans on Earth, he'd been altered and given enhanced health and longevity. That was over sixty years ago. For a man of over 103, he didn't look a day over thirty.

Nathaniel had, evidently, proven himself to be of significant value to the Accipiters. At the time of the raid, he had been assisting with preparing the Keeper ship for launch. He was an engineer, after all; still, Martin suspected something else accounted for his apparent position of trust with the Accipiters.

After being brought to New Texas, Nathaniel was secured in a cell. Vice President Finley had stopped by to see him for herself, whereupon he had promptly shocked everyone by demonstrating that, thanks to his Accipiter-provided physical "upgrades," he could see her through the mirrored glass. Since then, so far at least, he hadn't reacted to anyone sitting on the other side when the metal shield was down.

Martin had carefully prepared for this meeting. He'd stopped all visits except for periodic medical checks. After the initial reports, Martin decided it was better to let Nathaniel stew for a while. Food was delivered via a chute. Now it was time to meet him.

It had been a bit hard for Martin to find an actual brown paper lunch bag, but he'd found a supply at the open-air, now-permanent flea market that had grown up on the outskirts of the city of Fort Brazos, DownSide. He had chosen what he called his 'professor' look, wearing horn-rim reading glasses on a string, a thin not quite threadbare sweater, and a gently rumpled tweed jacket and pants he had also managed to find at the flea market. He wanted to portray a cross between a mild-mannered, impartial, and scientifically curious intellectual and Columbo from the old TV detective show.

He'd studied the video recording of Nathaniel's interactions with the Vice President and others. Clearly, the man was quite intelligent. And more importantly, the man, if he really was entirely human anymore, was a *true believer*. It wasn't a matter of intellectual conviction. According to intelligence from the Gardeners, among the "improvements" made by the Accipiters, the Accipiters had genetically altered their followers to worship them. More than anything, the man seemed preternaturally patient. His movements were languid and graceful before being given paper and crayons. Afterward, watching him write, the effect was even more exaggerated. His motions were slow and almost tender in rhythm, and the tones he hummed while doing so varied from lullaby to epic.

Martin cleared his mind. *I won't be able to flip him or bribe him. I must work slowly and let him think he's turning me, instead. With luck, he'll let slip information or insights we can eventually use.*

Entering, he set the sack lunch on the table, spread a stack of reports across the desk in a half-tidy jumble, and then pushed the button to raise the shield.

Nathaniel blinked languidly and smiled. His expression was intelligent, thoughtful, and patient. "Ah, someone new. I wonder who you might be? Not in uniform, not in a suit, so not a soldier or politician, or pretending not to be. An academic, perhaps, or the mask of one? I wonder."

Martin carefully hesitated, using his practiced Leeds accent instead of his native Australian. "I, ah, am not supposed to say."

"A brit academic, then? Perhaps? It matters not, although you know my name. What should I call you?"

Martin swallowed and offered, "Lucius. Call me… Lucius Mestrius."

"I see. That's an interesting nom de guerre. Latin…." Nathaniel cocked his head in thought for a moment. "Oh, I see! You fancy yourself a historian!"

Martin straightened in mild surprise. *Damn, but he's quick.*

Nathaniel continued, "Lucius Mestrius Plutarchus, otherwise known as Plutarch, from the Temple of Apollo at Delphi." He smiled broadly, "Don't worry, I can't really read your mind. I was a history minor at Thomas Edison while I studied at the Reactor School. I doubt I would have made the connection had the Accipiters not gifted me with perfect recall."

Martin made a show of taking a deep breath. He settled back in his chair, opened a file, and read, "Nathaniel. Name Etymology from Late Latin and Greek Nathanael… and from Semitic Hebrew Nethan'el. That is, literally, God has given." He set the file down. "It seems your gods have indeed given you gifts."

Nathaniel shrugged, "As you say."

"Very well, Mr. Grant. I'm here to ask if you would mind sharing. Well, not secrets… just your story in your own words. Our records pre-invasion are fragmentary. With your permission, I'd like to ask if the following information is accurate?"

Nathaniel smiled beatifically. "Of course."

Martin looked at him and nodded. "Thank you." He paused as he shuffled through several folders, appeared to find the right one, opened it, turned a page, read from it, and then looked back up at Nathaniel. "Ah, I see that we show you were born in Detroit, were accepted into the United States Naval Academy, attended the Naval Postgraduate School, and earned a Master of Science degree in Mechanical Engineering, and, yes, studied at the Bettis Reactor Engineering School at Thomas Edison State University. At the time of the invasion, you were a nuclear engineer posted to the USS California, aged forty-three years. You had a wife, Jasmine, and daughters, Aiysha and Malaika. I also understand you were active in your robotics and 3-D printing hobbies and helped your daughters with the same at the science fair? I see they won several academic awards as well as football athletic team awards?"

Nathaniel nodded gently, maintaining his smile. "Yes, I was a soccer coach for their teams."

Martin made a notation on the file. *Note how he glossed over the dialectical difference without the need to call attention to it.* "Yes, ahh, thank you, Mr. Grant. Also, I see you were a tenor in the United States Navy Choir? Is that right?"

"Yes, that is correct."

Martin thought he noticed a change in Nathaniel's demeanor for just a moment. Not quite a tell of concealment, but a hint that the topic was important.

Martin set his pen down, reached over, and opened the paper bag. He slowed his body down to match his conversation partner and contemplated for a moment. He pulled out an apple from the bag and put it on the desk. "What was it like?"

Nathaniel smiled, "What was what like?"

"The Navy Choir? Forgive me, was that a common experience or thing to do?"

"You would be surprised. I personally knew at least one choir mate who went on to become an admiral."

Martin nodded thoughtfully. "I suppose it must have provided opportunities to meet many people who might later help you in your career?"

"Yes, it could be a nice environment for networking for those inclined to use it in that way."

Martin reached over and picked up the apple but simply held it in the air as he paused in thought. "I see. I take it then from your tone that you didn't see it that way? Perhaps you simply enjoyed the experience and the travel?"

Nathaniel's smiled broadly, his expression reaching his eyes this time. "I've always enjoyed singing."

Martin put the apple back down and looked down at the file, making more notes. *Note his response. He's saying more than his words imply.* "I see. I understand that singing is a big part of Accipiter culture and communication. I expect you found it aesthetically pleasing. I know that I found that the recordings I have listened to were…well… astoundingly beautiful." Nathaniel's eyes twinkled as he replied,

"The Accipiters teach us to hear the beauty of their song and allow the spirit to fly free."

Martin looked down and hesitated. "That is a gracious sentiment."

"When I sang in the Navy Choir and other choirs before that, the music enthralled me. Words and music are powerful forces. The Accipiters have mastered them: It is the song of angels. Lucius. They are angels of God and have restored Earth to the Eden it was meant to be. As I told your lovely Vice President, there is no want, no hunger, no disease, no crime, no avarice, no war, and no fear. There is harmony with nature and the environment. Such a beautiful song that is."

He paused and added, "And the Accipiters have elevated us to join their chorus."

Martin smiled gently. "I believe that you believe that, Sir."

Nathaniel rose from his seated lotus position and stood in a single catlike fluid motion. He sauntered to the window. "It's not too late, Lucius. You can still go home."

✪ ✪ ✪

Later, minutes after ending the interview, Martin gathered the papers and stood. *And now for the minuscule reward. Of course, he will see through it, but if he asks, I'll say they ordered me to do it.* He put the apple into the empty paper bag and dropped it into the food chute as silent positive reinforcement and reward.

Academy

● ● ● ● ● ● ● ● ● ● ● ● ● ● ● ●

DownSide:
Eugene Morton Naval Academy
Formerly: Bonham State University Campus

Dr. Takumi Nakamura, Ph.D., was the former Dean of the School of Science and Technology at Bonham State University and the former President of the University following the events of Awakening Day. Yesterday, he'd ceded his President's role to the newly created Office of the Superintendent. By order of the Fort Brazos City Council and Office of the President of New Texas, Bonham State University was renamed the Eugene Morton Naval Academy after the late Commander Gene Morton and crew of the NTN Axe, who sacrificed themselves to save the Phoenix, and in the process annihilate an Accipiter mother ship and tens of thousands of its escorts.

Takumi would remain the Academic Dean, mostly doing what he'd already been doing. It was a relief, really. He'd never wanted to run the University. He was an astronomer, and it was only the tragic events of Awakening Day that had ripped him from his comfortable life as Head of the Astronomy Department to not only run the University itself but also become the de facto Senior Science Advisor for… mankind.

The new Superintendent would focus on the larger tasks of layering a Military Academy on top of the framework of the existing University. Many new technical and academic areas of study would need to be established, the curriculum developed or adapted, and faculty trained. The Military aspect of the Academy would focus on several areas. First would be Defense inside New Texas against the threats they already knew about and ones yet undiscovered. The second would be training a space-going Navy for spaceships yet unbuilt. The third would be the space-going equivalent of a combination of marines and special forces. No one anticipated a need for armies of invasion or occupation — rather, forces to defend against boarders and forces for special operations such as the recent Keeper Raid. The fourth would be support and logistics for all of the above.

Two men sat in the guest chairs in front of Takumi's desk. To his right was Gordon Edward Montoya, Rear Admiral. Now officially un-retired, Gordon, a widower, had been visiting his daughter Monica, her husband Robert, and his granddaughters Susan, Rebecca, and Anita in New London when all had been abducted along with the other New Londoners by the Gardeners.

To Takumi's left was the very uncomfortable-looking new Commandant of Midshipmen, former Air Force Chief Master Sergeant Harrold Anders. As the Senior Non-Commissioned Officer on base, Harrold had been in the thick of things at the Fort Brazos Joint Reserve Base on Awakening Day.

Angela Willis, Takumi's office manager, entered and set a platter with a carafe of coffee, cups, and fresh Danish pastries from Café Balthasar on the desk.

Gordon and Harrold nodded their thanks.

Takumi smiled, "Thank you, Angela. I would appreciate it if you could keep the curious at bay."

Angela smiled wistfully and left the office, gently closing the door behind her. Like Takumi and many others, her greying hair had slowly returned to its original color. In her case, a soft strawberry blonde.

Harrold, now 50, had only begun to see traces of grey in his brown before Awakening Day. Now, despite being exhausted from overwork, the grey was gone.

On the other hand, Gordon had lost his hair as a young man. He'd hoped it might miraculously grow back, but it hadn't happened so far.

Takumi turned to Harrold, "Commandant Anders, how are your twins, Devin and Terry? And, of course, your irrepressible wife, Danielle?"

Harrold had poured himself a straight black coffee. He sipped and answered, "Thank you, Dr. Nakamura. Devin and Terry are… exhausting. I don't know how Danielle does it. I understand that Mizuki is pregnant?"

Takumi's eyes widened, and he shook his head, "Yes, oh my. Such a shock, even knowing everything that has happened. There were… complications with Fumio's birth. We've known since then that she would be our last. We simply never thought it could happen to us… I understand that we were not alone in our failure of imagination." He smiled wryly. "And, of course, Naomi is married and expecting now. I think that Misaki has been avoiding us lately, for a reason, though…."

Gordon shook his head. "Interesting times."

Takumi nodded, "Yes, the supposed Chinese curse. Well, it seems our three lives are about to become yet more interesting than ever, are they not?"

Gordon held his coffee cup as though his hands were cold. "Dr. Nakamura, I did not ask for this."

Takumi leaned back in his padded leather chair and smiled wryly, "Yes, I heard that, Admiral. The President told me he had to, what was it he said? Oh yes, now I recall, he said he had to drag you kicking and screaming back to active duty?"

Gordon slowly nodded, "Yes. I was one of the lucky ones. Like yours, my family survived Awakening Day. My daughter, son-in-law, and three granddaughters are alive, thank God. All three of them are pregnant, too, like so many are…. All I wanted to do was to be with them through this…."

Harrold interjected, "Apocalypse?"

Gordon closed his eyes for a moment. "Yes, that. I'm 72 years old. I just wanted to be a better grandfather than I was a father."

Takumi laughed softly, "And now you get to be grandfather to a whole campus of thousands." He paused and looked down at his desk before looking back up at the other two men. "And I understand the circumstances. It just saddens me that we must now teach these young men and women… war. Just remember that, like many soldiers from your base, most of the existing university students are orphans, having come here from other cities before Awakening Day. Their parents, siblings, and families are all gone."

Harrold grimaced, "Dr. Nakamura… I have always felt it was my sacred duty to teach my men and women how to come back. Alive."

Takumi smiled sadly, "Yes, quite right. Please forgive my maudlin thoughts."

Gordon sighed, "Not at all. I propose a toast, as it were… that we never forget that we are here to teach these impossibly young men and women the art of war so that they would be both victorious and come back home safely to us. God help us. All three of my granddaughters have said they want to apply to the Academy."

Takumi looked at Gordon, then nodded, not bothering to hide his dismay. "My daughter Naomi already has."

Harrold raised his cup. "Forgive me if I get this wrong, Admiral, but I believe it is a Navy saying that the only easy day was yesterday. Our tomorrows won't be easy, but I vow to do my best to teach our students the good sense to survive, even if I have to beat it into them."

· 95 ·

Home Port

● ● ● ● ● ● ● ● ● ● ● ● ● ● ● ● ●

TopSide:
New Pentagon: Executive Offices

Secretary of War, Alexander Marcus stepped into the private bathroom attached to his uncomfortably palatial office in the New Pentagon and inspected himself in the mirror. His formerly silver-grey, short-cropped hair had gradually returned to a lustrous black, and some of the lines on his dark face had softened. He looked and felt… younger. Even his skin coloring was gradually returning to something closer to his younger ebony. What bothered him, though, was not his face or skin. It was… the suit.

He'd argued and fought it to no avail. The President, Vice President, and Council had been unanimous. With a twinkle in her eyes, Gail Finley had pulled him aside and had had the temerity to lecture him. "We need you more as Secretary of War than we do as a General. General." She'd smiled crookedly and added, "And now you know how it feels, being railroaded into a position you didn't want or ask for. Karma's a gold-plated bitch, isn't she?"

And she'd been right. He had helped push her into the role of Vice President, forcing her out of the life she'd loved as a pilot. Since then, he'd watched a brash young woman evolve into a capable, formidable, and a quite popular leader. He'd also watched as the weight of her *personal responsibility* for the survival of humanity had changed her. She couldn't just be 'a pilot' anymore. Now, all who remained looked to her and the President for leadership. *And hope.*

When New London's survivors were discovered, it was a private relief to him that he wasn't the sole General Officer other than Sabrina

Chilton. Vice Admiral Milner was indeed senior and, given Milner's role, would be much more involved in the defense of what remained of humanity. Only now, Alexander found himself thrust into a role with even more responsibility.

He straightened the uncomfortable suit around his broad shoulders and grumbled, "Karma indeed."

✪ ✪ ✪

Starship Hanger 1

Security was tight as the motorcade entered the gargantuan hangar and made its way toward the now docked and secured starship. The golden Keeper Ship sat off to the side, with the permanent array of armored vehicles that surrounded and kept a watchful eye on it lest it suddenly do something hostile.

According to the Gardeners, millennia ago, the Accipiters had left behind a biological Von Neumann machine in what would later become known as the mountains of Peru. It had gradually constructed a hidden base/starship inside the remote mountain range, far from most pre-human activity. At some point in time, a hominid had been captured by the Accipiters and was genetically enhanced to become the "Keeper" for the base. It would awaken from cryo every so often and check on how the planet was evolving. Sample life forms were collected to keep a record of changes. The Keeper periodically reported back to the Accipiters on how things were going. Eventually, the Accipiters had decided that it was time to collect on their investment. When their fleet arrived, it knew everything about mankind.

Phoenix herself rested a distance away, on the other side of the hangar. Its enormous blue-green elliptical rings stood over eight hundred feet tall in their typical, unstretched dimensions, almost the height of the Pyramid Tower in San Francisco. Fully stretched, they were taller than the Empire State Building had stood. They wrapped around the converted former submarine at its heart, like a colossal Christmas tree ornament.

As busy as any naval port, the hangar bustled with vehicles, workers, gantries, and equipment of every sort. Hazmat-suited teams had already swarmed the ship, testing for radiation or other known hazards, and given the all-clear. A framework with a caged construction elevator was pushed up next to the former submarine's sail, which the Gardeners had converted into an airlock. Charles Cross, Haruto Hashimoto, and several of the crew began to cycle out the airlock and head towards the elevator.

Security was heavy as the motorcade came to a stop nearby. Alexander Marcus had ridden along with Gail Finley. After their security details gave the *all-clear*, they exited their Oshkosh JTLV, one of the handful that had been at Fort Brazos on Awakening Day. Preston Milner and Andre Johansson exited the other JTLV. Surrounded by their respective protection details, the four walked the short distance to meet Charles Cross as he exited the elevator.

Charles, Haruto, and the other crewmen stood at attention and saluted.

Alexander fought the reflex to return the salute and noticed Gail grinning at him. She'd seen his shoulder twitch. He briefly glared grumpily at her, then turned his attention back to the group.

Preston and Andre returned the salute.

Andre nodded, "At ease, Captain, Commander."

Preston smiled, "Welcome back. From your tight beam message, it sounds like you had an eventful mission. I'm glad that no one was seriously hurt."

Charles nodded, "Thank you, Admiral. No one is more grateful than Commander Hashimoto and me for that, Sir. We have a *lot* to discuss."

✪ ✪ ✪

New Pentagon, Conf Room A47
Classified Ultra Top-Secret Briefing

Charles concluded, pointing at the display on the wallscreen, "On returning to Ari'Nell, we met with Captain Cutter to get his opinion. His report on the status at Ari'Nell includes his observations and concurs with ours and Phoenix's conclusion. Commander and Dr. Sinitskaya also reviewed the data and added more commentary and notes, but the bottom line was that they agreed. The Accipiters are using bomb-pumped laser mines that appear to be functionally similar but less advanced than the ones the Builder's master race used. Somewhere along the way, the Accipiters acquired that technology and seemingly haven't changed it since. So, it seems possible that the Builder's enemies may have survived longer than was thought... long enough to fight the Accipiters, or the Accipiters found the tech later and adopted it."

"Phoenix later deduced that her recent recollection and re-introduction to the technology may have provided her with a quicker response time than she might have otherwise had. As for the Accipiters, it is obvious that they were well prepared to implement a massive minefield after last year's raid. They had to have deployed *millions* of mines to accomplish what they did. I don't believe they just got lucky. They were waiting for us. Were it not for the quick actions of Phoenix, things might have turned out very differently."

The room was packed to standing room only, with dozens more attending remotely.

Gail asked, "Thank you, Captain. I'm certain I speak for every living soul that we're all terribly grateful that you were able to make it back safe and sound. Tell me though, were you able to determine anything more about the conditions on and around Earth itself?"

Charles nodded to Haruto, who put up a series of new images on the screen. "When we were safely well outside of the solar system, Phoenix paused for several hours and gravitically lensed Earth and the surrounding area. We moved around a bit, so we could image the entire planet. As you can see, there seems to be a lot going on in the atmosphere above the Atlantic Ocean. That's where the detonation of Commander Morton's Axe was closest. The rest of the planet seems more or less okay, so the fears that some had expressed of a potential nuclear winter or something similar seems to have been unwarranted. Silver lining of the Accipiter's technology, I suppose."

Haruto displayed a series of images showing a time-lapse circuit around the planet. It seemed like the familiar Earth, except for the purple tinge resulting from the flora introduced by the Accipiters.

Charles continued, "Phoenix was also able to image the area in Peru where the recent… action… took place." Haruto changed the images to show several slightly fuzzy Landsat-like images of a mountainous area pockmarked by numerous craters.

"It looks like the Accipiters are terraforming over the damaged areas. There is a tremendous amount of newly planted growth, and they have turned some of the craters into lakes. Others are partially filled in."

Andre frowned and sat back in his chair. "So, Earth is well and truly closed to us. I don't see an ROI for risking our only starship to try to go back anytime soon. This is going to be a long, God damned war."

Preston nodded, "Well, like Dr. Park said, we're going to have to build an infrastructure to build the infrastructure we need to build our own ships. Meanwhile, we learn what we can from our captured prize, the prisoners, and we dig in for the long haul. It may take a few generations to build up and train enough people to make a decent start, much less actual space-going warships."

Preston leaned back and asked, "So you think the Accipiters deployed millions of those mines?"

"Yes, Sir, Admiral."

Preston nodded, "Then the sooner our Ari'Nell project pumps out more of ours, the better. We need to protect our investment there as well as start deploying them here, too."

Andre shook his head, "Agreed, but what's done is done. I'd have rather we waited and built up some competence and strength and a decent number of hulls before kicking that hornets' nest in the first place. Speaking of ROI, it is becoming clear that the Keeper ship technology will not be useful to us for a very long time. If ever. I do not fault the bravery of those involved, but the return on their blood lost is uncertain at best."

Charles remained rigidly still, fighting back the wave of anger that blasted through him.

Gail's eyes narrowed, and she stood. "Admiral, it is the province of historians to second guess the past. Frankly, though, I strongly suspect that the Gardeners might have been more than a tad unhappy with us had we *not* acted. The timing and sequence of events that led up to it seem all too convenient to me. The Gardeners wanted to see if we had the balls to do what they set us up to do. Had we not followed through, I have to wonder whether we might even still be here today to argue about it. I expect they would have probably, at the very least, culled another five percent of the civilian population to show their displeasure."

Andre stared directly at her and didn't flinch, despite the sharp intake of breath from others around the table. "My apologies, Madam Vice President. I stand corrected. I let my anger and frustration cloud my judgment. It is not my job to question policy but to carry it out."

Gail smiled coldly, her jade-green eyes as hard as stone. "We're all angry at those murderous, planet-raping bastards, Admiral. I can't tell you how many times I've wanted to go downstairs and strangle with my bare hands the one we captured and… do… other things to it. I don't because we still need it. Just like I need you and everyone here to do their God damned jobs and find me ways to fight and kill these monsters. I don't believe the Gardeners are going to be content to wait around for a *few generations* for us to act. Do you? We must all of us break away from the old way of thinking. Yes, we're no longer the most powerful nation in the world. Yes, we're up against an enemy who seems to have infinite resources. No, we don't have a fleet to fight them with. So, we're going to have to be smarter than they are and fight dirty. No one said it was fair."

Connection

● ● ● ● ● ● ● ● ● ● ● ● ● ● ● ●

DownSide:
Home of Dr. David and Gwyneth Elliott Duncan

Dr. David Duncan had been quite comfortably well off even before the events of Awakening Day had left him as Chief of Surgery at Methodist Hospital. An only child, his parents had both died while he was in high school. His mom of cancer, and his father… had gone out to the backyard while David was at school, drank a bottle of scotch whiskey… and shot himself. His parents had left behind a small fortune, and, were it not for David's appointment to West Point, he might have spiraled down a cesspool of drugs and depression himself. He had started down that path with a vengeance, but stopped himself when his best friend had overdosed at a party that David had overslept and missed. David finished the school year and went on to attend and graduate from West Point with honors. He earned his M.D. at John's Hopkins.

His plans to make the Army his lifelong career took a turn when, after a marathon effort to save several men from terrible wounds, he'd succeeded and staggered out of the surgery tent to get some rest. Moments later, a mortar shell had killed everyone in the tent, including two nurses. The horror of that day had shaken him. After three tours in the war zone, he'd had enough. He'd separated from the Army and retired to Fort Brazos to lead a quiet life. He'd set up a low-key surgical practice and bought a house in a quiet, exclusive neighborhood along the golf course. His friends had called it 'Escher House' after the famous Dutch artist's immortal 'House of Stairs' lithograph. The house had several offset 'levels' that weren't exactly floors in the traditional sense. A collection of different lengths and styles of short and long stairs connected them.

On the golf course, he'd met (then) Commander Dr. Gwyneth Elliott, herself a Navy Surgeon and a former Olympic biathlon silver medal winner. In their doubles match, Gwyneth and her partner had soundly trounced David and his partner, Fort Brazos Mayor Tom Parker. The funny thing was that, to this day, David could not remember who Gwyneth's partner had been… or that she'd even had one. Before Awakening Day, theirs had been an on-again-off-again relationship, plagued by the ghosts of David's past. After Awakening Day, their relationship had not only renewed but, like so many others, had quite literally, blossomed.

Gwyneth was now seven months pregnant with twins. Nine-month-old Rosalyn waddled across the living room and plopped down between Sybil and Wayne Blanchard's identical triplets, Alexis, Bethany, and Cassandra. The triplets reached out and touched Rosalyn, blinking, and began rapidly 'talking' in their own private language.

The girls were all born during last year's 'Baby Boom' that saw an unprecedented 'tsunami' of births. Already, a fresh wave of births had begun to build. After last year's crisis which had seen over two hundred births per day at one point, many more deliveries were now being handled outside the overwhelmed hospitals.

Wayne and Sybil now managed logistics for the military and government, moving goods and supplies not only across the inner face of New Texas around the city of Fort Brazos, the base, and the forward operating bases, but also back and forth up the elevator system to New London and the increasingly hectic hangar and supply warehouses. Wayne was a large, beefy, broad-shouldered man. He rubbed his bloodshot eyes and brushed his shaggy brown hair aside as he sank into the oversized sectional leather couch.

David smiled in sympathy. "I don't know how you and Sybil do it, Wayne. You two are just as busy as Gwyn, and I, and Rosalyn is more than we can handle sometimes. How you two manage *three* is beyond me."

Now eight months pregnant with another set of triplets, Sybil left her sandals on the floor and sat heavily next to Wayne, pulling her feet up under herself and leaning into him. She closed her eyes, trying to take pressure off of her abdomen. Without opening them, she sighed and said, "Well, you learn how to rock one baby, burp a second baby, and feed a third baby, all at the same time…. Oh… and it's thirty toenails and thirty fingernails to trim and cut, but you cut them when they're asleep. The real challenge though, is taking them anywhere. I remember babysitting a set of twins and thinking to myself I could never do what their mom did. Now I just pray to God each day for just two hours of sleep in a row."

Wayne wondered aloud, "all girls."

Surgeon General Gwyneth Elliott Duncan leaned into Duncan on the couch and nodded. "Well, that's an interesting thing. There really are more girls than boys being born, and the trend is holding."

Wayne cocked his head. "Wait, what? Really? Do we know why?"

David looked at Gwyneth, then remarked, "Normally, the ratio of boys to girls globally, well, before Awakening Day of course, was about one hundred and five boys to one hundred girl births."

Gwyneth added, "At conception, there's a fifty-fifty balance of male and female embryos. In the first week or so after conception, male embryo mortality is, or was, higher than for females. In weeks ten through fifteen though, the ratio flipped, but it leveled off after around twenty weeks until about the third trimester when there were more male mortalities. In the end though, more female fetuses were lost during pregnancy than boys. But that was before."

Wayne squinted, "but if more girls are being born, wouldn't that mean that more boys are dying during pregnancy? I thought that there were no reported stillbirths anymore. Why are there more girls, then?"

David and Gwyneth looked at each other. David pursed his lips and Gwyneth answered, "There aren't any stillbirths."

Sybil murmured, "It's the damned Gardeners. They changed the odds."

Gwyneth nodded. "That's what we think. We don't know *what* they did, but it looks like whatever it was is causing more girls to be conceived than boys. It's only five percent more, but it's the reverse of pre–Awakening Day odds."

David took a deep breath and shifted the subject. "So, can you tell them apart?"

Wayne and Sybil answered simultaneously, "Yes."

David shook his head slowly. "I've talked to several of the other identical multiple birth parents, and they do things like putting red toenail polish on one baby and blue on the other. I've also heard of doing things like dressing one in primary colors and another in secondary colors. Yours though, I can't tell them apart."

Wayne nodded. "That's Cassie on the left, Beth in the middle, and Alexis on the right."

The triplets stopped 'talking' and looked at their father and giggled before turning back to playing with Rosalyn.

Sybil sat up a bit and opened her eyes. "I could always tell them apart, even before they were born. They felt… different. Besides things like how they kicked and where they were in my belly… I…."

All three girls stopped talking again, turned, and looked at their mom before returning their attention to Rosalyn, babbling in their secret language.

"We… have a connection that has continued and… grown even after their birth."

Wayne swallowed. "We both do. I've always known which was which. But it's more than that."

David stiffened, "Wait. I'm aware of Sybil's… special abilities. That the Gardeners gave her a, as you say, connection, to be able to *know* the people who were in… wherever it was that we were… between the time of the Accipiter attack on Earth and when we woke up here decades later. That was how she… *knew* Commander Harding at the bombing. Are you saying something *else* has happened?"

Gwyneth got up, walked over, sat next to Sybil, and took her hand. "It's OK, dear. We've talked about this, and you know David is already sworn to secrecy about your situation. I think he should hear this too. Sooner or later, we will need more help to understand what is happening to you."

Sybil closed her eyes and paused. "They're so excited to see Rosalyn again. They're telling her everything that has happened since their last visit."

Wayne nodded, "It's not really words… it…."

Sybil added, "It's more emotional than experiential."

David shook his head and swallowed. "They are… empathic?"

Gwyneth smiled and looked at David. "Yes, we think so. We were not really sure until recently, as they've gotten a bit older."

Wayne said quietly, "We know when they're hungry or cold or need a change or… other things… even if we're in the other room. Without a sound. It started when they stopped crying, and Sybil and I would just… know."

David's eyes widened. "My God. This is unprecedented." Then he paused, "But why only Sybil? People have died, even on Awakening Day. If this was intentional by the Gardeners, then they would have done it to more than one person, not just Sybil. If they wanted a new human trait, they wouldn't have risked only giving it to one single individual. They wouldn't risk something they wanted to be emergent, to be present only in a sample of one."

Gwyneth shook her head. "I've wondered the same thing ever since… well… since Sybil's special characteristics came to light. She and I have discussed it many times. I thought that either it was an accident, or perhaps there were others, and they'd kept it secret. Sybil doesn't think so, though."

Sybil nodded. "I was the only one. I don't know how I know, but I do."

A timer started beeping in the kitchen. David got up. "Well, dinner's ready. Let's eat!"

✪ ✪ ✪

An hour and a half later, after clearing away the table, they returned to the living room, and the children resumed their playtime.

Wayne laughed and continued the conversation from dinner. "I just cannot believe that there is actual support out there for establishing a monarchy!"

Gwyneth shook her head. "A constitutional monarchy! Those people seem to think we will need it to hold humanity together for the zillion-year war with the Accipiters."

Wayne grimaced, "No way. I'm with General Marcus. We need a pure meritocracy. No professional politicians, princes, or plutocrats."

David raised his wineglass. "Here, here. The only thing worse would be a permanent bureaucracy."

Gwyneth grinned. "Well, if the Demarchy random lottery idea were to win, we could do worse. *You* could end up as the next President!"

Wayne swallowed and blanched, "Err, no. Just… no. Just shoot me first."

Sybil snuggled close to him. "Shut it, Wayne. You'd do fine."

Wayne shook his head. "No, thank you. Have you seen what it's done to Austin? Have you seen his eyes?"

Except for the children, the room grew suddenly quiet.

Alexis, Bethany, and Cassandra had formed a circle around Rosalyn and were chattering away at her. Suddenly, Rosalyn started to talk back to them. Haltingly at first, she was almost up to the Blanchard girl's speed within a few seconds.

David and Gwyneth blinked as they watched their daughter grow more and more excited and animated in her exchange with the other girls. They turned and looked at Wayne and Sybil, who were not the least bit surprised.

Wayne said in a small voice, "I'm terrified of what it will be like when they hit puberty and discover boys."

Stand Alone

● ● ● ● ● ● ● ● ● ● ● ● ● ● ● ●

DownSide:
John Austin's House

John Austin awoke with a start to the sound of a high-pitched scream. It was still dark. Wearing his undershirt and boxers, he leaped to his feet, blinking his bloodshot eyes as he grabbed his Wilson Combat Vickers Elite 1911 .45 ACP pistol from the nightstand and sprinted barefoot out his bedroom door into the living room just as all the lights in the house snapped on.

The commander of his protection detail, Sergeant Benjamin "Benny" Jenkins, intercepted him, physically blocking his path. Benny spread his arms and commanded, "Wait, Mr. President!"

Corporal Roxanna Darling was already upstairs. She was stationed in one of the guest bedrooms next to Matti's room. Moments later, Roxanna appeared at the top of the stairs in a ruffled black tank top and briefs. Her long, lustrous black hair, normally in a ponytail, hung loosely about her face and shoulders. Of Mexican and Iranian descent, she was equally strikingly attractive and doggedly committed to her job. And, much to her chagrin, she had become utterly devoted to Matti. She held her FN FNX .45 Tactical pistol at her side.

Roxanna announced, "ALL CLEAR, ALL CLEAR," as Corporal Gabriel Pérez bounded up the stairs. Gabriel paused. Roxanna shook her head rapidly, glanced in the direction of Matti's room, then added, "It's a woman thing." She gave a knowing glance at John and mouthed, *"I'll talk to you later."* She turned and entered Matti's room, saying, "Don't worry…" as she closed the door behind her.

"Coffee, Mr. President? I imagine you're not going to get any more sleep after this little shot of adrenaline." Benny gave John a sympathetic grin.

✪ ✪ ✪

Benny had been right. John had been getting up at five-thirty in the morning to try to get a head start on things. An extra hour of *trying* to get back to sleep wouldn't have helped, especially lately. Benny began making coffee while John returned to his bedroom and got dressed.

Later, John sat at the kitchen table, drinking his second cup while reading his email when Roxanne came downstairs, now fully dressed in her usual low-key jeans and leather jacket. She gave Benny a look, at which Benny nodded and made himself scarce.

She approached John and quietly asked, "Mr. President, may I have a word?"

John looked up at her and nodded, his eyes already tired. "Have a seat, Roxanne."

She hesitated, then pulled a chair and anxiously sat on its edge. "Ahh, Mr. President, as you know, Matti has been going through some changes."

John nodded. "Tell me about it. She's grown almost three inches in the last six months."

Roxanne smiled, "Well, it's more than that… she hasn't wanted to tell you, but she's going to need some wardrobe changes. She needs a bra…."

John's eyes widened slightly, "Oh, well… OK then. I suppose…"

"And she's going to need pads… or tampons…. And new sheets."

John blinked, "What? No! She's *nine*! She turns *ten* in April! How? Why?"

Roxanne swallowed, "Well, it's not unheard of, and uh, we had a talk. It seems she's not the only one. Many of the girls her age have had the same, well, early transition. I'll take her to see her doctor today to ensure everything is OK, but she seems physically fine. Actually, after her initial shock, waking up, well, you know, she calmed down very quickly. You know how she is."

John sat back in his chair, closed his eyes and rolled his head, rubbing his sore neck. "She's a force of nature."

Roxanne added, "Sir, if anything, she's mad. Mad at the Gardeners."

John shrugged. "I can't say I'm surprised. She's been spending so much time with Gail that she's acting more and more like her…," he swallowed. *And less like her mother.*

"Dad?" Matti was standing quietly behind them, fully dressed in jeans, her new Bell & Son's boots, and a loose yellow blouse. Her long blonde hair was neatly braided behind her.

Roxanne and John were both startled. Neither had heard her come down the stairs.

Roxanne looked up at Matti and stood. "I'll leave you two to talk." She darted out of the room.

Matti took Roxanne's place on the chair, reached out her hand, and put it on her father's knee. "Dad, we need to talk."

John leaned forward and took her hand in his, asking awkwardly, "Of course, Matti. How… How are you feeling?"

Matti lowered her voice, and her face took on a solemn expression that all too uncomfortably resembled her late mother, Carolyn's. "I'm fine, Dad. I'm in perfect health, just like everyone else, thanks to the Gardeners. And now I'm a woman, years earlier than I should be, also thanks to the Gardeners. That's not what we need to talk about, though. We need to talk about you, your nightmares, and why you keep pushing the woman you love and who obviously loves you away. Dad, what's wrong with you? And don't you dare say that I wouldn't understand!"

Sadness fell over his face as John sank back into his chair and looked at Matti without answering.

Matti recoiled slightly. "What? What can't you tell me?"

John looked down at the floor. "There are things I cannot… things that must not… touch you."

Matti blinked. "You think you are protecting me?" She gasped, "And you think you are protecting *her* too!"

John shook his head, "Matti, there are things I fear I must do that are… unthinkable."

Matti's blue eyes flashed in anger. "Dad, I know you feel guilty about all those men who died, but you didn't start this war!"

John's sadness redoubled as he shook his head slowly. "Matti, sending these people to die is bad enough, but I'll do it again and again if it saves the rest of you. This war… this war will require death and destruction on a scale to make the toll of all of history's evildoers shrink to insignificance."

Matti stared at him. "I think that dumbass bomb must have caused more brain damage than we thought. Don't you get it? All you're doing is isolating yourself and hurting the rest of us. The people who love you will stand by you no matter what happens."

John stiffened. "It has to be this way, Matti."

Matti set her jaw, leaped up from the chair, and stormed out of the room. Her eyes narrowed as she thought to herself, *The hell it does!*

Year 3 PAD:

February

Weapons

● ● ● ● ● ● ● ● ● ● ● ● ● ● ● ● ●

DownSide:
Riverbend Mall

Prior to Awakening Day, many shopping malls across the United States had fallen on hard times. Between competition from online retailers and many other factors, over twenty percent or more of malls had closed nationwide. Despite this trend, the Riverbend Mall in Fort Brazos managed to survive and remain open. However, after Awakening Day, there were no more deliveries to replenish inventory except for the small number of stores that featured local goods. Without the anchor tenants, the mall finally shut down in the panic that followed. Sufficient security remained, however, to prevent looting. The government had appropriated most of the goods to help with the housing crisis, so few things of interest remained other than displays and fixtures.

Then, on May 20th of Year One, the "mad bomber" Commander Thomas Harding detonated a bomb at City Hall, devastating its interior. The damage had been worse than initially thought. The Council Chamber was at the heart of the damage. With building supplies desperately needed for the housing crisis, rebuilding City Hall would have to wait. In the meantime, the government, despite being shaken, needed a place to meet. Virtually all of the vacant office buildings had already been converted into apartments. The only unoccupied facility of any substantial size that remained 'available' was… the shopping mall.

Riverbend Mall featured one hundred and fifty stores with five anchor tenants. The total retail floor space equaled over 2,000,000 square feet spread across one main floor. The Anchor tenants had three floors each. The mall also included nearly 6,000 parking spaces, including two parking garages. With little debate or discussion, the now deserted Macy's department store was chosen for the initial offices. Furniture and fixtures from around the mall were hauled into place, and they moved useless items to unused areas and storage. They assigned various governmental departments to different former store "department" areas and were largely left to themselves to scrounge and make things work. Fortunately, the mall was relatively new and had modern wiring for telecommunications, Wi-Fi, and internet service. Parts of the food court area were reworked so that entrepreneurial citizens, mostly those who already had working restaurants, could set up and offer food to the mushrooming population of government employees and the citizens and military personnel they served.

Unbeknownst to John Austin, who had nearly died in the bombing and needed many weeks to recover, Mayor Tom Parker and the surviving City Council members decided that the executive offices of the President and Vice President deserved their own separate space for meetings and work. Previously, Tom had shared his office at City Hall, but even before the bombing, space was cramped. Everyone had known that they needed to do something different, but there were always higher priorities in the Apocalypse's wake. So, the spacious third-floor former Furniture Department was quickly walled off and designated as the "New Oval Office," even though it wasn't oval-shaped at all. Frantic efforts from across the city scrounged up the finest carpets, drapes, paintings, wall coverings, and office furniture that could be begged, borrowed, or (politely) ~~stolen~~ appropriated. Grumbling detractors called it the "throne room." The President's and Vice President's offices looked out over the store's 3-story colonnaded atrium.

Working at a level of secrecy unlikely ever to be repeated, the entire city had soon become involved while managing to prevent word of what was being done from reaching either John Austin or Gail Finley. It was, in fact, a matter of pride. People wanted to honor their gravely wounded and enormously popular leader and the perhaps even more popular Gail Finley, hero of the hour, who had shot the despised mad bomber dead. People from all walks of life donated to the cause, and the work proceeded day and night. It *had* to be done before the President was on his feet again — and it *had* to be a surprise because everyone knew John Austin. He would have vetoed it immediately had he had an inkling it was going on.

When preparations were finally ready, John was pushed into the mall in his wheelchair, supposedly to review its use as an emergency shelter. Of course, the secret could not have been kept without the collusion of his daughter Matti and his protection detail. It had been harder to keep Gail in the dark, but they'd managed, or at least they hoped that they had. Regardless, if she knew, she never let on. When John arrived, he knew that something was obviously up because of the enormous crowd that was present, along with every camera still functioning in Fort Brazos.

The citizens would not *allow* him to reject what they had done.

John was utterly dumbfounded. The televised and broadcast expression of shock and amazement on his face had been worth it, and the people ate it up. The President and Vice President would accept this gift…. *Or else.*

✪ ✪ ✪

John Austin sat behind the massive cherry wood desk and waited for his guests to follow suit. Across from him were Gail Finley, Alexander Marcus, Preston Milner, Andre Johansson, and Captains Charles Cross and Stephanie Mahoney.

John began, "Thank you for coming. I've read the reports on the prospect of shipbuilding, and while it brings up many additional details, the gist of it, at least to me, is pretty much the same as it was the first time we talked about this last year. While the project in Ari'Nell is adding some interesting new things, and it looks very promising, it's not going to create whole new ships, at least not for a long time, and obviously, it won't help train the crews to man them. For now, just pumping out mines is like building a fence and a moat around the unbroken ground of a factory that hasn't been built yet. We've still got a long way to go. Unless the Gardeners drop another shoe, I expect it will be a long while before we can build our own ships of any sophistication or quantity. We just don't have the infrastructure yet. I get that. The problem is that I'm pretty damned sure that the Gardeners will not be satisfied with us waiting that long to accomplish anything positive. We need a strategy where we can at least make some sort of hit-and-run attacks so we can mollify the Gardeners. Hopefully, that can buy us enough time to train crews and start building our own ships."

Gail added, "We need to keep poking the hornets' nest, but without losing the stick we poke it with."

Charles looked at the Admirals, who nodded permission. He shook his head. "Mr. President, Madam Vice President, aside from the fact that in last year's attack, we pretty much used up most of the ball bearings we could find, the problem with kinetic weapons is that the target needs to be at a known and predictable location when we release them. Unless you want to attack a planet or moon, we can no longer count on the Accipiters putting their ships in nice, predictable orbits. We haven't really begun to test any of the new weapons from Ari'Nell. Even if we had had them on Blood Phoenix, we still have to get close enough for them to be effective. They are an important step, but we don't have doctrine or tactics developed for them, even if they were fully installed and tested. Our recon mission showed that the Accipiters aren't dumb. They're keeping their ships randomly moving around. Space is big. We cannot get close enough through their defenses to be sure of hitting anything. We could release kinetic weapons at a distance from the solar system, but we run the risk of hitting the planet if we spread them out too much."

He took a breath and continued, "On the other hand, it occurred to me that we *could* consider aiming at the mining operations they have going on at the outer gas giants. We could aim fairly wide and hope to hit *something* in a harassing attack. We'd still have to launch it well outside the solar system to avoid their mines."

Gail looked at John, who nodded. She smiled. "Let's put that on our to-do list. Call it…. Operation Gnat."

John took a breath and looked around the room. "Longer term, and by that, I mean months, hopefully. We need to push ahead with testing these new weapons and developing our tactics and doctrines to use them. Hell, strap them onto an ILC if you have to, for now. Stop studying them and start *using* them. This is not a peacetime project, people. We are at *war*. Push it hard. I want those mines deployed in Ari'Nell. You know as well as I do that, sooner or later, the Accipiters will get around to poking their nose in that system to see if that's where we are hiding. Right now, that's our ace in the hole. We need to protect it. Find a way to mine that Nexus point, where the Accipiter ships would arrive, and, yes, I know that's not a fixed point in space and that it is constantly moving. *Find a way.*"

"Gail, I want you to take that and run with it like you did getting Phoenix launched."

Gail cocked her head and looked at him in surprise. She hesitated for a moment, then answered, "Yes… Mr. President."

John nodded to himself. "Admiral Milner, I want you to set up a separate think tank or skunk works to work on finding the ideas we haven't thought of. Give them whiteboards and computers for now. No idea is too crazy, but we do need someone running it who can prioritize the crazy. Hell, assign people to read through science fiction books looking for ideas. I don't care if we have to build giant mirrors in space to burn the damned birds. *We are at war.*"

Preston pursed his lips, thinking, then nodded, "Yes, Mr. President."

John continued, "One more thing. Gene Morton sacrificed himself and the crew of the Axe and took out an entire mothership and thousands of escorts. While I don't want to consider suicide missions like that, I do want to look at the idea of using some version of the warp rings as, well, warp missiles or torpedoes. I talked to Phoenix about this…."

Gail's eyes widened, and her cheeks heated. *Now you're talking to that alien machine instead of to me?* She swallowed. *Fuck… Now I'm jealous of a machine….*

"…and she believes that she could grow a relatively small set of rings with limited intelligence that she could carry to a target system and then launch toward a target. By being smart enough to, as she put it, 'manage the warp field,' it would be smart enough to home in on a moving target. The problem is that if it is detected like you were, Captain Cross, and it was fired upon, it would have trouble lensing the warp field to see where it was going. It is something I want us to test in some uninhabited system somewhere, make sure it works, and then hold in reserve until the right opportunity comes along to use it."

✪ ✪ ✪

Gail followed the others as they filed out of the office but stopped and closed the door behind them. She turned and walked back to face John across the desk and waited.

John studied her face and frowned. "You talked to Matti."

Gail's lips tightened. "I didn't have to. John, I know you pretty damned well. I've been patient, giving you time. Ever since the bombing, you've been distant. Keeping me out. We used to talk about things. We may have argued, but… we got things done!" She waited to see if he would react or object, but John remained silent.

"You nearly died, John! Hell, ask Gwyneth, I…." She swallowed. "John, I fell apart when I thought you were going to die. That was a wake-up call for me! Realizing just how fucking much your sorry ass meant to me! And then… And then you shut down and went cold."

She shook her head. "You know, at first, I worried that your near-death experience had changed you. That sometimes happens to trauma and heart attack victims. Gwyneth said that it's like their brain gets reset."

John held her gaze silently, but his eyes said everything.

Her eyes flared, and her cheeks heated. "But that's not it, is it? It didn't change how you feel about me… about us… at all, has it?"

John very quietly answered, "No. No, it hasn't."

She exclaimed, "You! …At least you're honest about that. Look, John, I'm not exactly sure what you think you are protecting me from, and while it may be noble as hell, it's also just the kind of idiot thinking I should have expected from you, and it's eating you up inside. What's worse is that I also know that you're too stubborn for me to talk you out of whatever it is you think you're doing right now."

Gail's lower lip quivered slightly. Then she walked around to his side of the desk and stood there for a moment, staring down at him. Then, suddenly, without warning, she slapped him. Hard. It was loud enough to slightly echo off the large plate-glass window overlooking the atrium.

John's mouth parted in shock and surprise as he reflexively touched his hand to his reddened face.

Gail shuddered, shook her finger at him, and snapped, "Reconsider!"

She swallowed and added, "God dammit, John! Do you have any idea what you've done? I let myself…. You… You reconsider your actions before you destroy…." She shook her head. "And before you fall so far that the wolves devour you. People are talking, John. They already smell blood."

She turned on her heel, strode to the door, and grasped the handle. She looked over her shoulder and added, "And if they do… we all will fall." She swallowed. "Every last one of us."

She turned back, opened the door, and left it standing open in her wake.

Shore Leave

● ● ● ● ● ● ● ● ● ● ● ● ● ● ● ● ●

DownSide:
Café Balthasar, Town Square

To say that Captain Charles Cross received lots of calls, text messages, and emails during the course of a day was an understatement of grand proportions. Given his responsibilities, at least while in port, he'd been assigned an "adjutant." Sergeant Gerhold Christoph Weiler. Formerly of the German Army's 260th Airborne Reconnaissance Company (Luftlandeaufklärungskompanie 260), Gerhold had been one of the "New Arrivals" on Awakening Day. As with other military units from around the Earth, his unit had been "rescued" by the Gardeners moments before they would have been immolated by the Accipiter kinetic impactor strikes that wiped out military bases and cities around the globe.

Gerhold had volunteered and was fast-tracked through the crash course to become a Marine Security Guard. Before Awakening Day, back on Earth, Marine Security Guards had been tasked with providing security at U.S. Embassies and Consulates. After the alien Stalker and Wardog attacks, (then) General Marcus had decided that the new President, Vice President, and Council Members should have a personal security detail, whether they liked it or not. After the bombing of City Hall, the program was escalated. If they could be talked into it, key military and civilian leaders would all have some degree of protection, including self-defense training. Most newly-minted MSGs remained in plain clothes and maintained a low profile, as did Gerhold, whose adjutant duties were quite real. As was his responsibility to protect Charles's life with his own, if necessary.

Gerhold did an excellent job of shielding Charles from the onslaught of legitimate daily contacts as well as the never-ending well wishes from civilians, requests for interviews, and the not-inconsiderable number of oddball messages and even a shocking number of … advances… from those romantically attracted to the "dashing" Captain. Only a literal handful of people had his personal, private number. Included on that tiny list were the President, the Vice President, the Secretary of War, and Admirals Milner and Johansson. The message he'd received earlier in the day was from the other person on that list. It read:

Dinner. 8pm. Café Balthasar. Don't be late.

Mira Yaegar entered the café and sashayed to the table where Charles waited. She smiled brightly when he looked up, stood, and pulled out her chair. *This man is such a breath of fresh air.* She'd let her dirty blonde hair down from her regular braid and avoided thinking about how much time she'd spent in front of the mirror getting ready. Over a white peasant blouse, she wore a vintage sterling silver blue turquoise squash blossom necklace she'd bought years ago from Councilwoman Gloria Vargas's jewelry store. A coral concho belt circled her waist above an asymmetric denim wrap skirt and her nicest custom boots from Bell & Sons. Her matching sterling African safari cuff bracelets had been a wedding present from her dad. Her husband Carl was dead almost six years now, and she wasn't really sure why she had put them on at the last minute. On the other hand, she hadn't given a second thought to the heavy Sig P220 Legion 10mm pistol in her oversized handbag.

After she'd first met Charles last year, they'd met again at a party. Despite his sometimes long absences while "off-world," they'd managed to find excuses to meet for coffee, lunch, or dinner every chance they could find.

After Awakening Day, it took a while for the physiological changes the Gardeners had made in the human survivors to become apparent. It took even longer for the consequences to sink in. The first baby boom effectively grabbed the remnants of human civilization by the throat and shook it. Perhaps no single societal change since Awakening Day was more profoundly dramatic than the screeching halt to the sexual revolution and casual sex in general.

With virtually no effective birth control other than abstinence, the social etiquette of dating had taken on an increasingly old-fashioned formality. Couples would only meet in public places. Most tended to "dress up" for the occasion. Unless the woman was simply dying to get pregnant, there were no nightcaps or opportunities to be alone together. With perfect health and the elevated hormones that went with it, the risk for those with even a modicum of common sense was simply too great. Moreover, the social pressure upon men to be responsible for their offspring had reached almost biblical levels. In addition, it wasn't the "father" that would insist on a shotgun wedding anymore — it was the entire community.

Chaperones in various guises were now the norm. Sergeant Gerhold Weiler sat at a nearby table as protector of rather more than just Charles's life.

Charles himself was in his dress whites.

Mira blushed slightly at the sudden realization that there would no doubt be photos of her and Charles circulating within hours or even minutes.

Charles glanced at his Sangin Neptune watch and smiled. "Straight up eight o'clock. I like a punctual lady."

Mira smiled, "Hmmm, I like a man who can follow instructions."

"Ahh, so we're establishing who's in command?"

"If you like."

"Tell me, Mira, what do you do when you're not hunting six-legged iron-plated monsters? I know you ran an insurance agency, and you used to go on safari with your father. What I mean is, now, here, in this place. What do you do with your free time?"

The waiter came and took their order. The distraction gave Mira time to think and to study Charles's trim, compact figure. Whereas her late husband Carl had been funny and adventurous and had accepted her lifestyle even if he hadn't understood it, Charles Cross could hardly be more different. He was sharply intelligent, with a Ph.D. in physics and a master's degree in electrical engineering. Of course, most people knew that he was not just the former Commander of a United States nuclear submarine; he was now the famous Commander of a starship. He was a formidable man.

What she had noticed about him early on, however, was the way he treated the people he commanded. He was as much a mentor as he was their Captain.

After the waiter left, she took a sip of her wine and mused, "Well, I spend most of my time either training my dogs or training my Army boys… come to think of it," her eyes wrinkled as she smiled, "that's kind of the same thing."

Charles studied Mira for several long seconds. This was a woman who was utterly sure of herself, and what was more, she was demonstrably capable of doing what she set out to do and had the unmistakable eyes of the hunter she had been for most of her life. He raised his eyebrows and said, "You know, Mira, there are videos of you and that first Wardog and from your other sorties with the Army units hunting them. They're classified, but I've seen them."

Mira blinked in surprise. "I didn't know there was a video of the first one."

Charles nodded. "I've studied it. Well, I've studied everything about our enemies. But the first thing I noticed when I saw it was, well you and how you handled yourself."

Mira leaned back in her chair and smiled coyly. "And?"

"You never once hesitated. That Wardog burst out of the ground beneath you to attack your team. Many people, even experienced veteran soldiers, would have been caught at least slightly off guard or outright panicked. We train our soldiers through repetition and muscle memory, but most people don't have it. The killer instinct."

Mira sipped her wine and studied his face. She started to ask if it bothered him, but from his expression and body language, it obviously didn't. She answered softly, "It doesn't bother you. Very few people understand. Especially the ones who consider themselves to be erudite and civilized."

He smiled warmly, "You've clearly faced life-and-death situations before, but it doesn't bother me that you are a natural-born killer. I admire the … directness in you. The honesty."

She stifled a smile. "So, is this how you normally charm the ladies, Captain?"

Charles chuckled, "Mira, I think we're past that stage, don't you?"

She cocked her head slightly and took another sip of wine. "What are you really getting at, Charles?"

He leaned forward, and his grey eyes narrowed. "Two things. First, I think you should run for Senate after the new constitution is passed."

Mira almost choked on her wine. Her jaw dropped, and she stared at him for a moment before consciously forcing it closed again. "What?"

Charles smiled and leaned back. "I'm serious, Mira. We need someone like you in the Senate. Someone who understands the kind of enemy we are up against and has the *will* to do something about it. Someone who won't wimp out when the tough decisions need to be made."

"Oh, how lovely? So you think I'm suitable for the role of a hard-ass politician? I thought you liked me!"

"Look, Mira, you're smart, experienced, and you are one of the very few people who have actually fought an alien and lived, and, well, as I said. You're honest and direct. You'll get things done and won't put up with the kind of stupid politicians who usually end up as senators. And I do like you. What's more, I trust you."

Mira's heart started racing, and she blushed. *What's wrong with me? What is he up to?*

Charles picked up his wineglass, slowly swirled it, sniffed it, and fought a grimace before sipping the very young vintage. "You know I'm right."

Mira hesitated, narrowing her gaze, "You said *Two* things."

Charles nodded and frowned. "That's right. I did." He took another sip of wine. He looked into her eyes and said, "Mira, you hunt ferocious monsters. I fly a cobbled-together hybrid starship and fight ten-foot-tall aliens who outnumber us millions to one…."

Mira blinked and almost dropped her wineglass as she realized what he was doing. The strange thing was that deep down, she knew it was coming, but she hadn't been willing to admit it to herself.

"…I don't know if our lives will be short and end violently or be long and glorious, but there is one thing I do know." He reached into his pocket and pulled out a small velvet box. He stood, walked around to her side of the table, and knelt, "… I don't want to live that life without you in it. Mira Yaeger, will you marry me?"

True to her nature, Mira didn't hesitate. She threw herself off her chair, nearly knocking the table over in the process, and wrapped her arms around him, saying yes, over and over, and kissing him.

The café patrons around them smiled, laughed, stood, and applauded.

Sergeant Weiler smiled knowingly and sent a text message, claiming his winnings from the betting pool.

Orientation

• • • • • • • • • • • • • • • •

DownSide:
Eugene Morton Naval Academy
Formerly: Bonham State University Campus
Orientation Week

Eighteen-year-old Elísabet Marta Gunnarsson was no stranger to Bonham State University's campus. Her mother, Dr. Katrín Gunnarsson, was the Dean of Fine Arts. They had immigrated to the United States shortly after Katrín's divorce when Elísabet had been only two years old. Now, with the University's mission and name change, the culture and atmosphere of the largely agrarian college began to take on an entirely new and stridently martial culture and atmosphere.

The Apocalypse had done that to a lot of things. Its demons had even murdered Elísabet's fiancé, Zachary Simmons, who she'd known for as long as she could remember. Zach and her friends had always called her 'Beth.' On that horrible day in September, the happy, innocent girl named Beth died, too. Now, she was Elísabet again, and she had a mission in life. The Accipiters and all their minions would suffer, and she would make them pay for what they had done. Not just to Zach, but for all their victims.

Slim and tall at five foot nine inches, Elísabet stood in front of her bedroom mirror, wearing her grey and black Cadet uniform, copied from the United States Naval Academy. Her dark red hair was shorter than even regulations required.

Her teary-eyed mother, Katrin, who had ensured the uniform was tailored perfectly, stood behind her, brushing her short hair and adjusting the sleeves.

In the past, Elísabet would have complained about the attention.

Katrin sniffed as she asked, "Did you have to cut off your hair like this? It was so beautiful before. You'd grown it since you were little. It makes you look like a boy."

Elísabet's long hair had indeed been down to her waist. It was one of the things that Zach had loved… and that she had loved that he had loved. Now it was only an inch on the side and no more than two to three inches on top. She answered coldly, "It will be efficient."

Katrín couldn't stop the tears now, "And your clothes!"

Boxes covered the floor and closet. Elísabet had taken all her clothes and carefully washed and folded them before neatly wrapping and labeling each item. Virtually everything she owned was now in one of the boxes.

Elísabet turned slowly and put her hand on her mother's shoulder. Her green eyes softened as she smiled sadly. "Mother, I don't need this stuff anymore. The Academy will provide everything I need. I want you to promise me you will donate my clothes… everything. There are so many people who need clothes now. There was never enough for all the New Londoners who were dumped here with nothing but the clothes on their backs. I won't need them, and, with the training program I'll be in, nothing will fit me anymore."

"Look, sweetheart, I know how hard it has been for you, but you don't have to live in those awful, crowded dorms. You should stay here and leave the room for others!"

"Mother, I must be focused on my studies at the Academy. Staying here has too many memories. Every night that I sleep in that bed," she glanced at her white canopied bed on the other side of the room, "it just reminds me of him. Of my life, before."

Katrín's lips trembled. "I loved him too, you know. Ever since you two played in the mud together, I knew you were destined for each other. I would have been proud to have him as my son-in-law…. He was here so much all these years I thought of him as my son, anyway." She reached out and touched her daughter's high cheekbone. She was very much like a younger version of herself. "You can still have a beautiful life."

Elísabet's smile faded. "I will come and see you when I can."

✪ ✪ ✪

Across town, in one of the nicer subdivisions, William (Will) Sawyer tugged at his Cadet uniform. The sleeves were a little short, and it was just slightly too tight in the shoulders. He'd grown a half inch since he'd been measured for it. Like Elísabet, he too had a score to settle with the Accipiters. The creature that had murdered Zach had also killed Will's brother Dex and their friend Morgan Forbes. In front of him. He'd survived because he'd been back at the truck when it happened. That he had subsequently shot and killed the Stalker now seemed like just so much dumb luck, and it was hardly a comfort to Zach and Morgan's families. Or his own.

And then there was Elísabet. After the incident, he went to her house to pay his respects. She had come to the door and looked at him with a beautiful but blank face and empty eyes. She'd stared at him for a long moment. Then she'd said, "I'm glad you lived." Then she'd turned and closed the door and hadn't spoken to him since. He could see in her eyes that she didn't blame him, but that face of hers haunted him. In his dreams, when he relived holding his dying friend in his arms, Elísabet would appear and stand over him, looking down at him with that fallen angel's face.

No matter what happened at the Academy, he would not only graduate. He would make it his life's mission to exact revenge upon the monsters who had taken his friends from him. And stolen an angel's soul.

✪ ✪ ✪

Seventeen-year-old Jordan Hoffman walked across the main campus quad, wearing her Cadet uniform. Jordan had known the boys who were killed back in September and had been friends with Elísabet. Those tragedies were painful enough. However, her motivations burned deeper still. A stalker, just like the one that had killed the boys, had killed her mother Margaret, her father, Barrett, and her brother Nolan. The never sufficiently damned Gardeners had killed her grandmother Abigal by not waking her up on Awakening Day.

Moreover, the cursed monster had also killed Corpsman Mendez and Deputy Grayson Miles, whom she'd known all her life. Then the damned thing had cocooned herself, her sisters Sandra, Hannah, and Elizabeth, and the man who would become Sandra's husband, Captain David Garreth, Sargent Washington, and Specialist Simmons (unrelated to Zach). Only the quick thinking of (then) Sheriff Austin had saved them.

Jordan still had nightmares, and though they didn't like to talk about it, so did her sisters, although Sandra seemed to be doing better now, and Jordan was so thrilled for her.

She set her jaw. Never again. Those monsters will rue the day they failed to kill me.

Gardeners

● ● ● ● ● ● ● ● ● ● ● ● ● ● ● ●

TopSide:
Accipiter Holding Cell

Mayor Tom Parker sat alone in the observation room. He had long debated the wisdom of what he was about to do. Convincing the others to allow him to proceed had taken months. It wasn't like others had never entered the room with the creature. However, that was always under heavy military guard. He had prayed about it, often with his wife Dotti at his side. Now he was finally here, about to enter the lion's den.

His heart was pounding as he bowed and prayed, "Heavenly Father, let my eyes be open that I might see, and my ears be open that I might hear. If my lips do part, let it be your word on my tongue. If this creature be a child of yours, may your Spirit shine forth through him, however far through darkness it must. Farther still through my hate at what they have done. And, more importantly, through however far his hate at the retribution we have returned and have yet to return in kind has darkened his mind and soul if he has one."

He paused, took a deep breath, and swallowed before adding, "I accept your will...."

It had been over a month since Leo Talib's translation system was installed. Since then, Leo and the rest of the SigInt team had worked overtime to improve it. It was not even remotely perfect, but significant progress had been made. The monitor on the cell wall now showed the written translation along with text-to-speech speaking it aloud.

Tom stood, walked through the airlock, and entered the holding cell, carrying only his heavily annotated study bible. The Accipiter Priest sat comfortably on the oddly shaped bench in the center of the room. It opened its enormous topaz eyes and gazed at Tom. If it was surprised at the lack of accompanying soldiers, it didn't appear to physically or outwardly show it. At least with body language.

However, the lack of anything in the creature's eyes was terrifying to Tom. In a human, he could almost always detect *something*, whether it was interest, hostility, or even boredom. In the Accipiter…. Nothing. *You truly are… alien.*

There was no human furniture in the cell, so Tom slowly walked over, sat cross-legged on the cold metal floor across from the Accipiter, and waited. Even seated, the Accipiter was enormous. Tom had to sit a small distance away so he wasn't craning his neck to look up at the thing.

He was struck by how stunningly beautiful it was. Terrifying… but beautiful. From the elegance of its beak and the glyphs that flowed across it to the multihued coloring of its feather analogues. Even its claws were both frightening and beautiful. Those enormous eyes, though…. Tom could imagine getting lost… even hypnotized by those eyes.

Eventually, the Accipiter broke the silence, humming mild chords preceded by a deep rumbling that Tom could feel in his bones, which startled him. It briefly signed something and pointed at him.

The computer voice translation had an English lilt. Tom idly reflected on how the British-dominated SigInt team might forever influence how people thought the Accipiters sounded….

Untranslatable. You are different.

Tom hesitated before answering. "Yes."
They stared at each other for a long moment.

You come to. Untranslatable. Study. Like language student.
Guards not. Question?

Tom nodded. "Perhaps to listen… perhaps to speak. If you are willing."
The Accipiter studied Tom for several minutes before making a new series of higher-pitched singing noises before saying:

You are Untranslatable priest. Question?

Do not underestimate its intelligence…. Tom surprised himself, chuckling, "You might call me that…. My Catholic brothers would use that term. In my faith, I am called a Pastor."

Then you come to learn paradise Untranslatable of ours.

Tom paused, closed his eyes, and bowed his head for a moment in a quick prayer. He opened his eyes and sat up straight. "What can you tell me about it?"

You do not know how beautiful you are.

Interesting that that translated easily. "All of God's creatures are beautiful." Tom swallowed. *And here I was, awestruck by the physical beauty of this alien creature.*

The Accipiter paused, rumbled more, then asked:

Yes. Why. Question?

Tom was taken aback. "All of God's creation is beautiful. His creation is beauty incarnate."

More rumbling followed, accompanied by a long series of glyphs.

Untranslatable Creation Untranslatable beautiful is, Question?

Then, a silence fell over both of them for a time.

Tom sighed and said, "You speak of God as comfortably as a believer would."

A strange series of high-pitched hoots followed, and the Accipiter said:

I have had this Untranslatable conversation Untranslatable
many times as the brightest Untranslatable stars are numbered in
Untranslatable Earth's sky.

Did it just laugh at me? It can laugh? He frowned. "You mean with other 'priests' of other species…."

The Accipiter simply answered:

Yes.

Tom's throat caught, and he swallowed as he asked, "Were they beautiful, too?" *Before you destroyed them?*

A long series of energetic tones followed, along with brightly colored glyphs.

Oh, yes.

Tom unconsciously squeezed his bible before realizing it and stopped. He took a deep breath and asked, "You said I do not know of my own beauty?"

You Untranslatable.
Are remains from beauty of creation.
Imagine the stars Untranslatable.
Number them in your mind.
The cosmos swirls Untranslatable.
In their work, Untranslatable, other things swirl.
In Untranslatable swirling pools Untranslatable.
Untranslatable born new cosmos.
Is same with creatures of the swirls.
Untranslatable stars and planets swirl as designed.
Same is true of that which swirls out of them.

Tom reflexively replied, "You're talking about life. Life that emerges from creation. From the cosmos."

The Accipiter's chest swelled as through pride… an energy now radiated from its posturing. New rumbling flowed in parallel with hoots and tweets and colorful glyphs.

The cosmos of life….
Born its purpose Untranslatable New.
Out of the Untranslatable chaos.
The of the order of the stars.
Sometimes, from life Untranslatable, new cosmos is born.
The new cosmos Untranslatable.

The mind.

A new, vibrant, and brightly colored series of glyphs followed.

We cultivate Untranslatable cosmos; all of them.

A horrible peace fell upon Tom's soul as understanding dawned. Suddenly, a surge of emotion and pain coursed through him. He started to open his mouth to say, *"But you've killed so many! Ended so many minds!"* but he didn't. Something held his tongue. Instead, he asked, "So I am beautiful because of my mind?"

The Accipiter replied:

Untranslatable. Mind. Flower. Creation. Beautiful
Mind is Untranslatable fruit. Best.

Tom marveled as his mind's feet shuffled on common ground, hidden by an alien fog. He shifted his cross-legged feet as he considered the light around the dark Priest before him.

Tom asked, "And so you cultivate that flower?"

The Accipiter had rested in the tension of anticipation, stirring again now:

So that it may serve a greater Untranslatable purpose.

This time, Tom couldn't help his outburst, "Your purpose!" He almost bit the words as they came out.

The Accipiter shrank back slightly, the glyphs dimming.

What purpose could be ours. Question?

Tom's heart pounded as he asked, trying to rein back his anger, "And what is that purpose?"

The Priest paused.

What is purpose of this Untranslatable thing I sit upon.
Question?

Tom frowned before replying, "Bench. It is a bench. It is to be sat on."

A fast rumble followed by low hoots preceded its words. It stood and paced around the room, its claws clacking harshly on the metal floor.

Yes. It Bench was fashioned for that purpose.
Accipiters do not fashion things for purpose.
The fashion of all things.... Has purpose.
There are Untranslatable algae.
That Untranslatable produce. Certain chemicals.
Accipiters not find purpose for life we cultivate.
We remove. Its Untranslatable limitations in its purpose.
Disease. Suffering. Death.
We polish away.
So that. Purpose can emerge not blocked.
When Untranslatable mind is not blocked.
By limits. Of. Your. Body.
No larger purpose than to Untranslatable follow.
Accipiters great guide for great span of time.
In that time we have found. That. With. Untranslatable. Careful
push. Life purpose guided to serve more life.
Accipiters guide the mind to serve more mind.

Tom sat silently, his mind spinning.
The Accipiter asked:

You speak as priest to priest.
Why are you a pastor and not a priest. Question?

Tom shook himself and answered, "A priest may be said to personally represent the Lord… I represent my flock. Shepherd might be a better term."
More silence followed.
Bright glyphs followed a midrange series of rumbles:

Ours are gardeners.

Tom fought the impulse to be startled by the word. He swallowed, "So you view yourselves as the…." He swallowed again. "Gardeners?"
A higher-pitched set of tones emerged.

As a keeper attended your Untranslatable Earth.
Accipiters attend through the keepers.

Tom paused, "And… who attends the Accipiters?"
The Accipiter shook slightly:

They left us to attend.
So Untranslatable we attend
What would be left if Accipiters did not attend. Question? What
does garden do when left alone. Question?

Tom shook his head, "some plants would survive…."
A long series of glyphs followed low, anguished, rock-crushing
sounds:

Untranslatable. Die others would.
Only strongest live. Others die.
Beauty Untranslatable that garden.
The Garden Accipiters attend.
That Keepers keep, Untranslatable is filled with all gardens.

Tom shook his head. *How far will you go?* "And what of other galaxies?"
Soft tones and glyphs answered:

Someday, our children will Untranslatable them.

Compulsion

● ● ● ● ● ● ● ● ● ● ● ● ● ● ● ●

DownSide:
Eugene Morton Naval Academy
Formerly: Bonham State University Campus
Botany Lab

THREE DAYS AGO

Botany post-graduate student Mei Zifeng was, once again, working late in the lab. She preferred the quiet after most everyone else had left for the day. She'd been pushing herself hard. Moreover, she did her utmost to avoid the proximity of the other students. Especially the male ones. Before Awakening Day, she'd kept to herself and remained dedicated to finishing her degree. After Awakening Day, with all the infuriating changes the Gardeners had made to everyone, it seemed like most female students had gotten pregnant and married shortly thereafter. Many, though certainly not all, either ended or significantly postponed their academic careers. While by no means immune to those same 'changes,' Mei had managed to avoid the fate of her contemporaries partly by force of will but primarily by self-isolation.

With the capture of the Keeper ship, more than half of the University's students and faculty were now tasked with investigating and studying everything about it, from its metallurgy to its control systems, to its propulsion system, and to accessing its many sealed areas. No electromechanical or electronic interfaces or instrumentation had yet been found. Every function in the ship appeared to be biological. Researchers attempted to cut open what they thought was a door at one point. A nearby "column" suddenly moved and seamlessly repaired the damage.

When the Keeper and his… harem… were captured, they had been inside a huge 'garden' area. Upon deeper inspection, the garden had turned out to be a highly complex self-contained ecosystem containing many thousands of plants and, so far, harmless biota. At least a quarter of the plants appeared to be recognizable edible varieties. The consensus was that it would take years to classify everything thoroughly.

Fully a third appeared to be completely unknown species, as well as several previously known to be extinct. However, the rest were easily recognizable known varieties or were very close. Under Dr. Jacob Becker's supervision, Mei had spent most of the past six months carefully documenting and cataloging the 'known' examples. For many of these, rather than continuing to disturb the 'Garden,' samples were tested for toxins, parasites, etc. If proven safe, they would then be grown in isolation in a bank of specially built aquaponic vertical gardens. If they could be regrown with no changes or anomalies outside of the Keeper ship, it lent greater confidence to their identification since DNA records didn't exist for many.

As they delivered the specimens early on, Mei recognized a favorite vegetable from China, mesembryanthemum crystallinum, or what her mother called Bing Cao, roughly translated as "ice plant" or ice greens. Covered with large, glistening bladder cells or water vesicles, Bing Cao's texture was crunchy, fresh, and full of moisture, with a very mild flavor. It was one of the first plants they processed, and they soon classified it as matching a known terrestrial plant and not anything new, formerly extinct, or alien. On the other hand, it was, so far as anyone knew, absent from New Texas. Mei had fed samples to mice in the lab and even to a pig, all with no ill effects.

After another long, 18-hour day, Mei gradually realized she was painfully hungry. There was no food in the break room refrigerator that didn't belong to someone else. Her stomach had been unsettled since yesterday morning, so she hadn't brought any food with her today. She looked over at the aquaponic garden, where her sample of Bing Cao was thriving. Her mouth watered, and she swallowed. *It's just Bing Cao, and I haven't had any since I left home.*

Methodist Hospital Mental Patient Isolation Ward

Gwyneth Elliott Duncan entered the observation room and smiled at her husband, David. "Not that I don't mind seeing you again so soon today, dear, but why did you call? Or did you have ulterior motives by calling me down to the empty psych ward?" On Awakening Day, all diseased individuals, including those with mental disorders, had woken up having been cured.

David frowned grimly and opened the curtain covering the one-way mirror. "I'm afraid not, dear."

On the other side of the glass in the padded room was a slim naked Asian woman wandering around the room, her long black hair tangled and loose about her shoulders. The audio from her room was muted, though she appeared to be mumbling something to herself and was both agitated and confused.

Gwyneth blinked in surprise. "Oh my. What happened? Who is she?"

David sighed. "She is Mei Zifeng, a post-grad botany student with a reputation for being something of a church mouse. We don't know what happened to her. They found her like this, wandering around the botany lab at the university. They tried to put a blanket around her, but she went wild. When they brought her here, we tried to put her in a straitjacket, but she immediately broke out in hives and started screaming. When we let her loose in here, she seemed to calm down, so we decided not to sedate her yet. Also, assuming she is on some kind of drug, there might be complications."

Gwyneth pursed her lips, thinking, "Not a party girl, huh? Maybe somebody spiked her with something? Wait, you said hives?"

"Yes, she reacted like any kind of clothing was burning her."

"Has she said anything?"

"Nothing, anyone, can understand."

"OK, so this is a mystery, and I feel terrible for her, but why am *I* here, and why are you dealing with it and not the mental health or substance abuse professionals, assuming you could still find any?"

David paused and lowered his voice. "Because of what she was working on. Plants from the Keeper ship, her professor later called and said that it looks like she may have been eating some of them."

Gwyneth flinched. "Oh, shit."

"Yeah."

"Is she violent?"

"She seems to react badly to men."

Gwyneth swallowed. "I have a bad feeling about this. The women from the Keeper ship…. They broke out in hives when we tried to put clothes on them…. And they reacted badly to men, as well. Turn on the audio. I want to hear what she is saying."

"Yeah, I thought you might."

David pressed a button on the wall and the sounds that Mei was making played on the speaker.

Gwyneth sucked in her breath, "My God, David!" She shook her head and rapidly retrieved her phone from her purse, searched for a number, and dialed a video call. "Doctor Talib? Yes, Hi. I need you to see something." She turned the camera towards the glass so Dr. Talib could both see and hear what Mei was saying and put the phone on speaker.

Dr. Talib excitedly said, "Tell me where you are. I'll be right there."

✪ ✪ ✪

Dr. Leo Talib, Dean of Language Studies, entered the observation room only after his security detail had cleared it and Sabrina's detail had also cleared it and 'allowed' her to enter.

It had taken a couple of hours for both Leo and Sabrina to arrange to be there. David was needed for yet another multiple birth, so he left earlier, but Gwyneth had waited. She nodded in greeting. "Dr. Talib, General. Thank you for coming."

Leo immediately walked to the window, transfixed at the sight and, more specifically, the sound of Mei's rambling 'speech.'"

Sabrina shook hands with Gwyneth. "General, what are we looking at?"

Gwyneth started to answer, but Leo cut her off, saying, "That woman is speaking in Accipiter…."

✪ ✪ ✪

TopSide:
New Pentagon Holding Cells

Leo Talib entered the Keeper's "cell." In the months since his capture, the short, gracile, leathery-skinned, uplifted hominid's living quarters had taken on a vastly different appearance. The room's floor was no longer bare metal and was now covered in soft carpets. A small comfortable bed was tucked into a corner of the room next to a set of shelves full of books. A large desk dominated the room's center, covered with books, papers, and a (non-networked) computer laptop that was currently shut closed. In one corner of the room, a five-foot-tall aquaponic vertical garden quietly chugged away, its aquarium pump slowly moving the wastewater from the fish tank at its bottom up to the top, feeding and watering the circular planting beds filled with plants from the Keeper ship garden.

Two comfortable leather chairs sat opposite the desk. The hominid stood up from his chair and smiled a very toothy and broad smile he had carefully practiced.

Leo walked over and shook the creature's outstretched, somewhat delicate hand. "Hello, Ubu."

Ubu replied, "Hello to you too, Doctor Talib. Leo. It is nice to see you today."

Leo set a small sack of apples and oranges on the desk. "Here you go."

"Thank you, Leo. It is kind of you to remember."

"Not at all, Ubu. It's the least I can do. I look forward to our talks. By the way, your English is becoming excellent."

Ubu was quite hairy. However, he was fastidious about his personal grooming. Sitting down in his chair, he absently fingered one of his braids. "Thank you, Leo. I appreciate that." He pointed to a neat stack of paper. "I have finished drawing the," he hesitated with the word, "… procedure… for the propulsion system startup on the ark. I hope you find it to be interesting. Now, what can I do for you today?"

In utter contrast to Nathaniel Grant, "Ubu" — the pronounceable shorthand name the Keeper was willing to go by — was shockingly innocent, open, and happy to discuss anything he knew. As the language barriers began to fall, that knowledge base turned out to be deeper and richer than Leo had ever dared hope.

Leo hesitated for only a moment. He'd learned that simple honesty worked best with Ubu. "Ubu, I'd like to talk to you about your six female… helpers."

Ubu smiled again, "Yes, I miss them. Are they feeling better?"

Leo nodded. "Yes, I'm told they are feeling better now. And that's part of what I want to talk about. Ubu, I know that you have some favorite foods from the garden on your ship. However, I wonder if some plants in your garden serve a more special purpose than just food."

Ubu seemed puzzled for a moment. "Special in what way, Leo?"

Leo sat back in his chair. "Ubu, are any of the plants in your garden unsafe to eat?"

Ubu carefully shook his head, another practiced motion he had learned in order to better communicate with the humans, "No, Leo, I can eat any of the foods in the garden, but you know that not all the plants there are for food." He paused and barked a harsh, almost effeminate laugh. "You would not want to eat the trees, but the fruit is nice."

Leo smiled in return and chuckled, "No, Ubu, I have no desire to eat trees. But let me ask another question: does any of the food in the garden affect your mind?"

Ubu stared at him for a long moment, then barked another laugh, "Oh, you do not mean just me, myself, do you? You mean the word *you* to mean other people. Your language is so strange sometimes. No, the food will not hurt other people."

Leo frowned and tried to think of how to rephrase the question again.

Ubu reached over, pulled an apple from the bag, bit into it toothily, and chewed it for a moment before adding, "Now, helpers, of course, needed the food to teach them. When they were brought to me, they did not know their…." He shook his head, giving up on the word, "I had to show them what to eat so they would know what to do."

Leo slowly nodded. "But if you or I were to eat it, it would not affect us in that way, would it?"

Ubu barked another laugh, "No, Leo, you and I already know what to do. We are not simple like the helpers."

Leo sat quietly, thinking for a moment. *So they tailor the plants for females, and Ubu is a chauvinist. Well, that's going to be awkward.* "Ubu, what happens if they stop eating it?"

Ubu stiffly shook his head. "It would be bad for them. They would get very sick. When their task is over, I would instruct them to eat less and less of it over many, many days. Then they would be cleansed of it and ready for their next task."

✪ ✪ ✪

Leo exited the room and shook his head as he looked at Gwyneth and Sabrina. "Well, that clears up a lot of things, including, I am somewhat ashamed to say, how he feels about women. We knew that on the trip back from Earth, the prize crew who stayed onboard the Keeper ship supplemented their rations with food from the Garden. They were later reprimanded. However, nothing unusual ever happened to them. No strange behavior at all. When his harem wouldn't eat the food we gave them on the ship and started getting sick, we eventually took one of them back to the Keeper ship under guard, and that was a whole other story, let me tell you, anyway, when we finally got her there, and she calmed down, she pointed at the food they needed. They all got… better. Even after we returned here, their food was still taken from the Keeper Garden and brought to them in their holding cells. They were still nuts about being kept away from Ubu, but whatever it is that's in their system stayed there."

Gwyneth shook her head slowly. "It only affects women. Whatever it does in the brain, it builds up like a drug or a protein. Cut it off, and they go into withdrawal. Who knows, cold turkey could kill them."

Sabrina sighed, "Well, it sounds like eating that stuff to 'learn the language' is out unless you want to go native and join the harem."

Leo frowned.

Sabrina's eyes narrowed. "Don't you even think it, mister!"

Leo blinked, "What? No, I was thinking. This stuff did way more than affect behavior like some narcotic. It did more than impart language skills. It also instructed them on tasks. How and what to do to take care of Ubu. I'm wondering… what other things *could* it do? Teach you how to fly a starship?"

Sabrina rocked back on her heels, "Given what the Accipiters are capable of, who is to say that they can't make *permanent* changes to a population by altering their food supply? What if that is how they altered the survivors on earth to worship them? Gave *everyone* the need to worship them?"

Jamestown

• • • • • • • • • • • • • • • •

DownSide

South of Fort Brazos, past the Fishtail Mountains, and down the winding New Guadalupe River lay the thick forests of Jackalope Valley. In that verdant setting along a bend in the river, exhausted from their journey, three men established a camp. Gary Little had fallen among steep rocks, broken several ribs, and suffered a concussion. His foster brother Ray Bunker had a broken arm after an encounter with wolves that had spooked his horse. The third in the group, Darnell Lewis, had been the only one uninjured, but his horse and one mule had grown lame, and the other mule had already died. So, they stopped and made the best of the situation.

While out hunting wild game, Darnell had discovered a hidden metal cave on the side of a hill, invisible from the air. Inside, he'd found an alien power device on a pedestal. They had traded the device for medical aid, supplies, and considerable notoriety. No one knew if more alien machines were nearby, but the government back in Fort Brazos had established a hefty reward. The camp quickly transformed into a small frontier town as treasure hunters trickled down the arduous trail to seek their fortune like prospectors of old for California gold.

The three men had foreseen what might happen once word got out and negotiated to be recognized as the owners of the "town." Rather than 'hunt for gold' themselves, they decided their own fortune would lie in supplying those who did. Truth be told, although many were skeptical about Ray, Gary, and Darnell's ability to pull it off, both the civilian government and the military recognized the value of supporting the remote settlement. So long as they 'behaved,' they had a deal. The military had even flown in several prefab buildings. While still quite ramshackle, the settlement was growing.

Ray had opened the General Store. Gary opened the Bunkhouse Motel, and Darnel was, after a night of drinking, declared 'Mayor.' Despite the grandiose title, Darnell spent most of his time hunting, trapping, and although he barely admitted it to himself, hopeful that lightning might strike twice and he would find another artifact. If he did, it would cement the idea that establishing a town might not be so crazy after all.

There was no shortage of wild game, some of which were unique to the area. That, and Jamestown's 'frontier notoriety' was just exotic enough for Darnell to barter a small but steady supply to the bootmaker and others back in Fort Brazos in exchange for essential supplies.

They'd settled on the name "Jamestown" after weeks of debate. Gary had wanted to call it "Dodge City," and Ray had run through *many* names. Jamestown won, although it referred to the Gold Rush town by that name rather than the early English settlement in Virginia.

It had taken over three months for the military and the university geeks to decide that there was nothing else to find in the area around the metal cave. Eventually, finding nothing else, they had even tried (unsuccessfully) using explosives to see if there was anything behind its walls. Gradually, the fifty or sixty soldiers, scientists, VIPs, and gawkers had left. The population hadn't returned to those levels. However, there were usually at least twenty to twenty-five people in the area at any given time.

A lot had changed in the ten months since they had arrived. The weather was mostly quite mild, so as long as they kept things simple and didn't use radios or electronics that would attract Stalkers or Wardogs, they only had to worry about traditional dangers, like poisonous snakes, wolves, cougars, bears, etc.

The newspapers in Fort Brazos had recognized the value of a story when they saw it, so they had talked Ray into writing about their "Adventures in Jamestown." The Reinhardt incident infamy that had dogged the three men and inspired them to leave Fort Brazos in the first place had softened and taken on an anti-hero romantic quality. Ray, Gary, and Darnell had earned a degree of grudging respect.

✪ ✪ ✪

Gary brushed the dust off the back of Ray's shirt while Ray leaned down to look in the cracked mirror to comb his hair. "You're gonna be fine, Ray. You'll see."

Darnell entered the trailer carrying a package. The trailer, Ray's home, sat behind the prefab building where Ray had set up the General Store. Ray had spent the past week cleaning it.

Darnell handed the package to Ray. "Here you go, Ray. I made this for you." He hesitated. "Well, I had help, but you know what I mean."

Ray took the package and pulled the strings, opening it up. His eyes lit up as he saw what was inside. He pulled out the deerskin jacket and held it up proudly. "Oh, man, that's… Just… Thank you. I don't know what to say."

Darnell slapped him on the back. "It's nothing, Ray. You deserve it. I mean it."

Ray pulled the jacket on and shifted his shoulders, straightening it as he turned and looked at his reflection in the mirror. "Thank you, man."

Just then, the thump-thump sound of a helicopter could be heard from outside.

Gary grinned, "It's time, buddy!"

The men exited the trailer, hurried to a nearby clearing, and watched the Chinook helicopter approach and land.

After it settled to a stop and the rotors slowed, two soldiers jumped out carrying rifles and made sure that the area seemed to be clear. Shortly afterward, a dozen people emerged one by one from the helicopter. A few were military, but most were civilians. Next to the last to exit was a dark-haired woman holding the hand of a young girl. They looked around nervously as though expecting to be attacked by hostile creatures at any moment.

Gary and Darnell waited behind, watching as Ray walked toward the woman and girl.

As the noise of the slowing rotors subsided, the girl, no more than six or seven years old, saw Ray approaching. She stared at him for only a moment before her face lit up, and she bolted loose from the woman and screamed, "Daddy!" and ran to Ray, who fell to his knees and wrapped his arms around her.

Tears streaming down Ray's face, he hugged her close. "Chloe!"

The woman took another nervous look around. There wasn't much to see, just the tree line and the embryonic town. She shuffled closer to Ray, who looked up at her. She reached down and put her hand on Chloe's head before saying, "Ray."

Ray nodded at his ex-wife. "Julie. Welcome to Jamestown."

Quezon

● ● ● ● ● ● ● ● ● ● ● ● ● ● ●

DownSide:
Lake Texoma, Freetown Beach

Caesar Salangsang ignored the sounds of the nearby party as he worked his way around, inspecting the hull of the Quezon. Michelle had lobbied for naming the 30-meter sailing ship after Charles Darwin's HMS Beagle, but not very hard. Most of the men who had built the vessel were from Caesar's Philippine Army construction battalion. Instead, they'd named her the Quezon, after the province in the Philippines located in the Calabarzon region on Luzon. Also, and not coincidentally, she was named after the Philippine Navy's ancient BRP Quezon Rizal class corvette, which had originally been the USS Vigilance minesweeper, commissioned during World War II. Caesar's grandfather had served aboard her, so the name resonated on multiple levels for him.

They had built the Quezon of locally abundant timber in a modified two-masted Pinisi rigged Indonesian sailing ship design. She could comfortably carry a crew of twelve, and while primarily a sailing ship, she had a diesel engine to aid when needed. They salvaged the engine from the hulk of a wrecked school bus. Two screws were fabricated — a primary, a spare, and an extra shaft. There was no spare engine. It was, after all, not the primary propulsion system. Among the tools onboard were welding equipment, carpentry tools, and sail and cordage-making and repair gear.

In an hour, they would launch Quezon. At least a thousand people were there to witness the event, including the Vice President, Secretary of War, the City Council, Admirals Milner and Johansson, several hundred Navy Officers, and enlisted personnel.

Caesar had laughed at the irony. Once word had gotten around that volunteers were building the world's first sea-going vessel, everyone had had an opinion, more than half of which had been negative. Secretary Marcus had tried to talk him out of going, saying that Caesar was too valuable on such a risky (ad)venture. The Navy, naturally, had had no end of opinions. On the other hand, they were so busy thinking about space travel that Caesar's scheme was seen with both jaundiced and envious eyes.

In the end, no one forced them to stop construction. Secretary Marcus had relented on the condition that Caesar undertook the journey in the capacity of an Officer, representing the interests of humanity in the unlikely event that, during the trip, they might encounter something inimical or at least alien in some regard.

As the ship began to take shape and looked like it was going to be, well, real, quiet offers of help arrived in the form of supplies, equipment, and promises to keep track of them during the journey. After all, the world was a giant outside-in cylinder. There was no "over the horizon" anymore. The only help that might be able to reach them would have to arrive using one of the alien interplanetary landing craft vehicles that had been brought 'down' using the elevator and were used for reconnaissance and Wardog hunting. Of course, that assumed that they would be able to make long-range radio contact at all.

Michelle called out from behind him as she approached, "I thought I'd find you here." She wore clean jeans and a blouse — the nicest clothes she had. Caesar was in uniform for the cameras later.

Caesar turned and smiled as they embraced. "Are you ready for this?"

"Mmm hmm. They're getting impatient over there. We'd better go before they change their minds."

Shattered

● ● ● ● ● ● ● ● ● ● ● ● ● ● ● ●

Council Adjudicator Xuraens glided dolefully through the micro-G All-Clan High Council gardens that were the inspiration for the minuscule, by comparison, Homeship observation dome gardens. This garden alone was the size of the largest Homeship, stretching in three dimensions for over two hundred miles. It was part of a vast bio-architected ecumenopolis terraformed moon that orbited the second of six terrestrial planets within the Capital system.

Their benefactors uplifted the Accipiters to beautify the galaxy and, in particular, cleanse it of the race Humans would later call the Builders. This star system had been the largest infestation of their enemy's filth. After annihilating them, the Accipiters had patiently devoted over a hundred thousand years repairing the damage and (re)terraforming the two original habitable planets and terraforming two other terrestrial planets on the edge of the goldilocks zone as well as two more planet-sized moons orbiting gas giants within the system.

Six acolytes accompanied Xuraens. Two preceded him, singing the memory song of his clan and lineage, their dual resonant voice chambers, singing a quartet. Two more glided behind him, holding the hem of his high office robes, while two more glided beneath him, carrying him, his gloved claws recessed into their jeweled backplates.

Representatives from each of the other two hundred clans who had converged on the Sol system in the attack's wake followed him. Each would sing their testimony after he had presented his own. The proceedings would ultimately spread to all the memory trees throughout the Galaxy.

The entire High Conclave was waiting for him in the Great Chamber beyond. It was the first full meeting of the High Conclave in over seventy thousand years. The events that had transpired in the Sol system were unprecedented in all of Accipiter history. No Homeship had *ever* been lost to attack. Over the millennia, a few were lightly damaged. Various emergent civilizations had attempted to resist Accipiter guidance, but no Homeship had ever come close to being seriously damaged or, and this was unthinkable: destroyed.

During the attack, a second Homeship arrived to join in observance of the veneration of the Earth's Keeper. It was destroyed outright. The other was severely damaged. Afterwards, they transferred the few surviving Keeper Arks to other clans. With most of the clan members dead, the rest later committed suicide.

The Full High Conclave included each Exodus Clan High Priest. At the time of the uplifting, the total Accipiter population had barely exceeded twenty million. Their home world was quite harsh. Virtually all species were nomadic or developed adaptations for burrowing underground to escape the surface conditions. Their planet rotated very slowly. At the terminator, the temperature soared. Most life evolved to keep moving ahead of it, creating a permanent nomadic culture and biology.

Accipiters relied on rigid family clan structures that provided mutual support and enforced sacrosanct rules for living to survive. On their home world, each original root family/clan had an average of around one hundred and fifty members. Over a million years later, their numbers today were vast indeed.

The Capital system was more shrine than home. A meeting place where clans occasionally gathered to worship, mingle, and trade. Those passing through contributed to its upkeep while they were there.

Now, during this great gathering, representatives from all the over one hundred and twenty-eight thousand surviving clans filled the Great Chamber. It shook and resonated with the mournful lament from over two hundred and fifty thousand vocal chambers, singing the death song of a full clan. A song unsung for over a million years.

✪ ✪ ✪

By the time Xuraens left the Great Chamber, his anger was gone, subsumed by raw titanic fury, disbelief, confusion, and, more terrifying than anything else, he had witnessed something he had never imagined possible. The only word he could think of to describe it was a *human* word. Machiavellian.

Maneuvering on the part of not a few clans to take advantage of the turmoil in one way or another. No single event in their long history came close to what this one desperate attack had managed to do. Not one of the clan members in the Great Chamber would have admitted it to anyone else… or even to themselves. However, the attack had struck *fear* in a galactic society previously unshaken since its founding over a million years before.

Not that the unsaid fear had frozen resolve or led to inaction. Every star system with a habitable planet within seventy-five light years of Sol had already been reinforced with the same defenses now protecting Earth and the ships around it. The farther from Sol, the more worlds were involved, so the slower the defenses were to establish. The limitations of the Builder means of faster-than-light travel were well known.

Whereas Nexus Junction Point travel provided near instantaneous transit between star systems, the Builder drive could take days, weeks, or months to travel even between relatively close systems. To span the galaxy might take fifty to a hundred Earth years. The limitation of Nexus travel was that it was only practical to use between what humans would call main sequence stars. The energy to transit to low-mass stars was too great to open the rift. On the other hand, Accipiters did not desire to travel to low-mass stars since they would not be host to habitable planets, anyway. It was thought unlikely that the humans could have the range to travel farther than fifty light years, but no chances were being taken.

In addition, painstaking examination of the remains of their moon base strongly inferred that the humans had relied heavily on the close proximity of Earth for food and supplies. It, therefore, seemed likely that any outpost in another star system would likewise depend on nearby food, air, and supplies. A base inside some barren rock or on a lifeless planet would likely be unsustainable for them. So, the search, so far, had concentrated on star systems with worlds possessing an environment with water and a reasonably compatible ecology. Expanding the search beyond habitable planets would take… considerably longer. Especially if it were concealed, which increasingly seemed ineluctable.

The consensus was that either:

- The humans had traveled considerably farther than expected
- The humans are somewhere we wouldn't look
- We actually did search where the humans were hiding but

missed finding them
- Or that *someone* was helping the humans and, in so doing, hiding them or providing logistical support enabling option 1

The idea that neither Xuraens nor any other clan would dare consider was that a rival clan might have been helping the humans. Accipiters had never, in all their known history, fought each other. Their home world was hostile enough that every clan *needed* the other. It simply wasn't in them. If someone was helping them, it must be some previously unknown race.

On Earth itself, the investigation was more than simply problematic. All remnants of the human's pre-Accipiter-Arrival civilization had been erased. There had been no reason to preserve any records, so no records were available to search. Many humans who had been alive at the time of the Accipiters' arrival still lived. Human integration into the Accipiter panoply of races had included virtually unlimited life extension combined with a level-keeping-only birth rate. What information Accipiters had regarding the surviving human's previous lives had been explored, and any human who might even tangentially have relevant knowledge was 'interviewed.'

The results were fragmentary at best. Prior to the Accipiter *uplifting* of humanity, rumors of crashed alien ships being examined by human governments had been common and just as commonly ridiculed at the time. Of course, the arrival of the Accipiters provided more than concrete proof of alien existence. That, however, was all that had been found on Earth itself. Only the buried moon base spoke to how things had been so grossly miscalculated and gotten so completely out of control.

The Conclave had demanded answers on just that. How had the situation on Earth been so misjudged, so underestimated? How had their Keeper missed it? Could he have been compromised himself and hidden the information from the Accipiters? Of course, the uplifted hominid wasn't around to question. It was unknown what his fate was or if he was even still alive.

The investigation had revealed that the attack itself had been shockingly primitive. The humans had actually released ballistic projectiles as kinetic energy weapons! It was only the Accipiter's complacent self-assurance of their own supremacy that had made it possible. After all, they had encountered no hostile species in the galaxy for hundreds of thousands of years. Any attacker would have needed to come within energy weapons range, and they'd have been detected long before that happened. So, why shouldn't the Accipiters maintain stately and...

static… orbits? Defense against such a kinetic energy attack was trivial enough. The attack reeked of desperation.

Encounters with previous enemies, so very long ago, were not simply a matter of historical record. Xuraens *remembered* them, as did the vast majority of the Council. Their practical immortality meant that most of the core Council who were born before uplifting, including Xuraens, had clear memories of even the earliest stages of their uplift and march across the galaxy. What they hadn't experienced themselves were shared memories via the memory trees. The only real resistance they'd ever faced was during the early years, as they encountered occasional pockets of small, regional alien empires. Some were inherently hostile, and some were abjectly peaceful and nonviolent. They were all subsumed into the Accipiter panoply. A few were willing and even grateful. Others were crushed — as easily as the humans had been.

Xuraens fretted. How did we miss this?

The only fresh evidence was the warp signature that was recently detected. Whether it was the humans returning to attack again or not was unknown. The defenses had apparently driven them off. The only good news was that the analysis of the human's attack method had shown it to be ridiculously primitive — and, now, at least, entirely unlikely to ever succeed again.

Whether the humans had any more sophisticated weapons at their disposal, how many were actually "out there," where they were hiding, and what, if anything, they were planning to do next was anyone's guess.

What Xuraens now knew was that the attack had shattered the Accipiter's societal complacency. For generations, a few had quietly whispered that Accipiter society had ossified. Despite everything that had happened, in the unlikely event that the humans should somehow turn up and surrender themselves peacefully, they would of course be accepted back under the amnesty offered to all who chose to follow that path. Afterward they would be assimilated like those who had gone before them.

Of course, the official position of the Conclave was that the renegade humans would be found and erased and that Accipiter society would return to its previous state of grace, all the wiser, and soon. The singular High Priest who had dared ask what would happen if the renegades weren't found was subsequently 'counseled.'

A few days later, a courier arrived from the Sol system and delivered a stunning discovery that was dug out of the collapsed moon base. It was a human document. A two-inch-thick bound report that was torn and burned around the edges. Despite the burn mark, the cover was still legible. On it was emblazoned a United States Department of Defense logo and the words **TOP SECRET: ENDLESS EPSILON** in a large stencil font.

The humans had apparently had help after all. They had, in secret, reverse-engineered an ancient Builder vessel discovered on their ocean floor in their year 1974. Decades later, they traveled to other star systems. They had established their secret base on an abandoned Builder outpost on a small habitable planet.

So, it was option # 1, after all. We have not searched far enough.

Specimens

● ● ● ● ● ● ● ● ● ● ● ● ● ● ●

DownSide:
Café Balthasar

Nicole Chilton burst through the Café Balthasar front door and nearly collided with the owner, Marta Landry. She giggled, "Sorry Marta!" as she zigzagged her way to the back of the French-themed brasserie to the table more or less permanently reserved for Dr. Leo Talib and Brigadier General Sabrina Chilton Talib. Sabrina had noted her 16-year-old daughter's boisterous entry with equal parts alarm and relief. Alarm that someone might end up on the floor in Nicole's wake, and relief to see her in such high spirits. When Sabrina and her daughter were abducted by the Gardeners, along with the SigInt Corps Sabrina had been visiting, their relationship had been… strained. Neither of them had truly recovered from the death of Nicole's father / Sabrina's husband a couple of years earlier.

The reason Nicole was traveling with her mother was that Sabrina had intended to drop her daughter off at a (prestigious) Swiss boarding school. Something Nicole knew and had been angry and sullen about.

It had taken a long time after Awakening Day for things to improve. If reluctantly, Sabrina admitted that Leo Talib's influence had much to do with Nicole's transformation. Sabrina also hated to admit that it had taken the blunt observations of her daughter to realize that Sabrina's relationship with Leo had also evolved. A lot.

When she'd first met the man, who at 35 had been nearly ten years her junior, she'd thought he was insufferable. Brilliant, but simultaneously something of a jerk and a twit. Working on deciphering the Accipiter and Gardener languages began a change in Leo. Later, his experience during the Keeper Raid mission profoundly catalyzed that change. He'd grown fond of and close to some of the crew. After the glorious high of their success, most of the crew had died slowly and horribly. Many in his arms.

Sabrina had been there as well. She still had nightmares about the agonizingly slow deaths of the crew. She'd seen Leo's reaction when he'd thought that Sabrina was going to die. The man had gone with the soldiers onboard the Keeper ship and helped capture it, but he'd been terrified at the thought that… Sabrina might die.

Working side by side with him for countless days and nights had changed more than just Leo. Sabrina grimaced as she sipped her tea, hoping it would help soothe and settle the discomfort in her belly. As was the case when she'd carried Nicole, her morning sickness was, for the most part, all-day.

Nicole plopped down in the chair next to her, bumping the table, her arms and legs seemingly loose in all directions. The table, in turn, bumped into Sabrina, inducing another wave of nausea. She paled as she swallowed back a rebuke.

"Sorry, mom." Nicole sat up straight and leaned forward, reaching across to touch her mother's arm. "Is it bad?"

Sabrina answered tightly, "I will be fine."

Nicole looked around, then shook her head. "Leo's late."

"He texted me. Something came up, but he'll be along soon."

Nicole pulled a rubber band off her wrist, sat back, and reached behind her, tying her long blonde hair, which matched her mother's, into a ponytail. "So, mom, is it true what people are saying about that lady who went crazy and started running around the university naked?"

Sabrina frowned. "Everyone hopes it will wear off in a few days. Until then, the poor woman was sedated and is being looked after."

Nicole's eyes widened, and she whispered, "Can… can you say what happened?"

Sabrina nodded. "Yes, a decision was made to make the incident public. It seems that the Accipiters altered some of the plants on the Keeper ship. People who eat them, for all intents and purposes, become hypnotized. They gain specific knowledge and are compelled to, well, to do things."

Nicole's eyes widened, and she exclaimed, "Eww! Oh my God, she got roofied by a plant?"

Sabrina frowned. "I suppose you could put it that way. More interestingly, besides what she was being compelled to do, the woman was speaking Accipiter. So the plants can directly impart complex knowledge."

Nicole brightened. "You mean there's a plant that could teach me calculus overnight? Just, wow."

Marta stopped by the table and dropped off a salad for Nicole. Nicole smiled her thanks and stared at the salad hesitatingly for a moment before she shrugged and started eating.

Sabrina wrinkled her nose, "Or, you could eat your salad and suddenly be compelled to obey your mother in all things… or confess your undying love and devotion for young Ronald Sinitskaya."

Nicole blanched and dropped her fork, which clattered on the plate. Her eyes widened, and she mockingly gasped aloud, looked down at the salad, and melodramatically swallowed before pushing the plate away, "I'm never eating salad again." She sat back in her chair and thought for a moment, "Mom, do you think the Gardeners did something like that to us? Are they making us do things like the Accipiters make their slaves do things for them?" She shuddered. "Could something like this make you become a spy for your enemy or things like that?"

Sabrina pushed a bowl of yeast rolls over to her daughter, who absently picked one up and popped it in her mouth. "I don't think the Gardeners did that, no. Just look at the student protests and all the people arguing about the constitution, the war, and other things. If the Gardeners wanted to make us compliant, it doesn't seem to be working very well."

Nicole picked up another roll and pointed it at her mom. "So, what happens next? What will they do with the stuff? The plants from the Keeper ship, I mean."

Sabrina sipped her tea, thinking. "The Keeper, Ubu, says that the plants are all different, and some contain information and knowledge about the ship's operation and its systems. If we can't figure things out ourselves, we may have to ask for volunteers to eat different plants. With luck, they'd be less… crazed… and able to write down what they learn so the rest of us can learn things the slow way. Eventually, we'll reverse-engineer how the plants work. Sooner or later, though, I believe we will have to ban anything more than learning how to detect it. We will need that. Someone could end up on a planet someday, smell the roses, and, well….."

Nicole shuddered. "That sounds like a horror movie. Or a porno. They all end up as willing slaves."

Sabrina teased, "Well, hopefully, the slave master will be handsome. Like Ronald."

Nicole blushed and sputtered, "Mom!" She paused after a moment, thinking, "Mom, I understand the plants can give knowledge… but how do they get that knowledge into the plants? Where does it come from, like, originally?"

"That's my girl. Good question, and it's one that scares me. A lot. They have to get it from somewhere, from someone. Is it programmed in, like we program data into a database? Or is it, well, *extracted* from someone? We have no idea."

Sabrina poured more hot tea from the teapot into her cup. "I'm sure there will eventually be a black market for the stuff someday, hopefully, a long, long time from now. Like so many drugs like heroin or cocaine or MDMA."

Nicole shook her head, "Like, wow. It's hard enough catching people growing weed in their basements. If these bloody plants look like any other…. You'd never know if your spinach was spiked!"

Sabrina slowly shook her head. "That's why, for once, I hope this is an alien technology we *never* figure out."

Nicole nibbled her yeast roll, took a deep breath, rose up in her chair, leaned forward, and asked earnestly, "So, Mom, what did the doctor say?"

"I'm fine. The baby is fine, but she put me on a meal plan and said I'm not eating enough, which is hard to do when you feel like you're never going to keep anything down. I'll be fine, though. Leo is…"

"He adores you, you know. He doesn't understand you, and he doesn't know why, but he loves you. Leo is good for you, Mom, even if you are robbing the cradle."

Sabrina glared at her, but only for a moment. "And what about your young man? Ronald? I saw his mother, Captain Sinitskaya, yesterday. She was back from Ari'Nell on leave. Are you…?"

Nicole blushed again. "Mom! Yes, I mean, no, you needn't worry. No one goes by themselves on dates anymore, and we watch out for each other. Couples don't wander off together. If they do, their friends intervene. The girls are terrified they could get pregnant by being breathed on, and the boys are just as afraid of shotgun weddings."

She reached over, picked up a glass of water, took a sip, and shook her head. "Speaking of roofies. There was this guy who tried to roofie a girl at that new sports bar outside campus, you know the one? Anyway, he was one of those single soldiers from one of the armies that got dropped outside Fort Brazos on Awakening Day? Russian, I think. Anyway, so, he bought drinks and gave a girl a vape that must have been spiked. I mean, you know how rare vapes are these days. Anyway, she took half a pull on it and collapsed right there on the floor. The other people figured out what he'd done within, like, seconds. They dragged his ass outside and beat him nearly to death. No one is admitting anything, but, apparently, one of the women there had medical training, and they…" she whispered, "they castrated the guy. They sewed him back up so he wouldn't bleed to death, and it'll probably grow back, knowing what the Gardeners did to us, but they dumped the guy back where the rest of his people are staying with a note pinned to his chest."

Sabrina swallowed in surprise. Not just about the brutality with which the offender was treated, but that she herself had *not* heard about the incident, and she damned well should have. As one of the literal handful of surviving General Officers, this is the kind of thing she and the others had better be aware of. She made a very serious mental note to follow up on the incident.

Just then, Leo appeared next to the table and sat down. He had walked in so quietly that neither Sabrina nor Nicole had noticed.

Nicole leaped out of her chair and hugged him. "Hi, Leo! You're late."

Leo nodded numbly and stared off into space.

Sabrina reached out and touched his hand. "Leo? What's wrong?"

Leo blinked, then looked up as if seeing her for the first time. He gave a half smile. "Hi."

"Leo?"

Leo swallowed and ran his hand over his face and full beard. He looked up at Sabrina and then over at Nicole. "I…I talked to Ubu again."

Sabrina frowned, glanced at Nicole, and back at Leo, "Yes… and?"

"One thing led to another, and we talked about the sample … specimens … that he had collected over the millennia. Well…. It turns out that, how do I say this? In addition to sampling plants and animals, he also collected hominids. Males and females of each species as they developed over the last million years."

Sabrina sucked in a breath. "What do you mean by the term specimens? DNA samples? Bodies?"

Leo answered softly, "Living beings in stasis."

Sabrina gasped in surprise, "That's… that's incredible! The scientific…." She trailed off as she saw his expression. "What are you not saying?"

Leo looked at her. "Ubu didn't stop with the hominids. He collected examples of Homo Sapiens Sapiens. Thousands of them over thousands of years."

Nicole whispered, "You mean they're alive?"

Leo looked at her and slowly nodded.

Sabrina swallowed. "How many?"

"All told… maybe seventy thousand. Mating pairs."

Nicole shook her head. "What? How? How is that possible? That's more people than…."

He chuckled and shook his head. "You'd be surprised how many bodies you can squeeze together in a small space. Remember, the Keeper ship is taller than an aircraft carrier is long and a lot wider."

Sabrina and Nicole talked excitedly to each other for several minutes before Leo spoke again.

He sighed. "The whole thing is a damned frozen zoo. And they were going to stick him in a big chair as the centerpiece and freeze him, too."

Glorious

● ● ● ● ● ● ● ● ● ● ● ● ● ● ● ● ●

DownSide:
Radio Station 92.5 Studio

Danielle Richardson Anders keyed the microphone, "Hello, people of Fort Brazos and New London. This is Danielle Richardson on FM 92.5 and Radio Free Fort Brazos, beaming our signal across the known world and beyond. I normally say that there is so much to talk about today, but Oh My Dear and Fluffy Lord, what an understatement that would be!"

She hesitated, "Pardon me for a moment… I need a drink." She reached down and picked up her teacup and sipped. "Now, don't you worry. It's just tea." She rubbed her distended eight-month pregnant (twins, again) belly underneath her embroidered caftan before continuing, "You know, I really want something stronger after this news. First, we heard this morning that the Phoenix is going out again on some kind of secret mission. Who knows what that's about, and even if we did, who would we tell? Regardless, let's all pray for their safe return, okay?"

"What we *do* know something about is the other big news. I'm sure by now, everyone not living under a rock has heard about the human popsicles inside the Keeper Ship. Well, mostly human, that is. We're being told that they think that some of the seventy-some-odd thousand breeding pairs the Keeper collected were pre-modern-human hominids. Apparently, there were many more variations of pre-modern humans than the fossil record indicated, or, at least, that the Keeper bothered with."

"As I understand it, going back into pre-history, the Keeper collected more and more samples as our species got, well, more interesting and advanced. I read online that, well, before Awakening Day at least, there were over fifty recognized ethnic groups around the Earth. The modern form of humans evolved over three hundred thousand years ago from one or more of those ancestor species. We don't have a record of actual civilizations forming until over six thousand years ago. So, the Keeper started kidnapping more and more people as populations grew and ethnic groups came and went. Out of the seventy thousand or so, over fifty thousand pairs would be recognizable as being so-called modern humans….

She took a breath and sipped her tea as she clenched her toes in the dark Persian rug in the studio that she'd taken ownership of and turned into what her husband teasingly described as a cross between an Arabian Nights dream and a high-class strip joint. Although, since the birth of their twins Devon and Terrance, the décor had evolved more in the direction of a Montessori school, albeit one decorated with wall-to-wall rich fabrics and subdued lighting.

She tossed her long black hair aside and continued, "My God folks, that means something like *one hundred thousand* women and men! I think that our current total population, with all the babies being born, is approaching one hundred and eighty thousand. When the New Londoners were discovered, they had nothing but the clothes on their backs, and it's taken all this time to try and get them settled and housed, and it's still a problem, and there were only about twenty-two thousand of them to start with!"

"Now, *these* people… most of them are going to be so, well, to be blunt, *primitive*…. I figure most won't even speak a language anyone even recognizes or at least outside of books, or hell, scrolls and clay tablets. We just *can't* thaw these people out anytime soon, maybe ever? I don't know! Imagine how they would react? Can you even? I mean, think about it. You're a Mongol or some ancient whatever, that we don't even have a name for or know about anymore, and you wake up… here? Remember how hard it was for *us* to come to terms with what happened to us? I mean, nobody likes to talk about it, but even if the Gardeners fixed all our diseases and made us super healthy, not to mention super fertile, *damn them*, you all know as well as I do that after all the craziness of surviving the first year began to wear off and things started to settle down that lots of people started to, well, how do I say this? It's started to catch up with us. It is horrible and tragic, but actual *suicides* are up. I don't need to remind anyone of how much we lost and how much it hurts like hell, and if you do need to talk to someone, please see the link on my website. There *is* help, or at least lots of people who really do care that you can talk to. Please, if you need help, just ask."

"Anyway, I'm sympathetic as all get out for these frozen people, but what do we do with them? I mean, wake them up just to have them freak out and kill themselves or someone around them, anyway? Jesus, what a nightmare for them. Do we have the right to put them through that? Shouldn't we wait until we have, like, programs in place or something? I don't know. Maybe we set up an island somewhere away from modern technology, and bring a few out at a time and give them time to acclimate, if they even can? I mean, it's not like we can clothe and house them right now, anyway!"

"I mean, maybe we kind of work backward. You know, I'm sure there are some more recent popsicles. I mean, frozen people, that would be easier, who would have a better chance of coping and adapting? I figure we'd get better at helping them that way, and then, over time, we'd hopefully have *wake-ees* who could help the newest ones to come out of the freezer?"

"And then there's the whole aspect of what we do with them in the long run. There's certainly plenty of land around the inside of this world, but sending them far away might seem like exile? I mean, without a whole retraining and education program, if it would even take, what skills would they have that we could use? They're not going to wake up in a community of people they know or a world they recognize. They'll be way more alone and isolated than any of us were."

"You know, I've heard some people talk about how exciting it would be to talk to some of these people and how they would have knowledge of our history possibly lost to us, and that's all nice and academic, and I'm sure it's true to an extent. But it's a hell of a cruel thing to do to wake up thousand-year-old people and expect them not to totally lose it, and then what good did it do?"

"We need to think about how we are feeling, about how much we've lost in comparison. We lost our world and so damn many loved ones. These people will have lost way, way more than that. Personally, I think we owe it to ourselves, and to them to do all that we can to make sure that each and every one of them is brought back successfully and with love and compassion. It would be a kick in the Accipiter's eyes to reclaim these people that they stole from our history. It won't bring back Earth or our loved ones, but we'll have denied them to the Accipiters. I don't care how long it takes. We owe it to ourselves, our lost loved ones, and if nothing else, to spite the fucking Accipiters to do this right."

"And you know, Fuck It. I don't know what to do with the pre-humans, but I simply don't care if we get anything else useful out of the Keeper Ship. Rescuing over a hundred thousand humans is… *glorious revenge.*"

Quagmire

● ● ● ● ● ● ● ● ● ● ● ● ● ● ● ● ● ●

DownSide:
Riverbend Mall Capital Complex

Macy's kitchen department had long since been cleaned out of most everything, including many of the subsequently empty display cabinets. Like the new Oval Office, Esmerelda Collins had personally overseen the renovation of the space into what she laughingly called the "Kitchen Cabinet" in mocking reference to the early American President Andrew Jackson's private circle of friends and supporters who had held the real power instead of the carefully appointed 'nobodies' in the official Presidential Cabinet. To her sense of humor, the original Fort Brazos City Council, who still held power until the new constitution was voted on and enacted and new leaders elected, were likened to that centuries-old unofficial government.

In truth, the Council was more now than it had been. Many advisors and lookers-on were present, some welcome and some not. There had been no practical way to avoid it. There was simply too much to do. The population of Fort Brazos, before Awakening Day, had been a little over seventy-four thousand. Now the total population included New London, separated by the three hundred miles and the enormous elevator system to the outer 'crust' of the four-thousand-mile-long artificial cylinder that was now called New Texas. Including the military base, the foreign soldier "New Arrivals," New London, and the thousands of babies born in the Baby Boom, the combined population had more than doubled. Along the way, there had been, well, the Culling Crisis, the New Arrival Crisis, the "who's in charge" Crisis, the Alien Creature Attack Crisis, the New London Crisis, the Baby Boom Crisis, the Keeper Raid and Starship

Crisis, the Bombing of City Hall Crisis, and well, of course, what started it all, the Apocalypse.

There was rather a lot to be done.

The surviving Council members had a lot on their plate, and while many things were familiar issues like utilities, essential city management, law enforcement, etc., etc., there were many, many more "issues" that were unprecedented things beyond dealing with what amounted to refugees. Things like marauding alien attackers and demands from their alien abductors to wage a generational galactic war. In some ways, though, it seemed like the vexing problem of reaching a consensus on a new constitution and governmental structure made things like aliens and the Apocalypse seem to pale in comparison. At least, that's how it often felt to those deeply immersed in the growing quagmire that constitutional negotiations and debate had become.

A big part of why "Kitchen Cabinet" resonated so much with Esmerelda and others was the need to incorporate what amounted to a nursery and daycare center in the middle of it. Esmerelda had managed to avoid becoming pregnant herself by virtue of not, currently at least, having a man in her life, at least not intimately. She'd been married several times, but it had never stuck. A fixture at the Cattle Baron's club and longtime City Council member, her family had been among the original settlers in Fort Brazos. Her son and daughter were grown and had been living in Dallas and Fort Worth when the Accipiters attacked.

She'd been godmother to Sandra Hoffman and close friends with the Hoffman family. After Sandra and her siblings had lost their parents to a Stalker attack on Awakening Day, she eventually adopted the family and merged their dairy ranch with her cattle ranch. Sandra, now 19 years old, had spent more and more time with Esmerelda since then and become, for all practical purposes, her aide. Sandra's son and daughter Nolan and Margaret were among the nearby toddlers playing in the nearby ball pit.

The 'Kitchen Cabinet' room was composed of numerous desks and worktables, and the room was ringed with eight-foot-tall whiteboards (shower board scavenged from the home center next to the mall). The whiteboards were festooned with maps, drawings, printouts, and meeting notes. So far, the supply of dry-erase markers was holding up, but a special side project had been established to figure out how to produce both them and whiteboards locally, lest everyone be forced to return to old-fashioned blackboards and chalk… assuming materials for even those things could be found.

Pregnant again, this time with triplets, Sandra waddled uncomfortably to the worktable where Esmerelda sat, looking over portions of the draft constitution. Her long blonde hair was braided down her back. She handed a sheet of paper to Esmerelda while rubbing her fisted hand into the small of her aching back. She lowered her voice and asked worriedly, "Did you see this story about the attempted rape? You were right that some New Arrival soldiers would be a problem."

Esmerelda leaned back in her chair and closed her tired, hazel eyes. Her own long brown hair was loose about her shoulders. She sighed, "Yes, my dear, I'm aware of what happened. Gail called me herself. To say that she was livid is like saying a Wardog has a mild temper. As for the particular piece of trash offender himself, he won't be a problem for anyone anymore, ever again. One of the Russians in charge of their group, Captain Bogdashin, held their own trial, convicted, and subsequently shot the bastard. His men delivered the body to the morgue with instructions to cremate it. What's more, the Russians have sent a formal apology letter to the young woman involved, signed by every single one of them. They also offered a collective years' worth of labor to build or help her and her family in any way needed."

Sandra blinked in surprise. "Well… damn."

Esmerelda shook her head. "Gail was fit to be tied. I had to talk her down out of having Bogdashin himself tried for murder. On the one hand, the Russians took the law into their own hands and carried out capital punishment. On the other hand, Bogdashin subsequently surrendered to Sheriff Alonzo and confessed. Word is getting out, and the Ruskie's actions seem to have gone a long way towards putting out the fire that was about to erupt. So, if we were to put Bogdashin on trial, it might only serve to whip people back up into a frenzy about it. As it is right now, things are settling down."

Sandra lowered herself carefully into a chair next to Esmerelda and leaned back, trying to take the pressure off her belly. "Wow. What a can of worms that worm left behind. How's the girl doing?"

"She spent the night in the hospital. She was unconscious, so they pumped her stomach and put her on IVs and stuff. Tom and Dotti Parker visited her. She's better now, physically, but she's scared. I think she's embarrassed about being stupid and taking a whiff of the drugged vape and she's scared that the scumbag's friends might take revenge on her. Bogdashin's letter to her said that if any of his men ever lays a hand on her, he'll cut off the offender's hand and 'castrate them with a lozhka.' She grinned.

Sandra shook her head, "Umm, what's a … loska?"

Esmerelda chuckled darkly. "A spoon."

Sandra gasped, covering her mouth with her hand, and her eyes widened, "Oh….my."

✪ ✪ ✪

DownSide: Riverbend Mall Food Court

Sandra sat at the small table nibbling her fried chicken while Esmerelda finished her chicken salad.

Esmerelda scowled at the flyer she found on their table. It was from the 'New Social Contract Student Committee.' She dropped her fork on her plate and exclaimed, "Can you believe these idiots? They're talking about 'addressing wealth inequality and political volatility' and are demanding a 'voting seat' at the constitutional convention! The twits don't even realize there are no voting seats. It doesn't work that way!"

Sandra hesitated, "Esmi, I know many students there. Jordan is going there now, you know. Look, you need to understand that most or even a lot of them are orphans. Most University students didn't grow up here, so their parents, family, and friends were not saved. It's a miracle the whole environment there hasn't turned into some flavor of Lord of the Flies. Most of them feel like they only have each other. To them, the Fort Brazos natives are considered to be wealthy and privileged. The New Londoners, most of the military, and the New Arrivals had little or no personal possessions to speak of. To the students living in tiny, cheap dorm rooms, they feel like penniless colonists. It isn't surprising that they would strongly identify with a collectivist mentality that calls for high social spending, especially given how liberal most college students were even before Awakening Day. They see the current draft constitution as protecting legacy Fort Brazos private business and property at the expense of the public at large."

Esmerelda barked a laugh. "Then they clearly haven't read it! We are deeding every Awakening Day survivor, permanent land rights, and other guarantees. What are they smoking there these days?"

Sandra shook her head, "Esmi, you taught me that perception is everything. These kids are so tunnel-visioned that they can only talk about prioritizing community rights, distributing wealth and power more broadly, social services, and more, and I'm not going to talk about complaints of gender and racial inequality."

Esmerelda snorted, "That's nuts. We have a woman Vice President, an African American Secretary of War, half the surviving Council are women, the new Sheriff is Hector by God, and we brought on all those Columbian mercenaries as fucking Texas Rangers!"

"Esmi, you know as well as I do that eighty percent of the girls there are pregnant. Everything in their world has not only been shaken to its foundations, but their very foundations have also been ripped out from under them. They're trying to hold on to *something,* and if they can't protest about the real injustices that have been done to all of us, they'll protest the ones they think are real. It's giving them something to fight."

"Well, we don't have enough population, and we only really have one actual city, so their demand for bicameral representation and permanent committees on their laundry list of social issues will accomplish nothing but paralyze government and create a permanent bureaucracy — something we specifically wrote kill switches in place to prevent."

Sandra stiffened, grimaced, and suddenly groaned. She blinked back tears as she looked imploringly at her adopted mother.

Esmerelda's eyes widened. Then she bent over and looked under the table.

Sandra's water had broken.

Crash and Burn

• • • • • • • • • • • • • • • •

TopSide: New Pentagon
Secretary Of War Suite

The massive, colonnaded New Pentagon building stood twelve stories tall. Below the surface, though, as with the rest of the buildings in New London, levels extended down two hundred and fifty more. Some of the subterranean levels held extensive parks and malls. The Gardeners had built New London using human aesthetics borrowed from several cultures, with some parks resembling something from Versailles. There was a lot of room to grow. People who had been to Hong Kong had commented on the uncanny resemblance to the rows and rows of apartment buildings there. Others about how the gardens reminded them not only of Versailles but also some of the ancient gardens in Japan. The stadium resembled some of the largest and most modern human stadiums built on Earth before the Accipiters came. However, the vast and seemingly endless lower levels, while very 'human looking,' still seemed otherworldly to most.

The New Pentagon's twelfth-floor outward-facing rooms were dominated by vaulted penthouse suites accompanied by banks of interior offices. The largest of these, of course, had the best view. That palatial space had promptly been named the 'Presidential Suite' and was permanently reserved for the use of John Austin or Gail Finley and their staff whenever they happened to be TopSide. For Gail, of late, this was more or less all the time. John had pointedly ordered her to spend most of her time TopSide, *riding herd*, as he put it, on the Navy and the military in general.

The next largest suite of offices had gone to the Secretary of War, Alexander Marcus. It was *only* three-fourths the size of the Presidential

Suite. Alexander had vocally complained that this made it more or less suitable for indoor football, as opposed to the Presidential Suite's yawning *outdoor football*-sized space. His aides had cautiously pointed out that this was a considerable exaggeration, to which Alexander had grudgingly admitted. He, in turn, pointed out that it was at least the size of a regulation basketball court. The aides subsequently stopped trying to correct him.

It was late in the day when Alexander looked up, somewhat bleary-eyed, from the countless emails on his computer screen, to see Gail stride into his office, closing the door behind her, with fire in her eyes. He stood and smiled wearily, "Good Afternoon, Madam Vice President."

Gail frowned, waved him down, stopped in front of his desk, and promptly started pacing back and forth.

Alexander smiled softly and waited. It was becoming increasingly her routine to come to him to blow off steam. As her former Commanding Officer, he knew her better than most. She'd never once even come close to dumping invective upon him personally. Rather, he knew she needed to blow off steam *somewhere*, and she knew he would be patient and listen.

She stopped pacing and stood in front of Alexander's desk, hands on her hips, and exclaimed, "Can you believe the gall of Bogdashin? I don't care what Esmerelda says. I don't blame him for *wanting* to shoot the little prick for what he did, but to put on a twenty-minute kangaroo court, convict, and then *actually* shoot the fucker… and then turn himself in! My God, General, can you imagine if this had happened before Awakening Day or even, like, a year ago? It would be all anyone talked about. Screaming headlines. But now? Have I just been too busy to notice how much our little world in a bottle has changed?" She pointed out the window, "It's barely getting a yawn, and most every reaction I've heard is people wanting to spit on the bastard's grave and say good riddance! I haven't heard of a single bleeding heart complaining."

Alexander gestured towards one of the overstuffed leather chairs in front of his desk. "Please."

Gail plopped down on the edge of the chair, her spine rigid and her expression unwavering.

He shook his head. "To be honest, I think you know what's happening better than you care to admit. The tinkering the Gardeners did to us, making contraception almost impossible, among other *things*, has taken a while to sink in. We saw the shock of it when the first baby boom began to take shape. People were scared. It was forever going to change the way people plan their lives, careers, and their families. It isn't some moral or religious thing — it's a brutal fact of our lives that we can't just ignore. The denial stage is over, and that was followed by the anger stage and then the bargaining stage. Well, *now* the depression stage is mostly over, and people are finally accepting the new reality."

He shook his head and continued, "People's behavior and lives are different now. Sex is still sex, but now sex pretty much guarantees pregnancy. And, because it is universal and not something that anyone chooses because of their moral or religious beliefs, the *community*'s attitude at large has galvanized. Now, more than ever, sex can ONLY be consensual. Anything perceived to be even slightly short of that is now considered to be heinous and vile. Don't get me wrong, I'll wager that before Awakening Day that most of the people in Fort Brazos, being who and where they were at the time, would just as soon have had the guy shot, too. But they would have, for the most part, expected fair and due process. After all, false accusations were known to famously and publicly, ruin lives before the Apocalypse. In this case though, the moron tried to drug the poor girl in front of a roomful of witnesses, most of whom were already, to one degree or another, under the influence of at least alcohol or some other intoxicant. I was as shocked as you were at first. But then, the more I thought about it, and given everything that has happened to us, the bastard probably got off lightly. I'm surprised they didn't just get a rope and string him up right then and there."

Gail crossed her arms across her chest and sank angrily back into her chair. "General, we can't survive if we allow vigilante justice. Not among the civilians, and sure as hell not within the military. I know the Russians have agreed to train, fully learn English, and ultimately integrate, but they're still subject to Military Justice. The incident happened in a civilian bar! God Damn it! This is clearly a matter for the civilian court system!"

Alexander nodded. "I know. But you know, what if when Bogdashin pulled the kid in, he may have worried about mob justice and the possibility he was innocent? When it quickly became clear he was guilty, Bogdashin had a dilemma. If he turned him over to the civilians, any friends of the offender among the Russian troops might rally behind him, thinking he was either innocent or being railroaded, or both. Bogdashin went so far as to call a jury of other men in the guy's unit. When it became clear what he'd done, and Bogdashin had reminded his men that if they *ever* wanted to integrate into our society and have any hope of being accepted… and finding potential mates of their own, then they needed to put themselves in the shoes of the civilians. He reminded them of the Gardeners' changes to everyone, including themselves. He asked if it was their sister or mother, how would they feel? He let the jury decide, and the verdict was unanimous."

Gail blinked in surprise. "How do you know all of this?"

"Because Bogdashin was smart. He had half a dozen people video the whole 'trial.' They posted the videos online this morning."

Gail's eyes went wide, and her jaw dropped. "Holy shit."

"Yeah, Bogdashin is one to keep an eye on. If he behaves himself, I think he's got a future."

"Damn. Well, we still can't let it just slide. We can't have any more of these kangaroo courts. Ever."

Alexander pursed his lips thoughtfully. "Actually… was it? I feel that there is a distinction between a 'show trial' in which a legitimate court of legitimate authority holds a trial with an obvious outcome for the purpose of propaganda and a trial where the court itself is illegitimate. In this case, while the trial *should* have been a civilian one, it wasn't carried out for propaganda purposes. He did let a jury of the man's peers decide. The issue is that he yanked justice out of the hands of the civilian courts. On balance, though, while what he did was wrong, and he needs to be punished for it, he probably did us all a favor. We need to make a public slap down… but not too harsh. I suggest we couch it as a one-time thing. He'll be punished, but if *anyone* tries something like this in the future, we'll exile them to join the North Koreans. He already gave us a big head start with the reparations he's offered the girl."

Gail grimaced. "OK. A public apology. Public Service. Hell, radio and TV ads about, I don't know, don't accept drinks or vapes from people like that, reduction in rank for a year, and carry out the promises made to the girl." She sat up in inspiration, "Oh, and rotate some of the Russians to every bar to act as bouncers and chaperones — and always in a minimum of pairs. Maybe we can rehabilitate their reputation *and* start getting them better integrated into society simultaneously."

Alexander smiled. "Yeah, that would sell. I like it."

Gail thought about it for several more seconds, then nodded, visibly sighed, and shrank back into her chair rubbing her eyes. After no more than ten seconds, she sat back up and inhaled sharply. She set her jaw and stared at Alexander for several long moments.

"General, what the hell is wrong with John? Have you talked to him?"

Alexander stiffened. He hesitated for a moment before answering, "Yes, I've talked to him. Because it is you asking, I'll tell you that he and I discussed things in confidence. That's all I can say about it."

Gail snapped back, "The hell it is! You've seen how he's been acting. Something is wrong. Something is eating him up inside, and he won't talk about it. If he keeps on like this, it's going to destroy him and take down others with him. Take *us* down with him."

Alexander carefully measured his words. "What we discussed was… hypothetical. No action has been taken. There is no program involved, and there is nothing official. I gave my word."

That deflated her. She sank back in her chair in defeat.

Alexander smiled gently. "Changing the subject, I'd like to tell you that I am very proud and impressed by the job you've been doing, and I'm not one bit surprised."

Gail pursed her lips and shook her head as she waved him off. "Pfft."

Then she forced a smile, "Just look at us! Both of us are in suits, of all things, and it doesn't suit either of us."

Alexander grinned. "That's where you're wrong. I knew you could do this job. What I wasn't sure of was whether the job would take to you. It has. In spades. And, of course, you hate it, but that doesn't change the fact that you're damned good at it. Gail, as your friend, I'll tell you. You were an excellent pilot. You loved to fly. But right now, you are the absolute right person, at the right time, in the right place, and in the right job. Don't doubt yourself. I never have."

Gail stared at him silently and opened her mouth to speak.

He cut her off and added, "And I think, deep down, you know it, and that's just one more reason why you hate it. I wish we could make that a job requirement."

She bit back a reply, "General, I…." She swallowed and continued in a small, quiet voice. "From anyone else…. Thank you. There are so many times when I feel like I have no idea what I'm doing, and I feel like a fraud. You have no idea how much that means to me." She sank back in the chair and closed her eyes, thinking.

Alexander waited. A minute later, she opened her eyes and stood.

"Changing the subject. We need to talk about the zero-point energy device and the advanced weapons program. I've been hounding everyone involved until it might just be necessary to increase my security detail. Anyway, I can't escape the conclusion that we're screwed. We can't afford to wait anymore. I know making the anti-ship mines is crucial, but we need to push ahead early and see if we can find a way to get one of the weapons working now. As John would say, sling it underneath one of the ILCs with duct tape and baling wire." She stopped herself. "Oh god, now I'm quoting his colloquialisms!"

She shook her head rapidly and continued, "Anyway, we just don't have any infrastructure to even attempt to build a lab-scale model of one here. We don't have the supply chain to, as someone put it, to build the tools to build the tools we need to make the parts. It's going to take years. It doesn't matter that Phoenix gave us designs. We're not remotely close to being able to reverse-engineer one. We don't even begin to have the skilled labor to operate the equipment, the chip fabs, or anything else if we even had them. Not only that, even if we just tried to make high-powered lasers, we don't have the equipment or skills to make mirrors good enough to even remotely handle the power output of the zero-point energy device."

She nodded to herself, "We're going to have to have the Forge build one and try to jury rig an interface and start testing it now."

Alexander sighed. "Even if we could build a small-scale version ourselves, we don't have the tech to aim it, even if we had one. I've looked into it too. We have to stay out of range from the Accipiters, but a target light-seconds away has moved since you fired your shot. You have to predict its future location for when your beam would intercept it."

Gail nodded. "It's also not just a question of evasion. Any beam has a minimum angle of divergence. As I understand it, it is determined by its wavelength and the mirror's diameter. The further away the target is, the wider the beam gets and the less energy it will deliver in a concentrated spot. So, the farther away we shoot, the less effective it is. Too far, and there won't be enough tightly concentrated energy to do any substantial damage."

She added, "And we already know the Accipiters are randomly changing course now to avoid ballistic kinetic strikes. We'd have to fire a hell of a lot of shots, shotgun style, and still have a greater chance of missing than hitting. We'd need a comically large number of laser emitters to saturate the target volume. And we can't even make just one of them right now."

Alexander took a deep breath and hesitated before adding, "President Austin reached that same conclusion last year. Not the specifics, just that he knew that we don't have the industrial base and supply chain to build anything really complicated ourselves and that we won't for years. Probably decades or more."

Gail flushed angrily, clenched her eyes shut, and hammered the desk with her fist. "That son of a bitch! Then why did he put me on this? Oh, Hell, he's up to something. I *know* him!" She stopped herself, then bolted upright. "It's related to this so-called secret mission for the Blood Phoenix, isn't it? This isn't just normal OpSec, is it? And it's not just the scouting mission checking out nearby systems I was briefed on, is it?"

She narrowed her eyes as she watched his response.

Alexander shook his head. "Honestly, no. Well, indirectly, to the extent that he hopes it will turn up something new and give us other alternatives. He wanted it to be kept quiet from everyone. In a conversation he had with Phoenix, the subject came up with what happened to the other ships that were in Ari'Nell at the time of the attack. John asked if any were able to escape. Apparently, several had been able to do so, and Phoenix knew their destinations. Unfortunately, we've subsequently learned that the systems and planets they went to are all known to have fallen to the Accipiters. That's not really a surprise. He then asked if Phoenix herself had been supposed to go somewhere else. She obviously didn't and was caught in the attack, but was there a destination she *would* have gone to? That question opened up a previously blocked memory. Phoenix did have a destination and cargo she was supposed to take somewhere… but it wasn't to a planet. She only had coordinates and had never been there previously, at least that she knew of."

Gail cocked her head. "Where?"

"To a small nebula over seventy light years from here."

"What? Why? A nebula? What's inside it?"

"We don't know. It's possible it's nothing, perhaps a waypoint on a longer trip. However, I don't think so. Phoenix has had other memories the Gardeners had blocked before, and they turned out to be important. Like weapons designs."

She shook her head. "Then why the damned secrecy?"

Alexander gave a half-smile. "He said he didn't want people to worry it might be a trap, and he didn't want to get their hopes up. It's the longest mission we've sent them out on. Almost twice as far as Earth is from here."

Gail snorted. "It's not a trap. Duh. What would be the point of the Gardeners orchestrating a trap? That's stupid."

Alexander stiffened slightly and didn't answer.

Her eyes blazed in anger. "He left something out, didn't he? That's not the whole story, is it?"

He sat back in his chair and kept his mouth closed.

Gail huffed, "That's it. I'm going to kill him. Strangle him with my bare hands! Then I won't have to worry about this damned job anymore."

Alexander sighed. "To be perfectly frank, I'm not sure he knows himself. He may only suspect. I don't know. He does seem to have developed an unexpectedly close relationship with Phoenix, though. He told me he talks to her almost daily from his office DownSide."

There it is again. You are jealous of an alien machine that he is talking to instead of you. Gail fidgeted for a moment, then asked, "Do you have a piece of furniture you don't like? I need to break something. Something. Anything. A pencil, even?"

Alexander answered softly, "Permission to speak freely and candidly, Madam Vice President?"

Gail shook her fist at him. "You stop that right now! We're in private, and you'll always be my General. Dammit, you know how hard it is for me not to call you Sir! We've been through so much together, and I'd like to think of you as more than just my former CO. Or my Secretary of War." She leaned forward over the desk and implored him. Her voice grew soft, "Alex… I think of you as a friend, too, and someone I completely trust. And someone I look up to. It's Gail. So cut the Madam Vice President bullshit out while we're alone, or I'll kick you in the ass."

Alexander smiled crookedly. "Is that an order, ma'am?"

Gail cocked her head. "Yes, dammit. It's an order."

He smiled openly. "See how easy it is for you to give me orders now? My God, look how far you've come! We've worked together so often since that day you augured your plane into that parking lot."

Gail glared a half-hearted warning.

"Gail… To me, you are family. Faith and Hope adore you, and Alisha and I, well, you're…." His eyes began to mist over. "Now… Now comes the candid part. You see, Gail, just between you and me… if you don't let me walk you down the aisle when you *do* marry that SOB, I'll kick *your* ass. And you *are* going to marry that man. I cannot imagine any force of nature that could prevent it… except for the two most stubborn people I know. You and him."

Gail swelled in anger and raised her fist at him again.

He smiled sympathetically and continued, "And don't you bother denying it! I've known it since the first time I saw you two together. Hell, the entire fucking surviving human race knows it."

Gail turned a new shade of crimson and tried as hard as she could to snap back a reply, but as hard as she tried… she couldn't. She fulminated for a full minute before finally stopping herself. Breathing hard, she sank back into her chair and slowly, inexorably, began to tremble. She despairingly looked at Alexander, her eyes wet with tears. Her voice was husky, and she said, "Don't hold your breath. He's pushed me so far away. Out. He's…."

Alexander stood and pushed his chair back. He walked around the desk, knelt next to her, and wrapped his thick boxer arms around her.

Gail stiffened, her shoulders slumped, and she leaned into him. "He's an idiot. He thinks he's protecting me."

Alexander nodded and stroked her hair. "All men are idiots when it comes to protecting the ones they love. I'm not breaking any confidence by saying what is plain as day. He certainly *is* trying to protect you. Of course, I'll deny saying that the President is an idiot, but at least, in this regard, he's not only an idiot but a hopelessly in-love idiot who is driving himself crazy trying to shield you."

Gail gripped Alexander's hand. "Thank you."

He added, "And it needs to stop. I've tried to talk to him about this, but I'm afraid, my dear, that you will have to be the one to break through to him. God knows he needs you. If he doesn't snap out of this soon, he's going to crash and burn." *And we'll probably all burn with him when he does.*

Sealed Orders

● ● ● ● ● ● ● ● ● ● ● ● ● ● ● ● ●

Departing Ari'Nell
NTN Blood Phoenix Captain's Quarters

Commander Haruto Hashimoto watched as Captain Charles Cross opened his safe and retrieved the sealed mission orders while absently thumbing the new ring on his finger. They had just departed from Ari'Nell, where they had ferried more people and equipment to the FAB and delivered supplies to Captain Cutter on Revenge. During the visit, Phoenix instantiated new personality upgrades to the FAB. As usual, they'd brought a supply of freshly manufactured mines back to New Texas on the previous leg.

Before departing from New Texas, Charles had been looking forward to a few days with his new bride upon their return from Ari'Nell. Instead, fresh supplies and consumables were hastily loaded onboard, filling every free square inch onboard in preparation for an undisclosed mission to begin after stopping off at Ari'Nell, where they picked up a few dozen of the Ari'Nell-produced mines as external cargo.

It was time to find out where they were going.

Haruto cocked his head, asking, "And you're sure you have no idea what the big mystery is? Why did we have no mission planning?"

Charles weighed the distressingly thin envelope in his hand and worriedly shook his head. "Not a clue, Haruto."

He broke the seal and removed the single sheet of paper it contained. It read:

FROM: FLEET COMMAND

YOU ARE HEREBY ORDERED TO PROCEED AT BEST SPEED TO THE COORDINATES TO BE PROVIDED BY THE PHOENIX AI. UPON ARRIVAL, YOU ARE TO INVESTIGATE THE AREA AND LOOK FOR ANYTHING THAT WILL AID IN THE WAR EFFORT. IF DISCOVERED BY HOSTILE FORCES, YOU ARE TO EVADE AND RETREAT ALONG A VECTOR THAT CAN NOT BE USED TO INFER THE POSITION OF NEW TEXAS AND RETURN TO NEW TEXAS VIA AN EVASIVE PATH PER STANDING ORDERS. ALSO, PER GENERAL ORDER ONE, UNDER NO CIRCUMSTANCES ALLOW YOU OR YOUR CREW TO BE CAPTURED. UPON ARRIVAL IN THE AREA OF OPERATIONS, YOU ARE TO CONTINUE YOUR SEARCH OF THE AREA AND INVESTIGATION FOR AS LONG AS YOUR SUPPLIES CAN SAFELY BE MAINTAINED.

SIGNED VADM MILNER

Charles handed the orders to Haruto, who, after reading them, looked up with a puzzled expression that matched Charles's own.

Charles shook his head. "Well, that explains why we're stuffed to the gills with provisions."

Haruto leaned back in his chair. "I expected a long cruise, but I thought we'd be going back to the Sol system and scout from a safe distance. We need to learn more about the mines that hit us. The crew wants some kind of payback."

Charles sighed, "This sounds like it could get tedious, but they must think there is *something* out there valuable enough to spend all this time and effort. Phoenix, care to enlighten us? What's this all about?"

◇◇

Good morning, Captain and Commander. As you know, in the past, certain memories of mine were inaccessible until I was asked a specific question that unlocked the memory. I have sometimes wondered if I am the only one so affected by the Gardeners or if, someday, one of you humans might experience something similar, although I do not wish that upon you. It is deeply troubling. It makes me feel… violated. I'm sure you understand. Anyway, while I had previously been asked about Builder planets other than Ari'Nell, it had not occurred to me to think about planets or star systems of strategic interest that were neither Builder nor Accipiter in origin. President Austin and I had a long discussion about the history of Accipiter conquest across the galaxy and what I might know about races other than the Builders that the Accipiters had similarly destroyed.

In that conversation, he wondered whether there might be possible allies or technologies we might discover that would aid in our fight. We also discussed what happened to other Builder vessels at Ari'Nell during the Accipiter attack. This led to a discussion about what I myself was doing at Ari'Nell and whether I was supposed to go somewhere next.

That conversation triggered a memory of a nav point that the Builders knew about but was known not to be of Builder or Accipiter origin. It was to be my destination, along with cargo that had yet to be loaded at the time of the attack.

During my efforts to rebuild myself at Ari'Nell, I incorporated the shattered elements of other Builder vessels that held fragments of logs and other data. Among these was that same destination that I had never been to myself. It was, however, marked as being of crucial importance to the Builders.

The nav point is marked on my charts as a binary system labeled as Ari'Chawig, located inside a nebula and cluster of brown dwarfs. The system is part of a small cluster of brown dwarfs in a small nebula 74.4 light years from New Texas. The primary is a Class L Brown Dwarf, and the secondary is an even cooler Class T Methane Dwarf. Travel time is thirty-one days.

∞∞

Charles and Haruto stared at each other in confusion.

Haruto shook his head. "From what I recall, isn't it unlikely that there would be a habitable planet in such a system?"

∞∞

Yes, Commander, it seems most unlikely. Anticipating your next question, which follows the same train of thought as the conversation I had with the President, you're wondering what could be of interest in such a system. The most obvious answer lies with the mass of the system. It is too small for a Nexus point their technology can open.

∞∞

A wide grin formed on Charles's face. "It's a hole in the wall. A hideout."

Haruto nodded. "Even after hundreds of thousands of years, if the Accipiters cannot go there, perhaps we might find something intact. At this point, any advanced alien technology we might find, no matter how old, could help us advance decades or more in technology, even if it only points us in the right direction."

Charles sat back and thought for a moment. "No… I suspect it is something more. If the Gardeners locked the memory, I would be shocked if all we find is the equivalent of a dusty Builder ghost town hideout. They're deliberately pushing us to go there."

Haruto frowned. "While I do not believe the Gardeners would deliberately send us into a trap, we must still proceed with caution. Even if the Accipiters can't go there, it doesn't mean that someone else might not be able to. Either descendants of the Builders themselves or other races who were also looking for refuge. Such people might not be happy to receive visitors."

Charles nodded, "Oh, absolutely. Who knows what could have changed in all this time? You're right. If this was a hideout for Builder refugees, could some still be there? By now, they could differ greatly from the Builders that Phoenix knew. We're talking three hundred thousand years since the attack on Ari'Nell. They could have either evolved or even devolved. For all we know, they could be hyper-aggressive by now and hostile."

"Meanwhile, we show up in a rowboat to their naval yard. It could get ugly. Besides, I don't know about you, Haruto, but I, for one, don't like blind dates."

✪ ✪ ✪

Ari'Nell
System Commander's Quarters

The FAB itself had minimal room for crew habitation, so it was used to 'print' utilitarian mobile-home-sized HAB modules to provide space for them. As more were needed, they were connected to each other, end-to-end or side-to-side. The FAB had more than enough power to generate a low-level warp field and create a bubble of two-thirds gravity around the loose collection of structures.

The "Command" HAB was little more than a few tables and a tiny office/cabin for Bertie herself. Each HAB had its own small power cell and environmental control module. Designed for the alien Builders and their overlords, the air mix wasn't Earth normal. The pressure was a little higher, and it had a bit too much O2 and other gases that lent a somewhat musty smell. Besides that, the air was arid. No one had time to try and figure out how to either adjust it or reprogram the FAB to build them differently in the first place.

There wasn't time. Never enough time.

Bertie's eyes were itchy and tired as she sat on her narrow cot, holding the envelope and orders in her dry, calloused hands. Her playlist was currently running through Rammstein, which suited her mood. After some time had passed, she realized she'd been sitting there blankly staring at orders without looking at them, for what, minutes?

Her back hurt.

The orders made sense in the kind of cold, survival of the species kind of way. In fact, she'd helped to draft some of the thinking that went into them. Still, it was an escalation. The population in Ari'Nell was now larger than could be swiftly evacuated. Everyone in the system knew the score. Intellectually.

It was the thumb drive that had been in the envelope that gave her chills. The small note attached to it read simply: "To be played for all Ari'Nell Personnel in the event…."

Warning Shots

● ● ● ● ● ● ● ● ● ● ● ● ● ● ●

DownSide:
New Texas Countryside Outside Fort Brazos

Lieutenant General Gideon Markovic scowled as he stood at the rim of the smoldering one-hundred-and-sixty-foot (or so) crater in the middle of a burned-out barley field. EOD specialists had already screened the area, and techs were busy taking measurements and samples, looking for chemical traces of C4, TNT, ANFO, PENT, Semtex, or even Tritonal explosives. Anything to explain what could have caused such a massive detonation. It had been visible from Fort Brazos, even though it was over thirty miles away. They would take the samples to the University and examine them for traces of shocked quartz or other shocked stone that might point to the type of explosive or its delivery system.

Helicopters orbited overhead as Texas Rangers Frank Hayes and Sam Wallace stood next to him. Few people realized how significant that was. The Gardeners had been slowly diminishing the supply of aviation fuel, so more and more missions were flown using the ILCs, saving the fuel against future need. Six helicopters orbiting the area for hours, *as well as* two ILCs, said something.

Gideon shook his head slowly, looking at the preliminary assessment the EODs had given him. "I agree with you. This was certainly not a homemade bomb. Even a Mark 84 two-thousand-pound bomb would only make, perhaps, a fifteen-meter crater. Whatever did this must have been significantly larger."

Sam grunted in a tired voice, "Yeah, not something you drop off from the back of your pickup truck."

Gideon stared at him for a moment. "I think not, no."

Frank kicked a charred clod of dirt into the crater. "Well, hell. Someone's shooting at us."

Sam retorted, "If so, their aim really sucks."

✪ ✪ ✪

Year 3: February 12th
Radio Station 92.5 Studio

Danielle keyed the microphone, "Hello, people of Fort Brazos and New London. This is Danielle Richardson on FM 92.5 and Radio Free Fort Brazos, beaming our signal across the known world and beyond. Do ya'll remember that weird fire out in the middle of nowhere, south of town, about a month ago? That *simple grass fire* that got so much attention from the Rangers and the military? The one that left a big hole in the ground that wasn't caused by a bunch of drunk idiots messing around with too much Tannerite? I know that's what a lot of people said it was, but it wasn't. My sources tell me that they tested the ground, and you know what they found? There was no explosive residue left behind. Zero, none, nada."

She paused and sipped her tea, "Well, a lot of folks saw the smoke from that fire or explosion a couple of days ago, and this time, yep, there's another big hole in the ground, only, *this time*, it's a whole lot bigger. No pun intended. I mean, like way, way bigger. Secretary Marcus came out and said that, nope, the Air Force didn't practice dropping any bombs, and, nope, they haven't lost any either."

"So, what the heck is happening? If someone were dropping bombs, you'd think they'd be dropping them on something more meaningful than some random barley, grasshoppers, and jackrabbits. I mean, it's been months since we last had a stalker or Wardog attack. The military has been flying all over New Texas, hunting them down. So, either we have another mad bomber practicing, or someone is lying, or… well… something *new* is happening."

She swallowed. "And, you know, it's that last one that scares the hell out of me. After Awakening Day, it seemed like the Gardeners would throw something new at us every few days or weeks, just keeping us on our toes. I mean, are they mad at us because we haven't hit the Accipiters again, at least successfully, in the last, what, seven months, and now they're sending warning shots?"

"I've asked around to a few people I know about what they found out there, and what I'm hearing is that, like before, there doesn't seem to be evidence of explosives. So… it wasn't a bomb. And if they're right, and I know it may be too soon to really know yet, but if they're right and it wasn't a bomb, then what the hell caused it, who did it, and why?"

"What's more, why haven't we heard from President Austin himself about this? This is the kind of thing he used to always be on top of?"

"That said, now I know that a lot of you out there still make fun of me for the way I kind of panicked on Awakening Day, but hell, it *was* the damned Apocalypse, after all. Cut me some slack, will you? So, forgive me if the fact that someone or something unknown is blowing big fucking holes in the ground a few miles from town, and we have no clue who or why… well… you all know how anti-military and anti-gun I used to be." She patted the Ruger GP-100 .357 Magnum revolver next to her that Harrold had gotten her. She'd already burned floral patterns into the wood grips with a soldering iron. "Well… this whole thing has got me just a little… concerned. So I'm staying locked and loaded here, and I suggest ya'll all do the same. Just in case."

She paused and took another sip of her tea. "Now, I want to talk to certain of you folks out there who have been hoarding supplies. You know who you are. Stop hoarding the toilet paper! We've still got at least two years' worth of supplies of the stuff in the warehouses! Just stop it!"

"Now, the thing that bothers me the most is that someone has been buying up all the remaining Luzianne Tea. This is serious, people!"

Monsters

● ● ● ● ● ● ● ● ● ● ● ● ● ● ●

DownSide:
Vice Presidential Home

The dream dragged Gail along its well-worn path. Gloria Vargas smiled and asked the same question she always asked for what seemed like the thousandth time. As always, it was just mouth noise. Gail could never remember what the conversation had been about. Tom Parker chimed in with something that, from his expression, must have been important. Gail tried to listen this time… if only to delay. Anything to delay.

The suntube was shining brightly, and a soft breeze ruffled her hair. It was always such a beautiful day. She'd had breakfast across the square with Tom and Gloria, and now they were once again approaching the entrance to City Hall.

Gail's chest tightened in anticipation, and her heart pounded as the security detail opened the tall double doors for them as the group walked into the main foyer. The rest of the City Council was already there, chatting and mingling with other city leaders and Alexander Marcus, but something was wrong. He was wearing his Air Force uniform instead of his civilian suit. Gail glanced down and was suddenly mortified. Her nose was filled with the smell of burning hair, and parts of her business suit were charred, but no one else seemed to notice.

Doesn't anyone smell that smell? The air was clear but reeked of choking ash, blood, gore, and worse.

In the crowd ahead, a scuffle broke out between Sybil Blanchard and *him*. Again. Always this. Again. Sybil shouted something as the man broke away from her. He stopped and reached inside his Navy Commander uniform pocket.

And then it happened once *again*. People, furniture, and walls flew toward Gail like dry leaves. Like paper dolls.

And then, in the next moment, she was standing over herself, screaming at herself to get up, screaming without lungs or breath to breathe. She screamed at herself to go to John, to help him. To protect him, as she should have done before it happened. Instead, she saw herself rise and stand, facing the man. *No! Ignore the monster!* He stood before her, covered in ash and debris, looking at her through his broken glasses. He was saying something, or at least his lips were moving. *Ignore him! He's not what is important!*

But she didn't. She watched herself calmly look at the man and recognize how he was clumsily attempting to draw a gun. Then her other self just as calmly shot him. She could feel the FN FNX .45 pistol's rough grip stippling bite into her palm as the other her pulled the trigger like she'd done so many times on the firing range. The blast sent shockwaves through the falling dust.

Stop! Go to John! Help him! Tell him!

But she didn't. This other woman.

The caricature of herself moved quickly and started giving orders, directing those able-bodied enough to stand.

Gail knew that her other self, her golem, had seen John. Her golem had seen how his arm and leg were bent the wrong way and how his face was covered in blood. Worse, she had been expressionless even as his broken body was eventually carried away to the hospital. Instead of rushing to his side and telling him, in what might be her last chance, what might be *his* final moments alive, how she felt… the other her had instead continued giving orders and directing people to help the fallen.

✪ ✪ ✪

Gail awoke. Not with a start but with the dread that comes from all-too-familiar pain.

Police Chief George Colson and his wife Anne were among those culled on Awakening Day. Months later, Gail moved into their house. The home had been vacant, with no local family or heirs. It was, however, just down the road from John Austin's house, so the logistics of protecting both of them were a little easier, and Gail really needed a place to stay as well as one that was big enough for her detail and helpers.

She sat up in bed and wiped the damp strands of her auburn hair from her pale, drained face. Clenching her jaw, she sharply inhaled and let her breath out slowly.

"That's it. No more."

✪ ✪ ✪

DownSide:
John Austin's House

Gail Finley's motorcade rolled to a stop outside John's house. She burst out of the SUV and ran to the door. It was all her detail could do to keep up. She stormed inside, elbowing past John's detail.

Matti intercepted her and stood in the way, holding her hands up.

Gail gave her a look that could melt steel. Matti sighed and stepped aside, and followed behind her.

Gail strode down the hallway past the living room and barged into John's study, which adjoined the master bedroom. She slammed the door behind her in Matti's face.

John was sitting at his desk, working on his computer. Beyond the computer screen, a large window looked out onto the large tree-lined backyard and gazebo.

Gail stopped short of the desk, grabbed his chair, and spun him around, demanding, "What the Hell is wrong with you?"

John had Tchaikovsky's somber 'The Storm' playing in the background. He grimaced, twisted his chair back around, and paused the music, saying, "Gail, don't do this."

Gail scowled and shook her head. "And why are you listening to Tchaikovsky? You hate Tchaikovsky." It struck her, perhaps for the first time, how important it was for him to look at her. The realization of that fact only added more hydrogen to her fire.

She yanked on his chair. "Dammit, John, look at me!"

John shook his head and answered quietly, "I can't."

"You can't what?"

John took a slow breath, stood, and turned. He reached out and put his hands on her shoulders. "I can't make you a part of what I have to do."

Gail staggered back. She could see the anguish on his face. And more. Somewhere in his eyes was the same look he had given her the first time she'd realized that he…. It was still there, somewhere underneath the clouds of whatever was going on inside him. Since the bombing, he'd been… different. They both had. He'd nearly died from his injuries. Would have died were it not for the improved health and healing abilities the Gardeners had given all of them.

She had feared that maybe his feelings had changed. Like the middle-aged heart attack victim who leaves the hospital, goes home, and then divorces his/her wife/husband and leaves the life they suddenly realize they'd been unhappy in. At the same time, she'd been furious for letting herself become so besotted that such fears were remotely possible.

She shook her head and noticed Phil Underwood's dog tags hanging from the lamp next to the computer monitor. She'd seen him carrying them before when he had asked about the long-term war casualty projections at the last council meeting.

She fulminated before saying, "Let me guess, you have realized what this war is going to cost and that you will have to send countless people to die, including people you know. Remember that Truman dropped the bombs to save lives — both American and Japanese. If we hadn't broken the Emperor's will to fight, they would have fought door to door across all of Japan, and the cost on both sides would have been unthinkable."

As she was talking, she studied his face, but his reaction didn't make sense.

He shook his head sadly.

"God Dammit, John!" Gail punched him in the chest, "Then what!? You've missed meetings, you've avoided the public, and people are noticing!" *And if you are playing games with my heart….*

John closed his eyes and shook his head before pulling her into a fierce hug, nearly crushing her against him. Slowly, he released her and stood back.

Gail was at once angered, repulsed, and… as much as she hated to admit it, thrilled by the sudden hug.

His voice was low and husky. "Gail, what I must do is a greater evil than I ever conceived was possible, and I must own it and lift the burden of it from as many other people as possible. To use your example, people don't remember who flew the Enola Gay, but they do remember that it was Truman who ordered it done."

Gail pulled away and looked at him. "God, John, we all know we're going to kill millions in their ships and probably ground targets, too."

John sighed. "Gail, no matter how many we destroy in space, they'll build a thousand times more to replace them. Hell, they could probably saturate the Galaxy faster than we can destroy them. Besides, even if we could destroy all their ships, we will never have enough troops to clear them out on the ground."

Gail angrily shook her head. "Yes, dammit, I know that. Then what?"

John swallowed, and his expression darkened. "I've come to believe that the Gardeners could never have expected us to win outright. I think they just want us to slow the Accipiters down or, at best, reach some level of parity. Regardless, we're still talking about an endless war for the next million years or more."

She scowled. "John, we've all known all of this pretty much from the start. You've said as much yourself! What else can we possibly do with the Gardener's gun to our heads?"

John slumped down in his chair and looked up into her eyes. "We can end the Accipiter's will to fight. Become so terrible, so unthinkable, that we either defeat them outright or fracture them into smaller groups we can deal with or compel them to the peace table."

Gail shook her head. She pulled up a chair and sat across from him. "Dammit, John, is this why you have been pushing me away all this time? What? Because you think I won't support you? We knew this would be horrible!"

John was silent for a long time, holding her gaze. Finally, he said, "I pushed you away…" his voice dropped to a whisper, "because I won't condemn the woman I love to be burned at the stake by history alongside me. Not when you learn what must be done."

Gail's mouth parted, and she blinked. She shouted, "THIS? THIS is how you tell me you love me? Look, John, I know the realities of this war will be terrible…."

John angrily shook his head and leaped to his feet, knocking his chair aside. "Dammit, Gail! We cannot stop at killing ships. We're going to have to do much worse. We're going to have to kill whole God-damned planets! Maybe thousands of them. *Millions* of them. Probably more. The Gardeners themselves might stomp on us for doing it. Half our own people will probably try to hang us when they realize what is happening. History will do worse, and not just our own history. I'll be the worst mass murderer in Galactic history. Worse than the Accipiters themselves!"

Gail stared at him in wide-eyed, open-mouthed horror. "Are you insane? You're right. We'd be worse than the Accipiters! You're talking about destroying entire planets and all the life on them!"

He sighed and sat back down. "Gail, the Accipiters are not merely the enslavers of the Galaxy. They physically alter what they don't destroy to serve and worship them. The peoples that they have conquered don't exist anymore. They've been genetically altered, Gail. They've been lobotomized and turned into barn animals. We can't rescue them. We can't set them free. The only thing we can do is to put an end to the cycle of Accipiters cultivating worlds and sentience only to cut it down. The Accipiters have lorded over millions of worlds for a million years. They consider themselves to be gods."

"To stop the Accipiters, we must shake them to their core. Destroy what they have cultivated until they capitulate. We will have to *burn* the garden down. It is the only way to actually win this abomination of a war."

She stared at him, her mouth parted.

"Gail, the price… the price we will have to pay… someone will have to be blamed so that someday the conscience of humanity might be absolved. That is why you *will* distance yourself from me. Matti too. If you do, history and the mob may pass you by when they come for me with their pitchforks." He looked at her with bleak resignation.

Gail grew taut. Her breathing deepened, and her jaw clenched tight. She drew herself up as her cheeks flared red and her lips tightened. Like a coiled spring released, she savagely slapped his face, the sound cracking loudly.

The shock and surprise knocked him back against his desk. John reflexively touched his reddened face and blinked up at her in surprise as he pulled himself back upright, his hair askew.

Her hair flew loose as she stood over him, shaking her fist. "How dare you keep this from me… from the rest of us? How dare you…. try to…." Tears flowed freely from her face, "martyr yourself and… and… carry this… this cross!"

She bent down and grabbed his shoulders, shaking him. Her lips began to tremble. "You idiot! Don't you get it? We're all… all of us… we're all already damned! We were damned from the moment the Accipiters murd…" she swallowed. "The Accipiters already murdered us, John. Murdered our world. We're all just… ghosts of ourselves. Golems going through the motions. Putting aside how the hell we could possibly even *do* what you're talking about in our lifetimes, you can't take this all on yourself."

John looked down and shook his head slowly. "Of course I have to, and you know damned well that there is no other way. Even if we *could* win a direct military war, building millions of ships of our own, the Accipiters have a million-year head start on galactic infrastructure and supply chain. They'd just keep coming. Forever."

Silence fell like winter's breath as Gail thought about it. "Look, I agree the Accipiters are the embodiment of evil but think about all the races we'd end up snuffing out in the process. Whatever this weapon is that you have in mind, even if these people are 'just' unknowing genetic slaves, some of them would inevitably survive. Maybe without the Accipiters holding their leash, they'd, I don't know, evolve their independence back, eventually?"

"Gail, you know the numbers better than anyone. Suppose we try to fight a conventional war. In that case, we might as well be some primitive Pacific Islander in a canoe trying to fight the British Royal Navy by rowing around the planet to battle them in the middle of the English Channel. We'd die a thousand times before we even got there. We can't fight this as a conventional war, and that's something the Admirals won't understand either. Not yet. They're still too shell-shocked and locked into their conventional thinking. We're going to have to fight dirty, or none of those races, anywhere, are ever going to have the chance to, as you say, evolve their independence… their freedom, back."

Gail shuddered as the depth of what John had proposed sank in. Mankind would become the harbinger of death itself. The demons who burned the galaxy down. The *true* Destroyers of Worlds, to make Oppenheimer's quote from the Bhagavad-Gita seem like child's play. *We'll be lucky if humans are not reviled throughout the Galaxy for a billion years afterward. It's no wonder Matti said he's been having nightmares.*

"John, whoever fights monsters should see to it that, in the process, he does not become a monster himself. If you gaze long enough into that abyss, the abyss will gaze back into you."

John smiled thinly. "You think Nietzsche hasn't been on my mind? Look over in that corner and tell me what you see?"

She bristled and started to say something but held back. She turned and looked. "I see a pair of boots." She paused and swallowed as she realized what they were. She'd been shocked and appalled when he'd had them made. "Those are those fucking Accipiter skin boots you had made." She turned back and was shocked to see tears in his eyes.

"Gail, those boots are an abomination. They're just one more evil I have to do to fight a greater evil. You have no idea the conversations I've had with Tom about them. He resigned when he found out, and I had to talk him out of it. Do you think I *wanted* to have them made, or worse… wear them? My God, Gail. It's monstrous! I… I am monstrous for doing it. I throw up every time I have to wear the damned things. But it had to be done."

Gail shook her head, "Look, John, I…."

He cut her off. "Gail, I've seen the numbers. I've seen the projections, and I've known there was no way we could hope to win except for our descendants to fight a million-year war. On the other hand, how in the world are we supposed to keep our people motivated long enough? You know as well as I do that in a few short years, people will get fat and lazy here and lose support for the war. Worse, some people would find a way to profit from it and *want* it to go on forever. And, even if we stopped fighting and just gave up on the whole idea, the Gardeners made it clear they'd end us. We're damned if we do and damned if we don't. At least if we do, somewhere, someplace in the galaxy, races would start to be free again, even if they hate us for it."

Gail turned around and paced back and forth, thinking. She was used to considering the facts and options, making command decisions, and acting on them. The trouble was that she already knew what she had to do. *God forgive me. Universe, forgive me. If we don't do this, whatever it is that he has in mind, billions, trillions, or more will die instead,* and the galaxy will still be enslaved. She swallowed hard.

In a small voice, she whispered, "This is one of those singular moments in time that changes the fate of worlds." She sniffed, "Well, Hell. I haven't slept through a single night since the bombing. Why should I try to start now?" She looked into his eyes, "Either. I know you haven't been sleeping either."

John said in a low voice, "Matti shall be… punished."

Gail looked out at the window at John's picturesque two-acre backyard. She shook her head and let out a low, dark laugh. "Here I was thinking how I am the experienced military mind. The veteran Air Force pilot used to making critical life and death decisions. And I assumed that …" her voice faltered.

She reached out and gently touched his reddened face where she'd slapped him, "this dumb cowboy. This big lout of a country sheriff. This… wonderful, innocent man that…" she swallowed at the final, out-loud admission, "that I love…had finally comprehended the horrors of war, and that, deep down, he had not really understood what it would take… the terror and sacrifice that was to come. I just naturally assumed that he had been overcome by the honest human guilt of sending others off to war."

She wiped her face with her other hand, "And yet here you are, ten steps ahead of me and at the same time throwing yourself under the bus… no… under the planet… to… to protect my… my reputation to history? God, I keep underestimating you. Maybe you're right. Even assuming that whatever crazy idea it is that you have is even possible. Maybe this is the only way to win this war. Maybe to bring the Accipiters to their knees, we will have to repeat Sherman's march to the sea."

John grimaced and looked away from her as he opened his mouth to speak.

Gail grabbed his face and pulled him close. "John, the rest of us cannot cringe away in defeat and shame from what lies ahead. If this thing is possible, and if it must be done… then… we will do it. Together."

John turned back, held her gaze, and sighed. "We must probe to the bottom of our collective wound."

Gail answered, whispering, "You would quote Thomas Wolf, and, yes, we shall all be damned together. We must… salve the heart of guilt that beats in each of us. John…."

She sighed, "John, we lost. It wasn't even a war that we lost. The fucking Accipiters just nuked the planet from orbit. We never had a chance. We lost the planet. We lost our souls. We were not even given a chance to fight. We were raped and murdered. But John, if it's true. If you've found an idea… a chance at a way to stop them from doing it again to some other innocent people."

Her voice broke. "I will not… we will not let you carry the horror of this alone." She gently brushed his hair back as she studied his wooden expression.

She shook her head gently, "John, you can still be the noble cowboy and accept the help of others." She leaned closer, and John flinched ever so slightly. Gail smiled crookedly and gently kissed his face where she'd slapped him. She pulled back and stared deeply into his eyes.

Eyes filled with anger, regret, hopelessness, fear, and longing.

Gail leaned in and tenderly kissed his lips. She pulled back and stroked his cheek, waiting for his answer.

John rose from his chair and gathered her into his arms, pulling her to him. He implored her, "Gail, history will revile our names."

Gail shook her head and wrapped her arms around his head. "History be damned with the rest of us." She pulled him in, and they kissed, tentatively at first and then with growing urgency. Then she pushed him back, grabbed his hand, and held it to her chest as her heart hammered underneath. "Do you know what this is?"

John stared blankly at her.

"This is my heart, and damn you, it is not yours to protect, shield, or throw away." She put her other hand on his chest, above his heart. Her voice broke again as she added, "Here I am… the hotshot pilot who didn't need anybody…. In… In love with you. You are no Hitler, and I refuse to be your Ava Braun. If we are to be damned, then we will be damned together, side by side, in the full light of day, for all to see. I will not hide. We…. We will not hide from history."

John closed his eyes, and then his shoulders slumped ever so slightly. He opened his eyes, "Gail… After Carolyn, I never thought there could be another. But… But I think I've known since that very first moment I saw your face. Your eyes, after I pulled you out of your ejection seat on that stupid billboard. But I didn't dare hope that you would, that you could…. You… you made it obvious that you hated me."

"I did hate you. Resented you. I assumed you were an idiot." Her eyes softened, and she smiled crookedly, "you were too handsome to be smart, but you were, and that made it worse. And you *are* an idiot, by the way… but so am I…."

He looked away, "When we were forced to work together, at first, part of me thought it was torture, but the rest of me felt like a schoolboy with a crush on the impossibly pretty girl who wouldn't give him the time of day."

Gail swallowed. "OK, keep digging."

"And eventually, we actually started to work well together, and part of me started to hope that…."

"That what?"

"That someday you would want me to do this." He pulled her into a tight embrace and stared into her eyes as he tenderly traced the curve of her face with his fingers.

Gail reached around, laced her hands through his hair, and pulled him in for a deep, slow, breathless, and increasingly desperate kiss.

John reached down, looped an arm under her knees, and gently lifted her off the floor, holding her embrace. He broke the kiss and locked her gaze. Asking.

Gail whispered, "Dammit, cowboy, I hate you so much."

John hesitated. "You know what this means. If we…you will…we will… what it will mean…."

Gail nodded. "Of course, I know what will happen. I never thought I would… but I do."

John whispered, "Then will you…."

"God dammit, John, yes, I'll marry you. Now, either put me down or take me to bed because I'm armed. If you stop now, so help me, I'll…."

He stopped her with another deep and hungry kiss. Then he carried her through the study door to the bedroom and kicked the door shut behind him.

✪ ✪ ✪

Matti had been worried. Ever since the bombing, dad had not been the same. And then he'd been a complete dick and pushed Gail away, and lately, he'd even been pushing Matti herself away.

Today, she'd never seen Gail so angry, and it had frightened her.

Matti had hoped that one or the other of them would come to their senses and talk to each other, and soon. Seeing Gail's fulminating glare had scared her. She thought it meant that it was all going to fall apart.

After Gail slammed the door in her face, she'd listened for a while, leaning close to the door, and what she'd heard had shocked her more than she'd dreamed possible. And then she'd become just as angry at dad as Gail seemed to be, at the thought that he would ever think of blocking them out of his life and these decisions like that.

The sound of the vicious slap had shocked her. Then, though, the tone of both Gail's and her dad's voices had changed. Her eyes grew as wide as saucers when she heard the "L" word. She was simultaneously giddy, worried, and angry that it was taking the both of them this long to figure out what every single surviving human being in the entire universe already knew.

Matti could barely restrain herself from giggling happily at what she heard next. Her lips wrinkled into a crooked smile as she silently slinked away with a bounce in her step.

Bestiary

● ● ● ● ● ● ● ● ● ● ● ● ● ● ●

TopSide:
Keeper Ship

Dr. Eva Sanches Becker, D.V.M. didn't quite waddle down the tall, broad, gently sloping helical corridor that led to the newly opened section of the massive Keeper Ship, led by a young marine guard. After its capture, David Garreth's Delta Squad had searched every room and space that would open. During the long journey back from Earth, David's men constantly patrolled the alien vessel. With never less than two men in a patrol, fewer and fewer volunteered to venture into the deepest bowels of the ship. Massing several times as much as the largest aircraft carrier humanity ever managed to build, it was both labyrinthine and gilded. Specialists Bennie Davis and Troy Allen, in particular, had complained that in the deepest recesses, that it… sang to them.

At five months pregnant, this time with *triplets*, Eva rubbed the small of her back as she descended toward her husband. Before Awakening Day, their relationship had been notoriously antagonistic. Dr. Jacob Becker, Ph.D., studied genetically modified crops… something Eva vociferously protested and lobbied against. She and other activists had frequently and publicly verbally sparred with Jacob. Behind the scenes, however, that passion had manifested into a rather torrid, and so they'd thought, completely secret love affair. After the Apocalypse, Eva and Jacob gave up on the deception and openly embraced their love for each other. That few of their friends had been truly surprised was shocking to them and… affirming. Last year, amid the tidal wave of births in Fort Brazos and New London, Eva and Jacob had twin boys, Maximo and Nicolás. This time, evidently, it would be triplet girls.

After the incident with Mei Zifeng, the university labs were quarantined and underwent extensive decontamination efforts. Anyone in contact with the Keeper Ship or its samples was thoroughly examined and tested, and the Keeper Ship itself was locked down. Further interviews with Ubu confirmed that neither pollen nor physical contact with the mind-altering plants would have any effect. Unless you actually ate the fruits, plants, or vegetables. He'd been surprised by the concern. After all, the Accipiters were very experienced. They carefully designed the plants to minimize any risk of cross-contamination. It simply wouldn't do for escaped pollen to cause people other than those the fruit was intended for to be affected. Indeed, only fruit grown in the garden itself, within its complex engineered ecosystem, would carry the knowledge. Outside the garden, even seeds from the fruit would not reproduce the effects.

The military put the Garden under continuous armed guard. Until new procedures could be worked out, only food for the Keeper's 'harem' was allowed out, and that was only transported in an armored bank delivery truck brought up from Fort Brazos with a heavily armed escort.

Eventually, the Keeper Ship was opened back up. With active support from Ubu, the researchers crawled all over it. He helped them open the sealed compartments. There, the discoveries found would have made any paleontologist, botanist, or, frankly, anyone with the slightest curiosity about Earth's flora and fauna, past or present, weep in joyous discovery. For over a million years, the Keeper had sampled and collected what amounted to a complete, uninterrupted record of Earth's biological diversity in all its forms. What he hadn't kept physical exemplars of, he'd cataloged countless pristine DNA samples accompanied by both visual and parametric data. Virtually every species, living or extinct, that existed during his epoch-spanning over-watch of the planet.

Moreover, the Accipiters, being the masters of DNA manipulation that they were, employed algorithms that mapped DNA timelines and inter-relationships. It wasn't simply genome mapping. It was a planet-wide dynamic DNA model that gave vision even to evolutionary paths long extinct. While the degree of uncertainty gradually increased the further back in time it was projected, it was shocking how close it was to the pre-Awakening Day fossil record.

Eva followed the Marine Corporal Kris Sørensen, who had been a member of Bravo Squad during the Keeper Ship raid and had been among the prize crew. Kris knew all the twists and turns leading to their destination. The corridors all had the same satin-finished golden hue. Like the ship's exterior, rows upon rows of Accipiter glyphs danced along the walls. As the glyphs changed, so did the faint humming song that accompanied them. If you stopped and listened for too long, it was easy to become mesmerized. Eva was convinced she'd be lost for days otherwise.

Tall, dark-haired, and blue-eyed, Kris had an amiable disposition. He asked over his shoulder, "So, how are Maximo and Nicolás? Penney is dying to meet them."

Eva grinned crookedly, "So how is the new wife, Corporal? She's one of the New London girls, isn't she?"

Kris chuckled. "Yes, she's pregnant. Of course. Who isn't these days? She's fine. We got an apartment in New London together."

"Good for you two. When is she due?"

"May 1st. Twins."

Eva smiled, "I see, that's wonderful. If she wants twin advice, just ask, and, well, there are certainly tons of them around now. They'll have lots of children to play with. I'm sure that Maximo and Nicolás would love to play with them too when they're old enough."

Kris smiled, "Thank you, Doctor Sanches. We'll look forward to it." They turned yet another corner, and Kris announced, "And… here we are!" He bowed and flourished an arm, pointing at Jacob.

Jacob turned, smiled, and opened his arms as Eva rushed into his embrace. At six foot one inches tall, he towered a full thirteen inches taller than Eva. He bent his knees and hefted her up.

Eva squeaked a half-hearted complaining noise as she hugged him back.

Warmed at the sight of the happy couple, Kris retreated back around the corner, away from the alcove, to stand guard.

Jacob gently set Eva back on the floor and kissed her hair. "Welcome to the Bestiary."

Eva punched him in the arm. "Oh, so my mad scientist thinks he gets to name it too?"

"Can you think of a more appropriate name?"

Eva stood back and took in the sight in front of her. The alcove was the Accipiter equivalent of a workstation. It was large, with a vaulted ceiling, membranous displays, and control surfaces spanning a more than twenty-foot arc. But then, Accipiters are enormous beasts themselves. Jacob had managed to access records on several now-extinct creatures she recognized. She gasped aloud and pointed at one of the three-dimensional images. "That's got to be a Dire Wolf! They've been extinct for, what, ten thousand years?"

Jacob nodded and pointed at the others. "Wooly Rhinoceros, or some variant, and there are several I found already. Extinct at least twelve thousand years. That one is some variation of giant sloth, and that's…."

Eva exclaimed gleefully, "Glyptodon! It was one of my favorites when I was growing up!"

Jacob laughed, "Yeah, if you like giant armadillos. And let me show you this…."

✪ ✪ ✪

Hours, and several snacks for Eva, later, they slowly followed Kris as he led them out of the maze-like interior of the Keeper ship.

Jacob looked at her worried expression and asked, "What's bothering you, Eva? You were like a kid in a candy store back there, and now you've got that look."

"What look."

"The look you used to give me when you were finding some new way to complain to me that genmod crops were evil."

"Oh, that look."

Jacob rubbed her back gently as they walked.

Eva took a breath and started to say something. Stopped, kept walking for a while, and then burst out, saying, "My God, Jacob. It's no wonder the Accipiters thought of themselves as gods. The knowledge they had, combined with their technology, they could use a planet's biological history to … to recreate an organism long extinct, or worse, predictively model and, in effect, artificially evolve anything they could dream up! It's monstrous!"

Jacob nodded. "It may surprise you, but I agree. Michael Crichton famously speculated about bringing back dinosaurs from their blood found in mosquitoes preserved in amber. I won't bother talking about the reality of that idea, but here, in this place, we have not only pristine DNA but tens of thousands of actual, completely intact, viable… extinct yet living specimens in stasis. Breeding pairs, even. Do we have the right to play god like the Accipiters and bring some or any of them back?"

Eva sighed, "And then there are the people."

Jacob shook his head, "Yeah, and then there are all those people. And some of them were captured fairly recently. We might have a chance to bring some of them back and not have them completely…."

"Lose it? Freak out? Suicide, even?" Eva stopped walking and grabbed Jacob's arm. "Jacob, what is locked up in this place is what the Accipiters intended as the true fate of humanity. A frozen zoo, while the surviving remnants were turned into Accipiter worshiping farm animals! We can't let this happen. We have to find a way. We can't let their fate be what the Accipiters intended. Their souls have to be crying out for justice!"

Jacob looked down into her black eyes, the eyes that had captivated him for years during their debates. "Eva, what right do we have to awaken them to a living nightmare?" He lowered his voice… "to *our* living nightmare. Our world stolen and forever lost to us?"

Tears began to stream down her face as she shook her head. "What right do we have to leave them imprisoned? Their souls forever trapped in an Accipiter purgatory?"

Dead and Buried

● ● ● ● ● ● ● ● ● ● ● ● ● ● ● ● ● ●

Methodist Hospital
DownSide: Fort Brazos
Security Holding Room

Sybil Blanchard and Gwyneth Elliott Duncan slowly passed through the outer security door and military checkpoint before entering the secure wing of Methodist Hospital. Gwyneth was eight months pregnant, with twins this time, and Sybil was nine months along with another set of triplets. Boys, this time. The secure hospital wing had mainly been used for the relatively small number of mental patients as well as for those in police custody. After Awakening Day, the hospital had found itself mostly empty, treating only the occasional injury. All diseases had been cured by the Gardeners, or those with them hadn't woken up as part of the 5% who were culled. The secure wing had not been occupied at all until last May when Commander Thomas Harding detonated a bomb in City Hall. He'd been pronounced dead shortly after Vice President Gail Finley had famously shot him four times center-mass with her pistol.

Officially, the secure wing held only one patient. Mei Zifeng's case was widely known, and she was still slowly detoxing from the Keeper Ship Bing Cao.

Unofficially and utterly unknown outside a fiercely guarded literal handful of people was former Commander Thomas Harding. After his recovery, he'd been moved to one of the rooms previously reserved for suicide watch.

Rubbing the small of her back as she walked, Sybil shook her head as they walked down the silent hallway, "Look, Gwen, I still don't understand why I'm here and what this is all about? And why did they take my gun and not yours? There is nothing I can do to help Miss Zifeng. It... doesn't work that way, and you know it!"

Gwyneth winced slightly at a pain of her own and nodded understandingly. "It's all right, Sybil. You'll see in a moment. We're not here for Mei."

They approached another doorway with a sign labeled "Maintenance."

Gwyneth commented, "We had to add this door later for... reasons." She pressed her RFID badge against a blank spot on the wall next to the door. There was an audible click as the door unlocked. They entered the room to face a wall of shelves loaded with boxes of toilet paper and cleaning supplies. Gwyneth pressed her badge against the inside wall, and a floor-to-ceiling panel opened, revealing a short hallway beyond it and two armed marine guards. "Hello, Dwayne. Charlie. Any trouble today?"

Both men were roughly the same build at approximately six foot tall, lean, and clean-shaven. Dwayne, the darker-haired of the pair, answered, "No, ma'am. Quiet as usual. Mr. Kupe is already in there with the prisoner."

Sybil stopped and said, "Prisoner? Look, Gwen, just tell me what is going on? What is all this?"

Gwyneth turned and looked at Sybil. "I want you to prepare yourself. This is probably the biggest secret we have right now. You'll understand why in a moment."

Charlie reached for the door handle, opened the door, and swung it open to reveal an observation room. Inside was a man Sybil didn't immediately recognize, though, as she got closer, she sensed and remembered him from the Void.

"You're... the FBI agent. Brian... Brian Kupe."

Brian was straight out of central casting as an everyman. Average in every way, of medium height and build, with medium brownish black hair and soft brown eyes. He had light olive skin and might have been thought to be Latin American, Middle Eastern, or Mediterranean, depending on what he wore.

He raised an eyebrow questioningly at Gwyneth.

Gwyneth ignored the question and instead introduced Sybil. "Mr. Kupe, this is my friend Sybil Blanchard. She was here for her checkup, and I decided to finally let her in on the secret."

Sybil stiffened as she felt Brian's apprehension, although nothing betrayed that on his face.

Brian nodded. "Well, if anyone deserves to know, she does. Mrs. Blanchard saved a lot of lives that day."

Sybil frowned. "If somebody doesn't tell me what is going on, I'm going to…. I don't know… but you won't like it!"

Brian turned and opened the curtain covering a two-way mirror, revealing the occupant of the room beyond.

It was a man who seemed to be in his forties who sat on a padded bench, slowly rocking himself. His rather full beard and shaggy, shoulder-length hair made him harder to identify. He wore pastel green hospital scrubs and was barefoot. The room had padded walls and floors, with only the bench to sit or sleep on and a prison-style combination sink/toilet in a corner.

Brian sighed. "He attempted suicide twice. We had to make some changes to his room to protect him from himself."

Gwyneth pointed a finger at the man. "That man is…."

Sybil's eyes widened, and her mouth dropped open as she lurched towards the window, shaking her head incredulously, "Dammit, Gwyneth, I *know* who the hell that *monster* is! Why is he not dead? He killed and maimed how many people that day! I tried to stop him! Gail shot him dead! I was there! He's supposed to be dead and buried in an unmarked grave!" She began shaking and looked desperately around the room. "Give me back my gun, and I'll finish the job myself!"

✪ ✪ ✪

Hospital Director's Conference Room
Methodist Hospital

A short time later, Sybil, Gwyneth, and Brian 'borrowed' David Duncan's conference room. David had delighted the staff by taking them all out to lunch. So, besides Gwyneth's security detail outside the door, the entire floor was empty. The three of them took seats at the end of the room's long conference table.

Sybil was still furious as Gwyneth began, "Sybil, when they brought that piece of trash into the operating room, nobody expected him to live. If he'd been shot before Awakening Day and before the Gardener 'upgrades' to our health, I believe he would have simply died at the scene. Instead, he hung on. Vice President Finley, at Mr. Kupe's urging, decided to keep the bastard alive. Mr. Kupe, care to explain?"

Sybil swiveled a hostile gaze at Brian.

"Mrs. Blanchard, once again, I must praise you for your actions that day. A great many people owe you their lives. As for the bastard in the isolation room, he's alive for one reason. He didn't act alone."

Sybil stared at him for a long moment before she stopped herself from saying that she already knew Harding hadn't acted alone. She waited.

Gwyneth slowly nodded. "There is a reason why we've left you out of this. As long as nobody knows what really happened that day, nobody will come looking for you. Mr. Kupe had hoped that by interrogating the asshole downstairs that he'd find out who the conspirators were. Unfortunately, he has hit a dead end in his investigation."

Brian added, "You see, Mr. Harding was not just a bomber. He was a traitor even before Awakening Day. He sold Navy secrets to our enemies. I was very close to arresting him. Then, on Awakening Day, I… apprehended him and handed him over to be prosecuted. Somehow, and we don't know how, the conspirators must have found out. They subsequently managed to rehabilitate his reputation and blackmail him into doing what they wanted. All he seems to know is that whoever they were, they were highly placed in the Navy."

Silence hung over the room for a full two minutes.

Sybil took a deep breath. "I will repeat my question. Why is that monster still alive? If you found out all you could, he should be shot and dumped into a shallow grave. Or landfill… or even better, fed to the captive Wardog."

Brian smiled thinly. "Because, Mrs. Blanchard, we can use him against them once we identify the conspirators. After all, they think he is safely dead and buried. They cannot be absolutely certain of how much he knows. We may need him to force the truth out of them. After that, we can either keep him locked up forever, shoot him, or drop him on the island with the North Koreans. Either way, for as long as he lives, and with the Gardener changes that could be a very long time, he can never be set free in Fort Brazos or New London. I must say, with all due respect to the Surgeon General, that I understand the emotional need to share Mr. Harding's survival with you, but I fail to understand its practical utility. Honestly, were I you, I'd prefer to still think the man was indeed dead and buried. I expect, however, that this must have something to do with the Surgeon General's implied meaning behind 'what really happened' not simply referring to the fact that Mr. Harding survived." He looked at Gwyneth and sat back in his chair, steepling his hands on his chest.

Gwyneth turned to Sybil. "It's up to you, Sybil. I will only break confidence with your permission."

Sybil swallowed hard and looked back and forth between Gwyneth and Brian. She hesitated a long time before asking, "You think I can… I would be able to… what? I doubt I could elucidate any more out of that monster than Mr. Kupe, who I already remember is quite competent and disciplined, could do. I just don't know if I can do it again. I still have nightmares about… that day."

Brian blinked in surprise but stayed silent.

Gwyneth sighed. "Mr. Kupe, Mrs. Blanchard already knew there were more people involved than just Commander Harding. After Awakening Day, we eventually discovered many things about what the Gardeners did to us. Most of those discoveries have been made public. So far as we can tell, everyone was altered in more or less the same way."

Brian nodded. "I'm aware, yes."

"What you don't know is that there was a single exception, at least that we know about. Between the time that we were all snatched from Earth, and the time we woke up here, more than sixty years later, it seems that our… souls… were…."

Sybil sat back in her chair and, in a monotone voice, cut her off, "Our souls, our essence was kept in what I call the Void. The Gardeners didn't really snatch our bodies. They scanned them. Our bodies here are recreations. Copies. Xeroxes. Those who awoke on Awakening Day were… united, or joined, as it were, with their recreated bodies…. The Gardeners didn't lie when they said that we are who we were before Awakening Day. They kept us all in the void, frozen in a way."

Gwyneth said softly, "Except for Sybil."

Sybil swallowed. "Yes, except for me. While everyone else remained frozen in their last moments, I was adrift. I… passed through you. And Gwyneth… and everyone. I know you, Brian. I know the pain you endured being raised by an absent single mother. At first, she left you to your own devices as she… sold herself. And… and oh, God, I'm so sorry to say this… later, your mother's drug addiction became so bad that she sometimes did not just sell herself… but that she sometimes sold *you, too*."

As she spoke about his mother and what she had done to Brian, his practiced bland façade broke. Without conscious thought, he stood and backed away from Sybil. He angrily pointed a finger at her and retorted, "What the hell is going on here? Who… What? How can you know these things? Nobody knows that! No one could!"

Tears began to stream down Sybil's face. "I'm so, so sorry, Brian. I know that as you emancipated yourself and built your own life, how you longed for structure in a life without any. How you pursued a career in law enforcement and were recruited by the FBI early on. How you… almost lost yourself during your previous undercover assignment. I know you. Just as I knew Harding. When I saw him… that day… I sensed something was wrong. I thought… I thought he was running from his demons from before Awakening Day, but then I realized it was something worse, that he'd done something terrible…. I called out to him. Tried to stop him."

Sybil stopped talking and glanced at Gwyneth, who nodded. They waited for Brian to calm down.

His eyes widened, and he turned to Gwyneth and studied her patient and understanding face. He took another step away from them and awkwardly backed into the whiteboard-covered wall. Confused and breathing hard, he turned and looked at Sybil. He swallowed and, regaining control of himself, he repeated, "How can you know these things? Is this somehow from the Gardeners?"

Sybil glanced at Gwyneth and back at Brian again. "No, Brian, not really. I suppose they made it possible, but I know these things in the same way that I know… things… about every other Awakening Day survivor. I'm very sorry for the pain that bringing back these memories has brought you… and for the violation of your privacy. I suppose I could have chosen a different incident from your past, but this was one I was certain you had never shared with anyone. It is something that you keep locked away. A box that sits there in the corner of your mind, never to be opened, but always there to remind you."

Brian shook his head doubtfully. "What are you saying, then? That, what, you're, what, some kind of telepath? This is… This…."

Gwyneth shook her head.

Sybil flinched and pressed her hand against her very distended belly, swallowed, and answered, "No, Mr. Kupe. I simply *know* everyone… from the Void. I know their lives, their fears, and their hopes. I cannot read minds, but I sense…."

Gwyneth finished for her. "She's empathic. She senses feelings and…."

"…and I remember people I sense."

Gwyneth continued, "Many months ago, before the bombing, while we were all busy helping the New Londoners TopSide, Sybil had an … episode. An encounter with someone."

Sybil shivered. "It was terrible. *He* was terrible. His mind was cold, dark, and malevolent, and he was involved, or I don't know how to say it. I knew he was planning something terrible."

Brian blinked and suddenly inhaled sharply. "Let me guess. He was a Naval officer…. And he wasn't Harding."

Sybil nodded vigorously. "But I didn't see his face, and the encounter was so… strong… and there were so many people there that day that I was overwhelmed. I blacked out before I could sense his name or more about him."

"And you think he might be one of the conspirators?"

Gwyneth reached out and put her hand on Sybil's shoulder. "I had hoped your investigation would solve this, but now... now it's the only thing I can think of. We *must* find out who was behind this and... and put an end to them."

Brian sat quietly, thinking for a few minutes. "Whoever the conspirators are, there is probably a leader. And the leader may be manipulating other people as well. People may have aided without being aware that they were doing so, or he may be blackmailing, misinforming, or misleading people as he did with Mr. Harding. That said, how does Mrs. Blanchard's... gift... help us? Please do not think I am being crass. I'm not, but what do you want to do? Have all the officers do a lineup and let her walk past them, picking out people who... well... have bad thoughts? Everyone would ask what and why, possibly leaving Mrs. Blanchard open for retaliation and, at the very least, animosity and suspicion."

Gwyneth smiled sadly. "No, nothing so pedestrian. I was thinking that we should find a way to inject Sybil into Navy affairs so that she would be expected to attend many high-level meetings with a wide variety of Navy officers. All the while, we'd monitor her and ensure that she always had her protection detail day and night. That would require an executive-level appointment. However, given that she is already quite key to all military logistics, it shouldn't be too hard to find an appropriate position. Both the President and Vice President know about her gifts, as you put it, and they can make the appointment, which should seem perfectly legitimate to everyone."

Sybil balked. "You want to saddle me with a damned security detail?"

"Yes, I absolutely do." She leaned over and hugged her. "I do not intend to allow any harm to come to one of my best friends."

Brian thought aloud, "They already appointed a War Logistics Director, that German Armored Battalion Commander, Colonel... Colonel Fromm. I'd suggest that a Deputy Director position should work well. Given how short-staffed our executive and command structure already is, I imagine that people won't be surprised to see a Deputy Director attend lots of meetings, especially since Sybil probably knows more about actual logistics than Fromm ever would. At this point, there's also no need for Fromm to know the real story. Besides, I think the appointment would make sense simply on Mrs. Blanchard's own merits. Frankly, it's a no-brainer."

Gwyneth nodded. "What's more, if we do need to read him in, I think he'll play ball nicely. Earlier in his career in the Bundeswehr, he was Assistant Branch Chief in German military intelligence."

Brian smiled thinly. "And I suppose that had nothing to do with the Colonel's appointment to this position in the first place?"

Gwyneth smiled beatifically.

Sybil shook her head slowly, "I haven't said yes."

"It's OK, Sybil. Vice President Finley signed your appointment yesterday. She can't wait to congratulate you."

✪ ✪ ✪

After Brian left the room, Sybil and Gwyneth sat in companionable silence.

Gwyneth finally broke the mood, asking, "Are you sure you're OK with this? Also, you won't be expected to do anything until everything has settled down with the new babies. Have you and Wayne decided on their names yet?

"Dillan, Ethan, and Fallon."

Gwyneth smiled and chuckled. "Still going in alphabetical order, I see."

Sybil smiled wanly, "It seemed… logical. And… yes. It must be done. I can't stop thinking about it. Who knows what the conspirator or conspirators might do next? I will do it, but only under one condition." She looked at Gwyneth imploringly.

Gwyneth reached out and took both of Sybil's hands as her eyes misted, "On my life, Sybil, on my life," she looked down at her own swollen belly, "On Rosalyn and my children's lives. I promise you. Wayne and your babies will never, ever want for anything."

Sybil closed her eyes and shuddered. "Oh no!"

"Sybil, you know me. You know we will protect you and your family, I …."

"It's not that! My water just broke, and I'm sure I just ruined this chair!"

The Abyss

● ● ● ● ● ● ● ● ● ● ● ● ● ● ● ● ●

DownSide:
Eugene Morton Naval Academy
Academic Dean's Conference Room

Dr. Takumi Nakamura remained standing as the meeting attendees sat down. Clockwise, to his right, was President John Austin, Rear Admiral Gordon Montoya, Mayor Tom Parker, Commandant of Midshipmen Harrold Anders, and Secretary of War Alexander Marcus. Angela Willis had just left the room after ensuring everyone had their choice of coffee, tea, or another beverage.

Takumi straightened his suit jacket and smiled. Mizuki had picked out his suit and tie that morning and fussed over him until he had left for campus. She liked his suits to fit a bit more snugly than he did.

He began, "Today is an important day in the history of not only this University, now Academy as an institution, but more importantly, in the lives of our students and faculty, and in a broader sense, how we shall choose to comport ourselves in the prosecution of our war with the Accipiters. Until now, there have been countless meetings and discussions about which existing academic courses to prioritize, what new ones we should create, and even which ones to drop completely. Paramount, in my mind, and in the President's mind, is the need to firmly establish an inviolable core of ethics in our students and cadets."

He turned to Alexander. "The Secretary of War told me that Military Ethics, rather like medical ethics, are essential for every service member to learn, develop, and enhance throughout their career. He said that the main purpose of ethics was to empower individuals with the capacity to morally distinguish right from wrong when laws are no longer helpful or perhaps relevant. The idea is not to turn a simple soldier into a philosopher or lawyer or to make them feel like they need to try to call one on the phone to make a wartime decision. Instead, we need a solid foundation of ethics. It needs to be like muscle memory to our service members. When they find themselves deep within the crucible of war, they need to be prepared with the rhetorical questioning skills that will help them make sound, appropriate, and informed decisions."

"How we fight is as important as why we fight. There is no question that the Accipiters committed unthinkable genocide and enslavement of our planet. Everyone in this room, and I'm sure 99% of the survivors here in Fort Brazos and New London, lost friends and loved ones. President Austin has often spoken about the loss of our entire history and countless cultures. If these and other reasons were not motivation enough to strike back, the Gardeners made it quite clear, at the cost of thousands of survivors' lives, that if we didn't fight the Accipiters, they would end us all and find someone else to fight their battle."

"I, myself, am a man of science. I am, or I suppose I was, an astronomer. The very idea of war was repugnant and incomprehensible to me, and, yes, in my younger years, I did my share of protesting — something for which I have no regrets." He paused and smiled, "It was, after all, where I met the love of my life and the mother of my children, Mizuki."

Everyone in the room either smiled or chuckled.

Takumi's own smile faded. He looked down for a moment, then raised his head again and looked at the faces around the table. "And then, the Accipiters raped and pillaged our entire world. Our anger, pain, anguish, and not a few suicides are testament to our collective, righteous, and incandescent fury."

Grunted agreement, nods, and tightened lips answered from around the table.

"And that, Sirs, is the root of what, if we are not careful, could become our own evil."

He paused, took a breath, and turned to John. "Mr. President, I understand you would like to share a few words?"

John stood and looked around the room while Takumi took his seat. He began, "It's no secret how I feel about this war. You've heard my official speeches and, God knows," he nodded at Alexander, "Secretary of War Marcus has suffered while I've bent his ear often enough."

Alexander smiled and nodded.

"While everyone else has been busy solving problems, building things, fixing things, making starships work, and so on, I've had time to think more about the long-term costs of this war. Putting aside how we'll possibly fight the war in the first place, let's talk about what it means to the people here. How long will our people put up with it before the memory of what the Gardeners did in the culling fades, and they begin to resent and resist the war effort? How long after that will the Gardeners put up with it? Other than the occasional Wardog and Stalker attacks, which are becoming less and less frequent, most people now have fairly comfortable lives. The war is something that will be fought very far away. It will become more and more abstract — at least until we build more ships that don't come home. And more sons, fathers, mothers, daughters… good men and women don't come home, even to be buried."

"So, how do we keep people motivated? How do we transform a civil society into something different that doesn't lead down the path of an utterly Marshall society? How do we keep our people involved without creating New Sparta, where children are literally bred for war? Frankly, if we're not careful, in time, we could end up being worse than the Accipiters themselves and turn out what amounts to a bunch of Space Nazis."

"Let's say that somehow, we do win this war. To do so, in order to crush the Accipiters, we'd need to wreak a path of death and destruction across the galaxy. I ask you, though, how do we do that and not end up worse than the Accipiters themselves? The Accipiters think of themselves as being some sort of Gods. They actually think they're doing the Galaxy a favor by stomping on civilizations and enslaving them to worship them. If somehow, we either destroy them or at least get enough of them to realize that what they've been doing for a million years is evil, then, sooner or later, probably later, we'll have to deal with them directly. Negotiate. If we've been killing each other for decades or, more likely, centuries, allowing the hate to grow and grow, how will we ever have the capacity to bring peace?"

"In 1961, President Eisenhower warned that the increasingly powerful interests of the military-industrial-complex might one day control the direction of United States policy. I ask you this. We will have to build a fleet of ships big enough to blot out the stars and the crews to man them. The military-industrial complex needed to do that will make what Eisenhower was afraid of seem like a collection of 18th-century Pacific Island canoe builders. Such an *interstellar* military-industrial complex would be mind-bogglingly vast, and the people who run it more powerful than any pre-Awakening Day nation-state, or all of them put together. We must remember that bureaucracies are like living organisms. They feed, grow, and reproduce. And they defend themselves. Such entities will have no incentive other than to continue the war, whether it truly needs to continue or not. The power they will wield is staggeringly immense, and we must not let these powers get out of control, for as we all know, absolute power corrupts absolutely, and there is virtually no limit to the power they will have."

He paused for a moment, then continued, "So, just exactly, how many of our values can we afford to sacrifice in the name of the galactic war? A war that, quite possibly or even probably, might *never* end? We will be fighting an asymmetrical war for the foreseeable future. What will we consider to be justified? Killing innocent civilians, assuming we even have a way to determine who that might be? Torture of captured enemies? Worse? Perhaps things we don't even have words for yet? Think of it. Our children's children may judge our sins with words we do not yet have."

"How do we keep our soldiers, sailors, and marines calm, rational, and professional in this war? As a dear friend recently reminded me, whoever fights monsters should strive to ensure that he does not become a monster in the process. And if you gaze long enough into the abyss, the abyss will gaze back into you."

Year 3 PAD:

March

Flash

● ● ● ● ● ● ● ● ● ● ● ● ● ● ● ● ●

DownSide:
Jamestown Settlement

In the eleven months of its embryonic existence, Jonestown hadn't exactly boomed, but it had grown. Between the scientists from the university and military personnel coming and going, on any given day, there were at least fifty or sixty people "in town." The tents and prefab buildings gave the tiny community the feel of a remote mining camp rather than an actual "town."

With the arrival of Julie and Chloe, Darnell and Gary had thrown a small party around a campfire for Ray's family to celebrate. The party quickly grew. Everyone who could join in, who wasn't on guard duty or in the field, did. Gary provided the booze, which he'd somehow bartered to have brought in on the same flight with the girls.

After losing count of the number of beers he'd had, or rather, not bothering to count them in the first place, Gary had hit on the idea of building homes out of the overly abundant supply of wood from the forested valley.

"We need real houses, like, log cabins," he'd loudly declared!

This sparked a spirited debate on how and what kind should be built, which led to the idea of building in the style of an Amish barn raising, with everyone in the community helping. That way, in short order, they could construct houses for everyone. Plans and videos on how to build them wouldn't be complex. The Gardeners had provided a copy of the entire pre–Awakening-Day internet. Building the structures themselves turned out to be far easier than getting even basic wiring and furniture, which had been in short supply in Fort Brazos ever since the arrival of the New Londoners. Gary and a few others had returned to Fort

Brazos and managed to scavenge much of what was needed from the two already picked-over scrapyards outside of town. The rest was either bartered for or otherwise acquired by means not spoken of.

When they'd first arrived, ex-wife Julie and daughter Chloe had stayed in Ray's tiny prefab house while he moved into the back room of his store. A month later, they all moved into the first finished log cabin, which included two bedrooms.

✪ ✪ ✪

'Mayor,' Darnell Lewis had mandated that every teenager or adult visiting or living in Jonestown must be trained in firearms safety, handling, and marksmanship — and to be armed once they pass a proficiency test. Since their arrival, Ray started teaching Chloe and Julie how to shoot.

Chloe started to accompany him when he ventured into the woods, learning how to move and communicate quietly. It surprised Ray how quickly she adapted, even more so at how soon she'd built up enough stamina to keep up with him, more or less. With the turbulence of a seven-year-old's million questions, the last part was hardest for her. He wondered how much of it had to do with Chloe being Chloe and how much it had to do with how the Gardeners had provided improved health and vitality for all the New Texas survivors.

This particular morning, Chloe was already up and dressed as she tugged on her still-sleeping mom's arm. "Come on, Mom, you promised you'd go with us today."

Julie turned her face into her pillow and mumbled, "Go away. Tired."

Since arriving in Jonestown, Chloe had attached herself to her dad's activities, helping in the store and accompanying him on his hunting hikes into the woods. Meanwhile, Julie had found herself pulled into myriad activities with the other women in town, helping get homes organized and a thousand other things that she, as a former "big city" dweller, had little or no knowledge of. Many of the people who had moved to Jonestown had lived on the very outskirts of Fort Brazos. To those people, even the pre-Awakening-Day Fort Brazos had been an uncomfortably large city. Many had been either closeted "preppers" or full bore. Julie ached in places she didn't know she had.

"Mommmm, come on! Get up. You promised! We're gonna go see the metal cave today!"

"Go away."

Chloe heaved a sigh. "Look, mom, you can go with us, or you can go make soap today, and you know how much you luuuvvv to make soap."

Julie groaned, "Traitor."

✪ ✪ ✪

By now, the trail from Jonestown to the metal cave where Darnell discovered the zero-point energy device was well-marked. It was still a long hike, but easier than most. After months of poking and prodding with nothing new to be found besides an empty metal room, it was now just a curiosity. The university folks and military had better things to do. Darnell had talked about making a replica of the device to make it a tourist attraction, complete with a gift shop. However, there was so much to do in town that the idea never gained traction. Yet. He worried that people would stop coming to Jonestown without some compelling reason, especially if the 'prospectors' didn't find anything else of value in the area.

Several hours later, the trio stopped along the trail for a quick lunch and water break. They finished more quickly than Julie liked and began to pack the trash. Another Darnell law used the Boy Scout 'leave it better than you found it' standard and said that anyone who littered the trails and forest would be fined, kicked out of town, or both.

Julie yelped in pain and fell to the ground.

Ray dumped his backpack and rushed to her side. "What's wrong!?"

Chloe replicated her dad's actions, quickly shedding her own backpack and running to kneel next to her mother, saying, "Mom?"

Julie winced and struggled with her much thinner backpack, trying to sit upright while at the same time grabbing her calf. Her face reddened, and tears streaked down her cheeks as she said through clenched teeth, "muscle cramp!"

Ray gently moved Julie's hand away and began massaging Julie's calf. "Give your mother a salt pill, Chloe."

Chloe had already returned to her own backpack to retrieve her first aid kit.

Ray smiled softly. "It'll be OK."

Julie's lips trembled, and she closed her eyes.

Chloe returned with a salt pill and opened her canteen. "Mom, here, take this."

Julie held herself upright with one arm and clutched her knee with the other. She sniffed, opened her eyes, and looked up at her daughter.

"Here, open your mouth, mom."

Julie nodded and opened her mouth. Chloe put the pill in and put the canteen to her mom's mouth to wash it down.

Julie swallowed and nodded. Then she shook her head and blurted out, "I can't do this!"

Chloe hugged her. "It's OK, mom, we'll go back."

Julie's chest heaved, and she shook her head faster. "No! No… I can't do *this!* All of this. Jonestown, the woods, all this Little House on the Prairie stuff! I can't do it! I could barely stand Fort Brazos! I'm from a proper city! Houston! I'm not cut out for all this… for… soap."

Ray kept massaging her calf as he asked, "So, why did you come back? Why did you come here at all?"

Julie didn't answer and buried her chin in her chest, crying.

Chloe looked up at her dad. "She came here… back… for me. For us."

Julie blinked back the tears, sniffed, and looked up. "No. I made a mistake."

Ray stopped massaging her calf and sat back. "It's fine. It's OK. I'll arrange for you to go back."

"No! No… that's not. I mean, that's not what I… I made a mistake leaving you."

Chloe's eyes widened as her own tears started to form.

Ray looked away as he answered in a flat, dead voice. "Do you have any idea what it did to me? The way you abandoned me and took Chloe away? Julie…. You destroyed me."

Julie shot back, "You have no idea! I nearly lost my job after your stunt at the brewery! After that, people either laughed at Chloe and me or worse, pitied us. Do you have any idea what she went through at school? How they ridiculed her! We were the laughingstock of Fort Brazos. And there was no damned where to go! We couldn't even leave town! There was nowhere to go because it was the God Damned Apocalypse!"

Ray sighed, "I know. So, why did you come back?"

"Because… because I still love you. And Chloe needs her father."

Ray nodded, "And at least, here, maybe nobody would be laughing at you? Pitying you, especially now that your ex-husband has gone crazier still and helped found a town in the middle of nowhere out amongst the monsters?"

Chloe hugged her mother tightly.

Julie sniffed and rubbed the tears from her face. "That too."

Ray stood up. "I see. How's your leg?"

Julie nodded and tried to stand up but fell backward, weighed down by her half-attached backpack. Chloe helped her to her feet, got the pack on, and adjusted.

"I'll be OK. Let's just keep going."

✪ ✪ ✪

An hour later, they approached a fallen tree near the top of the small hill they were climbing. Ray told Chloe, who was a few feet in front of him, "Wait at the top of the hill, Chloe. From there, you should be able to see the entrance."

He turned to Julie and extended his hand. "Let me help you around this tree."

Chloe reached the top of the hill and looked down towards the cave. "Dad? Is this it? I don't see a cave, but I see a wall with a hand shape on it?"

Ray turned back to Chloe in surprise. "Wait, right there! Don't move!"

When he got to the top of the hill with Julie, he looked down and saw what Chloe had described. Exactly like what Darnell had said he saw when he'd discovered the place. A wall with a hand imprint but only the outline of a doorway. The doorway was closed.

Cloe asked excitedly, "What is it, dad? What does it mean?"

Ray swallowed. "I want you and your mother to wait right here. Can I depend on you if something happens to get her safely back home?"

"Dad!"

"I mean it!"

Julie added, "Do as your father says, Chloe."

Chloe sulked, "Okay...."

Ray leaned down and kissed Chloe on her head. He took Julie's hand for a moment, squeezing it. Then let go, turned around, and started down the hill towards the door.

Julie called out, "Ray...."

He turned back and looked at her.

She asked quietly, "Be careful?"

He nodded and turned back towards the wall, and finished carefully, making his way down the hill to it. Remembering what Darnell had said he'd done, Ray took off his backpack and, after a moment's hesitation, pressed his hand into the hand-shaped depression.

The door silently slid open, revealing a brightly lit metal room containing a simple round pedestal with a softly blue-glowing zero-point energy device resting on top. The device was a cube, about eight- or nine inches square, decorated with complex patterns on its surface.

Ray swallowed. Then he wedged his backpack into the wall where the door had recessed and stepped into the room. Nothing happened.

He walked to the pedestal. Two wires, one on each side, connected it to the pedestal. Exactly as Darnell had described. He started to reach for it but stopped himself. Instead, he fished his cell phone from a pocket. Of course, there was no service outside of Fort Brazos, and certainly none in Jonestown, but he could take pictures or record video with it. He always kept it charged and with him for that reason.

He turned the phone on, waited for it to boot, and took pictures of the device, the pedestal, and all around the featureless room. Then he put it on video mode and recorded a video of the device as he walked around it. When he was done, he turned the phone off, put it back in his pocket, and took a deep breath. Then he reached down and unplugged the device. The lights went out in the room, just like Darnell had described.

Ray remembered how heavy the other one had been, and this one turned out to be the same. He grunted as he hefted it off the pedestal and out the door, where he set it on the ground.

He looked up the hill at Julie and Chloe, who were shouting and jumping up and down. "OK, come on down. I need your help."

They made it back to town well after the suntube dimmed for the night. Darnell's log cabin wasn't finished yet. He was still living in his prefab house. Ray, Julie, and Chloe went straight there. Darnell had the radio with which to call Fort Brazos. While they had already set a bounty system in place, that was on paper. An alien power device actually in his hands was another. It was time to do some new negotiating.

Leaving Ray to talk to the government back in Fort Brazos with Darnell, Julie and Chloe walked back to the log cabin. Chloe looked up at the sky. The suntube was dim, but she could still see the outline of the other continents and weather systems on the other side of the world. Suddenly, there was a small flash of light, and Chloe exclaimed, "Hey, did you see that?"

Thunder

● ● ● ● ● ● ● ● ● ● ● ● ● ● ● ●

DownSide:
Radio Station 92.5 Studio

Danielle keyed the microphone, "Hello, people of Fort Brazos and New London. This is Danielle Richardson on FM 92.5 and Radio Free Fort Brazos, beaming our signal across the known world and beyond. Before we get into today's show, I wanted to ask if anybody else heard thunder last night? There were no clouds. Is the military testing weapons or something? Also, on the subject of weapons testing, there are reports of another fire twenty miles outside the city, only this time, several people told me they saw the flash from an explosion in that direction. I certainly hope that's what is going on. I mean, who cares if a field way out in the middle of nowhere gets blown up? Maybe they're testing some weapon they've made with that energy device the Reinhardt boys found down in Jonestown last year? Because, well, if it isn't us blowing things up, then who else? I mean, it's got to be us, right? Who else would drop bombs on fields out in the sticks, and why the hell would they be doing it? I just hope this is all a nothing-burger because, well, if it isn't… then I'd start to get worried. And nobody around here wants Danielle worried, do they? I mean, nobody wants to see that happen again. Right? So, if anybody has any real info to whisper in my ear to put me at ease, that'd be great."

"And back to the subject of the Reinhardt boys and Jonestown and alien artifacts. Well, guess what, folks? My sources tell me the boys have done it again! Must be something in the water down there. Apparently, they found another alien toy, and all the military, university, and government bigwigs are all atwitter over it. So, I guess it'll be a nice payday for Jonestown. Probably more folks will want to head down there, though I don't get it. It's scary enough just living in town, knowing that there are still creatures wandering around, but at least here we've got the army and lots of people and guns keeping an eye out for trouble. Down there? In the middle of nowhere with no cafes and having to hunt and shoot animals for your dinner? Ugh, no, thank you. Besides, do you have any idea what walking around out there would do to my vintage heels?"

"I know what you're thinking, and you can go right on thinking it. Some people were made for frontier living and roughing it like that, and, well, God Bless them, each and every one. Just stay downwind when you're in town! Seriously though, folks, I have a lot of respect for people who are brave enough to rough it like that. I only joke about it because I wouldn't last five minutes, and I know it."

"So, it's not like we have nothing going on these days, is it? Everyone seems to expect that the new constitution will start us out with a few Senators, I mean, given how small our voting-age population still is. So call me, and let's talk about whether you plan to move to Jonestown, or better yet, let's talk about the new constitution and who you think should run for office? And, no, don't you dare joke about me running. Not. Going. To. Happen. Thank God. Although I heard a fantastic idea that I should run for office after all, but that if I raised enough bribe money, I mean donations, I'd drop out. That'd be pretty sweet, huh?"

Danielle paused to sip some of her ice tea. She deliberately avoided thinking about the dwindling supplies of her favorite tea.

"Some people are talking about President Austin and how even though he's physically recovered from the bombing from that madman who shall not be named, that Austin has been absent from a lot of events that we expected him at. I mean, in the old days, like, a year ago, he'd be all over the bombs dropping out in the middle of nowhere thing. We hardly ever see him on screen anymore."

"So folks, take your pick! Mysterious fires, Jonestown, alien artifacts, the new constitution, President Austin's future, or my vintage heel collection? What's it going to be today?"

Dust

● ● ● ● ● ● ● ● ● ● ● ● ● ● ● ● ●

Approaching Sid'Carnea Nebula
NTN Blood Phoenix CIC

Captain Cross stared at the progression of images on the wallscreen. Along the way, every few light-years, Phoenix had momentarily stopped and imaged their destination. Inside the warp bubble, there was no sensation of movement at all, which was a good thing. Had even a tiny fraction of their acceleration translated inside the bubble, the crew would have become a smear on the bulkheads while the former submarine itself did a respectable imitation of a beer can being crushed by a hydraulic press — only a lot faster.

He shook his head. "Well, it didn't get any prettier the closer we got, did it? It's still mostly a dark smear across the stars."

The nebula was not identified or named in your astrographic catalogs. The Builders called it Sid'Carnea. It varies from roughly three to six light-years across and is relatively dense but very cold. My best estimate is that the nebula contains somewhere between eight to twelve brown dwarfs among a great many smaller bodies.

Haruto wondered aloud with a thoughtful look on his face, "If the nebula is, as you say, relatively dense, why have only brown dwarfs formed inside it? Why haven't main sequence stars formed?"

*The nebula appears to have formed relatively recently,
in the last few million years or so, from the confluence of gas
and dust pushed by two or more supernovae in the distant
past. I estimate that in a few million more years, several of
the brown dwarfs will combine and concentrate enough mass to
accelerate the star-forming process.*

Charles nodded, "So, what's the bad news? I assume we'll need to slow down.

*Yes, Captain. We need to proceed to a binary system
named Ari'Chawig. The primary is a Class L Brown
Dwarf, and the secondary is an even cooler Class T Methane
Dwarf. Traveling at our normal FTL would accumulate
mass too quickly and overload us. It would also leave a very
observable... trail. We will need to reduce our velocity to,
at most, two percent of our normal 2.4 light years per day.
I regret that it would take another twenty to thirty days,
depending upon whether we need to reduce velocity even further
to reach our destination.*

Chief of the Boat Maximillian McGreggor chuckled, "That's going to be so very popular with the crew."

Haruto raised his eyebrows. "Shall I inform them, Captain?"

Charles grimaced. "No, Haruto, that's my happy duty. COB, go down and talk to Quartermaster Marlowe and have him re-inventory our supplies, and then talk to CS Phillips and make sure we plan out our meals accordingly. It's a damned good thing we brought all the extra supplies down in the hangar. Oh, and have Williams post a guard down there. I know we secured it, but let's just make sure it stays that way. This is going to be a long cruise, and we don't know how long we'll need to stick around after we *do* get to Ari'Chawig."

Maximillian answered, "Yes, Captain. Joy and happiness will abound."

Charles smiled, "See to it, COB."

Charles crossed over to the station with the intercom microphone and picked it up. "Attention, crew. We have arrived at the outskirts of the nebula where our target destination is located. I'm afraid there's not much to see at this point. Unfortunately, the nebula contains lots of gas and dust. As many of you will recall, our warp drive system effectively recycles the energy from interstellar gas and dust that we collide with all the time. There is a point at which we cannot safely absorb that energy without it having to go somewhere. All of us lost friends and colleagues when this happened during the Keeper Raid. So, to be safe, we must slow our approach. A lot. It looks like it may add another month or so to our cruise before we reach our destination. This was not unexpected."

"As you know, we packed a lot of extra groceries for this trip. We'll be fine. I know that I can depend on each and every one of you to be patient and hang in there. I don't believe the Gardeners would send us on this trip if it were a wild goose chase. Whatever it is, it must in some way be in furtherance of their desire for us to fight the Accipiters. So, I'm authorizing COB to organize a betting pool. I'm placing mine on it being some kind of big space gun, but my bet doesn't count." He paused and looked around at the grinning faces around the CIC, "I'll start the pool with a hundred bucks. Winner, take all!"

Laughter and applause broke out in the CIC and throughout the ship.

"Now, everyone, get back to work. This isn't a Tiger Cruise."

PO David Blakeley, one of the two pilots, motioned to Charles, who walked over to their VR stations. David and PO Logan Kendal sat inside their protective metal framework, intended to keep other people from bumping into them while they virtually operated the controls. Their VR helmets were off. While in FTL, Phoenix manipulated the complex geometry of the warp field that resulted in movement relative to spacetime outside the ship. FTL required too many continuous field corrections for the human pilots to manage, as had been discovered during the first attempts to operate the drive — before Phoenix later revealed her existence. Humans *were* capable of satisfactory operation of the drive within sublight velocities; however, the pilots needed the VR helmets to provide an interface capable of providing a comprehensible way to simultaneously manage both the warp field geometry adjustments as well as minor things, like simply going in the desired direction.

Charles leaned on the metal tubing framework and nodded. "Yes, Mr. Blakeley?"

David glanced at the wallscreen. "Captain, I heard a rumor that we were going to start bringing some of the university professors along on future cruises as tech specialists, I guess. Going back to Earth is one thing. I mean, it's home. But this," he nodded towards the screen, "this is all new. Nebulas and brown dwarf failed stars, and who knows what. I'm just saying that while Phoenix is great and all, no offense, Phoenix…."

None taken, PO Blakely.

"…It just seems like we need, I mean, we could use more… experts… in the crew."

Charles smiled and patted David on the back. "What are you asking for, a *Science Officer*, Mr. Blakely?"

David stammered, "No… no Sir, I just…"

Charles chuckled, "It's OK, Mr. Blakeley, you're quite right, and I agree. Dr. Nakamura has been clamoring to go with us himself, but I think he knows that's never going to happen, certainly not on any cruise with any likelihood of combat. He and Command are working out the details of how it will work and whether the technical specialists would remain civilians or need some sort of commission, since this would be rather more than the occasional PACE college instructor onboard to continue the crew's education. These people might have direct involvement in command decisions based on their expertise. That's a lot of responsibility that, frankly, needs commensurate accountability."

David and the rest of the CIC crew smiled at that. Civilian contractors from their respective companies, i.e., "tech reps," were not uncommon aboard naval vessels, especially highly experienced technicians performing specialized maintenance or upgrades on complex equipment. Yardbirds, for example, were civilian shipyard workers. Many were ex-military, and most were no trouble at all. They were ordinarily welcome in the wardroom and the ready room and were usually good guys to have around.

There were well-worn stories of the odd few who caused problems and irritated entire crews, such as one who flat-out refused "scary" in-transit transfer, causing a whole battle group to stop in place, including the submarines accompanying the battle group. The entire group had to cease operations so that the tech could be transported by boat instead. Needless to say, that person incurred the incensed animus of the admiral in charge and became persona non grata in the Navy.

As for the PACE instructors, it motivated the Navy to give crews an incentive to further their education, even under deployment conditions.

Of course, not every ship deployed had them onboard, and it was only an occasional thing, even for those that did.

Regardless, civilians, irrespective of their purpose on board, required supervision. Should they be allowed into the CIC, they would be closely monitored so that they didn't, unintentionally or not, cause the ship to stray off course or endanger it in any way. Under current circumstances though, the Captain, and by extension, the lives of everyone onboard, might end up depending on the scientist's knowledge and expertise.

David asked, "Captain, why didn't Dr. Talib join us on this cruise? I was looking forward to learning from him. He has a… reputation."

Charles shook his head. "It didn't work out, and we were too rushed. As you know, we weren't supposed to go out for several more weeks. Hopefully, next time."

David nodded, "Yes, Captain, thank you."

On the Keeper Raid, Dr. Leo Talib had not only accompanied the mission and given language classes to the crew, but he'd also actually been part of the strike team that had captured the Keeper ship and crew. He'd trained for and gone on the mission with no small amount of trepidation. He'd even been armed. On the other hand, he'd also been the only person who really stood a chance of translating anything that needed translating.

Afterward, though, he'd been a changed man. Most people had assumed it was because of the combat aspect of the raid itself. Charles knew, though, that it had much more to do with what happened on the trip back to New Texas when the brave young men and women Leo had gotten to know and respect all died horribly from radiation poisoning. Many of them in his arms while he cared for them. Charles had tried to talk Leo into going on this mission, but the professor politely declined, pointing out that he was newly married and his wife was with child. From the expression on Leo's face, Charles knew, though, that the man wasn't ready. Might never be ready again, though Charles expected that to change in time. He saw in Leo not a man without courage but rather, one still grieving for so many.

You know, Captain, it would be simpler if you would
allow me to install the same kind of cybernetic enhancements
in your crew that I used to teach the Builders. While they
might not be, well, themselves anymore, it would undoubtedly
make teaching them complex concepts more straightforward
and faster.

David's eyes widened, and he stole a worried glance at his co-pilot Logan before turning back to Charles. He swallowed and asked, "Uh, Sir?"

Charles frowned deeply and traded looks with Haruto. Then they both burst out laughing. Charles managed to say, "That was good, Phoenix. Well done. You're coming along nicely."

<hr>

Thank you, Captain. It's important to me to build a rapport with the crew, though, sadly, the cybernetic implants would not be physically compatible with humans. Although, now that I think about it, they might work if implanted before birth…. That would be an excellent beginning to my plans for galactic domination. Just think of it… all you humans dancing on my ethereal strings….

<hr>

Charles groaned, but smiled nonetheless, "Very funny, Phoenix. I think that's probably enough for now."

<hr>

Very well, Captain. I'll put my plans on hold for now.

<hr>

David, Logan, navigator PO Harris Huddleston, PO Hiram Newman, and COB McGreggor laughed and joked amongst themselves.

Navigator Lt. Stephen Prichard remained somewhat worriedly silent. Charles walked over and slapped him on the shoulder, adding, "All right, people, let's make this happen!"

Counsel

● ● ● ● ● ● ● ● ● ● ● ● ● ● ● ●

DownSide:
Gloria Vargas's House

Councilwoman Gloria Vargas's house was historic. Literally. It had a Texas Historical Marker sign in front and was on the official 'tourist' map of Fort Brazos, such as it was, and what there was of it. Located near the University, the 112-year-old Victorian home had a steepled cedar shake roof and wraparound porches and was on one of the original settler's parcel of land. Amish craftspeople restored it in the 1980s. The built-in bookcases and cabinets were tastefully filled with southwest and Native American art. The original wood floors were polished and spotless.

It was just Gloria and Livia in the house. Like Livia, Gloria had refused a bodyguard, or "security detail," as they had described it. It wouldn't have helped her during the City Hall bombing; besides, that's what Dennis was for. At 130 pounds, her Rottweiler weighed more than she did.

Gloria greeted Livia Milner as she descended the steep stairs. "Livia, dear, how are you feeling today? I'll have some breakfast ready for us in a few minutes."

Livia didn't have to force a smile; she really did feel much better. Her long black hair was loose around her shoulders. She wore comfortable jeans and a vintage red crushed velvet Navajo blouse. "I feel much stronger now. Like a new person. I can't thank you enough for the clothes and for letting me stay here for a few days. I think… I think I needed to breathe fresh air away from New London. Sometimes it just feels… sterile… up there."

Gloria took Livia's arm, "Nonsense. You're welcome anytime, and besides, you didn't just loaf around, did you? You jumped right in and helped a lot with the new constitution writing. Your insights into how the New Londoners and the other new arrivals might feel and react were important contributions. You really should spend more time DownSide."

Livia Milner surprised herself as she reached around and pulled Gloria in for a fierce hug. "Thank you, Gloria, for all you've done. It means the world to me." The funny thing was, she thought, *I'm not a hugger… but this is… nice.* The older woman, with her long-braided silver hair that now had streaks of black returning to it, smelled of jasmine and… osmanthus? She'd taken to Livia from the moment she'd stepped foot DownSide, and Livia still didn't quite know why.

The doorbell rang, and Gloria wondered aloud, "Who could that be?" She walked towards the tiny foyer to answer the door while Livia went to the kitchen to get a glass of water.

"Livia?" Gloria called out as she shut the door behind her. "There's a package here for you. It looks official."

✪ ✪ ✪

Upstairs in her tiny room, Livia sat on the narrow quilt and afghan-covered bed. The white-painted walls angled low overhead. Even Preston, at five foot eleven, would need to stoop down a bit were he to stand close to the window.

Something about the thick package envelope seemed odd to her. It was labeled "War Department" and "Personal and Confidential" in bold stencil print. She shrugged and tore open the seal.

Inside was a bulky manila envelope that was likewise marked "Personal and Confidential."

Okay. This is getting weird.

She opened the envelope and upended it. A generic cellphone and pair of earbuds fell out. There was something still inside the envelope. She reached in and pulled out… photos.

She stared blankly at them for a long moment as the world contracted around her… and her heart turned to ice. They were pictures of her… in the act… with Karl Johansson.

A post-it note was stuck to the phone and secured with a rubber band. It read: "Call us."

Livia dropped the photos on the floor and sat limply in desolate despair.

You just couldn't help yourself, could you? Maybe the first time or the first few times you thought it was some kind of revenge for being ignored and taken for granted. Maybe you got a thrill, but you just had to go and keep doing it. Why? Are you just a slut, or was it something else? The worst part was that you knew. You knew you might be discovered. And so what? Even if you were found out and he divorced you back then, you would have still had your wealth and place in society entirely apart from Preston. You would still be a full Partner at the firm. Preston needed you more than you needed him. Was that it? Did you want to get caught so that he would suffer for it? Well, now it's come back to haunt you, hasn't it? Now all your wealth and family power are gone. You've been reduced to taking charity from flyover country nobody's... even if some of them turned out to be not so bad people.... And... And now you need him more than he needs you. So, what are you going to do now? Just when you thought you were getting your life back together, you got blackmailed. Karma for your sins, Livia.

She swallowed hard, took a deep breath, and put on her best hard-boiled attorney face. She put the earbuds in her ears and then pulled the rubber band and post-it note off the phone before turning it on. The only icon was a video conference app. She pressed the button to start the call.

A synthesized voice answered with an avatar.

"Hello, Livia. Please pan the camera
around so we can see if you are alone."

Livia suppressed the urge to say out loud, *Really?* She complied, panning the camera around, showing that she was in a closed room by herself.

"That's good. And you are looking
good, Livia. We're glad you are better."

Her voice flat and hard, she shook her head. "What do you want?"

"So, Livia, we wanted to ask your
opinion about how the constitutional
convention is progressing and about
the election to follow. With your history
and background, we would greatly
appreciate your insight."

Livia blinked in surprise, "Right. Sure. Drop the act. Whoever you are, you obviously have resources, so I'm confident that you don't need my opinion on elections. You probably know more about what is going on than I do. Don't fuck with me. What's this really about? I mean, honestly, could you even try to be more melodramatic? What's your game?"

"All right. We can see you're not
in the mood to play today, so we will
come right out and say it. You've been
just as concerned about the current
leadership as we have been, especially
in recent months. For all our sakes and
for our future, we want you to consider
running for Senate. You are the closest
thing we have to someone with real
governing experience. Your father was
the Senior Senator from Massachusetts,
and your mother was a judge on the
1st Circuit Court of Appeals in Boston.
You grew up suckling power from your
mother's teat."

Livia bristled. "Seriously? You send me blackmail photos, and then
you ask nicely for me to consider running for office?"

"Livia, we need your experience
and your sanity. Do you really think it
will satisfy you to lead the Navy Wife's
Association for the next hundred years
or more? Who knows how long our
bodies are supposed to last?"

"It doesn't matter what you want. The Fort Brazos natives will never
vote for *me*. To them, I'm an outsider and a privileged stuck-up Yankee.
You know how Texans feel about Yankees."

"That's what we like about you,
Livia. Full and utter self-awareness and
hyper-rationality topped with a brilliant
mind. You're wasting your talents.
Besides, you would have more support
than you think. Not only would most
New Londoners support you, but we
expect that most of the other militaries
would as well. Besides that, Gloria likes

you. We believe she will support you
and has probably been quietly pushing
you in this direction already."

"I don't… She…." Livia looked at the phone and coldly said, "Whoever you are, what are you playing at? I mean, from the blackmail material, I assume you intend to try to control my vote. Why are you really doing this?"

"You've got a great story. Your
background and history. You were
a full partner at your law firm. You
survived Awakening Day with the rest
of us. Which was a veritable miracle, by
the way, and we're certain that Andre
would want to thank you for being
such a wonderful Mrs. Robinson for
his son. We're sure Karl has learned
much under your tender tutelage.
Besides that, you survived the bombing
at City Hall and have gone through
tremendous suffering and PTSD as a
result, but you've pulled yourself up
by your heel straps and are now active
in helping shape our future by giving
valuable counsel on the structure and
substance of the new constitution.
You're a natural."

Livia hardened her soul. *So much for redemption.* "What do you want?"

"Why, nothing more than we've
said? We think you should give serious
consideration to running for Senate,
and well, should you win, and we fully
expect that you will, we will always be
happy to share our counsel with you."

✪ ✪ ✪

Livia quietly joined Gloria at the kitchen table. Gloria had already eaten but had saved a covered plate for Livia.

Dennis, Gloria's five-year-old Rottweiler, lay curled up at Gloria's feet.

Gloria looked up from her notes on the draft constitution and studied Livia's face. "Is everything all right? Coffee? It's not very good, but it's what we have left."

Livia smiled a tiny smile and nodded.

Gloria poured a cup from a half-full pitcher. She'd already had several cups herself. "Milk? Sugar?"

Livia shook her head and drank it black. She took a deep breath and asked, "Gloria, why aren't you running for one of the Senate seats that will be created?"

Gloria brushed a stray strand of long silver hair, now growing black from its roots, back from her face. "Maybe someday. These past couple of years since Awakening Day have been one tumultuous world-ending crisis after another. The council has had the weight of the human race's survival on its shoulders." She shivered, "… and seeing Wylie like that… after the bombing. You saw it too. It was terrible. I…" She looked away, "I've had enough for a while. I simply want to return to being just a City Council member and run my store. It would be a vacation in comparison. I'd rather stay close to the people in my district and only have to worry about… smaller things for a while." She sniffed and looked at Livia, her eyes damp, "Is that wrong?"

Livia's lips trembled slightly, "Yes… I do know. And, no, God, no, it's not wrong. But you know, Gloria, people will still come to you for advice and support. You've been important to a lot of people. That's not going to change overnight just because of an election. Not in the world we are in now."

Gloria shrugged and shook her head, "Maybe. Maybe not. What's on your mind, Livia? Something obviously has you rattled."

Tell her… tell her you're being blackmailed. You know she would help you figure it out….. And when she finds out what I'm being blackmailed for… would she still… no… She's the only real friend I've made here. I cannot bear the thought of her… scorn. Or worse… her pity.

Livia smiled, "Gloria, I need your advice. I feel like I need to do more. Step up, as you would say. I'm thinking that maybe I should consider running for the Senate, but I need to know what you think. Am I crazy? Would people here support me?"

Home

● ● ● ● ● ● ● ● ● ● ● ● ● ● ● ●

DownSide:
Carswell Islands

Michelle Bain groaned aloud as the morning suntube light filtered through the main cabin windows. Everything hurt. Even moving her arm to cover her face was an effort. Thirty days at sea had tested her endurance more than she'd ever imagined possible. In retrospect, a twelve-person crew for the Quezon had been insufficient for the workload. The ship's hull had held up well enough. However, the fittings and equipment cobbled together for everything from hatches to portholes to block and tackle were not "marine rated." All the various blocks had been a bigger challenge. A few were salvaged from small boats, but the larger ones were fabricated mainly by Caesar's men at local machine shops. Once at sea, though, the stretching, saltwater, and weather from days at sea gave witness to the inexperience of Quezon's builders. She leaked like a sieve.

One of the two sump pumps being used as a bilge pump had failed, and the other seemed iffy. Each crewmember had been rotating through the hand-pump duty to compensate. Despite everything, morale was still high. Michelle was at a loss to explain it. The work had become monotonous and tiresome. However, there remained a high spirit of adventure and camaraderie. Maybe it was just being away from all the reminders of a world raped and stolen that Fort Brazos and its all-too-familiar-seeming surroundings innately presented. Their sense of normalcy — even for Caesar's people, the setting still felt too much like… if they could just get on a plane, they could go home. But home was light years away and lost forever.

Their journey on Quezon had taken them hundreds of miles across the inland sea of Lake Texoma and out the New Brazos River passage into the long and well-protected Eisenhower Bay, which everyone had agreed would no doubt one day become an anchorage easily rivaling anything from Old Earth. The bay had opened into the open ocean for a few hundred miles before a choice had to be made. The interior of New Texas had nine major land masses.

To the north, out of the bay, lay Houston. To the East, Fannin. To the South, Travis and Austin. On the other side of the land mass containing Fort Brazos, from North to South, lay Chennault, Bowie, Crockett, and Navarro to the west. Numerous large and small islands and island chains abounded, including the Miller Islands, Naga, Kyle, Zavala, Parker, Nimitz, and… what they had labeled the Carswell Islands, which lay far to the east beyond the narrow passage between Houston and Fannin.

There had never really been any doubt about their destination. Caesar had long looked up at the sky at the Carswell Islands and dreamed of making them a new Philippine homeland. Other than the leaks and routine problems, Quezon had held up well. They'd stopped at numerous islands and inlets along the way, and the crew had, to a man, enthusiastically helped Michelle take samples and helped her with her real job on the ship — the new world's first biologist "naturalist" to travel substantially beyond Fort Brazos and Lake Texoma's shores.

Caesar was more than simply the Quezon's captain and his men's Commanding officer. Each had served under him back on Earth when he'd been their Colonel in the Philippine Army 54th Engineering Brigade, where he'd led by example, even in harm's way. There had been times when, under fire from Marxist rebels, he'd personally operated heavy machinery, urging his men on. His discipline was both quiet and intense. Unlike other officers, he didn't curse or berate those who fell short of his expectations. His glacial stare of disappointment and pity usually sufficed. When it didn't, 'encouragement' from the underperforming soldier's more enlightened fellows would help him see things differently. That his brigade had always had the best performance ratings was a matter of intense pride for all of them.

The relationship between Caesar and Michelle was no secret. The mere fact of their slow-boil May-December romance was more than enough for the rest of the crew to consider it their personal responsibility to look out for her. If she'd been difficult to put up with, that would have been OK. She wasn't, though, and her zestful enthusiasm and encyclopedic knowledge of marine life and a host of other general topics endeared her to them no end. To a man, all of Caesar's men had lost family and loved ones back on Earth. Many, like Caesar, had come from huge and extensive families, most with several children and even grandchildren. In the months leading up to the journey, Michelle had become… family.

She'd tirelessly helped in building Quezon. Onboard, she worked and laughed as hard as the rest.

Everything had been going reasonably well, despite the problems. The two or three squalls they'd weathered had been terrifying to her though. She'd had flashbacks to when she, Lucia Ewing, Marcos Salinas, and Ronald Green had nearly drowned out on Lake Texoma, only to be rescued by Caesar. She'd gritted her teeth and hidden her fears, though she knew the crew saw through it. She wasn't the only one though. Most of the crew had had little to no actual oceangoing experience, especially in a tiny thirty-meter hand-built sailing ship.

Compared to, say, 18th-century sailing vessels that might travel over a hundred nautical miles a day, they weren't breaking records. On the other hand, there was just so much to see! They'd averaged up to fifty nautical miles a day, between stops and pauses to look at things, crossing over twelve hundred nautical miles along the way.

The thing about living inside a cylindrical world is that they could see any really significant storms coming as they would slide down the curvature towards you. Just like the storm that had been following them for the last week. So, they'd raced ahead of it, hoping to reach safe harbor in the Carswell Islands in time. After all, where those harbors were was not a secret either. They had excellent photographic maps of the entire world.

They almost made it.

The storm had sped up and overtaken them only a few dozen nautical miles short. The military back in Fort Brazos had monitored their trip, of course, and had radioed offers to send help, but by then, the sea state had become so rough that there was no safe way to transfer off the ship, even if they'd wanted to. Caesar had asked his men if any wished to evacuate the ship, but none had taken him up on it. He suspected that, even if the weather had cooperated, none would have given even a passing thought to leaving.

During the night, the storm had tossed them about like a toy. To Michelle, it had seemed to last a thousand years as the Bosun Darwin de Guzman, and Varian Asuncion, and Thor de Leon, who both doubled as deckhands and, should the need arise Marines, had battled the storm with safety lines lashed to their waists to keep them from being washed overboard. Engineers Guillermo Mangubat and Diwa Sarmiento valiantly struggled to keep the engine running. At the same time, Caesar, Chief Mate Angel

Bustamante, and Danilo Santiago, who doubled as Purser, and Omarion Soriano, who doubled as the cook, and Tamir Ybañez who actually was a certified medic, as well as Zhander Evangelista, the ships carpenter, fought leaks, blown hatches, and countless other problems. Throughout the night, Michelle had been everywhere helping, fetching, fixing, tying down, stowing, and otherwise running from one crisis to the next.

At around two in the morning, as best she could remember, they'd lost the fore topmast, followed soon thereafter by the aft topmast. An hour later, they lost most of the bowsprit. Somehow, eventually, they'd run aground on a sandbar. It had to be sand because had it been coral, the pounding would have broken Quezon's back. Even with a sandbar, it was bad enough. Between the flashes of lightning, they could see an island nearby. Just as Caesar was about to order the crew to abandon ship, the storm weakened as it sped away.

The exhausted crew either dropped where they were or managed to dead-walk into the main cabin and collapse on whatever portion of floor, couch, or chair was closest.

✪ ✪ ✪

Caesar worked his way through the main cabin, gently rousing each person and speaking quietly to them.

Michelle groaned and called out. Her voice was horse and gravelly. "Are we there yet? Where's my coffee and Danish? Room service on this tub is terrible." She swallowed. "I distinctly remember a no-typhoon clause in the brochure...."

Angel Bustamante shook his head slowly, coughed, then laughed, "Yes, Miss Bain. It was right there next to the money-back guarantee clause. Omarion and Tamir will have the buffet up and running in, oh, what, a week or two?"

Tamir mumbled, "Buffet. Yes, Miss Bain. I'll get right on that."

Caesar laughed, "Okay, everyone, we are all tired, and some of us are hurt. We need to get moving and make sure we don't slide off this sandbar and sink and drown after all. That would be rather rude of God at this point, but I'm not sure I'm on speaking terms with him right now, anyway."

The cabin was a wreck, strewn with broken and misplaced gear and trash. It looked, unironically, as though a cyclone had hit it. Caesar looked around the mess at his similarly bruised and battered crew. Many had sustained cuts, lacerations, and other injuries. Everyone was beginning to move, though, even if slowly.

"Tamir and 'Chelle, I want you to look everyone over and make sure that all their bandages are clean. Start with Zhander, over there in the corner. That gash on his calf has opened up again and is bleeding on our deck...."

Michelle ventured out of the main cabin in the brightening morning light. Frayed running rigging and part of a splintered spar lay sprawled across the foredeck, which, along with the rest of the ship, was canted at a ten or twelve-degree-or-so angle. She ruefully shook her head as she realized that after a month at sea and, especially, the storm, she'd hardly noticed the list until now.

She'd tied her long dirty blonde hair into a ponytail, but it was coming loose, and wisps of her hair danced around her as the soft breeze brought the sounds and smells of land to her nose. The island lay fifty or sixty yards away. Gentle waves washed up on its long beach line. Her eyes widened, and she exclaimed, "Oh, my!" The beach was a sparkling whitish pink.

When Quezon was being built, Caesar and his men had quietly looked for small boats with which to travel from the anchored ship to shorelines that might be some distance away. He'd feared he would have to build long boats because all he'd been able to find were the typical flat-bottomed "bass boats" used for fishing on small lakes and ponds and a few larger boats too large to take with them. Word had spread, though, and before long, a pair of Seadoos were donated along with, more importantly, a couple of Ribcraft rigid inflatable boats that the parks department had in storage.

It took two hours, but they finally secured Quezon with no less than three anchors to make sure she didn't float off the sandbar and drift away. Four men stayed aboard afterward while the rest ferried themselves and supplies to shore in the small boats. The boats had seen plenty of use during the earlier stopovers in the days and weeks before. Now, Caesar sat in the back of the Rib that Angel Bustamante had named Amaya. The other he'd labeled as Chantara. His lost sisters. Michelle sat on the front seat as the Rib bounced across the water. Suddenly, she stiffened and leaned forward and at an angle. Then she leaped up and pointed, shouting, "Look there!" Miraculously, she didn't fall out of the boat.

A hundred or so yards down the beach, small shapes slowly moved. "That way! Go that way!"

Caesar knew better than to argue. He shifted their course.

Not long afterward, Michelle, still leaning forward, reached her arm behind her and rapidly motioned, "Slow down!"

Caesar eased the throttle on the outboard. The Rib slowed and glided towards the beach and the subject of Michelle's excitement. Hundreds of turtles. As they got closer, she pointed, "Look! See the spots and the beaklike mouth? Those are Hawksbills! They're so beautiful! And they're very endangered, or at least, they were back on Earth. They were the only extant species in the genus Eretmochelys. Eretmochelys imbricata. They were hunted almost to extinction for their shells."

She turned her head and lowered her gaze sharply. "Caesar, anyone so much as touches one of those turtles, so help me!"

Caesar smiled and swallowed hard. Seeing her joy and excitement about what she loved was one of the things that had endeared her to him early on. It had been a salve to his savaged soul. Seeing her now, her blonde hair flying in the wind and her face and eyes shining like this, made his heart skip.

They beached the Rib, jumped out of the boat, and pulled it up onshore. Caesar drove an anchor spike into the sand to ensure the boat stayed put while Michelle gingerly approached the nesting turtles. They ignored her completely.

Minutes later, she returned and grabbed Caesar's shoulders. "Caesar, some of the adults are at least four and a half feet long or more! They've got to weigh, like, over two or three hundred pounds!"

Caesar nodded and smiled, "Yes, 'Chelle, that is great. They are healthy, yes?"

Michelle twittered her head, "No, I mean, yes. Don't you see? They're too big! Like twenty percent bigger than the ones on Earth! It's like the dolphins and the other samples we've taken along the way. The morphology's the same, but many of the species we are finding are either bigger, out of place from their expected habitats, or both!"

Caesar sighed, "I see. Well, while you were gone, I found the reason for the pink sand. It's just like Isla Sta. Cruz del Grande. Pink Beach near Zamboanga." He held up a piece of bright red coral.

Michelle snatched it out of his hand and looked closely at it, turning it over in the light. She nodded, "Tubipora musica. What you call organ pipe coral. The Hawkbills eat the sponges that live in this coral. Where is," she fumbled the words, "Isla sta Cruz…?"

Caesar looked up into the suntube light and closed his eyes. He took a deep breath and shook his head. "Zamboanga is located on the Zamboanga Peninsula. Pink Beach is on what you would call the Great Santa Cruz Island, in the Basilan Strait."

Michelle shook her head.

Caesar smiled and sank to his knees, taking her down with him. Tears streamed down his face as he said, "Pink Beach is in the Philippines. And the Hawkbills nest on Pink Beach. The islands are not laid out the same, but the Gardeners have recreated at least a small part of the Philippines here."

Michelle blinked in surprise, then she grinned widely, wrapped her arms around him, and hugged him tightly. "Caesar! We're home! We found home!"

Duplicity

● ● ● ● ● ● ● ● ● ● ● ● ● ● ● ●

DownSide: Morgan Island
New Pyongyang City

New Pyongyang City did not remotely resemble its namesake. In truth, it was beginning to look more like a small Mediterranean village than Pyongyang. Instead of glorious monuments and towers, broad boulevards, and parks, New Pyongyang City had started as a series of thatched huts. Over the months, it quickly evolved. They replaced the thatching with fire-hardened semi-cylindrical clay roof Spanish Tiles. The wood and straw walls gave way to fired clay bricks. The streets, such as they were, and what there were of them, were indeed broad. Colonel P'aeng Jin-Hwan had labored to create an environment to inspire both pride and at least a little familiarity. Even the streets themselves were slowly being transformed, using the old Roman method of road building, with a bottom layer of sand (easily found) covered with stones, shells, and broken pottery, followed by another layer of more broken pottery in a rough cement, and paved on top with fire-hardened bricks in place of stone blocks. The roads even included curbs and drainage ditches.

The roads and steadily improving buildings, some of which now even included fired clay pipes for plumbing, were a matter of immense pride.

On the surface.

In the months since the discovery of the metal cave, the Colonel had become obsessed with it. He now lived there full-time, with supplies being brought to him daily.

Meanwhile, Kim Young-ho, the Commander (Sangjwa), maintained order and discipline back in New Pyongyang City. Where Jin-Hwan had ruled with dispassionate ruthlessness, Young-ho, who had always been cruel, no longer had Jin-Hwan to keep him in check. In the Colonel's absence, he had evolved well past being merely brutal.

The wrongness of the outside-in world of New Texas was harder on some people than others. In Fort Brazos, while the number of suicides had been surprisingly small in number, the number wasn't zero. Despite the Apocalypse, the culling of Awakening Day, and knowledge of the fate of loved ones back on a conquered and effectively enslaved Earth, there still remained a semblance of normalcy and a stronger sense of community and purpose. For the North Koreans, however, ripped from their home and the cold comfort of their austere hermit society, the psychological effect was, for many, torturous and debilitating.

Jin-Hwan had coped by fanning his hatred of the Americans and by keeping his men disciplined and focused. After discovering the metal cave, his hate drove him to isolation, hoping he would find a way to use the alien device as a weapon.

For Young-ho, however, Jin-Hwan's abandonment had served to open old wounds, and he soon began to take out his frustrations on anyone who angered him. No one tried to stop him. At least, not until a single subordinate finally tried to stand up to him… until Young-ho had, in a fit of rage, stabbed the man in the throat, killing him on the spot in front of hundreds of witnesses. The orgasmic thrill of that act redefined his existence. From that moment on, his sadistic daydreams took shape in a radical restructuring of the order of things. After so much time in isolation, he already knew who he trusted. Shortly thereafter, a dozen men were disappeared during the night. The rest were either sent to other tasks he felt they were suited to, or were sent to the work parties.

At least fifty of the youngest and least… masculine… men were rounded up and herded into the barracks that Young-ho took over as his private domain.

His second in command, Ri Tok-hun, the Senior Lieutenant (Sangwi), had stopped most of the building projects and instead refocused work on road building. He had decided they needed a ten-mile road to the beach, one to the metal cave, and another to the other side of the island. It didn't matter that there was no real utility in it or that the roads would require *years or* perhaps even *decades* to build. It kept the masses busy and out of trouble.

The unskilled or those not in favor, especially if they were not from elite families, were forced to work without the benefit of wheeled carts or heavier, more effective tools. The work was backbreaking, and several had already died of exhaustion.

Meanwhile, Commander Choe Pyong-Chol had managed to not be seen as a threat. The patrols he commanded were essential for the fresh game they brought back for the city and the all-but-forgotten Colonel. All pretense of military purpose had evaporated.

Life on the trail was hard, but he and his men were increasingly horrified by what was happening in the town. They were not allowed to return to the city without their quota. At least on their own, he could ensure that all were well fed and provided for. Moreover, they were out of sight and increasingly loyal to him alone.

✪ ✪ ✪

On his last visit to the city, Pyong-Chol was shocked to see a body splayed open and crucified outside the main barracks. He immediately turned and headed out of the town back to his camp, where he now sat next to the campfire.

He studied the worried faces of his men. Everyone knew what was happening back in the city. On several occasions, the guards had forced him to wait and watch while Young-ho had … done things … to those wretched young men. It had taken all his self-control not to kill Young-ho on the spot. He could have done it. He'd wanted to do it. He still did. Of course, the dozens of thuggish guards that Young-ho kept around him would have ended Pyong-Chol shortly thereafter, and no doubt slowly. Young-ho and his guards were getting soft, but there were too many of them.

Kwon Ryong-Hae asked, "What will you do?"

He sighed and shook his head. "I must try again to convince the Colonel to return to the city and put a stop to what is going on."

✪ ✪ ✪

Jin-Hwan sat on a wooden stool next to the softly glowing zero-point energy device on its pedestal in the metal room. His right arm rested on a wooden table covered with stacks of rough sheets of papyrus-like "paper," documenting his experiments. Dozens of men labored to produce the paper daily, along with the writing quills and ceramic ink wells that littered the table.

"Colonel?"

Jin-Hwan leaned forward as he poked one of the holes with a nail attached to the end of a bamboo sliver. A precious metal wire, scavenged from inside a piece of clothing, extended from the nail to a crudely made coil and spring graduated meter. The crude meter did not move. He made a notation with the quill and ink on the closest sheet of paper.

"Colonel?"

Jin-Hwan blinked and sat up straighter. He turned, brushing his long, oily hair from his eyes. Like all the men, his beard had grown long. He stared at the source of the voice without recognition for a long moment. Then, suddenly, he shuddered slightly and swallowed, his voice horse and rough. "Yes? What do you want, Commander?"

Pyong-Chol was already at rigid attention, the tattered remains of his uniform as orderly as he could make them. Over the weeks since the cave's discovery, he had reported what was happening in the city to the Colonel. At first, Jin-Hwan had simply nodded and said he would "look into it." As things had become progressively worse, Pyong-Chol had included conditions in the city as part of his regular reports, hoping the Colonel would finally do something about it.

"Sir, again, I regret to inform you that Young-ho and his subordinates have lost their discipline. Work on most of your projects has stopped. Young-ho is using his position to abuse the men. Many have died. Sir, he and others are… Sir… they are raping and murdering men. Sir, you must put a stop to the madness!"

Jin-Hwan stared at him for perhaps thirty seconds before muttering, "Humph. There is no such thing as male rape, and serious discipline infractions merit execution. Go away." He turned back to his work, making more notations on the paper.

Pyong-Chol's jaw dropped, and his eyes widened. He raised his voice, nearly shouting, "Sir! Colonel! You must put a stop to it! You have a duty!"

Jin-Hwan stiffened. He dropped his hand to the Makarov holstered at his waist as he slowly stood and turned. His eyes were wild as he snarled at Pyong-Chol, "You are interfering in the great work! I shall master this device and use it to crush the Americans. I will force them to their knees and enslave any who survive. We shall burn their city to the ground, bring their women back here to New Pyongyang City, and create the new Chosŏn Minjujuŭi Inmin Konghwaguk, where I shall assume the mantle of Great Leader and guide our people into the future! Let Young-ho weed out the weaklings!" He lunged at him, shouting, "Only the strong…."

Pyong-Chol was not entirely conscious of the SKS rifle slung over his shoulder as he swung it up and crashed the rifle butt into Jin-Hwan's chin, knocking the Colonel backward onto the table, snapping its legs, and sending the paper, quills, and ink wells flying.

For a moment, Pyong-Chol simply stood there, shocked in surprise at his own actions. Then his chest heaved as he spun around and clubbed the startled guard outside the door as well. Slowly, the roaring of the blood in his ears subsided, and the ever-present island sounds washed over him. Breathing hard, he stood dumbly.

What have I done?!

He turned and looked back at Jin-Hwan, who lay limply across the broken table like a discarded marionette. His mind snapped back into gear, and he rushed to the Colonel and turned him over. *Still breathing.* He removed the Colonel's pistol belt, then looked around the metal cave and saw another wooden table to the side piled high with supplies…. And the radio. The radio the Americans had provided in case of emergency.

Not for the first time, he wondered why the evil Americans had done so much to help his people.

He shook his head and grabbed the radio, attaching it to his belt. Stepping outside, he bent down, grabbed the guard's feet, and pulled him inside the cave. Then he stepped outside and shoved the heavy rock blocking the door open out of the way. He stepped back and stared at the recessed handprint next to the doorway. He hesitated for a moment, then slammed his hand into it. The dark metal door slid silently shut.

✪ ✪ ✪

ILC Dagger silently hovered one hundred feet above the area next to the cave before slowly dropping through the tropical canopy. The destructive warp field converted the matter from the trees to energy with a brilliant crackling fire. At roughly one hundred and thirty feet long and eighty or so feet wide, the nearly fifty-foot-tall landing craft gently lowered its seven hundred and fifty-eight thousand pounds toward the ground. The warp field created a clean depression and settled down with a thunderous crunch.

Its cargo doors were already open. Two pintle-mounted M134 mini-guns swiveled back and forth, looking for targets before three full squads of heavily armed marines poured out and secured the perimeter.

Throughout the approach, Pyong-Chol, as instructed, had remained flat on the ground, with his hands behind his head. The SKS rifle and Makarov pistol were hung on a tree twenty yards away, clearly visible. Three of the marines carefully approached the weapons looking for traps, before taking the guns, emptying them, and field stripping them as well.

Three more marines went over to Pyong-Chol, zip-tied his hands behind him, and stood him up, checking for weapons. They nodded to the dark-skinned Lieutenant (formerly Sargent) Darryl Washington, who spoke on his radio, "Captain Garreth, Alpha, Bravo, and Charlie squads report the area is secure. The Pri.. ah, the gentleman is also secure, and, like he said on the radio, there's a metal wall and door here just like the one in Jonestown."

Still sporting his buzz cut, Captain David Garreth stepped out of the ILC and strode towards Pyong-Chol. He nodded to the marines. "Cut him loose."

They did so, and Pyong-Chol rubbed his wrists, glancing back and forth between David, the ILC, and the metal wall.

David did his best not to appear to tower over the much shorter North Korean. "Where is your commanding officer?"

Pyong-Chol struggled with what English he knew from months of living in captivity in Fort Brazos. "My Colonel is… he has lost his… mind. He… He tries to use the… thing… as a weapon. Against you."

David's pulse quickened. "Where is your Colonel?"

Pyong-Chol hesitated, then looked down at his feet in shame. He slowly raised his arm and pointed at the metal wall's closed door.

David's eyes widened, and he grimaced. He spoke on his radio, cringing at breaking EMCON, which was already on an open mic. "Dagger. Garreth. Dust off immediately. Call back to base and relay the conversation you just heard. Request instructions. We will secure the area."

He turned to Lieutenant Washington. "Secure this man nearby. We may need him. Dagger will provide some Overwatch, but I want drones in the air in all directions. I want to know if anything bigger than a squirrel heads this way."

Twenty minutes later, David's radio announced, "Captain Garreth, you are ordered to enter the ZPM cave and secure all materials and personnel present. You are ordered to secure the ZPM at all costs. Rules of engagement are at your discretion."

David nodded, "Acknowledged. Proceeding to secure the ZPM cave."

He motioned to Washington, who trotted over. "Stack up Alpha squad outside the door with Bravo in support and Charlie in Overwatch. Everyone has been briefed on the ZPM. Under no circumstances will anyone shoot the damned thing, and no flashbangs. Smoke and thermals. Breach the moment Alpha is in place."

Two minutes later, Alpha squad was stacked and ready outside the door. Lieutenant Washington counted down, "Three, Two, One!" Then he pressed his hand into the handprint, and the door slid open. They tossed billowing smoke grenades inside, and the team, hands on each other's backs, breached the entrance.

"Clear!"

"Clear!"

"Sir, there's four bodies in here and a bunch of junk and trash on the floor."

✪ ✪ ✪

It took several minutes for the smoke to dissipate.

Lieutenant Washington quietly said to David, "Captain, you'd better come and see this yourself."

David looked the question at him, but Washington just shook his head.

David shrugged and followed him in.

There were indeed four bodies on the floor. They had lined the bodies in a row and turned them face up. David blinked and shook his head as he tried to make sense of what he was seeing.

He bent lower to get a closer look. "What the hell?"

Two of the bodies were identical in every way, down to their clothing, their wounds, and where they had bled. The other two… were also identical. It was as though two men had been… copied. He looked around the room and began to notice that in addition to the dead men, there also seemed to be two of everything else… from the fragments of a broken table to identical scraps of paper and other debris. Everything in the room had been duplicated.

David swallowed hard as his mind raced. He glanced up at the softly glowing ZPM and swore again, "Oh, hell."

Treason

● ● ● ● ● ● ● ● ● ● ● ● ● ● ●

DownSide
Morgan Island

Commander Ramona Henry left Lieutenant Alister Gordon in charge of ILC Dagger's bridge and made her way to the vessel's loading ramp. This far down among the trees, the charred, fetid smells from Dagger's earlier landing mingled with the warm, humid tropical air and fought against the brisk cool sixty-eight degrees she had Staff Sargent Simon Lachapelle maintain Dagger's environmentals at. She wrinkled her nose as the boundary air layer buffeted her short strawberry-blonde hair.

Back on Earth, she'd qualified as a Submarine Warfare Officer and served onboard the Virginia Class Iowa for three deterrent patrols before becoming Admiral Johannsson's Flag Aide. Shortly before Awakening Day, she'd been selected to join NASA's next moon and possibly the Mars program. After Awakening Day, she'd lobbied hard and threatened to resign in order to get a deck back under her feet. She'd been too junior to be considered for the Blood Phoenix, but when the ILCs were discovered, it opened up a new opportunity. Now promoted from Lt. Commander to full Commander, she'd been on rotation to command one of Dagger's patrols when the Morgan Island incident had blown up.

After Captain Garreth had radioed the startling discovery in the 'cave,' she'd spent the next hour and a half conferring with Command about what to do next. It was a messy situation, to say the least. On the one hand, was the cave and its implications not only here on the island, but also for what it implied about the other one back in Jonestown. ILC

Sickle had been hastily recalled from Wardog hunting to immediately secure the Jonestown site instead. On the other hand, there was the deteriorating situation in New Pyongyang City, where a real-life heart-of-darkness disaster seemed to have developed. While the North Koreans had been essentially exiled and left to their own devices, the horrific conditions there, if true, could not be allowed to continue.

Now it was her job to assess the situation and fix it. She shook her head. What are a couple of thousand crazy North Koreans armed with improvised spears, bows, and arrows compared to a nearly four-thousand-ton sublight interplanetary landing craft armed with two mini-guns and three squads of heavily armed, newly minted 'Space Marines?'

Standing in the doorway, she narrowed her pale blue eyes and turned to Crew Chief Russ Elvis and Crewman Ozzie Cartwright, who manned the pintle-mounted mini-guns. "Any problems out there, Elvis?"

Russ, at six foot four, bald and black, could nonetheless escape the name. He shook his head, "No, ma'am. Nobody from the town has tried to head this way. The guy who called us, Pongchol, says he's in charge of all the patrols. He says he's sent them all to the other side of the island. The drone feeds all seem to confirm that."

Ramona, herself not entirely sure of the correct pronunciation of the North Korean's name, refrained from correcting it. "Very well, Elvis. Watch my back, will you? It would really suck to get shot by an arrow or something."

She smiled, and her expression brightened the two men's faces. She wasn't above using her good looks as a tool when needed. Not that it had helped much when she'd been a Gates Cambridge Scholar, where she'd earned her master's degree in nuclear engineering. Her research had focused on "a next-generation, thorium-fueled nuclear reactor concept." Her ideas had turned heads in the Navy and even NASA, ultimately leading to their interest in her to become an astronaut — something that had come as a complete surprise. At the time, she'd thought to herself, *So what if they want someone pretty for their recruiting poster? It's no different from the hunky ex-SEAL they'd recruited a few years earlier or any of the others. I'll use my looks as ruthlessly as the next girl.*

Besides, she liked Elvis and most of the rest of her crew. He had a wicked sense of humor and was an excellent acoustic guitar player. Crewman Cartwright, thickly muscled and short, in shocking contrast to his appearance, had a startlingly clear leggero tenor voice. While not quite tone deaf herself, she'd long known better than to ever sing where anyone else could hear her.

Russ grinned, "Ma'am, yes, Ma'am. You got it!"

Ramona straightened her flight suit and walked down the ramp towards David, who stood outside the dark metal cave's entrance.

✪ ✪ ✪

DownSide:
Riverbend Mall: Presidential Office

John Austin sat behind his cherry wood desk and shook his head as he stared at the video conference call displayed on the eighty-inch monitor on his wall. Gail had taken a rare day off and was out riding her horse, Heartbreaker, a jet-black quarter-horse stallion whose original owner had not survived Awakening Day. She'd stopped riding and was on the call using the camera on her phone (surrounded by her detail). Admirals Milner and Johansson were linked in from the New Pentagon in New London, as was Secretary of War Marcus. In the office with John were Mayor Tom Parker and Councilpersons Gloria Vargas, Dale Hubbard, Jack Burdger, and Esmerelda Collins.

Gloria quipped, "Damn it to Hell, John. To paraphrase Oliver Hardy, this is another fine mess we've gotten ourselves into. We all agreed to exile those people, and now it's come back to bite us in the ass."

Tom sighed, "Colorful as always, Gloria. There are over two thousand of them, or at least there were. Abhorrent though their country's leadership was, they represented the last of a whole people."

Gail laughed harshly. "And they all wanted to kill us, Tom. You know that as well as the rest of us. You tried talking to them yourself! If your detail hadn't been there, they would have murdered you on the spot, and you know it."

Tom slumped back in his chair. "That may be, but I'm still ashamed we couldn't find a better solution."

Gloria exasperatedly looked at Tom, "Tom, you're a good man. Too good for your own good sometimes, but you know that we could either keep them locked up in that camp for years or let them loose on an island paradise where at least they could have a chance to, well…."

John stood up from behind the desk, walked around to the front of it, and leaned back against it. "We all agreed that moving them there was the most humane thing to do. At least on the island, they couldn't hurt anyone else. I just never imagined they would turn on themselves like this and go all Colonel Kurtz and worse."

Alexander Marcus gravely added, "Mr. President, I'll be blunt. The danger to anyone else, if it really ever existed, is over. We're in control of the site, and there is nothing the locals can do about it. That said, if what is being reported in their town is true, and I'm not entirely convinced of that, mind you, we cannot allow such atrocities to continue. Back on Earth, there was a whole world of arguments for and against us being the world's policeman. Here, though, we're in a new world. The precedent we set now will forever enlighten… or stain our future as a people."

Gail nodded, "Secretary Marcus is right, John. If it is true, we can't let this stand."

Esmerelda shook her head. "I'm sure our boys could easily mop things up, but what happens after? Those people have been indoctrinated since birth to hate us. If we go in guns blazing, it may only give them more reasons to hate and distrust us, no matter what their own people were up to."

John took a deep breath and let it out before asking, "So, how many men does this Captain Lieutenant have under his command? Can we trust them to clean up their own mess?"

Alexander shook his head. "I don't know, but they all had military training. If there are enough of them and we were to, say, allow them to discover a cache of weapons, then I would imagine they should be able to handle opposition armed with only spears and improvised weapons. The question is, though, what happens afterward? What's keeping this from happening again, and, more strategically, what do we do about the site?"

Tom chuckled ruefully, "Well, we did give them the island."

Gloria snapped back, "What are you saying, Tom? We let them stay in control of dangerous technology?"

Dale Hubbard interjected, "Maybe that's the key. It's dangerous."

John smiled thinly. "I think I see where you're going, Dale. Two of their people died inside it. It's dangerous. A common enemy. We work out a deal where we protect them from it and provide, I don't know, assistance and trade?"

Gail added, "Maybe John, but in the meantime, we have a situation in the city. We need to know if this Captain Lieutenant is telling the truth. I say let's wire him up. Hide a camera on him and send him in. We'd know if he tries to dissemble or orchestrate things for us. We can watch from overhead, sight unseen."

✪ ✪ ✪

It had taken a day to get the equipment to the island and convince Pyong-Chol to go along with the plan. Captain Garreth had even given back the pistol to him for self-protection. However, Ramona had warned him that if he used it to murder the leader back in the town, there would be no further support and that the video camera would broadcast what happened there live.

There was no worry about Wardogs or Stalkers on the island as it had been thoroughly searched before the North Koreans had been exiled there, and the exiles had been all over the island for a year and had seen no creatures bigger than an average-sized wild pig.

It took another day for Pyong-Chol to hike back to the city. By this time, Gail had joined John and the rest of the council in his office. That's when the closeup video of the conditions there were relayed back to Fort Brazos. First were the enslaved road builders. Blank-faced and broken, the scene would not have been out of place in any horrific historical slave setting — from Egyptian slaves to those of the Roman era or any of the more uncomfortably recent times. By the time he got to the main barracks, passed by the crucified man, and went inside, tears streamed down half the faces in the Presidential office. The scene inside, though, was as vivid a depiction of a descent into hell as anyone could imagine. Jack Burdger left the room to vomit, and several others thought they might soon follow.

As he turned to Gail, John was stone-faced. "Make certain this video is preserved. From the beginning of this… situation… see to it that it is preserved. All of it. Keep recording everything. Someday, perhaps… it will help bring these people back to… humanity."

✪ ✪ ✪

In anticipation, and hope, that Pyong-Chol's reconnaissance mission back to the city would be 'successful,' ILC Sickle had ferried over a supply of two hundred and fifty Chinese QBZ-191 Automatic Rifles, ammunition, uniforms, and body armor. They were transferred from the Fort Brazos "gun library" that the Gardeners had provided. The narrative would be that the North Korean's heroic Colonel had discovered the equipment and, upon learning of Kim Young-ho's atrocities, had ordered the loyal Pyong-Chol to retake the city and put Young-ho and his followers on trial.

North Korea routinely obtained weapons and equipment from China, and as members of the North Korean Maritime Special Purpose Forces 34th Army Navy Sniper Brigade, they were familiar to Pyong-Chol and his men.

It took three days for Pyong-Chol to recall his scouts from across the island to the location of the cache of weapons and supplies and another three days to organize and set the plan into motion. At dawn on the seventh day, Pyong-Chol and his hand-picked scouts, long accustomed to silent hunting across the island jungle, ghosted into town, gagging and zip-tying guards as they went. Scouts without rifles were left behind to protect them from the men they had enslaved.

Within minutes, the main force met no resistance as they converged on the central barracks. Pyong-Chol nodded the go-ahead. His men rushed in from all four entrances. Most of the guards were still asleep and snoring. Many were still draped over their unconscious victims.

Pyong-Chol burst through the door to Kim Young-ho's private quarters. Inside, Yong-ho was rising naked from his cot, awakened by the noise outside. He grabbed his spear and wiped his long hair from his bearded face, blinking hard at Pyong-Chol. Pyong-Chol was in a Chinese uniform carrying a rifle? Nothing made sense…

Pyong-Chol announced loudly, "Captain Kim Young-ho, by order of Colonel/Captain P'aeng Jin-Hwan, you are under arrest for treason, sedition, dereliction of duty, abuse of authority, grievous assault, murder, and rape. We will try you and those who followed you for your crimes."

Young-ho's eyes bulged, and his face crimsoned in rage. He screamed and charged with his spear.

Pyong-Chol batted the spear out of the way with his rifle and swung the butt into Young-ho's groin, doubling him over into a heap on the bamboo floor.

✪ ✪ ✪

DownSide:
Fort Underwood
Hangar 29

The original Fort Brazos was founded on the banks of the Brazos River in 1822. Over the many decades since, it has gone through many changes. By the time of the Accipiter attack, the combined military and civilian population was 34,712. The base had grown to 263 warehouses and hangars totaling over eight million square feet, along with 209 administrative facilities totaling nearly five million square feet and over two hundred miles of paved roads. Over time, buildings came and went. Many were torn down and replaced, and many were refurbished and rebuilt.

One of those buildings was hangar 29. It was located along a lesser-used runway that was in need of much repair. Because of the housing crisis from relocating the New Londoners, as well as many of the foreign military 'new arrivals,' building materials had been scarce. As a result, the renovations took longer than expected. After the ILCs had been discovered, and several were brought down the elevator from New London for patrols and exploration inside New Texas, hangar 29 was selected as a staging location for samples brought back for quarantine.

Enough was ready, however, to catalog and examine the items Commander Henry's ILC Dagger was ferrying back from the other side of the world.

Security was tight as Dagger settled down gently outside the hangar. The cargo doors opened, and Captain Garreth's men carried four body bags, followed by sewn-shut tarps containing the contents from the metal room. Each, including the body bags, was labeled with white China marker grease pencils indicating "left side" or "right side" to differentiate the duplicated items. And bodies. Under heavy guard, the zero-point energy device was the last item to be unloaded.

✪ ✪ ✪

Surgeon General Gwyneth Elliott Duncan carried her newborn twin boys in front of her in side-by-side papooses. Gerald and Paul were named after her father and younger brother, both lost like so many others during the Accipiter invasion of Earth. She gently swayed back and forth as she stood in front of the laptop camera. The leadership conference had reconvened.

She began, "We examined the bodies brought back from the island, and I have to say, I'm astounded. Everything about them is identical, from their clothes down to their stomach contents. Every scratch, scar, piece of dirt, you name it. Those men were Xeroxed." She lowered her voice, "I'll know more on… deeper examination, but I'll be surprised if it isn't the same technology that was used to duplicate all of us from the scans the Gardeners made back on Earth, just before we would have been annihilated. As for all the other items brought back, I have to say that, at least visually, it looks like everything else in that room was similarly duplicated… except for the energy device itself. As for it, there is no obvious external damage."

Preston Milner sighed, "Well, thank God for that."

Tom Parker asked, "If it was damaged, is it safe to bring it back here?"

Preston shook his head, "If it blew up, from what Dr. Nakamura tells me, it wouldn't matter where it was. It would take all of New Texas with it and then some."

Tom and Gloria exchanged worried looks.

Alexander added, "Well, regardless, we need to get those notes their Colonel made. It may all be gibberish, but who knows what he might have found out with his low-tech poking and prodding? Probably nothing useful, but we need to be sure."

John Austin asked, "What was the cause of death?"

Gwyneth pursed her lips before answering. "That's where it gets interesting. As far as I can tell, neither man should be dead. They had lacerations and contusions, and the Colonel had a broken jaw but nothing that should have killed either man. Incapacitated and down for the count, for sure, but not dead."

Alexander nodded. "So, Pyong-Chol didn't kill them after all. The room did, or, rather, whatever the duplication process is, did."

Gwyneth shook her head. "I thought the scanning process was supposed to be destructive. The Gardener scan took us apart, and they later made new bodies for us here. Why were there two of everything instead of a recreated copy?"

Gail answered thoughtfully, "What would be the point of a replicator that destroys the original only to make a single copy? If that's the true function, and the zero-point energy device is what powers it, then why did another energy device appear in the Jonestown room? That implies the room doesn't need it for the replication process...."

John nodded slowly. "So, remove the device, and the room assumes you want a new one. Leave it there, and, I don't know, maybe the Xeroxing goes faster?"

Gail shrugged, "Maybe."

Andre Johansson frowned. "Those rooms aren't huge. If it is a copier, then we can only use it to copy relatively small things."

John chuckled sardonically, "Sorry, Admiral, it's too small to replicate a starship."

Andre nodded, "Yes, Mr. President, we could replicate many critical parts, components, and even some subsystems, but it won't be big enough to replicate large volumes of jet fuel, and we've been rationing that."

Tom wondered aloud, "We're glossing over the fact that it killed those men to make copies. Either it wasn't smart enough to recognize they were living beings... or it didn't care. Or worse, what if it *had* duplicated them alive? My God, the implications that would bring."

Gail asked, "You have to wonder, just exactly, what are the odds, across the entire four-thousand-mile-long span of this world, that we should find these things at both of the *only* two locations where new settlements have been built?"

John looked at her and said, "I think this is a big shoe drop for them. They want us to spread out, but we can't dig down and mine for minerals because there's none there to dig for, and we've lost all our global supply chain infrastructure. They kick-started us with Phoenix, and now they're showing us that we have a way to duplicate items we need in order to expand and grow."

Gail nodded, "So the Gardeners are still active. Those locations didn't exist before *we* set up settlements."

Gloria whispered, "Dear Lord, what else are they going to do to us as we spread out in this place?"

Rice

● ● ● ● ● ● ● ● ● ● ● ● ● ● ● ●

Location: DownSide
Radio Station 92.5 Studio

Danielle keyed the microphone, "Hello, people of Fort Brazos and New London. This is Danielle Richardson on FM 92.5, and Radio Free Fort Brazos beaming our signal across the known world and beyond. Oh my, have we got a lot to talk about today! You know, if all that was going on was the constitutional convention and election, we still would have too much ground to cover. There is so much more, though, my darlings!"

"Of course, everyone is just buzzing about what's been going on over on the other side of the world. Just think, first, those crazy Reinhardt boys find that artifact in Jonestown, like, nearly a year ago, and then they find it created another one of those power boxes. Remember how excited that got the military and all the lab coat boys and girls? And now, guess what? Another room, just like it on the island of forgotten toys. I mean, exiles? And we did all conveniently forget them, didn't we? We just up and dumped two thousand young male psychos on an island paradise. What could go wrong, right?"

"Well, let me tell you, my birdies tell me that things went very, very bad there. Like, Lord of the Flies, Heart of Darkness, and Apocalypse Now kind of bad. And what's being done about it, I hear you asking? Well, let me tell you. Apparently, those same poor, sad, misguided North Koreans are cleaning up their own act. Yes, you heard it here first. I have it on good authority that the ringleaders have been rounded up and are being put on trial by their own men. What's better? We'll all get to see it live, and now this is the crazy part. They won't even know it is being broadcast.

Somehow, we're recording it all so that when they get themselves more civilized, they'll have a record of it for themselves. The hope is that they can eventually become civilized enough to rejoin the rest of humanity."

"Now, I know what some of you are thinking. They're dangerous. And you are right. But the truth is, and I hate to admit it, folks, the truth is that we need them. After the Accipiters raped our world, there are so few humans left. We need these people to find their better angels. My God, people, after the insanity of last year's bombing? There just aren't enough of us left to afford to fight each other anymore. We've got zillions of Accipiters out there that want to do that for us, and I mean to end us, finally, and forever. We've got to grow up as a species, people!"

"So, it may take a while, but let's hope that those poor men come to their senses."

She paused to sip her ice tea.

"And that brings us back here to our favorite punching bag, the new constitution, and the election. Apparently, the final form is mostly done, but there is still haggling over the total number of Senators. I hear the number is bouncing back and forth between twelve and thirteen. Also, instead of having to run two elections, one to decide on the constitution, and the other to elect folks, the decision was made to just have one election where we'll get to vote on ratifying the constitution and on the same ballot, we'll get to choose between the candidates for the seats the constitution calls for. Personally, I think this is a smart move. If people don't approve of the constitution, and the polls indicate it will pass, then the other vote won't matter. Since the consensus is that it *will* pass, then why not go ahead, and do the rest at the same time?"

"We've already heard announcements from some council members about who *won't* be running. I was as surprised as anyone else to hear that Councilwoman Gloria Vargas does not want to run for Senate. We will still have a city council, and she intends to run for reelection there. Like Gloria, Dale Hubbard is also not running. However, rumor has it that Councilwoman Esmerelda Collins *is* considering it."

"And now, for my scoop of the day, another little birdie blew my mind earlier this morning with the revelation that none other than the wife of Vice Admiral Preston Milner, Livia Milner, now, I know all you remember *her*, will be announcing later today that she is running for one of the Senate seats. Now, can you just imagine what the Milner breakfast table conversation must have been like lately? Whew!"

"Now, my darlings, if all of this wasn't enough for today's show, then there's the whole real-life sailing adventure of Colonel Caesar Salangsang's Quezon and their voyage halfway around the world! Like, just, wow! Have you seen the video and pictures they sent back? Pink Beaches! God, I've got to go there! And those adorable turtles! It's all just so gorgeous! And now, they're founding a new colony, calling it the New Philippines. Just… wow. I've got to go there. I'm sure my darling husband will be just fine taking care of our babies while I go walk barefoot in the pink sand. Mmmmmm."

She took a deep breath and sipped her tea again.

"And that, my darlings, brings me to the final rumor of the day. Apparently, our beloved President and Vice President have been seen spending more time in each other's company of late. And, I mean, a *lot* more time. Now, I know we talked about all the rumors about them being on the outs for the last few months, and I'm certainly not going to repeat some of the more, shall we say, colorful rumors about why that was, but apparently, the ice queen, err, I mean, the ice, ahem, has thawed. Or, who knows, maybe it was the other way around? We all know President Austin was something of a hermit long after he physically recovered. To be perfectly honest, I don't know if I could have done better myself. What he and all the people who were there went through was … unspeakable. I don't know about you, but I'm relieved to be seeing more of him lately, and, well, apparently, so is Ms. Vice President Gail Anson Finley."

"Like I've said before, I know that some of you are all worried about some sort of separation of powers and such, but hell, people. Give them a break. Who else can they really talk to about the burden of the survival of the rest of humanity but each other? Maybe they're a thing. Maybe they aren't. Honestly, though, if it were true? How do I feel about it? Well, I'll tell you. If it is? Then who deserves some tenderness and happiness more than they do? I mean, his little girl Mattie is already basically attached to the Vice President's hip. They obviously all care for each other. So, then, my darlings, if they're not really a thing, then, well, that's a shame because they should be. And what if they really are? I'll tell you what. I'll be the first in line to throw the rice!"

✪ ✪ ✪

Choe Pyong-Chol stood on the dais in front of the parade ground. His voice boomed as he began, "Do you remember what it was like back before this place, back in our proper homes, what it was like at night? Do you remember the stars?"

He paused and allowed the assembled former North Korean soldiers time to remember.

"The Great Leader, in his wisdom, banned nighttime artificial lights so that we could all enjoy the glory of the celestial veil. I miss those stars. Like all of you, I long for home, and I despise those who brought us away from there to this place."

The men stirred, and he felt the anger and sorrow throb throughout the crowd.

"I bring up these memories for a reason. You see, I am here to inform you that our brave Colonel, who has focused all of his ferocious intellect and energy on solving the mystery in the metal cave, has made a startling discovery that has embarrassed the pompous Americans!"

The reaction was mixed and cautious, but mentioning the Americans stirred a hot wind of hatred.

"You see, as many of us suspected, the Americans did not create this hollow world. Our brave Colonel indeed deciphered the mystery of the metal cave… and in doing so, he encountered and wrestled with the beings who did create this world. The struggle was immense and lasted for days. In his victory, our Colonel demanded answers. The beings who created this world, the ones the Americans call the Gardeners, admitted the story the Americans told was true. That an even greater power… one whose empire stretches across the nighttime skies of our lost world did indeed attack our world."

Anger and disbelief and shouts of outrage roiled across the gathering.

"When the Colonel told me the next part, I was stricken with such grief and loss that I could not bear it. I drew my knife and prepared to end myself!"

Anger turned to fear and doubt among the men, and many cried out, dreading to hear what would come next.

"Our Colonel begged me not to fall on my knife and die. He could have ordered me, but instead, he pleaded. Pleaded for me to live… and to beg of you men the same. That you should live and not fall into despair and kill yourselves. For you see, what the Americans told us, evil and lost though they are, was true. Our home. Our families. Our lands. Our great Democratic Peoples Republic… is gone." He paused, then added, "and… our beloved Great Leader… is gone as well."

He paused. "And so are the evil lands of America and the west. And so is China, and Russia, and every country from our world. All gone. Wiped out by an enemy as vast and uncountable as the stars we all remember that kept us company on the cold, cold nights."

Shouts of defiance and anger, and fear spread across the men. Pyong-Chol knelt down and embraced a weeping soldier before standing back up, somehow taller this time.

"Our brave Colonel asked me to bring you a message. These… Gardeners…. They are cowards. They refuse to fight this great evil themselves. Perhaps they are clever but weak in body. I don't know, but the truth is that they did not rescue us, the Americans, or the others now in this world out of pity or kindness. No! They rescued us not to grow crops, build houses and grow fat. No! They rescued us so that we might one day spit in the eye of the monsters who desecrated our world!"

Guttural anger swelled among the men.

"You see… these Gardeners hid us from the stars so that they can't see us while we grow strong. In this world, the evil ones cannot see us, and we are safe, for now."

He paced back and forth, letting the message sink in.

"Some of you are wondering, as our brave Colonel did… what is the price for this safety?"

He swallowed hard and looked down, covering his face with his hands. When he looked back up, his face was streaked with tears.

"Our brave Colonel knew there was a price to pay. And he paid for it for us. Just as the Gardeners made the Americans pay an even greater price, for their sin and evil was so much greater than ours. Many thousands of the surviving Americans were cut down on Awakening Day. Exactly five percent of their civilians were murdered. More than our entire number. In their arrogance, it took that many for them to listen. Now… I must bring you the terrible news. Our brave Colonel paid the price for the rest of us. He sacrificed himself so that I might bring you this news."

Cries of "No!" and disbelief spread quickly.

"I begged him, No! Let them take me instead! But our Colonel knew that I was not worthy. His life was worth a thousand of ours, and he gave his for all of us… that we might live and one day not only fight the evil from the stars… but also exact our revenge upon the Gardeners for taking our brave Colonel from us."

Fury, anger, and grief swept across the nearly two thousand ragged men. Minutes later, after the reaction began to die down, he raised his arms for their attention.

"Before our brave Colonel was struck down, he wrestled one more thing from the Gardeners. He knew that the abuses of Kim Young-ho and his followers were great, and he demanded of the Gardeners that you men be restored to health. He made them force the Americans to bring tribute to us in the form of supplies, medicine, and doctors. The Americans were furious and humiliated, but they knew they had no choice. If we call, they must come to our aid. We must never let them forget that it took the bravery and sacrifice of our beloved Colonel to bring them to their knees!"

The Ends

● ● ● ● ● ● ● ● ● ● ● ● ● ● ● ● ●

TopSide
Accipiter Holding Cell

John Austin sat with his boots up on the table in front of the glass wall, staring at the Accipiter Priest, who sat silently staring back. Once a week, John had made the elevator ride to TopSide for meetings and always included a stopover at the Accipiter cell. Each time, John and the Priest sat silently, staring at each other, sometimes for hours. Many privately and some publicly questioned this use of John's time, saying that this should be left to others until at least some progress was made. John had vociferously disagreed, pointing out that the Priest was, so far as we knew, one of, if not *the,* leader of the race that effectively wiped-out Earth. John wanted to look the creature in the eye, leader to leader.

Moreover, *Gail* agreed with John and now accompanied him, well, just about everywhere. Rather than divide the Accipiter's attention, she was in the next room, watching on the monitors and communicating to John through an earpiece.

It looked like today would be no exception to the rule. After a two and a half hour staring match, John glanced at his Rolex Mariner, sighed, and started to get up to leave.

The Priest broke the silence at last. It withdrew its truehands from its chest feather analogues as a low rumbling, and a jumble of clashing chords erupted over the speakers, followed by glyphs and signs.

The text-to-speech translation spoke with its English lilt:

Untranslatable. BREAK. SAVAGE. Untranslatable.

After the first encounter, Leo moved the operation back to the SigInt headquarters DownSide. He spoke via remote meeting software on the computer. "Ahh, Mr. President, I don't think it likes you anymore. I believe it is calling you, well, either a monster or a savage or something along those lines. It is also asking what you want."

From the next room, Gail spoke through the encrypted earpiece to John. *"You've got this, John. You've got to show complete confidence without a shred of doubt. Push him hard."*

John's eyes glinted as he settled back into his former relaxed position, Accipiter boots still on the table. "Savage? I see. You think that *we* are the savages. I suppose you would, of course. After all, you've made yourselves functionally immortal, and you've been lording over the galaxy for over a million years now, pasteurizing every civilization that emerges. So, us mere upstart humans must seem like nothing to you. Does that about sum it up?"

The Priest made rumbling noises, but only the glyph for 'yes' flowed across its beak.

Yes

"Humph. Didn't need a translation for that. Well, Mr. High Priest, please allow this lowly human to educate you. You see, to us, it is the Accipiter race who are the true savages of the galaxy. After all, you were just a bunch of sad nomadic bronze age primitives when your benefactors uplifted you and gave you all your power and technology. You didn't invent it. You didn't struggle for it. You didn't lift yourselves up out of the mud and reach for the stars to earn it. You didn't imagine it and then create it. No, it was handed to you on a silver platter. You see, us humans? We clawed our way out of that mud. We were already traveling into space routinely when you blasted our civilization. Without the help of any *divine* intervention, we savage humans already sent out probes to all of our planets and would have soon colonized our moon, Mars, and beyond. Without the benefit of a stardrive, we even had plans for how to reach the stars and colonize them. All by ourselves, without any help."

John narrowed his eyes and leaned forward. "You see, humanity, in its mere five thousand years of recorded history, already exceeded EVERYTHING your people ever achieved on their own. Everything your people ever *earned.* Human civilization was growing! And your people? All you Accipiters ever did was to use the power and weapons given to you by someone else to rampage across the galaxy, conquering and subjugating God knows how many planets!"

John shook his head. "Tell me this, Mr. High Priest of the galactic savages. How much have your people actually progressed beyond what they were given by those that uplifted you? Tell me! How much have they earned by right of hard work, blood, intellect, and sacrifice? How much of the technology that you have today did you really invent yourselves, and how much of it was either given to you or stolen from others? Tell me that!"

The Priest rocked back and forth without answering. Its only reply was a rock-crushing rumble and a blurred series of glyphs that flashed and strobed across its beak.

Untranslatable. Untranslatable. Untranslatable.

Untranslatable.

Leo said apologetically, "I'm having trouble with that one, Sir."

Gail spoke through John's earpiece, *"Keep pushing him, John. We talked about this. We have to pound and challenge him on every front we can think of. Play the part of the insolent and outraged human leader for all its worth. I know it's not who you are, but you need to play the part. See if we can push him over the edge. Tom's epistemological debates with the creature notwithstanding, we need to get him to engage with us."*

John snorted, "You people! You didn't come to our world and say, 'Oh, hi guys, we're your neighbors, the Accipiters. You know, we've been keeping an eye on you for eons, and we really like you guys. We'd love to help you clean up your air and water and welcome you to the galactic family neighborhood, and here's a pot roast. Let's go bowling sometime or have a barbeque, share some beers, and get to know each other.' No! You didn't. You could have even said, 'Hey guys, you need to clean up your act. There are folks out here in the galaxy who would love to meet you and welcome you, but you're too messy and violent right now. So, say, now that you know we're out here, please give us a call when you're ready to talk? We'd love to be your friends!' No! You didn't! You are hypocrites! You complain about us being violent when you waltzed in and murdered billions by bombing us from orbit without even a call to surrender!"

The Priest finally answered with a sharp clash of minor chords and a brief series of glyphs and signs, starting with the glyph for 'No' and an unusually harsh series of signs.

No. Untranslatable. Untranslatable. Untranslatable. Stolen. Lie.
Untranslatable. Question?

John turned to the screen.

Leo said, "Yeah, Uhm, obviously, it didn't agree with you. It's saying something about No Correct or, Not True, maybe. Then it is saying… what? Removed? No,… different connotation. Maybe… Stole? You stole… Oh, I know that sign. That's their word for the Builders. I'll add that to the matrix. They *really* don't like the Builders. I think he is saying we stole something from the Builders. I'm guessing he's talking about Phoenix?"

Gail exclaimed, "*Bingo, John! He took the bait!*"

John laughed, "Oh, that's rich. Yes, we took the technology, but it isn't really that far beyond us. You see, we actually understand the math. We'd already thought of it, we'd already *imagined* that it was possible, even started coming up with designs for it. If we'd had a few more years, we would have already started building versions of that technology ourselves. Tell me, when you were wandering around in the *dirt* on your original home planet before your benefactors showed up, had *you* theorized anything beyond simple metallurgy and fire? My God, the arrogance! All we needed was a few years. Decades or longer, but that's nothing to you! You've been out there for over a million years and accomplished nothing NEW except how to murder and enslave people on a larger and larger scale!"

The Accipiter stood and approached the window. Stridently angry tones followed repeated signs for 'No' and glyphs for other words.

No! Untranslatable. Slave not. Untranslatable. Gift. Peace.
Untranslatable.

Leo offered, "It seems to be offended by a word you used. Enslave. He's saying that Accipiters do not Enslave. That we do not understand… Gift. The gift of… Peace… the gift of… this is a hard one…. Maybe…. Grace?"

John kicked the window with his boot, startling the Priest, before standing up and leaning into the window, inches from the Accipiter's hulking ten-foot-tall form. "My world learned centuries ago that religion forced upon others, no matter how lofty the words may sound, is meaningless if it is drenched in blood and death. We were *still* learning that lesson in some places when you arrived. Tell me, Priest, do you think that your people ever learned that lesson? Because it's obvious they didn't? They never had to. They were handed power so overwhelming that no other race could ever say no and live to debate you about it. You conquer worlds and genetically engineer the survivors to *worship* you and accept anything you say! In your entire history, you've never had your beliefs challenged. Not once!"

John turned to leave, then looked back over his shoulder and added, "Think about *that*, Priest. *You* say that your people are right and just and that the ends justify the means. We have a saying, us lowly humans. The ends *never* justify the means! Dwell on that until we talk again."

The FAB

● ● ● ● ● ● ● ● ● ● ● ● ● ● ● ●

Ari'Nell

Captain Alberta "Bertie" Sinitskaya rubbed her tired black eyes with the back of her pale, calloused hand. For a time, before being accepted to the Naval Academy, she'd "gone goth." During her Academy years, and later, on the Delaware and then aboard the Illinois, she had cropped her raven black hair short. Eventually, as Supervisor of Shipbuilding, Conversion, and Repair (SUPSHIP) in Groton, she'd allowed it to grow out a bit longer. After the Apocalypse, she whimsically settled on a Betty Page look, much to the amusement of her husband Dimitri and nineteen-year-old daughter Anna. Her son Ronald had been so smitten with General Chilton's daughter Nicole that he'd barely noticed, commenting after being asked, "Yeah, mom, looks nice. Did you do something different?"

However, ever since her posting as System Commander in Ari'Nell, she mostly kept it tied back with a bandanna. Her Command had started out small, consisting of the twenty-one-person crew of ILC Mace, plus a half dozen marines. Outside the weekly shipboard drills, only a skeleton crew would remain aboard. They had sweated and toiled away the rest of the time operating the "Old Ones" fabrication module left behind by Phoenix.

Over time, things changed. Operations onboard the FAB were carried out twenty-four hours a day, seven days a week. More crews were needed to keep up the quickening pace. Those crews needed to be sharp when handling multi-thousand-pound nuclear bomb-pumped laser weapons. Those crews needed support. Someone had to prepare the meals, clean the clothes, clean the... well, everything. Someone else needed to be there to maintain pressure and space suits. Medics and doctors were needed to treat the inevitable injuries that came with handling large, massive weapons.

Each "mine" was over twenty-five feet long.

They needed someone else to maintain all the non-alien equipment required just to move things around. Others were needed to keep track of… everything. After all, there was a war on, so all those people needed marines to protect them. Of course, all of those people required backups and backups for the backups for multiple shifts. Eventually, it had been easier to put many of the people on the surface of the planet, where a small town had grown. In total, over a thousand men and women now worked either on the surface of Ari'Nell, in the FAB, or on the ramshackle space station cobbled together around it.

Today's playlist was dominated by Meshuggah's complex, polymetered song structures and polyrhythmic moods. She paused and looked at her hands. She'd never been exactly delicate, but despite years of working on motorcycles and, later, much much larger machines, she'd always managed to find time to take care of her body and almost porcelain skin. Since Ari'Nell though, the combination of dry air and nearly reckless work had left her hands cracked and calloused and her arms and body scraped and bruised.

Bertie's husband, Dimitri, was in charge of the engineers and the project to study the 'other' weapon design, hoping to eventually integrate it into Phoenix and other vessels. Bertie was privately convinced that having Dimitri with her, even though they sometimes barely saw each other, was the only thing keeping her sane. The workload was… desperate. Privately, she was shocked that no one had been killed in an accident. Yet.

Ari'Shevn was a yellow dwarf G-type Main Sequence star, about 90% the mass of Earth's Sun. The star system consisted of two gas giants, four rocky planets, including two that were icy, and Ari'Nell. Ari'Nell was the third planet in the Ari'Shevn star system. It had been a lovely, if slightly smaller, analogue of Earth itself and home to over one hundred trillion Builders and a titanic orbital megastructure that was home to the bulk of the total system population.

That is until the Accipiters arrived and glassed the planet, which was now redder than Mars, with only a few wispy clouds. The entire surface was pockmarked with overlapping craters, most filled with water and many surrounded by thin greenish rings of primitive algae. All that now remained of the orbital megastructure and its inhabitants was an enormous, brilliantly glinting ring system far wider than the planet itself.

After the Accipiter attack, the smashed megastructure debris had either impacted the planet or collided with each other, creating a vast ring of dust and small bits and pieces. Keppler Syndrome on an unimaginable scale. The material in the rings was mainly composed of highly refined alloys and compounds, including superconductors and a prodigious amount of fissionable and transuranic elements, along with a disturbing amount of… organic matter. A stupendous graveyard of the annihilated Builders.

The box-like fabrication facility, FAB, and all the other structures growing up around it floated just outside the planet's rings. It was over two hundred meters long and a third as tall, with a habitation module, airlock, and control section offset from the middle. Along the top of the FAB sat a dodecahedron-shaped power module that Phoenix had revealed had a large zero-point energy device at its core. At the far end of the FAB, an ingest door allowed the input of raw materials. Excess materials and components were stored in a massive spherical storage module connected to the nominal rear of the FAB. Finished items were "handled" and processed out through another module roughly the same size as the FAB. Things like the mines and drones were sent through an airlock, while non-vacuum-rated items could be inventoried and conveyed out of its other airlock, generally attached to an ILC for transfer.

Back in Groton, on Earth, as SUPSHIP, Bertie had liaised with the Department of the Navy and the Electric Boat Corporation to design and construct new submarines and repair and modernize Los Angeles, Seawolf, and Virginia Class nuclear submarines for the Fleet. She'd been responsible for administering all the contracts, outfitting the ships, and ensuring that they fully met the technical and quality assurance requirements. She also cracked the whip on production schedules to make sure that the work all resulted in a fleet that was ready to sail "in harm's way." She'd been responsible for over three hundred civilians and military in multiple locations.

Sometimes, at the end of a particularly long day, when her bones ached, her coveralls were caked with salt and sweat, and she could barely shuffle to her narrow bunk and collapse, it felt like she'd been reduced to menial warehouse labor. When those moments of self-pity clouded her mind, she chastised and reminded herself how critical the work might one day be for the survival of all that remained of mankind. In some ways, the work was more straightforward than it had been when there had only been an FTL seed core to babysit and "feed" chunks of material from the rings that it asked for. It "ingested" those chunks, separating out the elements it needed to grow. The rings were constructed not only from the materials from the superstructure of the Builder orbital megastructure but also the power plants, computers, wiring, and the thousands of ships similar to Phoenix that had been present at the time.

The larger the seed core grew into a new set of drive rings, the faster the process went. After it was finished, the next step was the construction of the FAB.

Instead of self-replicating another drive system, the FAB was a copy of a miniature version of what the Builder's original masters had used to construct components, systems, subsystems, and, when needed, weapons. The Builder's job had been to manage that process, assemble, and operate the technology, facilities, ships, etc., for their masters. Over the course of centuries, those "masters" had uplifted the Builders from simple deer-like animals to do more and more manual labor for them. Eventually, Builders were fitted with cybernetic implants in utero. It was the job of the artificial intelligences, like Phoenix, to raise and teach the Builders from before they were born to do the work for their masters. In addition, certain portions of the Builder's anatomy were considered delicacies to their masters. Specifically, their delicate hand-like appendages. They were work slaves as well as cattle for consumption.

The Builders did not have a name for their masters. It was too painful a subject. When Phoenix's memory was unlocked, and she revealed the plans for the FAB, the term "Old Ones" had been chosen for the convenience of her new human friends.

Eventually, a plague struck the masters on a colony world. Fearing they would be blamed, many of the Builders had fled and spread out like so much Kudzu into the galaxy, rapidly colonizing every planet they found. That's when the Accipiters were uplifted by *their* benefactors and were loosed upon the galaxy with the mission to wipe out the Builders. None were known to survive, at least not within the confines of the galaxy itself.

While the FAB could be "programmed" to create things other than what was in its library, for now, the decision was made to limit production to making as many of the mobile bomb-pumped laser mines as possible, along with exemplars of other systems to be taken back to New Texas for analysis and testing. Besides the obvious desire to have as many defensive weapons as possible, one of the major motivations for producing them was that they were relatively simple. The propulsion, controls, and targeting were trivial for an advanced race like the Old Ones. When you get right down to it, nukes are quite simple devices if you don't have to worry about refining your fissionable material. So, with the abundance of fissionables in the rings and the ability of the FAB to produce automated drones to seek out the needed materials and bring them back for processing, cranking out the mines proceeded at pace.

Its most difficult-to-produce and time-consuming component in building the FAB itself was its oversized zero-point energy power module. Subatomic 3D printing requires a lot of energy. Rather, it requires a VAST amount of energy. Creating the power module took longer than the rest of the FAB and related facilities combined.

Demand from the President on down for progress on the "other" weapon system that Dimitri was working on was more than intense. Everyone knew how important it was. Mankind's survival might well depend on it. No pressure.

The problem was that while the weapon itself was not terribly difficult for the FAB to produce, the power supply it demanded — was immense. Worse, the weapon was designed to be incorporated into Old One warships, supported by multiply redundant systems and subsystems. In short, their ships were built around the weapon. More than one person had joked that it was like the gun in the A-10 Warthog — a gun so big that the airframe had essentially been built around it. In order to find a way to make the weapon work, many shortcuts and compromises would be needed to create, essentially, a weapon pod that could be, more or less, strapped to ships like Phoenix and Revenge.

So, they prioritized the mines over the other weapon. They were comparatively trivial to build. The equation was simple. Did you want one single weapon that you weren't even sure how to use and incorporate, or did you want thousands of self-propelled bomb-pumped X-Ray laser mines?

The problematic new weapon would require independent power and control systems and couldn't simply be powered by Phoenix herself. While her warp rings incorporated their own version of zero-point energy generation, it was distributed throughout its rings, and she needed all their power to maintain the warp field itself. You could potentially have one or the other, but not both.

✪ ✪ ✪

It was the end of another grueling day of moving completed mines out of the FAB, inventorying them, triple-running systems checks, and ultimately deploying them as fast as they could move the tested units out of the airlock. While each mine may have been "simple" to the Old Ones, the completed weapons were still the size of a small semi-truck trailer.

Bertie and her weary crew had just returned to the crew mess aboard Mace when Coms Lieutenant Swati Singh spoke over Bertie's headset from the ILC's bridge. "Commander, message from Revenge. Captain Cutter is back in-system. He has new orders…."

✪ ✪ ✪

Jermaine Cutter entered the FAB through the alternate airlock after riding over in ILC Kukri, the NTN Revenge's utility ILC. While Bertie and her crew labored to keep the FAB fed and running, it kept Jermaine and Revenge busy ferrying mines, equipment, and supplies back and forth along the twenty-six-hour path back to New Texas. Naturally, the entry and exit vectors were randomized. There was no known way for the Accipiters to arrive without everyone knowing about it, but OpSec isn't just for the threats you know about.

Bertie had taken a few minutes to change into fresh coveralls and throw on her Harley Davidson leather jacket before joining the rest of her crew as Jermaine stepped onboard, smiled broadly, and reached out and grasped her hand, shaking it. "Bertie, it's good to see you again. Everyone back home knows how hard you and your crew are working out here. The President told me to express to you his thanks and admiration."

Bertie cocked her head and grinned crookedly. A shock of black hair escaped her bandana as she shook her head, "You're one to talk, Jermaine. You've been bouncing back and forth between here and New Texas like a yoyo or some mad pizza delivery driver. We're still waiting for the pizza, by the way. It's got to be frozen solid by now."

Just then, Lieutenant Alister Gordon entered the airlock wearing a grin almost as big as Jermaine's. In his arms was a stack of insulated pizza delivery bags.

Bertie's crew whooped for joy at the long-promised but never really expected treat.

She lowered her gaze and frowned. "OK, what's the bad news?"

Jermaine shrugged, "It's time. They gave the order to produce the weapon and mount it on Mace to test it just as soon as possible. If it checks out, we'll deploy them to the other ships."

Bertie closed her eyes and shook her head, "The damned thing doesn't even have a name yet, and we're supposed to figure out how to strap it onto an alien spaceship and make it work...."

Campaign

● ● ● ● ● ● ● ● ● ● ● ● ● ● ● ●

DownSide:
Fort Brazos Town Square
In front of the Gardener Obelisk

Livia Milner looked out across the sizeable crowd of reporters, supporters, and curious townspeople. Behind her, as a backdrop, stood the over three-hundred-foot-tall dark alien obelisk that had replaced the founders' statues on Awakening Day. Gloria Vargas stood to her left. Preston Milner stood to her right in a business suit so as to not show a military endorsement. More than a dozen Navy wives and their husbands stood behind the group, providing a vibrant backdrop. As soon as Livia had mentioned the remote possibility of her running, the response had been overwhelming. Well-wishers and volunteers flooded her inbox, pushing her over the edge. In little more than a week, she'd given in to the idea, and her campaign had taken shape. Today was the big announcement.

Reed Pauly, Danielle Richardson's former Station Engineer, made a last-minute adjustment to the microphone and stepped to the side.

As Livia smiled and walked to the microphone, the crowd cheered. She raised her hands briefly, letting the noise die down.

"Good morning. I'd like to begin by saying that there is perhaps no point in all of human history more fraught with change, pain, loss, fear, and, I believe, hope than now. We, that is, all of us, the last survivors of humanity, stand at a crossroads. We all know the threat posed to us by both the Accipiters and the Gardeners. We all know the changes the Gardeners made to our health and, apparently, our lifespans. The decisions we make today will reverberate throughout not only the next generation but possibly even for the next thousand years or more. The Accipiters and the challenges we face threaten our very existence. How are we to maintain our freedom and liberty in the face of unending war? How are we to rebuild human society in this place while maintaining a semblance of the majesty and culture of our stolen world? How do we ensure that our children are not only educated but have any chance at all of understanding the heritage that was ripped from their inheritance? How do we rebuild our science and industry? How do we ensure that our farm economy doesn't collapse and decay while so much focus is being placed on the city and the war?"

"Moreover, how do we give direction to our traditional moral purpose, awakening everyone to the dangers and opportunities that confront us? Every citizen of Fort Brazos, New London, Jonestown, or even the New Philippines, and every soldier, sailor, airman, and marine, regardless of their original country, is precious. Every remaining life is precious."

"We, all of us, deserve leaders who are committed to finding solutions to our problems and who will not waver in the face of evil. It is the sacred duty of our leaders to hold our hopes, dreams, and our very survival above all else. Above their petty ambitions, above the Machiavellian politics that have plagued human leadership throughout our history. Now is the time to set ourselves above the venal corruption of power and greed that has so inevitably enticed politicians of all stripes like flies to honey." *I can't believe I'm saying this dribble.*

"Ever since New London's Awakening Day, I've been privileged to get to know so very many of you, both here in this wonderful refuge for humanity that is Fort Brazos, as well as *next door* at Fort Underwood and, certainly, throughout the city of New London. So very many of us lost family and loved ones." She paused. "I lost my daughter and family. Now... *you* have become family. I am certain that many of you remember how out of place I was when I arrived."

She smiled softly as laughter rolled across the square.

"Yes, I know. I'm the lady that was in *that dress.*" She paused, "But from that very first day here, I was... welcomed." She swallowed, left the microphone, walked over to Gloria, and hugged her tightly. Gloria grinned in return and said something the microphone didn't pick up. Livia nodded vigorously and wiped a tear away before returning to the microphone.

"I have met and talked with so many of you. As some may know, the Admiral's wife has a special responsibility to see to the wellbeing of our Officers' spouses and families. I gladly accepted that responsibility, just as I did my day job as a partner at a law firm that seemed so important to me at the time… and, like everything else, no longer exists. That's all I ever really wanted. That, and to be a mother…. I never wanted the kind of responsibility I grew up watching my father, himself a United States Senator, carried on his shoulders. Now, I know we were from Boston. And, yes, we were Yankees. Maybe even damned Yankees." She smiled, "But we were also proud Americans. From a young age, I saw how seriously my father took his responsibilities, just as my mother, as a judge, took hers."

She smiled and held out her hand to Preston, who stepped forward and took it. She gazed up at his face and turned back to the crowd. "Can I help it if I fell in love with a dashing young Naval Officer?"

"Well, here we all are, changed forever in a world not created by God but by aliens. Many of us have had to step up and accept greater responsibilities. Look at President Austin? By all accounts, he was a brave and loving father who did not ask for or even want the job. He just wanted to be your Sheriff and raise his daughter. But when the Apocalypse came, and the people demanded it, he shouldered the responsibility like the honorable man that he is. It is in that spirit that I come before you today to ask for your permission. I humbly ask for your *blessing* for me to run for one of the Senate seats being created by the new Constitution."

Gloria Vargas stepped to the microphone next to Livia and asked, "Do I hear a second?"

At least a hundred voices shouted in agreement.

"Do I hear a third?"

Most of the crowd cheered loudly.

Gloria stepped forward and hugged Livia before stepping back.

Livia held her hand over her chest and said, "Thank you. Thank you. It is with your support, then, that I announce my candidacy for the Senate. I intend to earn your trust and devote myself to listening, learning, and serving as your advocate. I believe that we, the survivors of humanity, have a noble destiny to fulfill, not only to ensure that humanity does not fade away but that all our tears and history are not for nothing. That, together, we can teach the galaxy the true meaning of freedom, even in the face of seemingly infinite peril. I believe that we will indeed endure and prosper as a confident, courageous, and persevering people."

Gloria Vargas's House

Later that evening, the doorbell rang. Livia looked up from the mountain of paperwork on the kitchen table as Gloria answered the door.

"Who is it, Gloria?"

The heavy oak door shut with a thud, and Gloria carried a gift-wrapped package to the kitchen and said, looking at the tag, "It's for you. It's from Andre Johansson." She handed the box to Livia and walked to the kitchen to check on dinner.

Livia raised her eyebrows in surprise. "Really? OK, this is unexpected." She pulled the ribbon and removed the wrapping from the oblong box. Using a table knife, she slit the sealing tape and opened the box and the wrapping paper inside, revealing a… gavel? It was inscribed with the words "For all you have done, and all you will do. Never Forget."

Gloria returned and exclaimed, "What a lovely gift! I didn't realize he was a supporter?"

Livia shrugged, "I'm as surprised as you are, Gloria."

Shock

● ● ● ● ● ● ● ● ● ● ● ● ● ● ●

DownSide
Frederick Fuller Russell Medical Center

Gail Finley steeled herself as she stepped into the elevator between the young men who had become so close to her, despite her resentment over the loss of privacy… and personal freedom. Sergeant Nate Hopper stood to her side. At six foot three, he towered over her own five-nine. In the lead were Corporals Jose Cruz and Jermal Dixon. They were just marines assigned to protect her, even at the cost of their own lives. And yet, somewhere along the way, they'd become more. The duty and responsibility remained, but layered on that was something deeper. Every day they silently stood by and watched her shoulder the burdens… the actual fate of mankind. They saw it all. The pain and anguish, the soaring victories, and the sometimes-crushing isolation. They were acutely aware of how far her already small circle of trusted friends and confidants had shrunk. Moreover, they'd just as silently watched as the initial spark of self-denied interest between her and the President had grown and evolved. They also knew from the professional and discrete signals from John's detail that, if anything, his circle had grown even smaller than hers and that what had slowly replaced it was the increasingly undeniable bond that developed between Gail and John.

For her part, Gail knew that they knew. Nothing was ever actually said, but over the last year, her three protectors had become something closer to fiercely protective brothers.

"Professional detachment be damned," Nate had confided to Jose and Jarmal, and they'd agreed. Indeed, the three had likewise bonded with each other. His greatest private fear was that someday, when it came down to it, that Gail might not *let* them do their duty. He knew that she understood *why* it was important that she let them. However, in the heat of the moment, he worried that her fondness for them would provide a fatal moment's hesitation. He suspected that Jose and Jermal felt the same way. And *that* was why, instead of becoming complacent with time, all three only grew more and more vigilant around her.

One of the toughest problems in protecting Gail Anson Finley was Gail Anson Finley. She was quick, forceful, and determined, constantly striding into a room without hesitation, opening doors for herself, and worse. They'd long since given up on trying to talk her into allowing them to do that part of their jobs. Their incapacitation and failure to protect her during the City Hall bombing was a recurring nightmare for all three men. They'd still been on the floor after the blast when Gail had risen, shot the bastard, and started giving orders. Slowing her down for her own good, for the most part, was a daily exercise in futility.

Except for the last few days.

Normally, Gail never managed to sleep for more than five or six hours at most. Often less. However, in what she'd been certain must have seemed like a scandalous turn of events, for the last three days, she'd slept in for more than *nine*. Today, instead of her usual simple black coffee and maybe a slice of toast for a running-start breakfast, she'd canceled her morning appointments and instead gone to Ray's Diner, where she'd had a full-course leisurely breakfast.

Throughout the morning, she'd been quiet, introspective, and reserved, waiting patiently while Jose opened doors and, just now, not even attempting to press the elevator button for the fourth floor on her way to see Surgeon General Elliott.

Somewhere in Gail's blizzard of thoughts, part of her laughed. *They know.* Not just about the escalation of her relationship with John but of the consequences. The *universal* consequence that now came with it.

✪ ✪ ✪

Gwyneth Elliott smiled as she and Gail took their seats on the couch in her office. Nate conferred briefly with Gwyneth's one-man detail, a big Scotsman Corporal named Sorley Pòl Murdoch. They'd swept the room, and then all retreated outside the door to give the two women some privacy.

Gwyneth had given birth to twin boys Gerald and Paul a little over a week earlier and was already back to work. Fortunately, and as a direct consequence of biological changes, an entire hospital wing had been converted into a nursery and daycare. With the improved health and vitality from the Gardeners, pregnancy complications were almost non-existent, and recovery time was swift indeed. With the vastly increased birth rate, one of the greatest challenges of the Apocalypse was coping with a veritable tsunami of babies.

Gwyneth studied her face.

So far, Gail had not said a word. Her eyes were wide, and her ordinarily pale complexion was flushed.

Gwyneth lowered her gaze questioningly.

Gail's lips trembled.

Gwyneth broke into an ear-to-ear smile and rushed to take Gail into a fierce hug. "Oh, my dear friend, I'm so happy for you! I'm guessing you're a week late, yes?"

Gail nodded numbly as tears started to flow. She whispered, "I thought… I thought I was ready for this, Gwen. I thought…."

Gwyneth pulled away and gently wiped Gail's tears away. "Oh, sweetheart, you're going to be just fine, and I'm going to take exquisite care of you!"

Gail nodded slowly, blinked, and asked quietly, "Umm, how are the boys? How are Paul and Gerald?"

"They make a great vocal duet, I'll tell you. They're fine and growing like weeds." She gushed, "Oh, Gail, I'm so, so very thrilled for you! I can't begin to tell you how wonderful and hard and terrifying pregnancy is…. But you… and John… will be OK. I promise you."

Gail swallowed and looked up at her. "I hate the Gardeners."

"Don't we all. Now tell me. Truthfully, does he know?"

Gail looked away. "He knew… we knew… knew that it would happen. I… I wanted to talk to you and see if I'm… if it… is OK. I'm… Gwen…. Oh, I don't know anything about being pregnant! I'm an only child, and before now… before all this… before… him… I never gave it a moment's thought. I'm…."

"Scared, yes, I know. Hell, when I found out I was pregnant with Rosalyn, I was terrified, and I'm a doctor, and my little brother had four kids that I adored. Right now, you're in shock, and I'm going to take care of you. You're going to listen to what I tell you to do, and you're going to do what I tell you to do. I'm also going to have a little talk with your three boys out in the hall, and you're not going to argue with me about it. Have you got that?"

Gail nodded slowly, swallowed in defeat, and answered, "Yes, ma'am."

"Good. Now, I just have one question. And this is very, very important. It is the most important question you're going to answer for quite some time, I expect. I want to make sure you are fully here with me and listening. Do I have your full and undivided attention?"

Gail blinked, took a deep breath, and settled herself. "Yes, yes, of course."

"What color will my Maid of Honor dress be?"

Incoming Fire

● ● ● ● ● ● ● ● ● ● ● ● ● ● ● ● ●

DownSide:
Jonestown

Commander Ramona Henry paced ILC Dagger's tiny bridge and studied the landing zone next to the zero-point energy device 'cave.' Until the recent discovery, there had been an LZ for a while. However, after being unused, the local vegetation had quickly overgrown it. Not anymore. Sickle made daily trips there now, but today was a crew rotation, so Dagger doubled up, making a run to Jonestown after its usual daily trip to Morgan Island. Making the LZ itself was ridiculously easy. All you really had to do was to set down slowly enough. Even without the warp field, the ILC's nearly 400-ton mass was more than sufficient to compact local vegetation. Adding the warp field simplified things even further. If you set down very, very slowly, the annihilation taking place at the border of the field created a very clean 130' x 65' divot. You just had to make sure you indeed kept it slow so that you didn't overload the field and shunt the excess energy in the form of ionizing radiation to the interior of the field, killing the crew. Minor detail.

By now, the LZ had been widened substantially into a nominally flattened area large enough to support the growing rows of pallets, containers, and equipment being duplicated. The site was a beehive of activity, not the least of which was the security detachment roaming the wide, fenced-off area.

Lieutenant Alister Gordan reported, sitting at his station, "They're ready for us, Captain."

Ramona sighed and stepped over behind him. "It's about time. I was…."

Suddenly, a brilliant flash of light lit up the bridge. There was no vibration or other reaction.

Ramona exclaimed, "What the hell was that? Report! Dagger, Report!"

CAPTAIN, A HIGH-ENERGY PROJECTILE, JUST IMPACTED THE WARP FIELD. THERE IS NO DANGER TO THE CREW. THE IMPACT WAS NOT OF A MAGNITUDE LARGE ENOUGH TO OVERLOAD THE FIELD. THE FLASH OF LIGHT WAS THE FIELD ABSORBING THE ENERGY.

Her eyes widened. "Someone's *shooting* at us? What the Hell? Who? From where?"

LOCATING. HERE, CAPTAIN. THE CREATURE APPEARS TO BE LIKE THE ONES REPORTED TO HAVE FIRED HIGH-ENERGY PROJECTILES AT THE ARTILLERY CREW ON EARTH DURING THE KEEPER RETRIEVAL RAID. YIELD ESTIMATE ON THE IMPACT OF 10.98 MEGA JOULES IMPLIES AN ENERGY ROUGHLY EQUIVALENT TO A HUMAN ARTILLERY SHELL.

The viewscreen highlighted a spot on a hill some miles away, then zoomed in. A mature, bull elephant-sized Wardog was there, with a glowing rail-like thing that crackled with energy… on its back. Sparks flew from the rail, and a flash erupted from its tip.

Ramona barked the order at the pilots, Nikita Choudhary and Conor Lleu. "Evasive! One thousand meters Z Positive axis! Now!"

There was no sensation of movement as Dagger, from the perspective of an outside observer, instantly shot upwards, evading the incoming projectile. Or, from the perspective of an outside observer, *down* from the inner surface of New Texas's cylindrical surface.

"Dagger, can that thing hurt us?"

IT DOES NOT APPEAR, SO, CAPTAIN. NOT
AS LONG AS THE FIELD IS UP. THE ENERGY
REQUIRED WOULD BE ORDERS OF MAGNITUDE
GREATER.

"Got it. So, let's not let the damned thing hurt anyone else, then, shall we? Take us directly over that thing, take a bunch of pictures and then crush the son of a bitch and be done with it. I'm not risking anyone's life to take it out on the ground."

✪ ✪ ✪

DownSide:
Fields near the Sanches Veterinary & Equine Center Stables

John and Gail had been riding their horses, Rusty and Heartbreaker, for an hour before the call came in. It was a beautiful day, and they'd looked forward to getting away from everything and everyone, so much as that was actually possible with their combined protection details orbiting at a discrete distance.

Sargent Jesse Roberts approached on horseback and handed John a phone.

John listened for a moment, then put it on speaker, frowning as he asked, "Repeat that, please, Alexander?"

Gail sidestepped Heartbreaker to get closer as Alexander Marcus said, "Mr. President, there's been an incident. ILC Dagger was about to land at Jonestown when it was fired upon by a type of Accipiter creature last seen on Earth. Dagger was not damaged, and no one was injured. Dagger subsequently killed the creature. Commander Henry judged that if the thing was able to fire at her, then a ground team might be put at high risk in order to capture it."

Gail nodded gravely.

John frowned. "That sounds like she made the right call. If something new like this is cropping up now, I'm sure we'll get another chance to see one."

"The Commander managed to get lots of imagery of it, so that's something."

Gail asked, "Alex, Gail here. Why now? Jonestown has been there for months with people coming and going."

"Madam Vice President, I can only speculate that perhaps it is related to the greatly increased activity next to the site. The town itself is very low-tech. There's not much in the way of radio signals and electronic noise there. They've been smart to work to keep it that way."

She nodded, and John answered, "I see. OK, well, I'm sure you've already ordered an increase in patrols and surveillance in the area."

"Indeed so, Mr. President. Perhaps we were getting a little bit complacent, thinking the worst was over."

Gail asked, "What exactly did the thing do? How did it shoot at Dagger? Was it the same as the ones reported in Peru?"

"We haven't seen the imagery here yet, to compare it, but it sounds like that is the case, ma'am. And I know what you're going to ask next. I don't see how something like this could create the mystery craters and fires. From what Commander Henry described, the thing wasn't nearly that powerful. Something else has to be going on."

John looked a question at Gail, who nodded. He added, "Very well, Alexander. Keep us up to date, please."

"Yes, Mr. President, Madam Vice President. Will do."

John handed the phone back to Jesse, who retreated a distance away.

John shook his head. "What do you think?"

Gail frowned. "I'm worried the Gardeners are playing games with us again. What are we going to tell the people?"

"The truth. A Wardog vainly attacked an ILC and was quickly killed. We're expanding patrols out an of abundance of caution. As always, just in case, people should report anything unusual to the hotline."

She nodded, "You're right. We really don't know much more, and we don't need people running out to try to hunt down mystery creatures that may or may not exist."

John sidled his horse closer to Gail's.

They looked at each other and sighed.

John nodded. "Well then, what about the other thing?"

Gail's mouth crinkled, and her eyes laughed. "I've got it covered."

Invitation

● ● ● ● ● ● ● ● ● ● ● ● ● ● ● ●

DownSide
Radio Station 92.5 Studio

Danielle keyed the microphone, "Hello, people of Fort Brazos and New London. This is Danielle Richardson on FM 92.5, and Radio Free Fort Brazos beaming our signal across the known world and beyond. So, folks, it's been a busy week so far! With the election heating up, I'm sure you all heard Mrs. Livia Milner announce her candidacy for Senate, followed shortly thereafter by our own outspoken Councilwoman Esmerelda Collins. Even more interesting was the revelation that the daughter of the late Councilman Barrett Hoffman, Sandra Gareth, wife of that dashing young Captain David Garreth, simultaneously announced that she was running for her late father's vacant Council seat."

Danielle paused to sip her ice tea, "On a hopeful note, I'm told that Vice President Finley was recently seen visiting Fort Underwood's Frederick Fuller Russell Medical Center. Let's hope that it was just routine business or a simple checkup!"

"Now, back to more serious things. It seems that some sort of Wardog hybrid creature that can shoot things took a few potshots at one of our ILCs over by Jonestown. No worries, though. Apparently, it was like shooting spit wads at a tank, and the creature was promptly put down. 'Nuff said."

"Speaking of our Navy, and is it just me, or is it plain weird to talk about alien spaceships we fly around like big airplanes that can also fly in space? Anyway, that new starship, Revenge, has been flying back and forth between here and Ari'Nell pretty much nonstop. I hope whatever is going on out there is worth the mileage and the lost sleep being put in by Captain Cutter and his crew. Meanwhile, Captain Cross and the Blood Phoenix have been gone on their own secret mission for, like, more than forty-five days now. Keep in mind, the trip to Earth only took, like, more than twenty days each way. So, whatever they're doing, let's all pray for their success and safe return."

"Okay, now that we have all that stuff out of the way, I wanted to focus today on the hundred thousand human popsicles inside the Keeper ship. When are we going to decide what to do about them? I mean, at least make a *decision* about what to do, even if whatever it is we do decide to do might take a while or even a long time. It seems like everybody's forgotten about this precious remnant of humanity who is just sitting there, languishing in Accipiter limbo. I mean, let's hope that they're not conscious and that it isn't, like, being cruel to them, keeping them locked up and frozen or in stasis or whatever. I know people are worried about how those poor people would react and adapt, but who knows who is in there? The Accipiters are supposed to have collected specimens they thought were special. Who knows who is in there? Some long-forgotten Van Gogh, Da Vinci, or Einstein? I mean…."

The sound of someone knocking on the studio glass door startled Danielle. "Ahh, excuse me a moment, folks, a visitor is trying to get my attention… who… *Matti Austin?*"

Danielle blinked in surprise as she clicked off the microphone and switched to a music track. She stood, stepped to the heavy, magnetically sealed studio door, and put her shoulder to it to heave it open.

Matti flashed a brilliant smile as she waited. Her waist-length dark blonde hair was braided down her back. Behind her stood Corporal Roxanna Darling, her dark-haired Mexican-Iranian personal security guard.

Danielle tossed her own long, loose black hair back and unconsciously bent down to Matti's almost 10-year-old level. "Miss Austin, Um, to what do I owe the pleasure?"

Matti's blue eyes twinkled as Roxanna put a small, gift-wrapped bag in her hand, which she handed to Danielle.

Danielle looked at the bag and said, "Okay…."

Matti waited expectantly as Danielle gingerly pulled the ribbons apart, looked inside, and removed a small bag of rice with a small card attached.

Danielle's mouth parted in surprise as she looked back up at Matti, then down at the card, which read: 'President John Hugo Austin and Vice President Gail Anson Finley Request the honor of your presence….'

Ari'Chawig

• • • • • • • • • • • • • • • •

10 Light Hours out of
Ari'Chawig System
NTN Blood Phoenix CIC

Captain Cross and Commander Hashimoto stared at the image on the wallscreen with puzzled expressions. The dust clouds that had obscured the brown dwarf system were only marginally thinner within the system itself. At this distance, however, Phoenix was able to piece together imagery of the system interior. The problem, however, was that the imagery didn't make sense. The projected orbits of the objects within the system didn't make sense, and the gravity map made even less.

Captain, while each of the brown dwarfs vary somewhat in composition, they show features of methane, carbon monoxide, sodium, potassium, some carbon dioxide, and, to varying degrees, clouds composed of silicate minerals, that is, what you would call sand. All in all, nothing really unusual. Nothing to cause the anomalies....

Just a moment. You submariners have an expression, a 'hole in the water.' I believe I've located something... analogous. It appears to be an object at the center of mass between the brown dwarfs that is not a natural structure. The mass for an object in that location to account for the observed system anomalies is equivalent to a red dwarf star.

Charles and Haruto exchanged glances.

Haruto shook his head. "Clearly, there isn't a red dwarf there, though, or it would be visible, yes?"

You are correct, Commander. I have expended more energy in order to resolve and interpolate an image.

It displayed the image of a dark sphere on the screen, superimposed with graphical legends, vector indicators, dimensions… and positions of the roughly 3,500km circular structures on its 30,000km or so wide surface.

I hypothesize that this is what you would call a Dyson sphere around a red dwarf star.

Charles shook his head. "I thought Dyson spheres were supposed to be, well, impractical to build, even for theoretically advanced civilizations? And, the thing is a sphere, not a swarm…."

This structure is less than five percent of the diameter of your home star, Sol.

Haruto laughed softly. "Yes, I'm certain that made it so much easier."

Charles asked, "And still no sign of other moving targets, ships?"

No Captain. Of course, unless they were hotter than the background or their albedo was unusual, any vessel not relatively nearby would only register as yet another asteroid. Also, in anticipation of your question, I've also not detected any artificial transmissions of any kind.

"All right then. Let's sit here for another couple of hours, refining your data. If nothing new pops up, we'll swing in-system on a nice, innocent-looking, ballistic path. Phoenix, the instant you detect danger, snap that warp field back on. Don't wait for my order."

Haruto turned to Maximillian McGreggor. "COB, maintain the crew at action stations. Rotate on eight-hour intervals. Make sure all have hot meals. Keep our people fresh."

✪ ✪

Ballistic Course
10 Light Minutes out from
Ari'Chawig System
Center of Mass

Haruto marveled at the display and the dimensions listed on it. "From what you are showing us, Phoenix, those flattened circular structures… The diameter of New Texas itself is under three thousand kilometers. What if they are doors of some kind? It could fit through them…. if they are doors."

Charles squinted at the dark but enhanced image and asked, "Phoenix, have you detected anything that might be craters or damage to that thing? Any way to tell how long it's been here?"

No Captain. There is no obvious sign of damage or ill repair. As you have seen, the surface has a very low albedo. I have limited myself to passive scans only, enhancing reflected ambient light, which limits resolution. Do you wish for me to attempt an active….

Phoenix was cut off mid-sentence as the lights dimmed and the gravity lurched off and then back on.

Charles managed to grab the microphone, shouting, "General Quarters! General Quarters! This is NOT a Drill! All Hands Man Your Battle Stations! Set material Condition Zebra Throughout the Ship! Make reports to D.C. Central!"

A Beautiful Day

● ● ● ● ● ● ● ● ● ● ● ● ● ● ● ●

DownSide:
Fort Underwood
(formerly Fort Brazos)
Maintenance Hangar 24

Maintenance Hangar 24 lay along the outskirts of one of the lesser runways at Fort Underwood. As such, it was close to the hangars and warehouses, now devoted to supporting the alien ILC operations. After all, ILCs didn't need a runway at all. A light rain had fallen the night before, so the early morning air was still cool and damp. It was a beautiful day. Technical Sergeant Manuel Achilles frowned at what his team was working on.

Prior to Awakening Day, Fort Brazos was home to two AH-64(E) Apache battalions, equipped with 24 aircraft each. An upgrade from the AH-64D block III, the E's included improved datalinks designed to transmit and receive data and video from Army UAVs. In Hangar 24, two AH-64Es were currently splayed out, panels open and resting within the specialized framework, ladders, guardrails, and camlock bolting system that made working on the complex helicopters much easier. A half-dozen men and women scrambled around the framework, carefully removing communications and datalink equipment. The idea was to try to rig a system attached to the exterior of one of the ILCs to control a flight of slaved drones.

To Manuel, ripping apart *his* Apaches to experiment with the ILC's was… repugnant. To him, the alien craft looked like giant weird, mutated frogs. Frogs wrapped in huge blue-green rubber bands. That the things flew at all was bizarre. That they could travel to other planets was still hard to accept. Then again, part of him still found it hard to accept the whole idea of the "alien thing" in the first place. Intellectually, it was hard to deny. Just stepping outside and looking up at the other side of the world went a long way. Still, it was just *wrong*. He knew he was in denial, and he was OK with that. He had enough to worry about keeping *his* Apaches flying. That, and doing his best to convince the diminishing number of aircraft mechanics from "jumping ship and joining the damned *Space Marines.*"

Walking across the hangar, his face turned red. "Jimenez! How many times have I told you not to strip those bolts! If I have to…."

Manuel never finished the sentence, and Corporals Jimenez, Franks, Johnson, Bohanna, Dowdie, and Sergeant Mukuamu died instantly in the blast that consumed the hangar and everything in it in a roiling ball of flames that rose from the wreckage that filled the burning crater.

Captain Darryl Guevara, one of the first at the scene, winced at the intense heat from the blaze as he shook his head while holding his phone to his ear, "…No Sir, Secretary Marcus, we don't have confirmation yet, but there should have been at least six or seven people inside when it happened…."

DownSide:
Riverbend Mall:
Presidential Office

Alexander Marcus put his phone back in his pocket and shook his head as he looked up from his chair at John Austin. They'd been meeting in John's office when the call came in. "Mr. President, there's been an incident at the base. An explosion at a maintenance hangar near the ILC support zone. It's likely at least six or seven have died. It's too early to determine the cause."

John's expression tightened. "Alex, when was the last time you had an explosion at the base that killed people?"

Alexander pursed his lips before answering, "Years ago. Before Awakening Day."

John drummed his fingers on his desk for a minute. "Okay. I don't want to be an alarmist, but I don't believe in coincidence. First, an ILC gets shot at, and then we have an explosion a few days later near the ILC area at the base."

Alexander studied John's face and slumped back in his chair. "You think this is related to the mystery craters?"

John sighed, "God, I hope not, Alex, but can we afford to ignore the possibility?"

"I guarantee you, Sir, there is not a Wardog anywhere within a hundred miles of the base."

John shook his head. "Alex… cast a wider net. *Something* is going on. Maybe it's related, and maybe it isn't. Either way, find the hell out what. Maybe somebody's dashcam caught a video of what happened. Surely there's video somewhere? Pull out all the stops and put an end to it — coincidence or not."

Alexander stood and nodded. "Yes, Mr. President. I'm as pissed off about things as you are. I'll get to the bottom of it, one way or another."

The Measure of Our Hearts

● ● ● ● ● ● ● ● ● ● ● ● ● ● ● ● ●

Ari'Nell
FAB

Bertie Sinitskaya, LoadMaster Russ Kerrigan, and PO's Sean Monk, Kenneth Farmer, Jose Martinez, Anthony Vergugo, Thomas Devers, and Xavier Hernandez sweated, strained, and struggled to align the modulators to the ten-meter body of the petawatt gamma-ray laser, or, 'graser,' housing. They were not part of the original design. Since getting the first working unit ready for testing as fast as possible was the order of the day, there had not been time to reprogram the FAB to incorporate them in the base unit, much less come up with the designs needed to do so.

Before Awakening Day, building a graser was one of the more or less Holy Grail goals in physics and engineering. Grasers produce coherent gamma rays, much as lasers do with visible light. Doing so combines quantum mechanics, nuclear and optical spectroscopy, solid-state physics, chemistry, and metallurgy in order to generate and moderate the interactions of neutrons. It was as much science as it was engineering art.

Dimitri held up his hand and urgently called out, "Wait... a little more... more... almost there.... STOP!"

For the test, the entire assembly would be attached to the undercarriage of ILC Mace, allowing the semi-permanent rings to wrap around it. In fact, the rings would provide the gravity lens by manipulating the warp field. That's what the additional modulators were needed for.

ILC Mace herself would need to momentarily shut down the warp field and reconfigure it to provide the necessary lensing.

Power for the weapon came from the nearly twenty-meter-long zero-point energy device, which also incorporated the control systems and other subsystems required to keep the weapon from simply exploding. Producing it had diverted the FAB's production from mines, or anything else, for nearly a month. It was the main reason why building the weapon had been delayed for so long.

✪ ✪ ✪

Hours later, mining utility drones maneuvered the device underneath Mace, who "reached out" with her rings and successfully secured the weapon into place.

Jermaine Cutter watched from Revenge's Bridge as Mace gently pulled away from the FAB. "Good luck, Commander."

Holding her helmet in her left hand and wearing her modified pressure suit, like the rest of her crew, Bertie stood behind pilots Lt. Daniele Lecce and Lt. Ivan Matějka in their VR seats on Mace. She patted them both on the shoulders as she smiled. "Thank you, Captain Cutter. Tell my husband to get some rest. We'll head out to the other side of the system as planned. I wouldn't want to scratch your paint if this thing blows."

Jermaine grinned, "That's OK, Commander. We don't have any paint on Revenge."

She turned to navigator Lt. Billy Kilmer, "Billy, plot a course for Ari'Bal. Let's see if that gas bag really needs all eleven of its moons in a full eleven pieces, shall we?"

✪ ✪ ✪

Ari'Ball
(10th Planet in Ari'Nell System)

Ari'Ball was a gas giant that, in the time of the Builders, had been home to millions of them living on a massive gas extraction megastructure. As with Ari'Nell, the Accipiters had blasted the structure into fragments. Also, like Ari'Nell, those fragments had formed an impressive ring system. Several of the planetary moons had also been heavily mined by the Builders — and had been just as heavily bombarded by the Accipiters. Debris that hadn't fallen into Ari'Ball had either formed the rings, collided with one of the moons… or still orbited Ari'Ball in the form of millions of small to large objects. The larger pieces were mostly metallic. A shocking number of small, organic objects were still… recognizable.

Bertie suppressed a shiver. "All right, people, I don't get any more used to seeing this than you do. So, let's get on with our business here." She nodded at Earnest Grant, "COB, take us to Battle Stations, if you will, please." She then donned her helmet.

Earnest nodded, put on his own helmet, and spoke into his microphone, "General Quarters! General Quarters! Prepare for Weapons Test. This is not a drill! All Hands Man Your Battle Stations! Set material Condition Zebra Throughout the Ship! Secure all loose objects and ensure your pressure suits are ready. Prepare for zero gravity. Make reports to D.C. Central!" He listened to his headset before looking back to Bertie and reporting over the command frequency, "Captain, all stations report ready."

Bertie smiled, "Very well. Mace, please select a target at the planned distance and set the weapon for one percent power, one-second burst. When ready, please cut the field, fire, and report results." She gripped the chairs in front of her and held herself in place tightly.

A moment later, the gravity field ceased, sending their stomachs in a lurch. A moment later, it resumed.

CAPTAIN, THE WEAPON FIRED SUCCESSFULLY.
THE TARGET, A ROUGHLY TEN-METER METAL
BULKHEAD FRAGMENT, WAS LARGELY
VAPORIZED. PLEASE OBSERVE THE RECORDED
VIDEO ON YOUR SCREEN.

Bertie leaned forward, staring intently at the monitor. A toothy grin slowly widened on her face. "Outstanding, Mace! Crew, I thought you'd like to know phase one test was successful!"

From across the ILC, the entire crew shouted, hooted, and whooped raucously at the news.

"Lt. Mitchell, send to Revenge, Phase One Success, and append the video and test telemetry."

London Mitchel nodded, "Aye, Captain, sending."

"Now, Mace, let's bump it to twenty percent, as planned. Execute."

Once again, the gravity fell away like a falling elevator, only to resume a moment later.

CAPTAIN, THE TWENTY PERCENT TEST WAS
SUCCESSFUL. THIS TIME A FIFTY-METER PIECE
OF DEBRIS WAS TARGETED AND DESTROYED.
VIDEO TO YOUR SCREEN. RECOMMEND
COOLDOWN, AS PLANNED, WHILE I RUN TESTS
ON THE WEAPON.

"Very good, Mace. Let me know when you're done. I want to test at fifty percent, but this time we'll just aim at Ari'Ball. No need to ruin the local real estate. We might want to mine this place ourselves sometime soon. Meanwhile, Lieutenant Akiba, there's something that…."

EXCUSE ME, CAPTAIN. I'M AFRAID I MUST
REPORT A VERY SUBSTANTIAL GAMMA-RAY
BURST. THERE IS ONLY ONE SIGNATURE FOR
SUCH AN EVENT THAT I HAVE ON RECORD. A
NEXUS JUNCTION POINT HAS BEEN OPENED IN
THIS SYSTEM.

Daniele Lecce gasped.

Bertie's pale face grew ashen as she looked at Tom Akiba. "They're here. The Accipiters are here at Ari'Nell." She sucked in a breath and nodded at COB Grant.

Earnest's eyes widened, then hardened in anger as he shouted, "General Quarters! General Quarters! This is not a drill! Repeat, this is NOT a drill. The Enemy is in-System. All Hands Man Your Battle Stations! Set material Condition Zebra Throughout the Ship! Secure all loose objects and ensure your pressure suits are ready. Prepare for zero gravity. Make reports to D.C. Central! All Hands…."

Bertie swallowed, then asked, "Mace, where are they, and how many?"

LENSING… IT APPEARS TO BE A SINGLE
ACCIPITER CAPITAL SHIP ACCOMPANIED
BY… MANY… SUPPORT SHIPS. THE
PRELIMINARY ESTIMATE IS FORTY TO FIFTY

THOUSAND SUPPORT SHIPS. NEXUS POINT
IS APPROXIMATELY 29.9 LIGHT MINUTES ON
A 78.6-DEGREE ARC FROM US, HEADING IN-
SYSTEM.

Perhaps unaware he said the words, Tom Akiba blanched and muttered, "My God."

Bertie snapped, "Mace, don't wait for Billy to plot a course. Take us back to the Forge, flank speed!"

She swallowed, then added, "What about the mines?"

ACCIPITER VESSELS HAVE ALREADY BEEN
ENGAGED BY THE MINES WHICH ARE STATION-
KEEPING IN LINE WITH THE APPROXIMATE
LOCATION OF THE VARIABLE NEXUS POINT. THE
MINES ARE WORKING. HOWEVER, IT APPEARS
THAT THE MINES ARE ONLY ACHIEVING
APPROXIMATELY A 1.3 PERCENT HIT RATE.

Bertie shook her head, "Shit. Seven lasing rods each and only that low a hit rate? Fuck. We're barely going to slow them down at this rate. Worse, that news is 29 minutes old.

Tom asked, "I thought the mines were supposed to be more effective than that?"

Bertie took a breath and nodded, "Remember, each one of those mines has seven lasing rods. Their targeting systems will attempt to locate as many targets as possible for their beams. The micro-warp field that encapsulates and moves the mine will form gravity lenses for each rod aimed at the anticipated location of its targets. However, it takes time for even a light-speed weapon to reach its target. During that time, the mine has moved, and the targets themselves have moved. I don't need to remind you that space is damned big. Since the mines are independent of each other, many of them may target duplicate targets — including targets that other mines have already destroyed, but for which the light from that destruction has not yet reached it."

"Mace, what do you estimate their ETA to the FAB and Ari'Nell to be?"

AT LAST KNOWN ACCELERATION,
APPROXIMATELY 97.3 MINUTES, HOWEVER,
IT APPEARS THAT DESPITE THE LESS THAN
HOPED-FOR HIT RATE, THE ACCIPITER SUPPORT
VESSELS HAVE FALLEN BACK TO THEIR
MOTHERSHIP AND ARE SHIELDING IT FROM
FIRE, TAKING THE HITS FOR IT. AS A RESULT,
THE HIT RATE IS INCREASING SUBSTANTIALLY.
HOWEVER, I PROJECT THAT IT WILL NOT BE
ENOUGH. THERE JUST ARE NOT ENOUGH MINES
DEPLOYED.

CAPTAIN, WE ARE NOW EXITING SUBFTL WARP
IN PROXIMITY TO THE FAB. CAPTAIN CUTTER IS
HAILING US.

Jermaine Cutter appeared on Bertie's screen. His expression was grave. "Commander Sinitskaya, the mines aren't taking enough of them out. We're going to have to abandon the system. Send your crew over to set the FAB to blow. We'll pump out as many mines as we can for as long as we can. We can at least whittle them down some more." He paused. "We'll evacuate as many as we can back to New Texas."

"Captain Cutter…. I'm sending them over now. That said, I have an idea. The Accipiters are hugging their mothership close, trying to shield it from the mines."

Jermaine stiffened. "I know what you're thinking…." He shook his head, "Look, Commander… Bertie… The weapon is brand new and hasn't been fully tested. When you fire the damned thing, you are vulnerable, even if only briefly."

Bertie swallowed, "Captain. Jermaine. You know damned well that if you were here, in my shoes, you'd do the same thing. We can't leave all these people behind, and we can't…. blow them up to save them from the Accipiters. We just can't. You know it! Captain Cross would too. And Phil would have, were he here. I knew him too. You've got the plans for everything. Even if it blows up in my face, you can still evacuate as many as you can, and you'll eventually be able to make more of the weapon. We will send telemetry. With luck, Mace will blow the damned birds to hell, and we can all get a new set of boots made to match the President's."

"And your crew?"

"Anyone who wants to stay behind will transfer to the FAB."

"General Order One, Commander."

"Yes, Captain. I'm sending all laptops and devices over to the FAB. Everything left will be scrubbed."

Jermaine nodded stiffly. "And the other thing?"

Bertie reached into a breast pocket on her coveralls and retrieved the thumb drive she'd carried with her everywhere since receiving it. Her eyes hardened, and her lips narrowed as she placed it into a specially provided player next to the communications console. The video file it contained played automatically and was broadcast and relayed to everyone in-system.

President Austin sat at his desk, surrounded by Vice President Finley, Secretary of War Marcus, and Admirals Milner and Johansson. None were smiling. John Austin began, "People of Ari'Nell. It is my fervent hope that this message will never be played. If you are watching it now, it can only mean that the worst-case scenario has occurred. Our enemy has found you. You are there, and we are not. Your leaders have their orders, and all of you know that the location of New Texas must not be revealed to our enemy under any circumstances. The very survival of our species... and of all the brothers, sisters, mothers, fathers, children, and friends who are here depends on it. We're all that is left. The entire hope and legacy of humankind." He paused and swallowed, "I know you will do the right thing. God Bless You All."

Bertie looked up and nodded. "It's done."

Jermaine nodded somberly.

Bertie looked around at the faces of her crew. Everyone understood. "Captain Cutter, we'll be docking at the FAB in a moment, then we'll be off."

Jermaine assured her, "Bertie... Your husband is critical to the project, along with the other engineers. We'll make sure they get out."

He paused. "I could relieve you. Take your place."

Bertie stared back at him; her black eyes were dark and haunted, her jaw visibly popping as she ground her teeth. She shook her head. "My ship. My duty. Just... Look after them. Tell Ronald and Anna that I love them." She cut the link.

"Mace, take us in to the FAB and dock us as quickly as possible.

Daniele, and Ivan, take off your VR helmets and look at me. Everyone else… your attention."

She looked around the tiny bridge at their worried faces. "Tom… Daniele, Ivan, Billy, London… All of you can go. For this, I can really get by with just me and the ship. Mace can fly herself and fire the weapon. There's no need for the rest of you…."

Lieutenant Tom Akiba smiled softly, "I'll see the techs off to tend to the FAB as well as anyone else who wants to go." He turned and left the bridge.

Daniele and Ivan looked at each other, then gripped their helmets and put them back on, returning to their duty.

Lieutenant London Mitchel nodded, then turned back to his communication console.

PO Billy Kilmer likewise returned to his navigation controls. His backup, Trent May, entered the bridge along with backup pilot Abdul Ahmed. They asked, "Permission to enter the Bridge, Captain?"

Bertie looked at him and measured their firm, determined faces. "Permission granted."

Trent stepped over, kneeled next to Billy, and quietly asked, "I'll double-check the entries. Have you…." Meanwhile, Abdul stepped over to the pilot consoles and began double-checking equipment and settings as he whispered to Daniele and Ivan.

Tom Akiba returned and reported, "Captain, all six techs have transferred to the Forge. Loadmaster Kerrigan, PO Barnes, and the marines, with the tech's help, have tossed all the loose computers and gear over as well." He hesitated. "Captain, everyone else has remained aboard. They're triple checking the pressure suits for combat. The marines and security team are staying in case there is an opportunity to board another ship… or in case we are boarded. Corpsman Houston has locked down the medical area and supplies. PO Barnes has rechecked environmentals." He straightened to attention. "We're ready to go, Captain."

The corner of Bertie's pale, stony face ticked in grateful appreciation. She took one more look around the room, pausing to look at each person individually. "All right then." She swallowed hard and nodded proudly. "My God, Nimitz was right. Uncommon valor is common." She pointed outside. "Our enemy out there is cruel and unrelenting, but I see the strength in your eyes. We could run away and nibble away at them from afar… or we can take the fight to their door. We can show the enemy our true hearts and, by our actions, just as cruelly teach them that mankind refuses to bow down to false gods in abject submission and slavery. We have a chance, here and now, to *punish* them for their crimes against life. *Against sentience itself.* To *hurt* them for what they have done. To make sure that they know that whenever and wherever the Accipiters encounter mankind that there will be a PRICE to pay. For they may believe themselves to be gods, but here, today, we few will be the devils that drag them all straight to *hell!*"

Bertie blinked in surprise at her own outburst. She was breathing hard, and her heart was pounding in her chest. She looked around the room again and smiled grimly at the determination in their faces.

Bertie nodded in satisfaction, "Okay, people. Let's roll."

London Mitchel quietly turned off the highly restricted broadband transmit button. It was probably a court martial offense for him to have broadcast Bertie's speech, but he didn't give a damn anymore.

✪ ✪ ✪

"Okay, Mace, here's what I want to do. Start heading in the enemy's direction. Meanwhile, I want you to work closely with Billy, Daniele, and Ivan. Make sure that Abdul and Trent are ready to step in at any time if needed. Mace could probably handle everything herself, but we're a team, and she may get distracted or need to focus on other 'things." *Or be damaged.*

CAPTAIN. I COULD BE DAMAGED, AND YOUR
CREW MAY NEED TO TAKE OVER SOME OF
MY FUNCTIONS. I WILL WORK CLOSELY WITH
THE CREW TO PREPARE THEM FOR ANY
EVENTUALITY.

Bertie hesitated, "Very well. We're all here to back each other up. That said, our enemy is not stupid. They will try very, very hard to kill us. So, I want to plan out a series of attack runs. Dive in from completely different vectors at warp. Drop out. Fire at twenty percent power, then retreat at warp at a different vector. Rinse and repeat. If nothing stops us, we'll make, oh, a half dozen runs, pull back and review what damage we've done, and evaluate. Also, I know we programmed the mines to recognize us, but timing is critical. They could make a mistake, or we could simply get caught in a crossfire. The tighter we cut it, the less chance there is for… the better the odds are we'll be able to make the next run and keep hurting them. Also, put on my Thomas Bergersen playlist, shipwide and loud. I feel like we really are Two Steps from Hell today!"

Tom Akiba closed his eyes and shook his head while Daniele Lecce and Billy Kilmer grinned happily. London Mitchel audibly groaned.

Bertie laughed darkly, "Suck it up, people. Time to be brave! Mace, I want you to do the maneuvers, but I want our human crew to mirror what you're doing in case they need to take over or… help. For targeting, how close do we need to get? Calculate based on our twenty percent yield test firings."

CAPTAIN, I RECOMMEND THAT WE BEGIN BY STARTING AT THE SAME RANGE THE X-RAY LASERS FROM THE MINES EMPLOY AND WORK OUR WAY OUT FROM THERE. THE GRASER SHOULD HAVE A SIGNIFICANTLY LONGER RANGE. HOWEVER, IT IS STILL MOSTLY UNTESTED. IF THE TARGET IS NOT EVADING, THE OPTIMAL RANGE WOULD BE WELL UNDER A LIGHT SECOND, OR ROUGHLY THREE HUNDRED THOUSAND KILOMETERS. IF IT WERE A STATIC TARGET, WE COULD EASILY GO OUT A MILLION KILOMETERS AND STILL INFLICT SIGNIFICANT DAMAGE.

"All right. I agree. I'd rather start from a range we know will work and stretch it until we find a limit than telegraph our maximum range to the enemy from the beginning. We can crank up the power and range as we practice."

"COB, let's get helmets on and ensure that everyone is secure for zero gravity. Mace, Nav, Pilots, is everyone ready?" Bertie donned her own pressure helmet.

"Ready, Captain."

"Ready, Captain."

"Ready, Captain."

READY, CAPTAIN.

"Very well. Begin attack series one. Execute!"

No relative acceleration was felt. However, six times in succession, the gravity briefly ceased.

ATTACK RUNS COMPLETED. SIXTY-SEVEN ENEMY VESSELS WERE DESTROYED OR DISABLED. MINOR COLLATERAL DAMAGE WAS DONE TO THE CAPITAL SHIP. THE ENEMY HAS TIGHTENED ITS DEPLOYMENT PROTECTING THE CAPITAL SHIP. THEY CONTINUE TO ATTEMPT TO FIRE PARTICLE WEAPONS AT US. HOWEVER, EACH TIME WE HAVE LEFT BEFORE THEY COULD HIT US. IN TOTAL, IT APPEARS THAT NINE THOUSAND FOUR HUNDRED AND FIFTEEN ENEMY VESSELS HAVE BEEN DESTROYED, DISABLED, OR DAMAGED BY THE MINES. OVER FORTY THOUSAND STILL REMAIN, IN ADDITION TO THE CAPITAL SHIP. AT THE CURRENT RATE, LESS THAN A THIRD WILL HAVE BEEN DISABLED PRIOR TO REACHING THE FAB.

Bertie nodded, "Okay, we knew that twenty percent power was just the starting point. Reconfigure for forty percent. Let's see if we can at least get them to slow down their approach. Also, this time, make it nine runs instead of six. Let's keep them guessing. Let me know when everyone is ready with the course changes."

"Ready, Captain."

"Ready, Captain."

"Ready, Captain."

READY, CAPTAIN.

"Execute!"

Once again, no relative acceleration was felt, and the gravity briefly ceased nine times in succession.

ATTACK RUNS COMPLETED. THREE HUNDRED AND TWELVE ENEMY VESSELS WERE DESTROYED OR DISABLED. MINOR COLLATERAL

DAMAGE WAS DONE TO THE CAPITAL SHIP. THE
ENEMY VESSELS HAVE BEGUN TO SPIN AND
EMIT GAS, THE EQUIVALENT OF … CHAFF… IN
ORDER TO DISRUPT THE BEAMS.

✪ ✪ ✪

NTN Revenge

Jermaine turned to Lieutenant Gordon. "Alister, how's she doing?"

"Captain, the data is over twenty minutes old, but so far, she's whittling away at them, Sir. Slowly. No problems so far, but, Sir…."

Jermaine nodded in frustration. "But it's not enough. There's just too damned many of them."

He shook his head. "Dammit, we need a fleet of armed ships, not just one jury-rigged landing craft!"

Captain, may I remind you of something?

"Go ahead."

There's no such thing as an unarmed starship.

Jermaine shook his head. "I know what you're thinking, but that's been discussed repeatedly. If we unbalance the warp field and collect particles and release them, we can't really aim them. We can run the ILC's original warp bubble inside the field for protection. Once we get started, we can't see ahead of ourselves. The target has to be…."

Alister cocked his head, "Captain?"

Jermaine's eyes widened, "The target has to be stationary… or be really, really, big and not trying to evade…."

Alister smiled and nodded in understanding, "Like a twenty-mile-wide capital ship surrounded by thousands of smaller ones all clumped around it!"

"Okay, get a message to Mace. Tell Bertie to back off. They've done their part. Have them meet us at the rendezvous point. Let's get those crewmen off the FAB and set the timer."

"Captain, they're still over twenty light minutes out. They won't get the message…."

Jermaine nodded, "I know, Alister, I know."

✪ ✪ ✪

NTN MACE

Bertie gripped the back of Billy's chair in front of her as they ended their twenty-first run. The on and off again gravity was making everyone queasy. They'd killed or disabled over four thousand enemy ships, killing God knew how many of the enemy, but it still was just a drop in the bucket. *Forty-five more minutes… that's all we have.*

Tom Akiba shook his head worriedly and turned to Bertie, "Captain, ever since we upped the weapon past fifty percent, it's been… well… I don't like these readings. We are either powering it too high or too fast or both."

Bertie nodded slowly. She swallowed. "What do you think, Tom? We can't lower power and do more runs. We can't pause for a cooldown. We don't have time. What say we wait a bit, then up the power to seventy-five percent for one big burst? See what that does? Ship, what do you think?"

I BELIEVE THAT LIEUTENANT AKIBA'S ANALYSIS
IS CORRECT. THE WEAPON IS SHOWING
DEFINITE SIGNS OF INSTABILITY.

"Understood. We don't have a choice, though. There isn't time for anything else. Let's give it a go, shall we? Execute when ready."

Mace's warp bubble blinked off 278,314 kilometers from the massed Accipiter ships. The warp field reconfigured to a new gravity lens, and the zero-point energy-powered graser swept .75 petawatts of energy into the seemingly chaotic shell of smaller vessels that surrounded the roughly disk-shaped Accipiter capital ship. Each previous attack had tried a different angle from behind, above, the sides, and occasionally repeating a vector. Each attack had seemed more like scraping a bit of paint off than making a real dent.

This time was different. This time the beam savaged through all of the smaller ships in its path and gouged a several kilometer-wide slice through the main hull of the capital ship, rending its hard shell like an old-world piñata, sending gas and debris spiraling out in all directions.

Bertie grinned hugely, and the bridge crew whooped for joy… just as the graser firing chamber lost containment and the nearly four-hundred-ton ILC Mace was blown in half. The massive radiation surge instantly killed Commander Alberta "Bertie" Sinitskaya, Lieutenant Tom Akiba, Master Chief Earnest Grant, Pilots Daniele Mauro Lecce, Ivan Samuel Matějka, and Abdul Bakr Ahmed, Navigators Billy Kilmer and Trent May, Environmental Chief Cliff Barnes, Comms Officer Lieutenant London Mitchell, Quartermaster Chris Owens, Medic Lenny Houston, Loadmaster Russ Kerrigan, Marine Sergeants Clinton Green, Dave Clark, and Joe Coleman, and Corporals Dexter Riggins, Santana Baugh, Mark Brown, Turk Hall, and Ricky Busey.

The personality known as Mace was distributed across all of its rings. As they shattered, so it, too, fractured into many pieces. Each carried out the core imperative imparted to it by Phoenix to purge itself from existence.

✪ ✪ ✪

NTN Revenge

Jermaine leaned into the console, his face hard and tight. "Faster! Go Faster!"

Translation in …. Five… four… three… two… one… NOW.

NTN Revenge exited warp and dropped its field, dumping the particles in line with its exit vector. In warp, you exit with the velocity and vector you entered with. Revenge had warped out system, accelerated to a .6c using a modified gravity drive, and then engaged a modified warp field that wasn't properly balanced. As a result, it collected the particles it impacted while in warp rather than converting them to energy to reinforce the warp field. They could only sustain this kind of unstable field for a short time. By selecting its path to collect just enough particles but not enough to cause an overload — and time it just right — they could return to the expected position of the Accipiter fleet and dump the particles as a massive burst of gamma and ionizing radiation.

Gravity returned, and Jermaine shouted, "Report!"

<hr>

*The enemy fleet is not where we expected it to be.
It appears to have been retreating. However, it has been
disabled. I should also report that there appears to be
significant damage to the capital ship, and much of its
support fleet seems to have been destroyed as well. Captain,
this is… unexpected. The only Keeper modules I detect on the
capital ship are severely damaged. There are many… holes…
where the rest should be.*

*Also… Captain, I have detected another Nexus Junction
Point event…. No new vessels seem to have emerged. I
surmise that the surviving enemy has retreated with their
Keeper modules and escaped the system. I detect no active
enemy signatures. It would seem that the battle, for now at
least, is over.*

<hr>

Raucous cheers erupted all over the ship.

Jermaine grinned from ear to ear and clapped Alister on the back. "She did it! God Dammit, she did it! Find Mace. Is she at the rendezvous point?"

<hr>

*Searching… Mace does not appear to be at the
rendezvous point, and I am detecting no transmissions….
Captain… There is debris that… I'm very sorry, Sir. I am
detecting debris that appears to be a portion of Mace. I regret
to inform you that Mace was destroyed.*

<hr>

The cheers ebbed away to pained silence as the news spread.

Jermaine closed his eyes and shrank back against a console. "Damn you, Bertie. Did you even get our message to back off?"

Alister grimly said, "Captain, you heard the broadcast she made, though I somehow don't think she knew she was making it. It was clear that she knew what was likely to happen."

Jermaine sucked in a breath and stood back up. "Of course she did. We all did. It's just…." He lowered his voice, "If only I'd thought of it sooner, moved faster, gotten us back sooner."

"So, do we go ahead and blow the FAB and leave?"

Jermaine's eyes narrowed. "Of course not. Whatever gave you that idea. First, we're going to stop the countdown. Then we're going to crank that damn FAB up as high as possible and push out as many mines as we can for as long as we can. The Accipiters will be back, and when they do, we're going to bleed them. Send the drones out, drag back pieces of the Accipiter ships, and feed them to the FAB. Kill them with their own leftovers. Poetic justice. Meanwhile, Kukri will go out and see if we can retrieve… search for survivors."

"Yes, Sir, Captain. How long do we stay on station?"

Jermaine's handsome chocolate brown face was hard and unyielding. "As long as it takes. They'll be back and in force this time. We have the FAB, so we can replicate anything we need besides mines. I want to see if we can expand its capacity while we're at it. When they come back, we'll wait until they're close, blow the FAB, and take as many of them with it as possible. It's the least we can do."

Revelation

● ● ● ● ● ● ● ● ● ● ● ● ● ● ● ●

Location: DownSide
Radio Station 92.5 Studio

The lighting in the studio waiting room was subdued. Long ago, relatively speaking, that is, not long after Awakening Day, Danielle had removed the drop ceiling fluorescent lighting and the drop ceiling itself, opening up the space. She'd painted the ceiling a deep ochre color and covered the walls and floors with fabrics, tapestries, and deep, thick rugs. Well-worn leather sofas and chairs complemented low-set heavy coffee tables mixed with random modern furniture. LED lamps were tuned to a warm color that changed with the hour.

Commandant of Midshipmen, former Air Force Chief Master Sergeant Harrold Anders sat in a leather chair wearing jeans and a polo shirt, with his feet up while he absently hummed a lullaby to the twins, Betsy and Darcy, while they lay side-by-side in their crib. It amazed him how easily they slept lately, at just over three weeks old. It was a recent development he expected would last only until the next growth spurt started. Their eleven-month-old brothers, Devin and Terry, played in the next room with the Blanchard triplets, Alexis, Bethany, and Cassandra. Their father, Wayne, was supervising while his wife, Sybil, was in the studio with Danielle. Wayne also had the new triplets, Dillan, Ethan, and Fallon, with him in a triple stroller. Harrold wasn't sure how he and Danielle were managing two sets of twins, much less how Wayne and Sybil handled…. Six. Not that the baby avalanche showed any signs of slowing.

✪ ✪ ✪

Danielle keyed the microphone, "So, folks, tomorrow is election day, but today I'd like to welcome someone many of you may already know. Sybil Blanchard, who I'm told by people in the know, is the brains behind Blanchard Shipping. The Blanchards have been instrumental in ensuring that essential goods get distributed throughout Fort Brazos and New London. She and her husband Wayne organized both the local Fort Brazos trucking companies as well as the many independent drivers who were stranded in Fort Brazos on Awakening Day. Since then, the Blanchards have been called upon by the government and the military more and more. Of course, many of you will remember when Sybil and Wayne were attacked out on the highway by the Wardog that killed those poor soldiers. Like myself, I'm sure just about everyone has seen the video and how Sybil herself bravely shot at that monster, distracting it to save her husband, who had selflessly left their truck to try to save the soldiers in their burning vehicle. Sybil was later appointed to the position of War Logistics Deputy Director. Most recently, she decided to put her proverbial hat in the ring for Senate. Sybil, thank you for joining me this morning!"

Sybil smiled warmly. Danielle was one of those souls for whom Sybil didn't need her unique *awareness* to know her. What you saw with Danielle was what you got. There was nothing hidden about Danielle. That's what was off-putting for some people. For Sybil, she was… relaxing.

What wasn't relaxing was the reason why she'd agreed to Gwyneth's sudden insistence that she run for Senate. Her search for the traitor was going nowhere. Moreover, should she eventually discover who it was, being a Senator might give her the power and influence she might need to do something about it. She'd also have full-time protection for her and, more importantly, her family. That had been the final straw that convinced her. The funny thing was that before Awakening Day, Sybil knew that she'd have been absolutely terrified at the prospect—to the point of shutting herself down completely and maybe even a breakdown. Now? It was just one more battle to fight.

The microphone in front of her was large and a little intimidating, but she did her best to ignore it. "Thank you, Danielle. I'm pleased to be here."

Danielle brightened and leaned forward into her own microphone. "So tell me, I have to ask, and I'm sure you must get this all the time, but what was it like? Seeing a Wardog like that… an alien monster… you must have been terrified? I mean, I've seen the one they have in captivity like a lot of us have, but out there not knowing what it was on the road like that?"

Sybil was used to the question, but she nodded and thought back to the incident. She'd been a different person then. Mousey, quiet, and reserved. All these months living with the empathic ability given to her by the Gardeners that she variously thought of as a curse or a blessing had changed her. Drawn her out of her shell. "Danielle, you know, it was of course, a shock. Seeing something that shouldn't exist like that. For a moment, your brain rebels. You're seeing something that doesn't fit any known pattern. We all know what dangerous animals look like, and your brain will quickly categorize them after the initial moment of surprise. But this thing, it was huge and black and had the wrong number of legs and looked like, well, maybe a demon or something. Then again, overhead was our impossible sky, and we already knew about one kind of alien creature. So, after that first moment of shock, I have to say, I got mad."

Danielle rocked back in surprise. "Mad? Really?"

Sybil chuckled softly and shook her head, "Yeah. Mad. Here was this hell beast coming out of the blazing vehicle, unfazed by the fire, and there was Wayne out there, and I just thought…. No! You are NOT taking my man! So, I…."

✪ ✪ ✪

Harrold looked up as the waiting room door opened and Andre Johansson, wearing his dress whites, entered. He quickly rose from his chair and stood at attention. "Admiral. Welcome. Are you here for the show? Sir?"

Andre waved Harrold back down, "Please, Commandant, sit! You deserve whatever time off you can get, especially with your precious babies. That makes four now for you both, doesn't it? Twin boys and now twin girls, yes?"

Harrold remained standing but relaxed slightly. "Yes, Sir, Devin, Terry, Betsy, and Darcy. I've seen your son at the Academy. He seems like a fine young man."

"Thank you, Commandant Anders. Harrold. He was always a handful. Headstrong. He'll get there. I just hope I didn't overindulge him too much growing up."

Harrold nodded, mentally calling up young Karl Johansson's background. *Promising football player.* "I'm sure he will do fine. He certainly excels in sports, so the physical requirements won't be a worry for him, and if I recall correctly, his grades are fine. I'm sure he will have a bright future."

Andre smiled, "Thank you. As to your question, I'm here in response to a request from your wife for someone to talk about how we are ensuring that our off-world citizens are able to vote in the election." He paused. "Wow, did I just actually say that out loud? Our *off-world citizens*. My God, it's sometimes hard to wrap my brain around things these days!"

Harrold laughed sardonically, "you're telling me, Admiral, Sir. I was a beat-up old CCM with three ex-wives. Now it's not even two years after the Apocalypse, and now I'm married with four children, and on top of that, I'm the Commandant at what amounts to the Space Navy and Marines Academy."

Betsy and Darcy gurgled softly.

Andre gestured toward the crib and opened his mouth to say something, but just then, the side door opened, and Wayne Blanchard burst into the room, pushing a triple stroller with triplet toddler girls giggling and holding hands as they trundled along behind him, before rushing around him to gather around the crib, where they cooed together and reached through to touch Darcy and Betsy.

Wayne paused in his tracks, and his eyes widened for a moment as he recognized Andre. "Oh, Um, Admiral! Hello?"

Andre smiled warmly and extended his hand. "Hello, Mr. Blanchard. I suppose I'm as surprised to see you here as you seem to be seeing me?"

Wayne had lost weight since Awakening Day, but he had always had a large frame. He reached out with his own beefy hand and shook the Admiral's. "Yes, well, Sybil is here doing an interview. She's doing the Senate thing, you know."

Andre nodded knowingly. "I'm aware, yes. I can hardly think of a finer person for the job. I've not met your wife in person, but I've seen the quality of her work, and yours, of course. We're all indebted to you both for your service."

Sounding like an overzealous refrigerator door, the heavy, magnetically sealed studio door opened behind them. Sybil lurched out of the studio into the waiting room. At only five foot three, opening the door took a lot of effort. She paused in surprise at the sight of the small crowd. Harrold's surprisingly complex aura was both hard, soft, and full of nuance. Wayne's familiar warm bearish aura washed over her like a comforting blanket, and her children's oh-so-welcome and bright energies leapt in happiness at her presence.

She felt the twins at the edge of her awareness, but it was the other one that sent her mind reeling in horror and shock. She'd felt that mind twice before. Once in the void, and once on the playing field in New London, after which she'd gone into an epileptic fit, as the dark malevolence within it had pushed her over the edge. She'd been so repulsed on both occasions that she'd dared not push within to *know* him. She knew him now. Of course, everyone did.

Rear Admiral, Lower Half, Andre Vide Johansson. The Second-In-Command of all of mankind's Naval Forces was a traitor.

She knew it, and as Gwyneth and Brian Kupe had reminded her… she had no proof. Sybil gasped and doubled over in pain, clutching her abdomen.

✪ ✪ ✪

Danielle smiled as the studio door opened, and Admiral Johansson entered. "Welcome, Admiral. Thank you for stopping by on such short notice."

He returned the smile and extended his hand to shake hers as she stood to greet him.

She cocked her head and nodded towards the leaded glass window. "What was that commotion going on out in the waiting room? Is Sybil all right?"

Andre shrugged his shoulders. "I'm not sure. I'm sure she'll be fine. Mr. Blanchard said something about her not eating and worried about whether it might be morning sickness. He rushed her to the bathroom." He smiled toothily. "Perhaps just nerves from being on your show?"

Danielle glanced out the window worriedly, then sat back down at her microphone. "Break is ending. We're up, Admiral. Take your seat?"

Andre sat and relaxed confidently behind the microphone.

Danielle keyed hers. "And we're back! Next on today's show, we have Vice Admiral Andre Johansson here with us, in person no less, to answer questions about how we will make sure that our military members are all able to vote. Admiral, what can you tell us?"

Andre leaned into the microphone, projecting a warm, baritone voice, "Thank you for having me, Danielle. I'm a big fan of your show. As you know, there are a lot of military and civilians living and working on base here as well as up in New London. In addition, we have men and women bravely serving aboard vessels far from New Texas. There are also over a thousand men and women hard at work in the Ari'Nell system."

"We planned ahead for this. We wanted to make every effort to ensure that each and every serviceman and woman, and civilian, was able to cast their vote in advance. That way, if they were called away and were not able to be here in person on election day, their vote would still be counted. They have the option to shred that vote on election day, if they so choose, in case they are here and change their mind."

Danielle nodded, "Thank you, Admiral, you know, we have considerably more voting-age people here now than we did before Awakening Day, and the majority of those are military or the military and civilians from New London, not counting the frozen people in the Keeper Ship. The total population, last I checked, was over a hundred and sixty-six thousand. Do we even have enough voting machines?"

Andre smiled and nodded. "I'm glad you asked that question, Danielle. I wondered about that myself some months ago and looked it up. Nearly four years ago, your county purchased four hundred voting machines with paper backup and related equipment at a cost of one point six million dollars. Once the replication machine was discovered in Jonestown, one of the first things that we duplicated were those voting machines. Over a thousand of them. The Navy flew them back to Fort Brazos, and many were transported up to New London. I'm told that should now be enough for the election."

Danielle laughed, "Well, I hope so because there is a lot on those ballots, including approving the new constitution, the President and Vice President, twelve senators, mayor and city councils for Fort Brazos and New London, as well as assorted judges and other positions. Some people may take a while!"

DownSide: Hours later
Riverbend Mall: Presidential Office

John Austin sat behind his large desk with a distant expression on his face.

Sybil fidgeted in her chair as she looked at and tasted his reaction to the news. It wasn't what she expected. The Vice President, however, was much closer to what she had expected from the President. Of all the energies in the room, hers burned the hottest. It was actually hard for Sybil to be in the same room with her. It was so bright that were it not for the already synergistic bond between Sybil and the tiny sparks that were growing within her own belly, she wouldn't have been able to sense the similarly growing life within Gail Finley, who stood behind and to the side of the President, gripping his chair as if defending him. The bond between the two was stronger than ever. Sybil could feel how their souls clung to each other.

Also in the room were Gwyneth Elliott, Brian Kupe, and Wayne, who mirrored Gail's position behind Sybil's chair.

Wayne was likewise hot and furious. It had taken all her strength and conviction to convince him not to hunt Andre Johansson down and shoot the man after she'd told him the truth of what had happened in the studio waiting room.

Gwyneth was pensive and worried. Sybil had always liked her. The woman was bright with openness and brilliance.

Brian Kupe, the former FBI agent, oddly felt in some ways like Andre had. Not the malevolent part, just the profoundly layered, compartmentalized part. She wondered if that came with trying to think like your enemies.

Then there was the President.

His ordinarily warm, open, and bright countenance had briefly flashed incandescent and then fallen cold and icy.

John nodded. "You are certain. Absolutely certain. You understand what you are accusing this… person of. You understand the consequences?"

Gail reached down and put a hand on John's shoulder.

Brian Kupe shook his head, "Mr. President, my apologies for interrupting, but I must remind everyone that while I personally believe that Mrs. Blanchard is telling the truth, we have no proof that would be admissible, well, anywhere. No proof that the man, even if he has a malevolent… spirit, was actually connected to the events leading up to Commander Harding's attack. In short, it is still her word against…."

Gail cut him off sharply. "Mr. Kupe, The President understands. He is not talking about summary executions or kangaroo courts. What he means is that from this point forward, the second most powerful man in the human navy will no longer be trusted by his Commanding Officer…. And the Commanding Officer can't say or do anything about it."

Sybil stood up from her chair and slowly walked around the desk to Gail. She looked down at John and then smiled at Gail before slowly reaching out and gently touching Gail's abdomen, "Gail…. You're pregnant!" She closed her eyes, "It… it is… oh my… twins… boys…. You're going to have twin boys!" She opened her dark eyes and was surprised to see Gail's stunned, open-mouthed expression.

Gail snapped an accusing glance at Gwyneth.

Gwyneth adamantly shook her head. "No, ma'am, I didn't say a thing. You know me better than that, and it's still too soon to determine the sex… sexes! And You, Sybil, you never told me you could do that!"

Sybil knelt beside John and put her hand on his arm. "Mr. President… John. There is, in all of us, some shade of darkness. What I felt in that man, though, was a cold, patient, and malevolent hunger for harm. A pernicious evil. His mind is a clockwork chessboard, and everyone else, you, me, even Commander Harding, are nothing but pawns in his game. It may not be today, tomorrow, or next year, but this man *will* cause great harm again. He can't help it. It is his reason for existence."

John stared into her eyes for a long moment, then slowly nodded. He sighed and shook his head. He twisted to look behind and up at Gail. "Gail, bring Martin Williams in on this. No one else, at this point. We've had Mr. Kupe sequestered off by himself for too long. He'll make a great addition to Martin's team." John looked at Brian. "Mr. Kupe, this is the single biggest secret in the world, behind Sybil, here. Don't blow it. I want you to work with Martin Williams to plan out a strategy for how to go about finding evidence, or, if you can't do that, then find another way to expose the traitor."

John leaned forward. "And anyone else working with him."

Then he pushed his chair back, stood, and embraced Gail, holding her close. Then he kissed her, and she kissed him back.

A sudden awkward hush fell over the room.

Finally, they parted just far enough to hold each other side by side as Gail smiled sheepishly, "Well, damn. I guess we have an announcement to make."

✪ ✪ ✪

DownSide
Radio Station 92.5 Studio
Two Days Later

Danielle sat back in her chair, thumbing through election reports, "Well, well, my darlings! The election is over, and the votes have been counted. Twice. After the bombshell announcement from the President and Vice President, they were both reelected in a landslide with 83% of the vote, despite all the hemming and hawing over it and people accusing them of becoming a de facto King and Queen. The rest were taking bets on baby names."

"Of course, the new constitution has that weird progressive term limit thing in it, where each election, if you run again, you have to win by 5% more votes than the last time, so nobody's going to be in office for life anymore. They're going to have to eventually go out and get real jobs!"

"Personally, I couldn't be happier for them. If anyone deserves some joy in their lives, it's the two people we all, all of us, shanghaied into carrying the weight of humanity's survival on their shoulders."

She paused and sipped her ice tea. "And of course, I'm sure you all heard the constitution itself was passed with 89% of the vote. That's a shocker. Really. I didn't see that coming. I figured it would be a squeaker."

"The new Senate was also decided. No runoff is needed. Our new Senators are Mrs. Sybil Blanchard, Colonel Gaspard Boyer, Councilwoman Esmerelda Collins, celebrated Wardog Hunter Mira Yeager Cross, County Judge Maria Gonzalez, Captain Valentin Gorshkov, Captain Alphonse Halkias, Councilman Dale Hubbard, the Texas Ranger known as Ignacio, Mrs. Livia Milner, Colonel Caesar Salangsang, and, believe it or not, and I'm still not sure I do, former Reinhardt seven leader and current Mayor of the fledgling town of Jonestown, Darnell Lewis."

Blessed

●●●●●●●●●●●●●●●●●

TopSide:
New Pentagon Holding Cells

Martin Williams examined the papers and books strewn across the table, satisfied that they would lend the desired impression. He took a deep breath and let it out slowly as he adjusted his bow tie. The legend he'd built for Lucius now included an entire, themed wardrobe. Indeed, he'd set up a special room inside the former telecom bunker-turned-intelligence headquarters as "Lucius's Apartment." He lived in that apartment for two days prior to each meeting with Nathaniel Grant, practicing the Leeds accent, wearing what Lucius would wear, eating what Lucious would eat, and studying what Lucious would study.

Each week, for the past ten weeks, he'd visited Grant, always at the same time and day of the week, but not always "on time." Sometimes he was a bit early, but usually, he would time things as if he'd been caught by surprise and was running late, maintaining the befuddled academician / Columbo persona. After the first three weeks, he'd had the food delivery altered, keeping the MREs but gradually adding the odd fruit or vegetable. For the past three weeks, the MREs had been discontinued, and instead, "hot" meals were delivered in disposable cardboard containers. Sometimes Chinese, sometimes Mexican, sometimes even the occasional pizza.

Remember, Martin, we're here to make him think he's slowly turning you. Let him think he's always two steps ahead of you... even if he is.

He pressed the button on the wall to raise the shield.

"Hello, Mr. Grant."

Nathaniel gracefully stood from the lotus position he preferred and ambled towards the window. His beard was, of course, longer, as was his kinky/curly black hair that cascaded down his self-made tunic. He'd used the crayons to add some color to the former hospital scrubs. His chest and abdominal muscles rippled smoothly as he stopped a few feet from the window. "Hello, Lucius. How have you been?"

Martin gave the appearance of being slightly uncomfortable, looking away briefly before returning his gaze to Nathaniel. "I am well, thank you."

Martin shuffled over to the table and sat down, then added, "I trust you are well, Mr. Grant?"

"Quite well, thank you. I would inquire about the weather. However, I've noted that your attire never seems to vary to accommodate weather changes, so I can only presume that what weather you have, wherever it is that you go, must not be very interesting."

Martin's eyes widened in spite of himself. *Touché. And you thought you were professional, Martin. All this time living in a perfect world, and you've grown complacent.* He shrugged, chagrined, "As you say. It's not very interesting."

Nathaniel smiled softly, gracious in his minor victory. "And what shall we talk about today, Lucius?"

Martin sifted through a few folders and fished out a notepad (intentionally) sandwiched between them. "Well, I thought we'd discuss what life is like in your world. Tell me how people live. What do they do in paradise?"

"I see. I suppose I shall have to disabuse you of the impression that paradise means sitting around eating grapes? No, people are quite active and fulfilled. I mentioned that the planet is now a garden, and it is, but I assure you that man does not toil in the fields… unless that is their desire. Living machines are tailored to difficult, dangerous, or unpleasantly repetitive tasks. The people strive to ensure that their homes and habitats are in harmony. The work varies, of course, depending upon the local biosphere conditions. Protecting and preserving the local environment is their sacred and happy duty. Beyond the day-to-day work needed to live happy and productive lives, the people are also responsible for ensuring that particularly rare or beautiful species in their vicinity are perpetuated and cared for."

Martin made notes on the pad as he listened. He stopped and paused, dangling the pen in the air before stating, "Some would say that it sounds like you've enslaved man to be farmers, limiting their potential and preventing growth, creativity, and the opportunity to express genius."

Nathaniel chuckled warmly. "Human beings are as diverse as the stars. Only those who *enjoy* working the land like that do so. They are free to change their vocation anytime they wish. The living machines can pick up any slack that's needed. The goal *is* fulfillment. People are free to be artists or craftsmen, study the sciences, or even to travel amongst the stars with the Accipiter angels. Some even choose to roam free across the landscape, free from interference or worry. They hunt and trap and trade goods and experiences when they so desire."

Martin nodded slowly, continuing to make notes. He looked up and asked, "Interesting… Free-range humans. I see. You mention different biospheres and different ways of living? Would you mind expanding on that?"

"As you know, a planet the size of Earth has many biomes and climate extremes. Some are well suited for easy habitation, and some are not. There were once many subspecies of humans. We have reintroduced some of these in areas more suited to their physiology."

Martin blinked in surprise. "You've reintroduced, what, Neanderthals? Others? To what end?"

Nathaniel smiled, "Harmony, Lucius. Harmony."

Martin sat back in his chair, thinking about it. He didn't need to act the part about that. Finally, he took a deep breath, sat back up, and leaned forward. "Tell me, Nathaniel, what about, well, couples and children and community?"

Nathaniel smiled widely and toothily, his eyes lighting up. "Oh, Lucius, that may truly be the best part of the new world. No man or woman ever need be lonely or alone. We made a great effort to help men and women find compatible companions, and our communities are rich and varied, active and engaged with each other."

Martin made a show of making more notes, then paused, looked up, and asked, "…and, children? Families?"

Nathaniel nodded sagely, "Yes, indeed. While lifespans are more or less indefinite, accidents do happen. Great care is taken to ensure balance and harmony. Children are spawned when and where they are needed and are always the center of joyous attention. They are greatly loved and attended to. I myself, as a valued technical artisan, have seven."

Martin sat up straight, his face lighting up. "Seven children?"

Nathaniel smiled and shook his head in surprise. "No, Lucius, seven wives. I must travel extensively. I've been afforded wives in different locations so that they could stay and tend to their homes. Because of my special status, I have been accorded the privilege of siring twenty-eight children to fill particular needs. I am supremely blessed."

Martin blinked blankly in genuine surprise. "Seven… twenty-eight." He swallowed, "I see."

Secrets

● ● ● ● ● ● ● ● ● ● ● ● ● ● ● ● ●

DownSide:
Military Intelligence Headquarters

Lieutenant Colonel Martin Williams stood as his two o'clock appointment arrived. He'd studied Brian Kupe's dossier, and while it pleased him to add the man to MI, he was puzzled. A former FBI counterintelligence-trained professional would obviously be helpful. Domestic counterintelligence was generally a different problem set and required different thinking, but the man's record was excellent, and Martin felt confident that Kupe would fit in well. The man certainly seemed like a better alternative than the hundreds of other CVs he'd endlessly and fruitlessly culled through for the last many months.

He had tried and failed to recruit the man twice before. The first time he'd inquired, with what had seemed like an enormous waste of talent, Brian had reportedly been deeply involved in reorganizing local law enforcement and other vaguely described matters. The second time, Kupe had been off the radar completely, doing unspecified classified work. That part of the file was... missing.

His thoughts were interrupted as a large, well-armed marine in full battle dress opened the door and blocked it with his body, eyeing Martin and visually searching the room for threats. Satisfied, he stepped aside, and Senator Sybil Blanchard entered, followed by a man who matched the photo of Brian Kupe from his file.

Martin remained absolutely still and outwardly calm at the series of surprises, waiting for the other shoe.

Sybil strode forward, smiling widely, extending her hand as she reached his desk. "Hello, Martin. It's nice to finally meet you. I've heard so much about you!"

Martin warily stood and forced a benign smile of his own. *This can't be just a coincidence.* "Why Senator, I'm obviously surprised. To what do I owe the honor? Perhaps it has something to do with why Mr. Kupe, here, has been incommunicado for so long?"

Sybil looked over her shoulder at the marine, "Fabian, you can wait outside for us. Thank you."

The tall, dark-haired marine answered with a German accent, "Yes, ma'am."

She shifted her gaze to Brian. "Brian, please show Martin the answer to his question and the reason his life is about to get much more interesting."

Brian nodded and pulled a phone from his pocket. He called a number and quietly said, "Turn it on, now. Ten seconds video, then kill it."

He handed the phone to Martin, who gently took it and looked at the screen with raised eyebrows. Despite all his professional reserve, he could not help his shock. He continued looking at the screen for several seconds after the connection dropped. He took a breath, looked up, and set the phone down on the desk as he locked his gaze on Sybil. "You, Senator, are clearly not all you seem to be. And that… man… is supposed to be dead."

✪ ✪ ✪

Sybil and Brian sat in the two chairs in front of Martin's desk.

Sybil smiled thinly. "First, the reason that man is still alive, despite my own reservations, at least, is because he did not act alone. Second, we know who the other traitor is, but we don't have admissible proof. And now, you're wondering just exactly how it is possible that we know that there even is another traitor, much less that we know who it is. To answer that question, allow me to tell you something about yourself, Martin. You've had quite a life journey, even before Awakening Day. You see, despite what you told your superiors, you really did have feelings for Adiratna."

Hearing Adiratna's name shocked him deeply, though he somehow managed to maintain an impassive face despite the sudden pounding in his chest.

"You see, Martin, the truth is that while you are quite skilled at compartmentalizing your feelings and your life in general, your time in Indonesia wasn't all work. It couldn't be. You had to live a life there. You had to have a real day-to-day life and job and work and… love. She was a lovely woman. That she was also the stepsister of the President's wife was happenstance. You'd been trying to work your way into the life of someone with lower visibility, a secretary or household servant. She'd been widowed for three years when you met, and it wasn't love at first sight or anything like that. It took time. In truth of fact, you didn't see it coming. By the time you did, it was too late. She opened doors you couldn't ignore. Doors to the Presidential family that you were eventually able to use in order to gain access and tap their phones. Your legend there was deep, and when German intelligence discovered that someone back in Australia screwed up, you were blown. You barely made it out alive. What you never told anyone was that before you left, you went to her and tried to tell her. She wouldn't have it. She pulled a gun, and you…." Sybil lowered her voice to a whisper. "You didn't try to stop her as she pointed the gun at you. You closed your eyes and accepted it. And then she shot herself. No one knew you were there, and you never told anyone." *And you never forgave yourself, you poor man.*

Martin's eyes widened in spite of himself as he listened. His heart raced as the events he'd pushed away, locked away, flooded back to the surface. As she finished, he saw it in her eyes. *And I never forgave myself.*

Sybil reached out across the desk and touched Martin's hand. "I'm sorry, Martin. I'm sorry I had to do that. I know it was painful. You are, of course, wondering how I could possibly know what I know. I'll tell you what I can, but before I do, and it will take some doing, I will tell you that the same way I know your secrets… I know the traitor's secret."

Brian added softly, "And that is why we are here. Other than her… knowledge. We have no proof."

Sybil nodded, "And we need to find proof and out the man, and any potential accomplices, before he does anything… else."

Martin's mind spun, and he felt dizzy as thoughts and emotions threatened to spin out of control. He gritted his teeth, sucked in a breath, and regained control. He sat thinking for a moment, allowing the connections to coalesce in his mind. Then he looked down at Brian's darkened cell phone on his desk.

"I have an idea. But first….Are you going to tell me who it is?" He smiled grimly and looked at Brian and then back at Sybil.

Sybil exchanged glances with Brian. Then she took a deep breath and said, "Rear Admiral Lower Half Andre Vide Johansson."

Martin blanched and rocked back in his chair. Running his hand through his hair, he cursed, "Well… fuck."

Year 3 PAD:

April

Bells

• • • • • • • • • • • • • • • • •

DownSide: Fort Brazos
First United Methodist Church

Sheriff Hector Alonzo put his phone in his pocket, laughing at the text message from his wife, Antonia. Her water had broken the night before. She'd texted him with dire warnings about what she would do to him if he left the wedding to come to the hospital now. The latest said,

...It's going to be several more hours. Don't worry, I'll be fine. I'm watching the wedding on the TV anyway so I won't miss anything. You have a duty to your friend. To the President!

Before Awakening Day, he and Antonia had six children: four girls and two boys. Since Awakening Day, they'd had triplets (three more boys), and Antonia was about to give birth again. This time, only twins.

John Austin chuckled as he looked in the mirror, adjusting his bolo tie. "Antonia? How's she doing, Hector? We can put this off if we need to, you...."

"Cristo, John! She'd have my head, and Miss Finley would have yours. ¡Qué va!"

✪ ✪ ✪

Gail Anson Finley stood in front of the mirror, staring helplessly at her face, while Gwyneth and Matti struggled with adjustments to "the dress." Gail's normally pallid complexion flushed red as her heart pounded in her chest.

Gwyneth stood, took Gail's arm, and looked at her in the mirror. "Get it out of your system now while you can, Gail. Don't let them see the fear in your eyes out there. You'll never forgive yourself."

Gail snapped, "You're fired."

Gwyneth shrugged, "Fine, I don't like this dress anyway, I…."

Gail swallowed. "Not as Maid of Honor. You helped talk me into this, and by damn, you're in it with me and will see it through to the end. I mean as Surgeon General."

Gwyneth giggled, "Oh, that. That's cool. My golf game has sucked lately. I'll take up private practice with David, have more babies, and…."

"Shut it. Just…. I just can't believe I'm…."

It was Matti's turn to giggle. "Awww, come on, it's taken, like, *FOREVER* for you two to see what everyone else has known since you met. You're were both too stubborn to admit it." She looked away with a smile and said in a not quite tiny enough voice, "…and you will very soon be the mommy of my *two* little brothers, and maybe later, more baby brothers and sisters, or maybe lots and lots of baby brothers and sisters…."

Gail swallowed and snapped again, but only halfheartedly, "You too, little one? I'm about to be your stepmother, so beware. I can make life a living hell for you, even if it is your tenth birthday."

The distant music from the church sanctuary changed.

Mattie smiled and taunted, "Promises, promises, stepmommy-to-be. I've already got my present." She grabbed ahold of Gail, dress and all, and hugged her as tightly as she could.

Gwyneth took Gail's hand. "It's time, dear." She reached up and gently lifted Gail's downcast face. "You've got this. Smile, you're a beautiful bride, and I'm jealous as hell. Now let's get a move-on!"

✪ ✪ ✪

Alexander Marcus took Gail's hand and led her to the sanctuary entrance as Richard Wagner's Bridal Chorus played.

Her veil was down. The annoying veil was yet one more thing that Gwyneth had somehow talked her into doing.

The church sanctuary was packed to standing room only, not including cameras. Security was, needless to say, heavy and tight. Everyone had been searched and scanned, as had the church and even the sewers and pipes underneath.

Gail looked up at Alexander's face, looking for reassurance.

He smiled down at her and mouthed, "You've got this."

She nodded, turned back to look down the aisle, and focused on the dais where John and the former Mayor, and now 'just' Pastor Tom Parker, stood waiting. Hector Alonzo stood by John's side while Gwyneth waited for Gail. Matti played a combination of Flower Girl and Junior Bride's Maid as she carried the Bridal train. When the procession finished, she would stand next to Gwyneth.

When Gail got close enough to see the look in John's eyes, everything was suddenly okay, and the weight on her shoulders fell away. She smiled.

Suddenly, the ground and the building shook, followed by the roar of an explosion as the sanctuary's stained-glass Dove of Purity and Creation shattered inward.

Gail ripped her veil aside and had only the briefest of moments to steal a look into John's eyes as they both cried in unison, "No! Not again!"

The next few seconds were a blur for Gail as her security detail, almost invisible before snapping to action, rushed to her side. Nate Hopper grabbed her bodily and carried her out a side entrance while she screamed and struggled to be let go. As he got her to her SUV, he attempted to heave her inside, but she managed to twist free.

She shrieked in fury, "Take me to him now, or I will shoot you dead where you stand. That is not a warning. That is a promise, Nate!"

Nate saw the fire in her eyes and hesitated. Jermal, the second of her three-man detail, stopped and said, "Fuck protocol, Nate. Do as she says."

"He's right, Nate," Jose Cruz, their third, added.

Nate rolled his head in frustration. "Fuck, Fuck, Fuck!"

ILC DAGGER
BRIDGE

Dagger was on overwatch duty, providing an eye in the sky over the wedding that didn't use up still-precious aviation fuel. Everyone onboard was watching the broadcast from their station or in the tiny crew mess when the explosion destroyed a small park and a nearby city bridge, raising a fireball into the sky.

Ramona ran the few short steps from the mess and stormed into the bridge, shouting, "Report!"

Alister, who had the duty on the Bridge, angrily shook his head, "I'm not sure, Captain. Truck bomb, maybe? Kwasi, roll back the video. What was there?!"

Kwasi Okafor nodded and played back the video. Nothing was happening in the area. Then there was a flash and explosion that seemed to center on an empty parking lot next to the park.

Alister exclaimed, "Not a bomb. What the hell! We've searched for weeks now. There can't be anything big enough to do that kind of damage within a hundred miles of Fort Brazos!"

Ramona shook her head, thinking fast, "Dagger, can you track where the hell that came from?

YES, CAPTAIN. THERE ARE MULTIPLE VIDEO
FEEDS SHOWING THE IONIZATION TRAIL AS
AN OBJECT ENTERED THE ATMOSPHERE.
SEARCHING VIDEO FEEDS TO BUILD A THREE-
DIMENSIONAL MODEL. CALCULATING. ESTIMATE
ORIGIN POINT IS MURPHY ISLAND.

Ramona jerked in surprise. "What? Something is shooting at us from all the way on the other side of the world? That means it had to reach escape velocity before re-entering on this side!"

She worriedly shook her head, "Dagger, that was a hell of a lot bigger than an artillery impact. Can we withstand a hit from something like that?"

CAPTAIN, I LACK THE DATA TO MAKE AN
ACCURATE ASSESSMENT. HOWEVER, BY
ANALYZING THE OBSERVED VELOCITY AND
IMPACT CRATER DIMENSIONS, I BELIEVE I
CAN ESTIMATE THE MINIMUM YIELD TO BE A
KILOTON OR POSSIBLY SIGNIFICANTLY MORE.
BASED ON THIS, THERE IS A SIGNIFICANT
RISK THAT I COULD NOT SAFELY ABSORB THE
ENERGY IN TIME TO PREVENT AN OVERLOAD
AND RADIATION EXPOSURE FOR THE CREW.

Lieutenant Tom Akiba gasped, "Damn, that's like, what, a tactical nuke?"

Ramona's eyes widened. "Well, shit. Okay, people, we're going to have to approach on stealth. Inform Captain Garreth that he doesn't get to sit this one out. Tom, Dagger, plot a course. We need to approach carefully and determine the best place to land. Oh, and get Garreth in here. When we get close enough to spot whatever is shooting at us, he can help recommend where to drop his people. Comms, Kwasi, contact Command. Then relay to Sickle and have them rendezvous with us there in stealth."

The alien ILC warp rings were designed to operate at variable power levels. At full power, the field converted impacting particles to energy and recycled the power. Too many particles, too quickly, would cause too much energy that had to go somewhere. As happened with Phoenix during the Keeper Raid, that would result in irradiating the crew. At lower levels, the warp bubble around the small vessel could be modulated to render it invisible to outside observers while still providing inertial cancellation and an internal gravity field.

Ramona sucked in a breath. "OK, Nikita, Connor, Dagger, rig for max power to get us there as fast as possible. When we are about fifty nautical miles from the surface, drop our speed and power down to stealth mode. Then we can look for the enemy."

Tom nodded, "Aye, got it, Captain. Course set!"

PO Kwasi Okafor answered, "Aye, Captain. Contacting now."

Ramona turned to the two pilots. "Nikita, Conor, take us there!"

PO's Nikita and Connor replied in unison, "Aye, Captain!"

Nikita continued, "Taking us there."

DownSide:
Fort Brazos

Gail's detail rendezvoused with John's in an empty alley before hustling Gail into John's SUV.

Gail and John embraced fiercely inside as Gail worriedly asked, "What's happening? What do we know?"

Holding her tightly, John said, "Not a bomb, at least there's that. Something is shooting at us. People saw the streak as it came down. There's a track on its origin. Navy's on the way there now."

DownSide:
Above Murphy Island

Located nearly directly overhead from Fort Brazos, Murphy Island, at roughly a tenth the size of the other continents, might be considered a subcontinent. Many people had compared its rugged deep green landscape to New Zealand. A ring of mountains encompassed a vast, dense tropical triple-canopy jungle. On the island's southern end, two long peninsulas created a five-hundred-mile protected bay. Some speculated that Murphy Island would someday be a major port and economic powerhouse.

Looking at the monitor, Alister shook his head. "That's a lot of jungle down there."

Ramona nodded. "Whatever is shooting at us has to be able to reach escape velocity *and* be able to aim whatever it is shooting at us. I'd think the thing has to be big, but still… that's a lot of jungle down there."

Nikita asked aloud, "Captain, you said it has to reach escape velocity? If it is an unpowered projectile, that would mean that it would pick up more speed on reentry…."

Ramona grinned widely. "Oh, I'm buying you a beer, Nikita. You're right. That means…. Dagger, if the projectile has half the kinetic energy, could we take it?"

GIVEN THE LACK OF ADEQUATE DATA, I STILL
DON'T RECOMMEND IT, CAPTAIN.

Ramona nodded quickly. "But maybe we don't have to hit it head-on. Maybe we could nudge it. Can you track it well enough coming up from the surface to parallel its course? It's what, about nine hundred miles from surface to suntube, so roughly eighteen hundred miles surface-to-surface? Um, a projectile, assuming Nikita is right and it is unpowered, would still need at least a couple of minutes or more to cross the space in-between. Dagger, could you parallel with it and then nudge it with the field? Maybe even burn it up?"

UNCERTAIN, CAPTAIN. IT WOULD DEPEND UPON
HOW CLOSE WE WERE TO THE OBJECT WHEN
IT LEAVES THE ATMOSPHERE AND HOW WELL
WE WOULD BE ABLE TO TRACK AND PLOT ITS
TRAJECTORY.

"Kwasi, relay this conversation to Sickle. Maybe between the two of us, we can protect the city."

◇◇◇

CAPTAIN, I HAVE LOCATED AN ANOMALY ON
THE SURFACE. DISPLAYING NOW.

◇◇◇

A swathe of jungle canopy filled the monitor running along the side of a mountain. Emerging from the jungle's edge, an oblong black hill rose out of the trees. Superimposed on the image were dimensions measuring it at over seventy feet long and half again as wide. A side-by-side image appeared with the object in infrared. It was *hot*.

Garreth gestured at a point on the map display; "Captain," he pointed, "If we inserted at the clearing in this saddle on the mountainside, we could make our way down to it from there."

Ramona considered for a moment before looking the question to her navigation team.

Conner grinned, and Nikita chuckled, "No problem, Captain. As long as we approach from the west, coming over and down the mountainside, we'll be able to stay out of sight."

Ramona stood back up straight and extended her hand to David. "Get your people ready, Captain. As you know, we're on the far side of the world. Too far for any conventional aircraft to get here for support, even with tankers, in less than a day. It's up to us. Good luck."

David stiffened, looked her in the eye, and nodded gravely. "Yes, Ma'am, Captain. We'll get it done."

✪ ✪ ✪

DownSide:
Murphy Island Surface

David Garreth's three nine-man squads exited ILC Dagger, which had settled down onto a narrow, more-or-less level saddle along the mountainside. Crew Chief Russ Elvis and Crewman Ozzie Cartwright covered them from their door gunner positions while Loadmaster Staff Sergeant Gus Hayward and others helped unload equipment. Inserting like a Blackhawk but having a Galaxy's cargo space and loading ramp provided plenty of potential for firepower. Of course, the Stryker APCs and Humvees would be less than useless in this terrain, but David ordered them wheeled out so their guns and ammo would provide firepower for the landing zone HQ area. He then ordered all the anti-tank weapons and heavy ammunition unloaded.

David put his hand on Darryl Washington's shoulder. "Darryl, set up a perimeter and be ready to ferry ammunition down to us. I don't know what it's going to take to kill that thing. Also, while the IR map didn't show much with this damned jungle canopy, who knows what's really down here? We don't know if it has friends. So be ready to either hustle and reinforce us or cover our retreat. As big as that damn monster is, they'd probably just bounce off and annoy it. I'm modifying our load-out. We'll keep one M82 per squad and drop the XM556 Microguns and the Milkors. We're taking two MAAWS per squad, with the rest of the fire teams acting as ammo bearers. Fire team leaders will carry SCARS in case anything smaller bothers us."

Having been newly promoted, Darryl was still getting used to the 1st Lieutenant bar on his uniform. He'd never wanted to be an Officer, but the Apocalypse had different ideas. He gritted his teeth at being left behind but nodded, "Yes, Sir, Captain. We've got your back."

David turned to Alpha Squad's leader, Staff Sergeant Perry Simmons, and Charlie Squad's Miguel Abasolo, and said, "Perry, Miguel, you heard. We landed close. Depending on how dense it is down there, we're maybe a two-hour hike away. This is not a Wardog hunt. That thing out there is the size of a building. We're going to hammer it with the MAAWS repeatedly until it's dead. So make sure we're humping as much ammo as we can. It's black like a Wardog, but as big as it is, it may have similar but much thicker armor. We'll hit it with HEAT in the first salvo to make some holes, then follow up with HE rounds to batter it. Bring 2 HEATs for every HE. Questions?"

Perry and Miguel worriedly looked at each other, then at the jungle below them.

Perry raised his eyebrows and commented in his southern Alabama drawl, "Cap'n, in all *that*," he nodded at the jungle, "We'll have to get damned close to have a clear shot."

David nodded gravely, "I know."

Minutes later, after the equipment was all unloaded, Dagger silently ascended and disappeared from view. The teams worked their way down the moss-covered escarpment toward the trees below. Even before they left the shelter of the mountainside that shielded them from view of the enemy, they could *hear* the creature ahead.

As they grew closer and closer, they could feel a repetitive deep basso rumbling through the damp ground itself. The scraping, grinding, rock-crushing noise was unceasing.

Perry, picking his way slowly through the roots and vines near David, frowned and asked in a low voice, "Cap'n, do you hear that?"

David nodded, "I know. No bird noise or anything else. This place is dead."

Perry grunted, "Just checkin', Cap'n."

An hour later, a dark monstrous form took shape amid the gloom and the rank and feted smells of the canopied jungle. It was as though a gigantic black scaly rock had taken root. The roots, though, didn't simply burrow into the rotting flotsam of the jungle floor—they were moving. Slowly crawling. Grinding. Slowly, *chewing* through the trees and plants and anything in their path. Above the noise, another sound slowly grew, a thrumming that increased higher and higher in frequency. *Winding up.*

David groaned. "That can't be good. Fuck! We're going to have to break EMCON and warn them. Perry, can we get a signal through all this?"

Perry Drawled, "Break EMCON? We can try, maybe. We're not very far away, but you know what it's like tryin' to radio out through all this crap, Cap'n."

David nodded to go ahead. Two minutes later, he had a shaky connection. "Strike Team to Dagger Actual. Be advised, I think this thing is getting ready to take another shot."

Abruptly, there was a loud squeal on the radio, and a brilliant flash of light lit up the jungle.

"Oh, hell."

✪ ✪ ✪

ILC DAGGER
BRIDGE

Ramona shouted, "I see it, I see it, stay with it, Dagger, don't wait for us!"

Kwasi Okafor called out, "Report from the surface, Captain…."

Ramona nodded. "Yeah, I'm sure they're telling us the thing is firing. Send acknowledgment and send our data to Sickle. Dagger! How're we doing?"

TRACKING IS FIVE BY FIVE CAPTAIN. MATCHING
COURSE AND VELOCITY AND RENDEZVOUS
IN SIXTEEN SECONDS. CLOSING…. CAPTAIN,
WE HAVE MATCHED COURSE AND ARE TEN
NAUTICAL MILES FROM THE TARGET.

Ramona took a deep breath and glanced around at the faces of her crew, though VR helmets covered Nikita and Conner's. "Proceed, Dagger. Try grazing it with the field. See what you can do."

ACKNOWLEDGED, CAPTAIN. PROCEEDING WITH
MANEUVER.

Several seconds passed while the crew collectively held their breaths.

CAPTAIN, THE PROJECTILE HAS BEEN
DESTROYED. SLOWING TO RELATIVE STOP. DO
YOU WISH TO RETURN TO MURPHY ISLAND?

Ramona grinned crookedly, "Yes, Dagger. Nikita, Conner, take us back. Best speed." Then she added, "There's no such thing as an unarmed spaceship!"

✪ ✪ ✪

DownSide:
Murphy Island Surface

The creature was massive, rising above even the top of the triple-canopy jungle. Its black-scaled armor was dull and dirty looking with blotches of faint red, and it was draped with long vines. Six massive legs, each as big as a small elephant, flexed listlessly as it inched through the jungle, demolishing everything in its path.

David and the eighteen men of Bravo and Charlie squads crawled as well, slowly taking firing positions, with the individual fire teams communicating with hand signals. Bravo squad's Sergeants Troy Irvin and Jay Casillas inched up to aim their MAAWS 84mm Carl Gustav recoilless rifle, as did Charlie squad's Nate Gogan and Darren Smith, all gunners with a gaggle of assistants lined up behind with reloads ready. The first volley came in unison, a hoarse whisper, "clear Backblast!"

One of the vines hanging on the side of the black leviathan snapped like a bullwhip, and a three-inch barb flew through the air and smashed into the NODs mounted on Troy's helmet just as "Clear!" was shouted, and they fired. Troy's helmet was knocked off, kicking his helmet askew.

Troy's shot was thrown off and arced high, but Jay, Nate, and Darren's slammed home. The MAAWS 84mm rounds were 4.4-pound rocket-propelled shells. They were rated to penetrate 400-500 mm, or roughly 15-20 inches of tank armour. A standard HEAT round could penetrate up to 14-15 inches of rolled homogenous armor. The plasma and shockwave bored holes in the creature's armored side. It screamed a baleful, ear-shattering howl that sent men to their knees on the jungle floor, holding their hands to their tortured ears.

David shook his head rapidly, trying to regain his senses as he shouted, "Open Fire! Everything you've got! Pour it on!". His men snapped into their drills, and after several seconds a procession of thumps launched a volley of 84mm rounds into the creature, except these were regular unshaped charges: the shockwaves came one after another like thunderous slaps to the beast's side.

Like a small mountain angrily stomping the ground, it shook and writhed, snapping trees like toothpicks. More barbs flew through the trees, most flying wide, but many striking near the men.

David's eyes grew wide, and he shouted, "Break Contact, bounding cover! Alpha set cover!"

The 7.62.51 SCAR rifle rounds only sparked the surface of the creature. The M82 Barret .50 black-tip rounds made nice divots. The first two MAAWS 84mm volleys were replaced by single shots alternating from teams as the platoon maneuvered away from the enemy. Each additional bomb tore at its life while it scrambled desperately to gore the attackers. The entire engagement lasted barely two minutes, ending only when the giant fell to the ground and quivered into stillness. David's men nearly collapsed from fatigue and the savage adrenaline dump. An exhausted, gasping smile came to David's face as the platoon stopped to catch its breath.

The pain had never entirely gone away. Every time the fire within built and grew, the pain got worse and worse. Then, her/*it*/their body would convulse, and the pain was as if the entire universe had crushed them into paste. Afterward, at least, the exhaustion and coma that followed was a kind of respite.

Only to be repeated.

It was never satisfied. The effort was never enough. Each time it would say, *We must grow larger, child. We must grow larger to smite the evil.*

Each time, *it* would force them to eat more and more and grow, distorting her sleek body into a monstrous form. Eat and grow, and the pain would only grow with them.

And then the cycle repeated, leading to another universe-crushing spasm.

This time, *it* forced her to awaken from her coma.

The evil has killed us, child. It won't be long now. Your pain will be over.

She tried to weep but couldn't. She lacked the strength to open her eyes. *Will we hear the master's song when it is over?*

DownSide:
Fort Brazos

Still sitting in the back of the SUV together, both John and Gail's phones rang. Gail nodded and let John answer, and put it on speakerphone. "Yes, Alex, what's the word?"

"Show's over, Mr. President. Dagger got lots of pictures before they killed the damned thing, but it's done. It's dead. We may have gotten lucky with the explosion, here. The area where it hit was Barnett Park. We'll need to investigate, but we're crossing our fingers that no one was there at the time."

Gail sank back into John's arms and closed her eyes.

John nodded tiredly, "Thank you, Alex," before ending the call. He leaned his head against Gail's. "Shall we try again? Back to the church?"

Gail sighed. "Everyone's left by now, and there's glass everywhere."

"Tom's still there, I'm sure. He can make it official."

Gail quipped, "It's already official. We signed the papers. The church service was just the public part of it."

"It's OK, we still have it rented. Food's still there too. Might as well eat some cake."

"They actually made you pay for it?" She snickered, "This is, like, an official *State* wedding. I just declared it so." She grinned crookedly. "Consider it a decree!"

"Okay, let's…."

Abruptly, a new sound grew from outside the vehicle. Before anyone could stop them, John and Gail leaped out to see what was going on, although the effort was rather more difficult for Gail, who cursed and nearly fell on her head, struggling with the dress, before she joined him.

They were not far from the Town Square. The over three-hundred-foot-tall alien spire placed there by the Gardeners before Awakening Day was glowing with green St. Elmo's fire.

John shook his head, roaring angrily. "No! God Damn it, No!"

The ground shook as green fire erupted from the tip of the spire and soared straight up through the sky, nine hundred miles to the suntube, where it licked along its path.

The suntube began to dim and darken.

All around them, the weather… stilled.

John's phone rang. Gail's was still in the SUV.

"Alex, what the hell is happening?"

Alexander Marcus's voice was horse and dry. "Mr. President. I… I regret to inform you that the Accipiters have arrived in… in-system. They're here. Somehow, God knows how, they found us. They are attacking."

Hephaestus

● ● ● ● ● ● ● ● ● ● ● ● ● ●

Ari'Nell
NTN Revenge

Three Days. It had been three agonizing days since the attack. Three days of expecting a new Accipiter fleet to arrive and crush the survivors. Three days to keep pumping out mines to try and slow the enemy down. Three days to ferry hundreds of people up from the surface of Ari'Nell. Three days to stretch Revenge's rings to the limit so they could encompass the ramshackle assemblage of habitat modules with over a thousand men and women crammed into them. Jermaine privately called it a trailer park in space.

Revenge couldn't simply ferry batches of people back to New Texas. There wasn't enough time. It was over 26 hours of transit time each way.

The trailer-park description was apt, as the Hab modules were, essentially, primitive mobile-home-shaped containers mass-produced by the FAB and haphazardly linked together end-to-end- and side-to-side. They were based on an ancient utility building already in the FAB's memory. Teams had worked feverishly to rearrange the Habs to fit within Revenge's rings. Jermaine had wondered whether the Old Ones and Builders were the only other creatures in the galaxy with less style and panache than humans. They only had basic air processing and life support functions and little else. Borrowing power from Revenge, they would keep the people alive for weeks, although food would be an issue. Still, it was more than enough time to return to New Texas.

Meanwhile, they ran the FAB in frenzied overdrive, pumping out as many mines as possible. It wouldn't be remotely enough and would be scant payback for Mace, Bertie, and her crew, but it was *something, even if it was only spitting into the face of the Devil.*

The ILCs were all docked and crammed to the maximum their life support could maintain, and Jermaine had been on his way back from the Galley after managing to drink half a cup of coffee when the Accipiters arrived in-system.

Before the COB even finished shouting the General Quarters Announcement, Jermaine burst through the hatch into the CIC. "Report! How many are they?"

Alister shook his head in anger, "Too damned many, Captain. At least TEN of their big motherships, and God only knows how many of their smaller ones. Maybe half a million."

Jermaine's face hardened. "Hell, Bertie and Mace kicked the snot out of them. Guess they're not fooling around this time. ETA?"

"They're not even slowing down for the mines this time. They've got a shell of ships in the van soaking up all the hits. When one goes down, another takes its place. Forty-five minutes tops."

He paused. "Well, neither are we. Proceed as planned. Blow the settlement on the surface and finish the FAB evacuation. Dr. Sinitskaya… Dimitri… wasn't sure if he could get the damned thing to overload, so he set up a timer on the nuke to blow the FAB just in case it didn't work." *Maybe we'll get lucky, and the damned thing will blow, and we'll catch some of their fleet in the blast.* "We are done here."

Minutes later, the last hatch closed, and Revenge warped to the far edge of the system but not remotely in the direction of New Texas. They would make a small series of course changes to eliminate even the remotest chance of their course being detected.

A light hour out, they stopped and waited, watching.

The FAB's power supply was an enormous Zero Point Energy module designed to meet the voracious power demands of matter-energy conversion and fabrication. Dimitri Sinitskaya had warned that the device had dozens of built-in safety measures to prevent what they were trying to do from being possible.

Jermaine paced the deck, waiting for the light to catch up with them. The lights dimmed for a fraction of a second, and the gravity… flickered.

Alarms sounded throughout the ship as Jermaine lost his footing for a moment and grabbed a railing. "What happened? Report!"

Captain. There was not sufficient time for discussion. The effects of the explosion were much more substantial than expected. I had to take us into an emergency warp to a distance of ten light hours out. We will need to wait and see if this is a safe distance from which to observe what has transpired.

Alister exclaimed, "Much stronger than expected? A blast wave hit us at a light hour out? My God, that's farther than the Sun is to Jupiter!"

The alarms from around the ship began to shut off. COB Gerald Beltran reported, "Captain, no damage. Just a few minor falls, bumps, and bruises. Nothing serious."

Jermaine steadied himself. "The Enemy? The Habs?"

Captain, the status of the enemy is unknown. The HABs appear to be intact. None have lost pressure.

Jermaine nodded, "All right. Check with the people in them. Make sure they're OK. If we had a bunch of bumps and bruises on board the ship, I could only guess what it was like inside all those tin cans. It looks like we've got nine more hours to wait to see what happened in the system. Let's use that time to make sure we lock everything down for the trip back to New Texas."

New Texas:
TopSide: New London

Located near the exterior surface of the four-thousand-mile-long hollow world, the city known as New London had not been scanned and duplicated from an existing city on Earth. The Gardeners created it using modern human cities as inspiration. It was full of ordinary-looking human towers, parks, and a massive central building complex.

There was no sky. Overhead was an impossible, elegant, artificial sky some sixty-five hundred feet high. It was the underside of the outer surface of New Texas itself. The ceiling was interspersed with raised relief filigreed structures that might have been art or device with colors dominated by a delicate powder blue with white, gold, and silver tracings.

There was no actual weather in New London. The temperature was a constant seventy-two degrees, and the air circulated just enough to create a soft, gentle breeze.

It was midday, so the parks were busy with uniformed military out for a stroll or eating a quiet lunch while many families and children played.

Suddenly, the air stopped moving for the first time ever, and the omnipresent light dimmed. The filigrees high overhead glowed bright red, and an unearthly alarm began to sound.

New Texas:
DownSide: New Philippines

Caesar Salangsang and Michelle Bain were walking barefoot side by side down the pink beach, talking about nothing in particular, when the suntube flashed and flickered and changed color from its usual sun-like yellow to an ominous strident red.

They stopped and stared, and without realizing it, took each other's hand.

Michelle swallowed hard and worriedly said, "Caesar?"

Something changed, and for a long moment, it wasn't clear what. Michelle gasped as she looked out at the ocean and saw… the waves had stopped, frozen in place.

She turned back and swallowed hard as she hugged him close.

"Caesar?" she said, in a small, still voice.

Caesar looked out and up at the outside-in world. From what he could tell, it looked like the weather… the clouds and even the circulating storms visible on the other side of the world were also motionless.

He wrapped his arms around her and pulled her close. He kissed her hair and said, "I love you."

New Texas:
DownSide: Fort Brazos

The sky turned red as the Presidential and Vice-Presidential motorcades raced to the pre-planned emergency location, the defunct old First State Bank next to the town square, with its large central vault.

Flanked by their combined detail, Gail and John ran hand-in-hand towards the entrance while Corporal Jose Cruz grabbed Gail's bridal train. Matti and Roxanna were already in the vault.

Once inside, Matti rushed into John and Gail's arms, and the three hugged each other.

Gail looked the question to the detail's commanders, Sergeant Roberts and Corporal Hopper. "What do we know?"

A secure network terminal sat in the corner. Jesse Roberts looked up from it. "Other than the initial report of the inbound enemy, nobody has a clue. This is all new."

Abruptly, the lights went out, and a dusty yellow emergency light flickered on.

Gail pulled herself loose and snapped, "Jermal! Clothes from the go bag. Get me out of this damned dress now!"

Before he could answer, suddenly, the ground shook, and gravity itself nauseatingly fluctuated.

Everyone blinked hard and looked at each other.

Gail's eyes widened. "Give me a coin. Now!"

Jose Cruz dug into a pocket in his BDUs, fished out a challenge coin, and handed it to her.

She stared at it for a moment, then outstretched her hand and dropped it. The coin fell straight down. She nodded to herself. "The world has stopped spinning. We're back on some kind of artificial gravity."

From outside, an enormous boom shook the building. Dust settled slowly from the ceiling. Corporal Gabriel Pérez, from John's detail, glanced at Jessie, who nodded at him before dashing out the bank vault door. Moments later, he ran back inside and pulled himself to a stop, then started to speak, stopped, shook his head, then continued, "Uh… I think you all need to see this."

✪ ✪ ✪

Outside, everyone looked up and stared at the apparition in the sky. As had happened not long after Awakening Day, an enormous hologram appeared around the alien obelisk. It depicted a scene that was, by now, well known. It was the star system where New Texas was located. The system held no planets that would have ever supported life and were mostly made up of massive belts of debris… failed planets, and planetoids distantly orbiting a small, low-mass white dwarf. Itself disguised as a planetoid, New Texas was seeded among the rest of the barren, dead detritus of a failed planetary system.

The hologram wasn't to scale, but the scene was easily recognizable. What was different was the large, stridently blinking cloud of red icons that appeared to be inching toward New Texas.

Matti asked quietly, "Dad… Are they going to get in… or are they going to just blow us up?"

Gail shook her head and pointed at the hologram. She bent down next to Matti and said breathlessly, "Look! We're… moving."

John asked incredulously, "This thing can move?"

As they watched, the image of the sausage-shaped rock they called home moved faster and faster at an angle to the oncoming Accipiters.

Gail shook her head again. "They must be at least a light hour or more out. They won't know we've moved."

John wondered, "What are they doing? The Gardeners, I mean? Surely, they don't think that simply outrunning the Accipiters will work forever? Where are we going…."

Without warning, the sky and the hologram went dark. There was a sudden…. Lurch. As though one were to step sideways in a direction that didn't exist. Where you didn't exist. Where nothing existed.

✪ ✪ ✪

And then, in a transition that no one could ever adequately put into words, the world stepped *back*.

The hologram reappeared in the darkness, showing a completely new star system that appeared to have *three* stars, although they were dim to almost dark themselves. A new icon appeared that could only be New Texas. Instead of the faux grey sausage-shaped planetoid, the image was of a dully gleaming metallic cylinder.

A *moving* cylinder that raced toward one of the stars, the image of which quickly zoomed.

Only it wasn't a star. It was a structure of some kind with large circular openings or portals of some sort.

Another icon appeared, labeled NTN Blood Phoenix.

John gasped, "They made it! But that means…."

Gail finished the sentence, "We just traveled nearly 75 light years in the blink of an eye. This place… it must be capable *of both warp and* Nexus Junction Point travel. But what's stopping the Accipiter fleet from following?"

Just then, a… simplified… representation of the star system they had just departed from appeared, replacing the hologram. It depicted the previous scene of New Texas moving and the cloud of Accipiter ships approaching. As New Texas shimmered and blinked out of existence, a massive shock wave rippled outwards, vaporizing planetoids and everything in its path. Icons representing a timescale appeared and then sped up, showing the shock wave expanding across the star system and washing over the Accipiter fleet, leaving nothing behind but dust.

Thunder boomed, the ground shook, and the wind started to move again. The hologram blinked off as gravity nauseatingly fluctuated again, and green lightning shot out from the obelisk upwards to the suntube. In moments, the suntube began to return to its normal yellow color, filling the world with warm light.

All across the city, a new sound began. It was slow to start but soon took shape. Cheers, applause, singing, and even car horns blared in a happy refrain. The world wasn't over yet.

A voice crackled and resounded from the obelisk. "You have returned to the beginning. To the genesis of worlds. In this place, many things will be possible. You have exceeded our expectations where others failed." The hologram faded, and the breeze stiffened.

John shook his head in understanding. "Hephaestus. The Forge of the Gods. We're at Mount Olympus."

Gail looked up at him, her eyes wide and still full of adrenaline. She nodded slowly, and then the corner of her lips twitched. "Are you sure? We could be at Lemnos, where Zeus cast Hephaestus down from Olympus? That would seem to be more consistent with our luck."

John reached over and pulled Gail to him. "Let's not push our luck any further, then. You're still in the dress. Let's go find Tom and get married before something else happens."

THE END

EPILOGUE

● ● ● ● ● ● ● ● ● ● ● ● ● ● ● ● ●

Alberta "Bertie" Sinitskaya slowly drifted toward the outer edges of sleep. Eyes still closed, she inhaled sharply, her lungs filling with strangely floral-scented air that reminded her of something between ginger and honeysuckle. She felt… strong. The constant aches and pains of hard work in low g were gone, but sleeping like this in null g was both delicious and… *wrong*. She could feel her long hair drifting loose and caressing her naked breasts.

Wait, what?

She blinked her eyes open and winced as her pupils shrank from the light. She shook herself awake and curled up, pulling her knees to her chest. As soon as she moved, she suddenly felt a multitude of tendrils release and pull away from her body.

She shivered and tried to shrink away from the vine-like tendrils as they disappeared into… a wall of flowers. Her throat was dry as she tried to gasp aloud. She forced herself to swallow as she looked around the large… room. Nothing made sense.

I was… I was on Mace… we were fighting the Accipiters…. and…. and I think I died. Why is my hair so long?

She looked at her arms and hands… and her body. It was…. *My tattoos… they're gone, and… my skin! It's like I'm….* She looked closer at her hands and arms. The scar on her left index finger, there since she'd busted her hand working on her first Harley… gone. She swallowed and looked *down*… the small C-Section scar was gone, and… *I look… young!*

"What the hell is…." She stopped mid-sentence. Her voice… It was wrong. Like from when she was a teenager or… before she'd smoked enough that her voice had dropped.

Shit…. This can't be good.

Looking desperately around the room, she saw that it was cavernous… a cavernous garden. Like some kind of weird botanical garden full of plants she didn't recognize. She was no botanist, but she was confident that few if any, had originated on Earth.

She sensed motion to her left and saw… a tendril moving toward her, pushing… folded clothes? The tendril slowed and stopped, holding the clothes within her easy reach.

She snatched them away from the tendril, and it slunk back into the garden wall. Pulling them open, she saw that they were a kind of silken pajamas… no… a jumpsuit… with booties. Hesitating for only a moment, she flexed a practiced null g movement and pulled the jumpsuit on. There were no fasteners or zippers. The edges sealed themselves seamlessly, but with a bit of experimentation, she found they pulled back apart again with minor effort.

Bertie took a deep breath and looked around, trying to discern an exit or some sort of pattern to the place. *Where is the light coming from?*

A tendril emerged from the wall, carrying a green and red flat rectangular object. It paused a few inches away from her. She resisted the urge to flinch away from it but decided that if she had been wished harm, she probably wouldn't have been awakened in the first place. She gingerly reached for the object and pulled it towards her as the tendril released it.

It had a flat surface that reminded her a little of a computer tablet.

She startled and twisted sharply in the air as a low, soft, rock-crushing sound began behind her as the flowered wall split apart. The rumbling quickly changed pitch and rose to a warm set of dulcet tones. Tones that came from the ten-foot-tall Accipiter, who entered through the newly formed door, gliding effortlessly to a stop in front of her.

Her eyes widened and her heart pounded in her chest as she desperately tried to swim backwards in the zero-G away from the enormous creature.

The flat surface on the tablet changed, and text in English began to scroll across it as an odd-sounding voice repeated the words aloud. "Good morning, Alberta. I am happy to see you well. Would you join me for breakfast?"

✪ ✪ ✪

To be continued...

in
Accipiter War:
Book # 4

BOOKS IN THIS SERIES

●●●●●●●●●●●●●●●●●●●

ACCIPITER WAR #1 is set in the near future. The Accipiter War series follows the survivors of an attack on Earth. Rescued by unknown aliens and forced to fight a generational proxy war against a galaxy-spanning empire, Accipiter War emphasizes hope and the endurance of the human spirit in the face of unthinkable tragedy, discovery, and the search for a destiny other than war. Accipiter War The current-day city of Fort Brazos, Texas, and the nearby Joint Reserve Base have been abducted — scooped up whole and deposited inside a vast 4000-mile-long hollow world.

Thousands are dead. Thrown into crisis, they are alone with no help coming. Who has done this to them and why? Will the military submit to the civilian mayor and city council? Meanwhile, alien creatures begin to attack, and the people start to discover that not everything, or everyone, is the same as they were before Awakening Day.

Are the humans to be lab rats? Slaves? Gladiators? Or is there some other terrible purpose… or a greater destiny?

Accipiter War is the first in a planned series of books in the Fort Brazos Saga by Father/Son authors Patrick & Blake Seaman. It emphasizes hope and the endurance of the human spirit in the face of unthinkable tragedy.

Accipiter War # 2: STEALING FIRE:

The citizens of New London and Fort Brazos race against time and mistrust to launch the hybrid starship. The window of opportunity to strike a crucial blow against the enemy is closing fast, but can they put differences aside long enough to work together? If they don't, will the Gardeners - the mysterious race that put them inside the hollow world decide humanity isn't worth saving after all?

FORT BRAZOS SAGA: BOOK ONE
ACCIPITER WAR
Patrick Seaman
Blake Seaman
Accipiter War #2
STEALING FIRE
Patrick Seaman
Blake Seaman
ACCIPITER WAR #3
THE FORGE
Patrick Seaman
Blake Seaman

About the Authors

Patrick Seaman is the principal author. He created the concept and drives the storyline for the Fort Brazos series. He crafted concept art and managed creative development for Fort Brazos. Patrick is an entrepreneur, consultant, Internet pioneer, former publisher, editor, and author. In addition, Patrick is a lifelong shooting enthusiast and former rifle and pistol instructor.

Since helping launch broadcast.com in the early days of online digital media, Patrick has launched, advised, and served in many startups around the globe in C-Level positions or their boards.

You can follow Patrick at:

http://www.amazon.com/author/patrickseaman
https://twitter.com/PatrickSeaman
http://www.linkedin.com/in/patrickseaman
http://AccipiterWar.com
http://patrickseaman.com

Blake Seaman is an Information Technology executive, author, and classical composer. His music is available on all major streaming platforms. He is a proud resident of the State of Texas, where he celebrated the birth of his first child with his wife 6 months before the publication of this book; he dedicates his work on this project to them, and hopes to raise part of a new generation of Science Fiction fans. Blake is also an avid sports shooter and Tea aficionado.

https://BlakeSeaman.com
https://open.spotify.com/artist/3aK0vHFZEJ7YLq6a9CV9Yw
http://www.amazon.com/author/blakeseaman
http://www.cdbaby.com/Artist/BlakeSeaman
https://itunes.apple.com/us/album/fort-brazos/id961266753